Praise for Candice Fox

"This engrossing new variation on *The Fugitive* sets a female U.S. marshal every bit as relentless as Sam Gerard against a runaway prisoner as compelling as Richard Kimble. . . . This one is her best yet."
—*Booklist* (starred review)

"One of our brightest crime fiction stars."
—Adrian McKinty, *New York Times* bestselling author of *The Chain*

"If you haven't read Candice Fox yet, you're missing out! I can't wait to read what this talented writer does next!" —Chevy Stevens

"A bright new star of crime fiction."
—James Patterson

"Definitely a writer to watch." —Harlan Coben

"Sign me up as a big-time Fox fan!" —Lee Child

CANDICE FOX

THE
CHASE

Tor Publishing Group
New York

THE CHASE

A Forge Book
Published by Tom Doherty Associates/Tor Publishing Group
120 Broadway
New York, NY 10271

www.tor-forge.com

Forge® is a registered trademark of Macmillan Publishing Group, LLC.

ISBN 978-1-250-79884-8

Our books may be purchased in bulk for promotional, educational, or business use. Please contact your local bookseller or the Macmillan Corporate and Premium Sales Department at 1-800-221-7945, extension 5442, or by email at MacmillanSpecialMarkets@macmillan.com.

First U.S. Edition: March 2022
First U.S. Mass Market Edition: February 2023

Printed in the United States of America

0 9 8 7 6 5 4 3 2 1

For all the aspiring authors. Never give up.

THE
CHASE

CHAPTER I

From where she sat at the back of the bus, the driver's death was a confusing spectacle to Emily Jackson.

She had a good view down the length of the vehicle from her position, leaning against a window smeared with the fingerprints of happy children. Her seat was elevated over the rear wheel axle, so as she rode she could see youngsters jumping and crashing about the interior, playing games and teasing each other across the aisle, occasionally throwing a ball or smacking a catcher's mitt into a rival's head. Half of the other parents on the bus were ignoring their children's activity, gazing out the windows at the Nevada desert, some with AirPods in their ears and wistful looks on their faces. Others were making valiant attempts to dampen the chaos and noise: confiscating water bottles, phones, and toys being used as weapons, or dragging wandering toddlers back to their seats. Forty minutes of featureless sand and scrub beyond the garish structures and swirling colors of Vegas was a lot for kids to endure. When the bus bumped over a loose rock on the narrow road to the prison, Emily saw all the other passengers bump with it, the bus and its riders synchronized parts of a unified machine.

She didn't have to nudge her son, Tyler, as they approached the point at which Pronghorn Correctional would come into view. Tyler had been coming to the annual pre-Christmas softball game at the facility since he was a kindergartener, and had only missed one year, when his father strained his back fixing the garage door and couldn't play second pitcher against the minimum security inmates as he usually did. Tyler's familiarity with the journey seemed to give him a sixth sense, and she watched as he flipped his paperback closed, shifting upward in his seat. No landmark out there in the vastness told mother and son they were approaching the last gentle curve in the road. Hard, cracked land reached plainly toward the distant mountain range. Then the pair watched through the bus's huge windshield as the collection of wide, low concrete buildings rose seemingly out of the sand.

"Who's your money on this time?" Emily asked the teen. A five-year-old in the seat in front of them started pointing and squealing at the sight of the prison up ahead. Tyler considered his mother's question, watching the boy in front of him with quiet distaste, as if he hadn't once been just the same, so excited to see Daddy at work.

"I'm betting inmates," Tyler decided, giving his mother a wry smile. "Dad says they've been practicing during yard time for months."

"Traitor." Emily smirked.

"How 'bout you?"

"Officers," she said. "If you're going for the cons, I've got to go for the correctional officers or your father won't sp—"

A thump cut off Emily's words.

It was a heavy, sonic pulse, not unlike a firework exploding; a sound Emily both heard and felt in the center of her chest. Her brain offered up a handful of ordinary explanations for the noise even as her eyes took in the visual information that accompanied it. *A blown tire,* she thought. Or a rock crunching under the bus's wheels. Some kind of spontaneous combustion in the vehicle's old, rickety engine, a piston or cylinder giving out due to the rugged terrain and the desert's usually blinding heat.

But none of those explanations aligned with what Emily saw.

The driver slumped sideways out of his seat, caught and prevented from falling into the stairwell only by the seatbelt over his shoulder. A fine pink mist seemed to shimmer in the air before dissipating as quickly as it had appeared. Emily grabbed the seat in front of her and held on as the bus swung off the road and slowed to a stop in the shrubbery.

Her eyes wandered over the scene at the front of the bus. The passengers in the first two rows were examining their hands or touching their faces as though they were damp. Hundreds of tiny cubes of glass lay over the driver, the dash, and the aisle, the side window having neatly collapsed and sprayed everywhere, exactly as it was designed to do. Emily recognized Sarah Gravelle up there, rising unsteadily from her seat and walking to the driver's side. Emily could see, even from her distant position, that half of the driver's head was gone. Sarah looked at the driver, and everybody watched her do it, as if they were waiting for her to confirm what they already knew.

Sarah stumbled back to her seat and sat down.

Emily's tongue stuck to the roof of her mouth, her body suddenly covered in a thin film of sweat.

Sarah Gravelle started screaming.

And then everyone was screaming.

Grace Slanter put down her pen and pressed the speakerphone button to answer the phone that was ringing on her wide desk. Few calls came to the warden's office without first being channeled through her assistant's office in the room down the hall, so she was expecting someone familiar on the line: her husband, Joe, or the director of Nevada corrections, Sally Wakefield, a woman she spoke to almost daily. When the line connected, there was a second click she'd never heard before, and her own voice gave a ringing echo, as if it was being played back somewhere. *Robocaller,* she thought. But that was impossible. This was an unlisted line, not the kind that could appear on a database in some sweaty underground scam-mill.

"Hello, Grace Slanter."

"Pay attention," a voice commanded.

Grace felt a chill enter her spine, high, between her shoulders, as though she'd been touched by an icy finger. She looked down at the phone on the desk as though it held a malevolent presence, something she could see glowing evilly between the seams in the plastic.

"Excuse me?"

"There's a bus stopped in the desert half a mile from the prison walls," the voice said. It was a male voice. Soft, clipped. Confident. "If you go to the window behind you and look out, you'll see it sitting on the road."

Grace stood. She did not go to the window. The warden had been trained to respond to calls like this one, and though she'd never before had to put that training into action, the first thing she remembered was not to start following the directions of the caller until she had a grasp on the situation. She went to the door of her office instead, the furthest point from the window, and looked down the hall. There was not a soul to be seen.

"Are you looking at it?" the voice asked.

Grace stepped up onto the couch against the wall, to the left of the desk. She could see the bus out there, a distant white brick in the expanse of land beyond the concrete walls and razor wire of the prison. It had one wheel off the road, the vehicle tilted slightly, leaning, as though drunk.

"Okay," Grace said. "I see it. What's your name? I want to know who I'm talking to."

"On that bus are twelve women, eight men, and fourteen children," the voice said, ignoring her questions. "They're the families of guards inside the prison. Your employees. Your people."

"Jesus Christ," Grace said. The annual softball game. Inmates versus officers. The families always came to watch. It was an event designed to appease the prison staff stuck minding vicious criminals during the holiday season while their families gathered at home. The peacemaking gesture usually lifted the dismay after the rosters for Christmas Eve, Christmas Day, and New Year's were drawn up, so that officers went into those shifts with at least half a smile on their faces. After the game there was lunch and drinks for the unlucky families in the conference building outside the prison walls.

Grace staggered down from the couch and gripped the edge of the desk. Her training was forgotten, her senses blurred. She went to her chair and fell into it, relieved by the familiar feeling of her own warmth on the seat, something comforting in the chilling seconds that passed.

"The driver of the bus is dead," the voice on the phone said.

Grace tried to remember the location of the panic button on her desk, the one that would send an alarm to her colleagues inside the building, and an automatic "assistance needed" call to the nearest law enforcement agencies. All she had to do was remember where that single button was. But her mind was spinning, reeling, and for a long moment it was a struggle just to breathe.

"Are you listening, Grace?"

"I'm . . . I'm listening," she said. Grace drew in a deep breath and then let it out. She found the button under the desk by her knee and pushed it. A red light came on above the door to her office, but no sound issued. In seconds, her assistant, Derek, was there, huffing from the run up the hall, two guards right behind him. It only took one look from Grace to send them sprinting away again.

"What do you want?" she asked.

"I want you to let them out."

Grace had known the words were coming long before they were spoken. She drew in another deep breath. Across the two decades she had been in senior management at Pronghorn, she'd run over this scenario in her mind a hundred times. She knew what to do now. She was regaining control. There was a procedure for this. She grabbed her pen again and started jotting down notes about the voice and the time of the call, keeping an eye on the window as she sat twisted sideways in her chair.

"Which inmates are we talking about?" Grace asked. "Who do you want me to release?"

"All of them," the voice said.

CHAPTER 2

Celine Osbourne smelled smoke. On Pronghorn's death row, tobacco was a controlled substance. Level two contraband. Any inmate found in possession of it was punished with the same severity as if they were caught with cocaine, heroin, marijuana, or ice. She stopped in her tracks halfway down the row, outside serial killer Lionel Forber's cell, and sniffed. Forber was curled in his bed, asleep beneath a blanket, the seventy-seven-year-old predator as motionless as a snake under a rock. Celine followed the smell forward, past a serial rapist crocheting a blanket, a child killer reading a romance novel, and a cop killer watching television. The smell was not tobacco burning, she realized; it was wood. And when she found the source, a dark, worn smile crept over her lips.

"How come I knew it was you?" she asked.

John Kradle was bent over the small steel shelf bolted to the wall of his cell that acted as a desk. On the floor, at his feet, a battered silver toaster sat plugged into an extension cord that ran out of his cell and down the length of the row, where it turned a corner and disappeared from view. Kradle had a piece of smooth pine stretched across the desk, and he was using a wire that ran out of the top of the toaster as a makeshift soldering iron to burn ornate lettering into the wood's surface.

"How come you what?" Kradle grunted without looking up.

"How come I knew it was you?" Celine repeated. "I smelled smoke and I knew somebody around here was up to no good, and I immediately thought of you."

Celine examined the device in his hand. Kradle had fashioned a handle and a burning prong out of what looked like scraps of wire and wood and duct tape, elastic bands, and folded cardboard. He was just rounding the second "e" in the word "*feet,*" having already spelled out "*Please wipe your*" in skillful, near-perfect cursive.

"I don't know, but if I had to guess I'd say it's because you're obsessed with me," Kradle said, flicking the iron upward gently to finish the letter with a fine line and a coil of gray smoke. "I'm never far from your mind. You smell smoke, you think: John Kradle. You smell breakfast, you think: John Kradle. You smell your boyfriend's cologne, you think: John Kradle."

The toaster at his feet popped and the piece of wire in his iron, which was glowing red, dimmed to black. He shunted the toaster handle down with the toe of his shoe and it began glowing again.

"Is that the kind of delusion that gets you through the cold, lonely nights here?" Celine asked. "Most guys turn to Catholicism, Kradle. It's more realistic."

"Uh-huh."

"Who the hell rigged this up for you?"

Kradle looked at her through the bars for the first

time, a weary glance that said prisoners didn't snitch, even against guards, and that was a fact she should have learned within five minutes of arriving on her first day on the job. She sighed.

"Give me that." She beckoned for the wood.

"Nope." Kradle swiped back his gray-streaked blond hair and started on the "t" in *feet.*

"What? 'Nope'? You don't say 'nope' to me, inmate. Ever. Give me that piece of wood. That's an order."

"I've been given an order already today. It was to create this sign here." He nodded to the wood in front of him. "I've got a few conflicting orders during my time in prison. You people holding the keys have a lot of trouble deciding what you want, sometimes. So, when that happens, I go with the one I like best. And right now, that's working on this sign."

Celine bit her tongue, turned away, and smiled. The smile held no warmth and was an automatic reaction, something burned into her from years as a correctional officer. *Never let them see your anger. If you get angry, smile. Make them think you're in control. That you expected this. That it's all going to plan and you couldn't possibly be happier about it.* But even her false smile was too good for John Kradle.

"I bet you think standing there smiling like an idiot is going to make me think you're not angry," Kradle said, behind her, as though he could read her thoughts. She turned back. He was still bent over his work, his big hands moving skillfully. "You're wrong. I know you're mad."

"You do, huh?"

"Yeah," he said. "Because you know who rigged this setup for me. You know what the sign is for. It's for the warden's office. It's a peace offering from a certain lieutenant who took the warden's directive in last month's staff notices about trudging sand into her office to heart."

The toaster popped. Kradle shoved the handle down again.

"And you're also mad because you know it's a good sign. It's pretty," he continued, gently blowing the tendrils of smoke away from his face as they rose from the wood. "It makes you mad to know that even though the warden is going to figure out an inmate made this sign, she's going to hang it outside her office anyway because it's so attractive. And for years to come, maybe decades, every time the warden calls you up for something—a promotion or a sector review or a captains' meeting or whatever the hell—you're going to have to look at this sign and know that your most loathed inmate made it and you couldn't do a damn thing to stop him."

"That's a fairly advanced narrative for a brain the size of a peanut to handle," Celine said. "You better give me that piece of wood and go lie down."

"Make me."

Celine grabbed the cord running from the toaster out through the bars and yanked it free of the extension cord. She stormed toward the control room.

She slowed as she neared Burke David Schmitz's cell. The neo-Nazi terrorist, an unrepentant mass shooter, had the highest number of confirmed victims of all the men on Celine's row. There was a kind of thickness in the air around him. A coldness. The feeling touched the cells on either side of his, which for now were empty. She peered sideways as she walked by and saw him sitting on his cot, straight-backed, looking at nothing, as he often did. The young blond man gave Celine the sense that he could see her even beyond the reach of his line of sight as she passed by.

Lieutenant James Jackson was there, as she expected him to be, slouched sideways in his swivel chair, his feet up on the control panel, clicking between the cameras on the screens before him. The coldness Schmitz had left her with was gone, and she was hot with anger again.

"Did you give John Kradle a soldering iron?" she asked. Jackson's round face was lit by the light of the camera screens, highlighting the bags beneath his eyes.

"I didn't give it to him. He built it himself."

"But you gave him the parts. You gave him the toaster," Celine said. "That's the toaster out of the break room. The old one. The broken one."

"Well, he didn't have a visitor smuggle it in up their asshole, that's all I can tell you, Captain," Jackson said. His assistant, Liz Savva, choked on her coffee.

"Help me understand." Celine leaned in the doorway, her arms folded. "I'm trying to get into your frame of mind. You let a man who shot his family to death in their home before setting the place on fire take possession of a toaster and misappropriate its mechanical parts so he could use it to burn things. Is that what you're saying?"

"Look, Captain." Jackson leaned back in his chair and stared at her. "These guys on the row? I don't sit around thinking about their crimes. If I did, I couldn't work with them. I just think of them as miserable sons of bitches who spend twenty-three hours a day locked in a cage." He pointed upward, in the direction of the warden's office. "Warden Slanter's been looking at me funny since I messed up the new carpet in her office. I was telling Kradle about it and he came up with the idea of the sign. And I think he's doing a good job. So why don't you just lay off the guy? He's helping me out."

Celine sighed.

"It'll look good for the next inspection," Jackson continued. "The inmates doing arts and crafts."

"Kradle should be bumped down to finger-painting level," Celine said. "That way, he's less likely to hurt someone."

"What's your problem with Kradle?" Savva mused, peering into her coffee mug as if the answer might lie in there. "He's one of the least confrontational inmates we have. It's like you hate him even more than the guy in six who ate all those old ladies' faces."

"I'll tell you what I hate." Celine put her hands up, ready to paint a mental picture, but a dull ringing interrupted her. At first she thought it was the phone on her hip. Then she followed the sound to the speaker hanging from the ceiling in the corner of the room. She'd never heard a phone ringing through the PA system before. There was a click, and a noise like a desk chair creaking.

"Hello, Grace Slanter."

"Pay attention."

"Excuse me?"

"What the hell is that?" Celine asked.

"It's the warden," Savva said. The gentle ex-teacher and death row rookie was slowly rising from her chair. "Sounds like her phone's being picked up by the PA."

"Oh, shit." Jackson laughed. "She's left her mic on and taken a call."

"There's a bus stopped in the desert half a mile from

*the prison walls. If you go to the window behind you
and look out, you'll see it sitting on the road.*

"Are you looking at it?"

"Somebody better get up there and tell her the
whole prison can hear her," Liz said. "Before she
starts—"

"Shut up," Celine said. "Listen."

There was a strange silence on the line. A silence
that had flooded through the speakers and infected the
entire prison. Celine stepped back through the doorway and glanced down the row. It wasn't this quiet
in E Block even in the dead of night. She heard Grace
Slanter huff into the phone.

*"Okay. I see it. What's your name? I want to know
who I'm talking to."*

*"On that bus are twelve women, eight men, and
fourteen children,"* the voice said. *"They're the families of guards inside the prison. Your employees. Your
people."*

"Jesus Christ."

"The driver of the bus is dead."

"Oh my god," Celine whispered.

"Hey!" an old man in the cell nearest the control
room called out. Celine looked. He was holding a
shaving mirror out through the bars to see her. One
gray eye was scrutinizing her, its brow hanging low.
Roger Hannoy, the face-eater. "What's going on out
there?"

"Are you listening, Grace?"

"I'm . . . I'm listening."

Celine dashed down the corridor to the row of windows along the east side of the block. Beyond the furthest concrete wall of the prison, she could see the
bus out there in the desert, stopped just off the lonely

road that led to the facility. The voices on the speakers above them carried on. Jackson and Savva arrived beside her. Jackson gripped the bars.

"My family's on that bus," Jackson breathed. Celine saw all the blood rush from his face into his neck and then it was gone, leaving him gray as stone. "Tyler. Oh my god. Tyler. Tyler. Tyler."

"Who do you want me to release?"

"All of them."

"This is . . . ," Liz began, but her words fell away and her mouth simply gaped.

"Don't panic. Let's not panic," Celine said. "It's, uh . . . It's a drill." It seemed important to simply interrupt what was happening, to throw something, anything, under the wheels of the train as it came hurtling down the mountain, even though she knew it was impossible to stop it completely. The interruption didn't last long. Jackson met her eyes, and they both knew that captains were briefed on all drills. The fear on Celine's face crushed her lie the second it was out of her mouth.

"I can't. I mean, I can't do that. That's not doable." Slanter's voice was bouncing off the thick walls. *"You can't just . . . What do you—"*

"You've got four minutes to empty the prison. We're watching, and we're looking for a particular inmate. When he appears outside the prison walls, I'll call my shooter off."

"Who's the inmate?"

"We're not going to tell you that. You'll have to release everyone."

Jackson's radio crackled on his belt. Celine watched him try to grip it, work it awkwardly from its holster, but he failed, his hands numb. Celine pulled it free.

"Are you guys up in E Block hearing this?" a voice on the radio asked.

It sounded like Bensley from H Block.

"Is this real?" came another voice. All call signals were abandoned. All procedures thrown into the trash. Celine knew that was one of the first signs of mass panic. People forgot their training, became scared animals working only on instinct, fighting to return to reason.

A gaggle of voices and blips came out of the device in her fingers. Calls from all over the prison, fighting for airtime.

"My husband is on that bus!"

"Can anyone tell me what the hell is going on? Is this a drill? Is this a drill?"

"This is Issei in Watchtower Eight. Somebody tell me this is a drill. Has anybody got a captain on deck?"

"Is this for real, Celine?" Jackson asked. He'd grabbed her bicep so hard his nails were biting through the fabric of her shirt. Celine tore her arm away.

"I . . . I . . . I don't know." She couldn't force the words through her lips fast enough. "Just, uh . . . just get back into the control room. Send up a code red, and—"

"*What you're asking is not possible,*" Slanter was saying. "*Okay? This is not how this works. Give me some time.*"

"*You don't have time. Meet our demands or we kill the passengers.*"

"*You're not killing anyone. If you want to negotiate, we can negotiate, but—*"

Two pops. So dim Celine couldn't tell if she imagined them, or if her brain took in the distant puffs of dust in the desert and the sight of the bus lurching sideways, and added the sounds, knowing with sickening clarity what she was seeing. The shooter had taken out both of the bus's left tires, causing the vehicle to collapse sideways and resettle, tilted, like a listing boat.

She thought she heard screams on the wind. But maybe not. Maybe they were in her mind, too.

"Three minutes, fifty seconds. That's how long you have left, Grace. Then I instruct my shooter to fire at will."

"Did you guys see that?" came a voice on the radio. "He took out the tires. He took out the fucking tires!"

CHAPTER 3

Sarah Gravelle gripped her seat with her fingernails, staring at the stairwell of the bus, the mess there. It looked like cheap horror-film special effects: the blood, brain matter, and flecks and splinters of who knows what mixed in with the broken glass. The people on the bus around her were screaming in thirty-three different ways, everybody with their own distress song, toddlers squealing and men bellowing and teenagers wailing, clawing at their shirt collars, reduced suddenly to the wide-open-mouthed kids they once were. Sarah stood again and held on to the rail that separated the front passenger seat from the stairwell. Her legs were jelly as the screaming began to be punctuated by individual voices, some young, some older.

"Is it an active shooter?" a child cried. "Mom! Is it an active shooter?"

"Everything's fine! Everything's fine! Just stay down! Stay down low, honey!"

"Daddy! I want to get off! I want to get off!"

"Holy Mary, mother of God, pray for—"

Sarah gripped her way along the handrail. She told

herself to keep her eyes on the prison, half a mile away, as she stepped numbly down the stairs.

"What are you doing? Sarah! Sarah? Sarah, no! There's a shooter out there!"

Sarah looked back. A woman was vomiting into the aisle. A man rambling into the phone to 911. Kids and adults were under the seats, jammed into tiny spaces, tight bundles of terrified humans.

"I've. Got to. Get off," Sarah said. Her voice was flat, ridged only with weakly hitched breaths. "We. All have to. Get off."

Two explosions. The bus lurched sideways, throwing bodies into the aisle. Sarah grabbed the door and pushed it open, let in the crisp desert air.

In Watchtower Seven, Marni Huckabee was staring down the scope of her rifle at the desert. She spent a good five or six hours a day on the tower, some of it staring through the lens at the gates, the fences, the yard, the walkways, and the cages. Once or twice a week, maybe, she lifted her scope to the desert beyond the razor wire and tracked a rabbit or coyote or tortoise out there on the plains. But she was looking now at something she had never before seen, never imagined her crosshairs trembling over as she gripped the weapon with bone-aching tension. A bus door popping open. Someone's wife or girlfriend, a woman she didn't recognize, hesitating as she stepped down from the leaning doorway like a shaken-up child exiting an amusement park house of horrors.

"Oh, god!" Marni's tower partner, Craig Fandel, gripped her arm. "They're going to run for it."

"Don't do it," Marni whispered. She could feel a droplet of sweat making the rim of the rifle scope wet beneath her eye. She swept her hat off, wiped her face with it, pushed her eye against the scope again. "Woman, please, don't do it!"

Marni and Craig watched the woman push off and sprint into the desert, running for the prison gates. Craig let go of Marni's arm.

"Give her cover! Give her cover!" he cried. Marni twisted the rifle sideways on its point, aiming into the hills, where the shooter must have been—the same side as the shot-out tires. For the first time in her career, Marni flipped off the safety and opened fire.

Warden Grace Slanter saw the flash of white gunfire from tower seven, felt the delayed booming in the pit of her stomach. A lone figure was running from the bus across the desert, the unsteady, hunched, desperate running of human prey. Puffs of dust rose and gunfire cracked. Slanter watched the woman fall and slide and tumble in the sand.

"Did you shoot her?" The words felt sharp and hard in Slanter's throat, almost unutterable. "Did . . . did you . . ."

The caller said nothing.

Slanter watched the woman struggle to her feet, turn, and run back toward the bus, throwing herself through the doorway.

"Take me," Slanter said. "I'll walk out into the hills. No one will follow me. I'll be unarmed."

"We don't want you."

"*Who do you want?*" she cried. "*You can have any-one!*"

"Two minutes, forty seconds," the caller said. "We're not playing."

* * *

Celine Osbourne watched the activity in the desert play out through the barred windows of death row. She hardly noticed when Jackson snatched his radio back from her fingers.

"This is Jackson, on the row," he said. "My son is out there. He's thirteen. My wife is also on board. Can anybody in the towers see the shooter? Can we . . . Can we take him out?"

"Nobody disarm their doors! That's a direct order!" a voice said. Celine recognized it as Mark Gravelle, from the gate. "That woman, the runner, that's my wife. We have to get through this, people. We can't empty the goddamn prison. Okay? We just can't. I don't care what's happening out there, we gotta keep these guys in. Some of these men—"

"Fuck you!" Jackson's hand was gripping the radio so tight the plastic case was creaking. "That's my family! We can recover the fucking inmates! I'm not burying my son!"

"Don't disarm!" came another shout across the airwaves.

"We've got every fucking killer in the state locked—"

"—leaving my babies out there—"

"—go to hostage protocol! All officers—"

"Look." Liz Savva's sweaty finger bashed on the window, through the bars. "Look. Look. There are guys running. They're unlocking the yard!"

Celine stared at the alarm lights mounted in the ceiling, the bell on the outer corner of the control room. Stillness. Silence. Just the stutter of gunfire from a distant watchtower. No one had announced code red. Because this wasn't a code red. This was something far, far worse.

"Celine," Jackson said. "Open the row."

"No," Celine snapped. All the hairs on her body were standing on end. She was suddenly so cold she was shivering. "No, Jacky, we're not doing this."

"I'm opening up," said a voice on the radio.

"Who is that?"

"This is Brian over in C Block. I'm doing it. You got women and children out there. My fiancée and my two girls. I'm opening the goddamn doors."

"This is Amy, in-in-in tower five. My husband just called me from the bus. This is real. Th-th-this is real. Open it up, please, everyone. Please. My baby boy is out there. Please!"

"If C is opening, we're opening, too."

"Me too."

"D Block here. We're opening up."

"No!" Celine gripped the bars on the window, stood on her toes so she could see the barred door of F Block below. She watched an inmate, someone she didn't recognize, push open the security door.

With his hands.

His own hands.

The man walked out of the door on the side of the building. He took a few steps, looked around, took a few more steps. No officers with him. No other inmates lining up behind him. Just a prisoner, on his own, where he should never be on his own. It might as well have been a zebra in a pink tutu walking out of F Block. Celine blinked but couldn't comprehend it.

She reached out for Jackson, but he was gone. So was Savva. Celine swallowed bile at the back of her throat. She sprinted back to the control room.

"No, no, no, no!" She grabbed the handle of the

door just as Jackson slammed it shut in her face. "No, we're not doing this! No, no, no!"

Celine heard a sound that she had never heard before, and that was because it had never been made. It was a loud, thundering, rolling series of clanks.

It was the sound of all the death row cell doors being unlocked at once.

The monsters emerged slowly. She knew them all. It was clear in one horrifying instant how well she knew them, because as each man slid open their disarmed cell door, Celine's mind was flooded with images of their crimes. The face-eater. The strangler. The mass shooter and the slayer of innocent children. Celine watched John Kradle step out into the hall, hesitant, like a wild animal venturing into a clearing. They locked eyes. She saw the terror and excitement in his face.

"Get back inside!" she called, but her voice sounded pathetically small in all the commotion. Some men were calling out to each other, asking what they should do. Others had ducked back inside to gather a precious item. One or two had sprinted away toward the iron-barred door to the stairwell.

She turned and bashed on the door to the control room with her fists.

"Jackson, shut the doors! Shut the doors! Shut the doors!"

Men were running by her. They were going to the windows to check that the bus was really out there. That this wasn't some sort of prank or test.

Celine then did something she had only ever imagined doing. She took two steps to her office, stepped inside, ripped out the bottom drawer, and grabbed the revolver she kept strapped to the inner wall of the desk. She went back into the hall and raised the weapon.

"Get back in your cells!"

They turned, looked her over, laughed. Big Willy Henderson, who had doused his wife in gasoline and set her alight. Ainsley Sippeff, who had opened fire on his colleagues at a bowling alley and killed two teenagers and a parking lot security guy.

The men brushed past her. Celine had never been on this side of the barred doors with any of the inmates she worked with unless they were wearing cuffs. They put the cuffs on in the cells, walked the inmates out to the yard, then uncuffed them in the cages that were there under the sunshine to let them roam in a slightly bigger space for an hour a day. Big Willy's arm touched Celine's as he went by. She felt ice tumble into the pit of her bowels.

The last men ran out into the stairwell, heading for the yard. Celine went back to the windows. Men were flooding out of the prison buildings, rushing toward the gates at the front of the complex, a mass evacuation, a sea of denim flooding out into the desert. A wave of nausea hit her and she doubled over, resting her hands on her knees. The sound of the release had been deafening. Now the halls were quiet but for the words falling out of her own mouth, panicked moans.

"No, no, please," she huffed. She straightened, trying to breathe, but the nausea hit again like a punch to the gut. "Please, god, don't do this."

The monsters were gone. All of them. Out into the world. She turned away from the windows, knowing that, with each second that ticked by, the state's most dangerous men were edging closer and closer to their next victims.

She had failed. For a decade and a half, all Celine had wanted to do was keep the bad men in their cages where they belonged; away from the world, from each other, from the people they had hurt. And all of it had been for nothing.

A man turned into the hall. Celine raised her gun. It was Jackson, pausing briefly before he ran.

"It's my family." He gestured weakly, then disappeared. Liz followed him. She heard their footsteps on the gravel outside.

She went to the control room, stepped numbly into the space, which was lit dimly to accentuate the contrast on the surveillance cameras. She touched the cell discharge button and some other dials vainly, as if she would be able to reverse the last few minutes somehow if she just found the right switch. The screens in front of her showed no movement. She turned and looked at the screens by the door that gave glimpses of the yard. Remaining inmates were being hustled reluctantly toward the gates by prison staff. These were likely the elderly, infirm, or mentally ill prisoners, or some perhaps merely scared men who were close to their release dates and didn't want to step outside the prison walls and have their sentence extended for an escape attempt. Celine marveled at how seamlessly the mutiny had unfolded. Once the first call had come through announcing someone was opening up, it seemed that most of the other staff had fallen into line. When a colleague's family was in danger, you stepped up, it seemed. Even if that meant endangering everyone else out there by releasing the worst of the worst into their midst.

She decided she would go out into the yard, to see the big gates of the prison standing open. It was something she had never witnessed before. The twenty-foot-high iron gates, as thick as truck tires, usually only ever opened as far as was necessary to let vehicles into the outer enclosure. But she supposed there was no need for that now. The gates would be thrust wide, useless.

The figure that appeared at the edge of her vision was tall and slender. Her mind, still failing to comprehend the new reality of the animals running wild outside their enclosures, told her it was Jackson. But it was not.

Willy Henderson grabbed Celine by the arm and shoved her back into the control room.

CHAPTER 4

John Kradle stood in the staff parking lot of Pronghorn Correctional Facility and felt the sunshine on his face. It occurred to him that he had never in his life stood on this spot, though he was positioned a mere hundred yards or so from his cell back on the row. On the night he had been driven to the facility, the truck had come in the back way, through the rear gate, a less impressive fifteen-foot-tall iron affair on the south side of the complex. He'd hardly noticed the facility taking in the bus on which he sat, like a giant whale swallowing a fish. He'd just been sentenced to death for murdering his family. Minute by minute, he had simply been trying to resist the urge to scream.

As well as standing somewhere he had never stood before, he was also standing somewhere that he had never considered he would be able to stand. His feet on the asphalt. His hands by his sides. The sun on his cheeks. One hundred yards, give or take, into the free world.

Men were running past him, yipping and cheering as they went. Kradle was initially surprised at just how many of the inmates were able to smash the windows of the cars in the lot, get in, and get the engine running in mere seconds, but then he supposed being able to hotwire a car was among the most common skills within the populace at any prison in the world. He watched alliances forming almost wordlessly, inmates flagging down and packing into the back of cars, horns honking as the vehicles took off toward the road. In the distance he could see civilians cowering against the side of the tilted bus as cars full of criminals zipped past them, trailing dust.

Every vehicle was headed the same way: out onto the service road that led to the highway. When they reached the highway, Kradle knew, the cars could turn left toward Vegas or right toward Utah. Kradle could guess which way most would be turning.

He looked at the huge, open gates of the prison before him, standing open like welcoming arms. A cluster of staff was gathered there, gaping at the spectacle of the mass breakout with their arms folded and mildly defeated looks on their faces. Some were on their phones, pacing back and forth nervously, trying to warn loved ones of the coming tidal wave of criminality.

"Take the kids and go to my mother's place," an officer was saying into his cell phone. Kradle didn't recognize him. There were only ten staff who worked on the row, where he had lived for the past five years. "Get in the car and drive there now, Cherie. Right now. Don't stop anywhere."

"Go down to the basement and don't come out until you hear my voice." A female officer passed Kradle, on her phone, her gun out in front of her, finger on the trigger. The pistol's aim wavered over him as she moved, but her eyes didn't meet his. His was just another criminal face in the horde that was running rampant. Kradle watched her get into her car, parked at the furthest end of the lot, and shake the gun at some inmates to get them away from the driver's side door. She started the engine and sped away.

Celine hit the floor of the control room so hard that all the wind was smacked out of her lungs. The gun clattered out of her fingers and slid under the control room desk. She crawled a few paces, trying to suck in air, but Henderson snatched her ankle, dragged her back to him, started pulling weapons off her body and throwing them away. He took her baton from its sheath and smashed her a few times, the pain so sudden and all-consuming she didn't even know where she was being struck. Everything blazed with pain. *Wham-wham-wham.* There was blood in her eyes. Her vision blurred red just as her thoughts came back into focus: her brain told her she needed to be very strategic now, true with her aim, calm and cool and moving like a machine that ran on instinct and training.

She squeezed her eyes shut, and in the darkness felt him kneel on top of her. He was within swinging distance now. Celine struck out and felt her knuckles smash against the bridge of his nose.

Right on target.

She'd spent a second in offensive mode, and now reeled back into defensive mode. *Get to safety; recover; plan; strike.* She covered her face with her arms, locked her fingers protectively around her skull and waited for the barrage of rageful punches to ebb. When it did, she slammed her knee upward into Henderson's crotch. He bent double instinctively, his body folding, anticipating the pain, his sweating forehead pressed between Celine's breasts. He let out a groan, high and ear-drum rattling. She clawed at his neck and head until he rolled away. She rolled as well, gripping her way toward the door, but he was back on her before she could move more than a foot or two, and he seemed somehow stronger, as if the rage generated by the knee in the crotch had only given him power.

His arm came around her neck, thick and wet and hairy, and squeezed so hard she felt the pressure of it behind her eyes.

And then, with a crack, the pressure was gone.

He's snapped my neck, she thought.

The words in her mind were hellishly clear. She curled her toes, expecting to feel the terrifying numbness of paralysis down her body, but she found that she could move. Henderson's arm had slithered away. More cracking sounds came. Celine rolled onto her back and watched John Kradle standing over the big man who had attacked her, his arm reaching up and then swinging down, the toaster in his hand smashing into Henderson's face like Thor's hammer, shiny and dented and covered with blood.

Celine watched Kradle beat Henderson half to death, her limbs refusing to move, seized by shock. Weird thoughts drifted through her; about the blood splattering up at Kradle's face, about how he gripped the toaster with his two fingers in the slots and his thumb around the base of the machine, as if he were holding a bowling ball.

All at once her body and mind recovered, and Celine scrambled under the control desk, picked up her gun, and swung around. Henderson wasn't moving.

Kradle was standing there with the toaster in one hand and her baton in the other.

"Are you—" he managed before a yelp of surprise and a look of horror. Celine fired three times. The bullets smashed into the wall behind Kradle's head, the last missing his ear by an inch or less. He cowered, the toaster and baton at his feet, forgotten.

"Sweet *Jesus*!" he howled when the firing had stopped. "I'm trying to save your ass here!"

"Get down!" Celine growled. "On your knees, inmate! Put your hands on the back of your head!"

"You're crazy." Kradle stood, backing up. "You want to shoot me, go ahead and shoot me, Celine. I only came back here for my stuff."

She didn't shoot. He turned and walked out of the control room. Celine pulled herself up to the observation window. She watched him jog back to his cell. He emerged what seemed like seconds later holding a pillowcase stuffed with items. She watched him disappear through the door at the end of the row that led out to the yard.

Celine crawled back to Henderson. She couldn't bring herself to look at his mangled face and head. The hands that cuffed him were slick with blood, her own and his. She snapped the restraints on the big man, gathered up her weapons, and limped slowly in the direction Kradle had gone.

Raymond Ackerman had been sitting listening to all the hubbub outside his cell. The phone call patched over the PA system, then the hoots and hollers of excitement from the inmates, the crash and clatter of chaos erupting beyond the bars. Two female guards stopped right in front of his cell, yammering in terror and gripping each other, and he watched them lock themselves in a storage closet only seconds before all the cell doors slid open. He was stirring a pot of noodles on his little camp stove throughout the entire affair—picante beef ramen—the thin, lifeless packages lying discarded on the iron desk by the toilet. He thought long and hard, but couldn't remember anything like this going down during his time at Pronghorn, or in any prison he'd been at, as a matter of fact. Seventy-seven years on the planet, forty-two of them behind bars, or steel mesh, or bulletproof glass, or whatever the hell they decided to keep him in, and he'd never witnessed a mass breakout. Pretty special. He stirred his noodles and waited for it all to die down, until only the clink of his spoon against the side of the pot could be heard.

Nobody came to see if "The Axe" Ackerman had joined the breakout. People tended to forget about Old Axe. He was quiet, slow-moving, didn't want for much. When fights broke out in the chow hall he tended to back away. When his cell was shaken down he stood with his arms by his sides, face against the wall, just as he was told. He sat now, enjoying the quiet of the empty cell block, eating his noodles, thinking about how good he'd got at eating noodles with a spoon over the years. They didn't have forks in H Block—as though, without forks, guys wouldn't have anything to hurt each other with. As if without forks, everybody was safe.

Stupid.

Axe got up after a while and went to his cell door, looked out across the cluttered common area. The men had trashed the place as they fled, like they thought they'd never be back. There was toilet paper festooned around the place, hanging off the ceiling fans. Books and cups and other stuff lay about everywhere. A cell down the hall was on fire. Axe figured most of the block would be right back where they started within twenty-four hours, and the screws would make them clean up all that mess with their own toothbrushes.

Axe had no real plans about going anywhere. He saw the outside world on TV and didn't much care for it. It seemed pretty noisy and weird. People on sitcoms were rude and mean and dressed stupid, and there would be a whole bunch of things he didn't understand about how to be in society. Seemed to him that just to get a decent meal you had to order it on a phone and pay for it with a cloud, and he didn't have either of those. He figured he'd only get a hundred yards outside the gates before a flying drone would turn up and scan his face, and then he'd be turned right around and marched home to his cell. It was all too much effort for him. He was a tired sort of guy. Liked to conserve his energy. But, he thought, he'd wander out into the yard anyway, just to see the gates hanging open, and then maybe raid everybody's cells for noodles.

When he got out into the yard, there was nobody there. He went to the gates, put a hand on them, felt their warmth from the desert sun. He took a couple of steps out, just for the hell of it, and rolled a rock under his shoe. Most of the activity seemed to be clustered around a bus parked in the desert, maybe a half mile from the facility. People hugging. Kids moving about. Axe hadn't seen a kid in almost four decades. He watched the scene for a while with his hands in his pockets.

Axe hung about, not doing much, waiting for someone to notice him standing there, but nobody did. There were the unattended noodles to think of. Dozens and dozens of packets, probably. But he decided in the end that there was no sense in making the screws' jobs easy by sitting in his cell for the entirety of the breakout. He turned and started heading for a Joshua tree he could see standing all alone at the foot of a rocky hill. He figured he'd go there and check it out. Axe hadn't seen a tree up close for half his lifetime. It was something to do with himself.

CHAPTER 5

The desert sun beat on the back of John Kradle's neck. It worked its way around his ears, up into his scalp, hot fingers trying to climb around his skull. In the Nevada desert there was no winter, not until the sun went down. He kept his head down and pressed on over the cracked and dry land, one step at a time, spiky plants scraping at his pants. It wasn't long before his white rubber prison shoes were brown and rubbing at the back of his heels. They were shoes made for walking on polished concrete floors, no more than a couple of miles a day; shoes that had no hard internal structure, not so much as a shoelace eyelet that could be taken off, bent, sharpened into a tiny blade. The shoes began to squeak as sweat rolled down his calves into them. Kradle kept on, glancing back now and then to see the prison shrinking and shrinking.

A helicopter flew overhead, low enough for Kradle to feel the beat of its rotors in his chest. There were cars in the distance soaring up the service road to the facility, cars of every color and shape. It would be an all-hands call to law enforcement. Kradle figured

Las Vegas Metro police and Nevada Highway Patrol would be there, and in short order SWAT, FBI, and the US Marshals would be too. Every Pronghorn staff member would be called to help out. Kradle planned to be in the mountains by the time things really ramped up. He figured he had about five miles to go before he hit shade.

It was while he was looking back, checking on the growing activity, that he spotted the man on his tail. Kradle knew he wasn't from the row. He'd seen everyone on the row, even if he didn't know their names. At home in his cell, Kradle had been able to physically call out and communicate with guys three or four cells to either side of his, and one Christmas had passed a kite six cells down to negotiate the barter of two bottles of hand cream for a Snickers bar. The other guys he only saw when they were being escorted past his cell to visits with their lawyers or family in the cages.

For a while he simply hoped the guy would peel off, head into the hills another way. Maybe Kradle had picked the only sensible path from the prison to the walls of the shallow valley in which the facility lay. The shortest path. But when the man on his tail hadn't disappeared, hadn't lengthened or shortened his proximity in about twenty minutes, Kradle stopped.

The man stopped.

"Get your ass here!" Kradle called.

The man approached. The last thirty yards or so, Kradle expected him to stop growing in size, but he didn't. Somehow the outside world had added a foot and a half of height to Kradle's approximation of him, a worrying thickness to his already huge, muscular frame.

"You can't be following me," Kradle said, in a voice that was far less confident than the one he'd used already. He pointed to a fork off into the mountains. "I'm heading this way. Give me some space, okay?"

"I want to come with you." The guy smiled, showing a big gap between his front teeth that made Kradle think of a toddler. "You look like you know where you're going."

"Are you . . ." Kradle shook his head and tried to think. "Are you kidding me? I don't even know you, man."

"I'm Homer Carrington."

"Look, the smartest thing for everybody to do here is strike out on their own. And I'm heading—"

"Pretty clever." Homer ran a hand over his buzz-cut black hair. "Head for the hills. Everybody else will be going off to Vegas. Why go into the hills? It's rocky up there. Dangerous. There'll be snakes. Probably big cats. It'll take you so long to get through, everybody else will be rounded up by the time anybody even thinks to look up here."

"That's . . ." Kradle shielded his eyes from the glare of the blazing white sun. "That's exactly right. Okay? You get it. We get each other. So now that you understand my reasoning, you can split off and go your own way."

"You're a smart guy." Homer smiled again. This time he showed all his teeth. Big, white, square teeth with that sizeable gap in the middle. Kradle was at once softened by the smile and also a little creeped out. Kradle thought of a plush-toy tapeworm he saw once at a school science fair, its cute, buggy eyes and coiling, pale body.

"Thanks," Kradle said. He decided to try a different

tack. "But you don't want to hang out with me. I'll be one of the top priority targets in the search."

"Oh, man." Homer stepped back a little. "You're not a serial killer or—"

"Very dangerous serial killer." Kradle nodded gravely. "John Kradle. I killed twelve women. Some of them young girls. And men. I've killed nine men. Very violently. So I'm going to be right up there on the hit list. I'm just going to try to get out of here as fast as I can."

"I guess that means I'll be high priority, too," Homer said, a little sadly. He looked off toward the rise beyond which the prison lay.

Kradle felt the hairs on the back of his neck stiffen in unison. "You're . . ." He couldn't use the words.

"Probably best if we stick together," Homer said. He walked up and passed Kradle, thumping his shoulder in a way that made Kradle even more aware of the man's dense, heavy, tree-trunk arms and the huge, skull-crushing hands hanging off them. "Two heads are better than one."

In her time as a US Marshal, Trinity Parker had seen some colossal fuck-ups. She'd once attended a near-miss mass shooting at a courthouse in Brampton, in which a guy had been able to smuggle a cache of sixty-five weapons into the building via a doughnut cart. He'd been wheeling parts of guns, knives, and boxes of ammunition right through the front doors in Krispy Kreme boxes and stashing them in a dis-used broom closet not twenty yards from the judges' chambers. The whole plot had only been discovered when an old lady buying a Boston cream to go with her cappuccino dropped the doughnut and spotted the barrel of an AR-15 poking out from under the cart. Another time, Trinity had seen a group of six sheriffs chase a serial rapist into a carnival, only to lose him in the mirror maze. It was like something out of a *Scooby-Doo* cartoon.

But as she stood surveying the scene at Pronghorn Correctional Facility, it occurred to her that she might be witnessing the greatest failure of privatized incarceration in the history of the state of Nevada, perhaps even the country.

As with all fugitive hunts, the ground zero action plan had been born on the hood of a patrol car, and had quickly grown and evolved across the facility as officers, information, and documents were added. The planning site now encompassed the prison chow hall. As Trinity commanded from the officers' watch station on a raised platform at the front of the great room, a loud, unsettled gaggle of men and women ebbed and pooled at different steel tables around her. Many of them were facility staff in tan and green uniforms, commiserating, retelling the story of the breakout from their various perspectives, gesturing wildly, some of them with bleeding noses or split brows, or with chunks of hair torn off in fights to keep inmates contained.

Among these correctional officers were newly arrived deputy sheriffs, highway patrol officers, and volunteer officers from the surrounding towns and counties, many of them listening to the tales of the breakout with incredulity. There was a special collection of people in the corner of the room: civilians in plain clothing, some of them still weeping quietly into phones or typing out long messages to family and friends. The bus people. Trinity saw toddlers bawling and traumatized teenagers madly reciting the experience to the outside world via their phone cameras.

Trinity turned and watched through the large barred windows as a couple of choppers landed outside the prison gates. SWAT, maybe, or journalists. A few leftover inmates and officers stood together, watching, at the fences, united in their bewilderment. She took the coffee that someone handed her and glanced at the slew of maps that had been placed on the table in front of her, a feast of information.

"First thing I want is for someone to stop those kids," she said, jutting her chin at the livestreaming teenagers. "Take all the phones from the bus passengers. Information about the breakout needs to be locked down. And I want the prison closed again. No press are to enter those gates."

A couple of deputies nodded and dashed away.

"Now that I'm here, we can take the fluffy-bunny initial response and give it some teeth and claws," Trinity said, looking over the maps. "The cordons—push them out by fifty miles and beef them up. I'm giving shoot-to-kill approval for any vehicles that try to rush the barricades. Most of these meatheads will be headed straight for Vegas to have a good time before they're rounded up. The really dangerous ones will go to ground, try to go on the run for the long-term. They'll be taking hostages in cars and houses, looking for supplies. Money. Clothes. Food. Licenses and papers. Put up the heat-seeking drones and send out alerts to cell phones in a five-hundred-mile radius."

People were rushing everywhere to enact her commands, phones to their ears, repeating her words. Trinity looked for a cookie to go with her coffee, but there was not a single bite of food visible in the entire chow hall.

"Someone get me something to eat, and someone drag in some partitions," she said, sipping her coffee. She waved toward the long east wall of the food hall. "I want a wall of photographs erected of the inmates we have on the loose. I want to see all their faces. I'm a visual person. Somebody categorize them by security level. The really dangerous cases up this end of the room, by me."

More people rushed away, and others took their place around her. Everyone wanted to be near Trinity. She'd experienced it before. The attraction of a calm island in a tumultuous sea. Wayward boats were drifting in, taking shelter but also wanting to witness her undertaking the plainly unfathomable task of cleaning up a mess as breathtakingly ridiculous as this.

And it was a spectacular mess. It wasn't so much the number of prisoners set free that concerned Trinity. Sure, it was the biggest mass breakout she'd ever dealt with—but the response was immediate. If she got a proper grasp on the personnel assigned to her, and they all followed her directions, there would be a huge number of inmates scooped up within the first few days simply because they were idiots who didn't know what to do when presented with sudden freedom. There would be clusters of inmates to be found in bars, brothels, and casinos all over Vegas. Trinity had worked on a mass breakout in Chicago—twenty-one prisoners escaped from a transport vehicle—and the week's delay in calling her in had meant Trinity was trying to hunt down some of the guys as far away as Venezuela.

No, it was the high-profile inmates on the loose in this particular case that filled Trinity with a sense of unease. Three of them, in fact, should never have been in Pronghorn at all.

There was Abdul Hamsi, the failed terrorist, who had wound up in a state prison rather than a federal control unit because the one death he had actually managed to chalk up was a parking-lot security guard he'd run over with his getaway car.

There was Burke David Schmitz, who should also have been a federal inmate, but who was saved from a fed stay in Louisiana, where his crimes were committed, because he also killed while on the run. Schmitz had shot two Black police officers who tried to pull him over in Nevada as he headed for California. He was not extradited back to the state where he'd conducted a massacre for fear he would be a travel security risk.

And then there was serial killer Homer Carrington, who had confirmed kills in several states, which had landed him in a federal prison in north Nevada. Until an attack on a guard had him temporarily shipped to Pronghorn for containment.

The biggest tickets on Trinity's bill should have been rapists and wife-killers. Instead she was chasing mass murderers and terrorists.

She rubbed at her temple, trying to subdue a growing headache.

A slender woman in a tan and green uniform appeared by her side, and Trinity could tell from the collapsed look of her frame and the restlessness of her hands that this was probably the warden.

"Grace Slanter." The woman gave a dead-fish handshake. "This is my disaster."

"An excellent choice of word," Trinity said. "Disaster. Congratulations, Ms. Slanter. You're about to make history as the world's worst prison warden."

"In defense of myself, and my staff"—Grace held a hand up—"we never anticipated anything like this. No one was trained in this. All our hostage protocols are designed to deal with inmates inside the facility taking control of staff. We were presented with a situation today in which—"

"Let me get this straight," Trinity said. "You put thirty-four civilians—the family members of prison staff—on a single unarmored vehicle and let them drive toward the facility without any kind of protection?"

"The annual softball game is something we've had in place at this prison for eleven years," Grace said. "There's never been an issue."

"Okay." Trinity nodded. "So not only did you wrap a bunch of children in meat and send them unguarded into shark-infested waters, you made sure you did it on the same goddamn day eleven times in a row."

"Well—"

"If I'm to understand my briefing correctly"—Trinity shifted some blueprints of the prison on the table in front of her—"on that bus you had the wife of a watchtower guard, the wife and son of a death row guard, the husband and two daughters of a gateman, and a family member of at least one guard from every single accommodation block in this institution." Trinity looked at a list of staff members with names highlighted in bright yellow ink.

"That's what I'm led to believe." Grace swallowed.

"Well." Trinity widened her eyes, shook her head in astonishment. "I don't know whether to send you home to enjoy your last few moments of professional anonymity, or to put you in a room with a couple of my investigators so that you can be questioned about any possible leads on who your inside man was."

"The inside man?"

"Yes." Trinity sipped her coffee. "Obviously."

"Marshal Parker," Grace said carefully. "Nothing is obvious to me right now. I'm still recovering from this morning's events."

"Ms. Slanter, every hostage on that bus was linked to a key staff member inside the prison," Trinity said. "That was deliberate. Somebody arranged that. Otherwise you might have had all the guards in one cell block falling over each other to meet the shooter's demands and no one else willing to do so." Trinity squinted, examining Grace's face. "Are you following me, dear?"

"I am," Grace said. "I just—"

"Go home, Ms. Slanter." Trinity gave a thin smile and patted the older woman on the shoulder. When she looked away, there was a petite woman with a bloodied, bruised face standing at her elbow. Trinity jumped, almost dropping her coffee. "Jesus!"

"You Marshal Trinity Parker?"

"The very same."

"They tell me you're heading up this operation." The woman scratched at dried blood on the collar of her uniform. "I'm Captain Celine Osbourne. Death row supervisor."

Trinity looked the woman over. Trinity was tall, which suited her, because she found herself most effective when talking down to people. But even then, the Osbourne woman was particularly short. Trinity felt the muscles in her neck tightening as she looked down at her, something she decided she didn't want to do for very long.

"So you're the one who let the worst of the worst out." Trinity turned her back on Grace Slanter, who was still hanging around for some reason. "Congratulations, you—"

"Ma'am, don't start in on me. I didn't let *anybody* out," Celine said. "My second-in-command locked me out of the control room and flipped the switch. In fact, we've got one inmate already back in his cell on the row. Willy Henderson. Wife killer."

Trinity cocked her head, reassessing the short woman with the pixie-cut blonde hair. "Uh-huh. I see. And was it Henderson who . . ." She twirled a finger around Osbourne's pummeled face.

"Yup."

"Right." Trinity beckoned a deputy with her finger. "You. Yeah. Write a statement for this woman to give in front of the cameras. Osbourne, you tell the media you single-handedly fought off one of your most violent inmates to keep him contained."

"I don't want to fuck around in front of cameras." Celine flapped a stapled sheaf of papers she had been holding by her side. "I want in on the hunt for the top fugitives. They'll all be from my row. I know these guys. Top priority needs to be a man named Kradle. I can give you the lowdown on him, and—"

"That's not the best use of your time right now." Trinity held up a hand. "We need to get out in front of this. We've got a female warden in this story. Understand? I don't care how much she actually had to do with letting the inmates out"—Trinity glanced at Grace Slanter—"but she's going to be the face of this thing. It'll be *Woman Warden Released Killers Into*

Public. Woman Warden Responsible for Slaying of Dozens. This fiasco is going to decimate the progress of women in management positions in law enforcement for the next two decades unless we can change the narrative."

"I couldn't give a shit about narratives!" Celine pointed at the partitions being dragged to the side of the room, the photographs of men already being pinned up. "I want to catch those guys before they hurt anyone!"

Trinity gestured with her coffee cup, kicking an offer over to the mouthy little shrimp. "Do a five-minute bit to the press and you can be part of the lead team."

"Deal," Celine said, just as Trinity expected her to.

Trinity took the papers the woman had been waving around and started spreading them out on top of the maps and blueprints on the table before her. Thankfully, Grace Slanter took the hint and slumped away. Trinity's eyes flicked between the papers as she laid them down. She had seen plenty of prisoner profiles in her time and skipped right over the names, sorting them into piles according to body count. She flipped a couple of sheets to the corner of the desk, and Celine snatched up one of those before it could slide onto the floor.

"This is the guy who should be top of the shit pile." Celine smacked the sheet down in front of Trinity. "John Kradle. He—"

"Three victims?" Trinity cocked an eyebrow. "You kidding?"

"He came home from work one day and blew his wife and kid away. Sister-in-law, too. This guy is a cold, calculated—"

"Look." Trinity straightened. "I know you're new to this. You haven't been trained for anything like this before, blah blah blah. But I'm going to be looking for the terrorist who organized this whole clusterfuck."

She pointed to the room around them, two hundred people working like ants.

"I don't know for sure who he is, yet," Trinity said. "But he's got to have connections. We know there was a man, possibly more than one, on the inside. We know he recruited at least two people on the outside, the shooter and the caller. Probably a driver and a lookout, too. So, 'top of the shit pile,' as you so eloquently put it, is going to be someone like this." She picked up a sheet and waggled it in front of the woman's eyes, then turned it back toward herself. "Burke David Schmitz. White nationalist neo-Nazi terrorist. Mass shooter responsible for fifteen deaths and eighteen injuries." She picked up another page. The shrimp's face was slowly filling with color. "Or this guy. Abdul Ansar Hamsi. Islamic State. Killer of—"

"John Kradle is a family annihilator," Celine snapped. Trinity waited. The little woman just panted and looked aggrieved.

"You use that term like it's supposed to mean something to me," Trinity said.

"It means he slaughtered the people he loves most," Celine said. She snatched up Schmitz's paper and crushed it in her fist. "These guys? We can go after them. I get it. They're an extreme danger to the public. But they kill the people they hate. Kradle murdered his own child in cold blood while the kid was taking a shower. He gets equal weight in the hunt."

"No, he doesn't," Trinity said.

"Yes, he does, or I don't do the bit to camera."

"You do the bit to camera or I'll have you imprisoned in your home," Trinity said.

"You can't do that."

"Oh, yes I can. I'll put three agents on you. Dear, you said it yourself. These are your guys. It was your row. It's reasonable to expect that one of them might come after you, so perhaps the best thing to do is put you in protective custody for the duration of the hunt. There are a lot of inmates on the loose." Trinity widened her eyes, blew out her cheeks at the sight of the papers before her. "Might take months, a year, to round them all up."

Celine had started shaking. Trinity felt a flush of pleasure roll over her. She liked putting people exactly where they belonged. It was no different to organizing her linen closet, or stacking cans in a cupboard. She liked order. Celine had started crawling up the shelves, and now she had been taken down and tucked away in her spot. The woman turned and stormed away, and Trinity shook her head in disbelief for the benefit of anyone who might have been watching.

1990

He found her in a newspaper.

He would always find something interesting on his trips into town. They were rare enough at that time that something special always happened. Interactions with people who weren't gator hunters or the swamp witches they married were always ripe for magic. Once, when John Kradle came onto land because the rudder on his houseboat had cracked, he found a pair of hapless Russian tourists on an unnamed back road. He'd been walking to his favorite shack bar and saw the woman sitting on a log, fanning herself in the choking heat. The guy was in the driver's seat of their RV, trying to interpret a hand-drawn map probably given to them by some gas station attendant, which had led them to this exact spot. Nowhere. A subtle little "New Iberia is not New Orleans" message the locals sometimes dished out. Kradle made his case as a trustworthy local, jumped into the vehicle, and saw the Russians back to the main road, which took him well out of his way. But they paid him a hundred bucks, which bought the supplies to fix the rudder and get a beer afterward.

He was sitting at the back of the bar, a corrugated iron and scrap-wood affair close enough to the river that it always stank of fish guts, when he saw the ad she'd placed in the classifieds section. He had been thinking he would need to do a few jobs before he could get away into the weeds again for any decent period of time, but he hadn't been looking for the kind of work she was offering. He was more of a porch-painting, bee-hive-removing, motor-oil-changing sort of guy. Most of his clients were old ladies who had deathly concerns about getting up a ladder. But he was intrigued, so he used the phone behind the bar to call her.

When he heard her voice, like a bass guitar wire thrumming, he decided he was going to do whatever he had to in order to get the job.

"What kind of camera do you have?" she asked.

"Well, here's the thing," he began. Marty, the bartender, sweat beads sticking in his arm hairs, rolled his eyes as Kradle made the play. He'd take his pay in advance, go get the camera, then do the job. Christine wasn't buying it, so he shrugged casually, as if she could see him through the phone. The shrug was really for Marty.

"I'm not trying to scam you, lady," Kradle said. "I'm going to hang up now. If you get any interested parties who already have a camera, fine. If you don't, come down to the bar on Second Street and you can see what you think of me face-to-face."

"What's the name of the bar?" she asked, but Kradle hung up, because he'd said he would, and the place didn't have a name anyway.

An hour later, she was there, wearing a flowy, leopard-print number that made Marty hang his head back and look down his nose, like he was trying to decide if he was really seeing what he was seeing. Kradle didn't know what kind of fabric it was, but he did know Southerners didn't wear it. He could see sweat rolling down her sides through the oversized armholes. He could also see her lacy pink bra. She asked Marty if he served daiquiris, and he laughed and laughed before putting a vodka Coke in front of her.

"So you didn't get ten other guys wanting to come help you catch demonic activity on film?" Kradle asked when she sat down.

"You can stop right there," Christine said, pointing a finger at his face. She pushed back her brown curls, composed herself. "I won't work with anyone who doesn't take my profession seriously."

"Wait, so you mean the demon thing is real?" Kradle said. "I was sure it was a cover."

"A cover for what?"

"Porn."

"Oh, Jesus." She shook her head. "No, honey, it's not porn."

"Well, whatever is it, I'll try to take it seriously, then." He hid his smile with difficulty.

"The couple I'm providing consultation to live over in Erath," she explained, her eyes locked on her drink, defensive. "They've had an entity threatening them for some weeks. I haven't confirmed it's demonic, because I haven't visited the residence yet. I'm just guessing. Could be we're dealing with a returner, not an outer-worlder. But I need to film all my interactions with the dwelling and its inhabitants, because the footage can sometimes prove useful in analysis of the entity's residency."

"So what happened to your last camera guy?" Kradle asked.

"He got scared off." Christine looked at him, challenging.

"Well, it would take a hell of a thing to scare me off," he said. She thought that was just the funniest thing anybody had ever said; kept saying, "Hell of a thing," and clapping. Marty gave a big, long sigh and poured himself a big, long whiskey.

It was supposed to be just a fun way to spend his afternoon. An easy four hundred dollars and a job that maybe wouldn't get him filthy with oil or covered in bee stings. But she liked to talk, and it had been a long time since he'd listened to anybody, so he sat in the bar with her all night, feeding her vodka Cokes and nodding along to her tales of ghosts and bogeys and possessed people. He learned the difference between a returner and an outer-worlder, and left pretty convinced that the previous camera guy hadn't been scared off by anything supernatural. The plan was to get a cab to a pawnshop to look at cameras, but then they figured it was too late and the place would be closed, so they ended up arriving at midnight at the little dock where he'd parked his houseboat.

When he woke up in the morning he expected her to be gone. Instead he walked out onto the back deck and found her there, sitting on the plastic chair, buck naked and dangling a handline in the water.

CHAPTER 6

Kradle was thinking about his houseboat as they hit the base of the mountains and pockets of shade began flooding over him. Long stretches out of the sun bathed him in coolness, or the illusion of coolness to a mind desperately trying not to focus on fire, burning, searing, bones cooking down to ash. The threat behind him urged him on. The man named Homer kept maybe ten yards back, his head down and his long legs crunching into the dry earth. Kradle would just get himself into the safety of his memories—of the Louisiana rain hammering down on the corrugated-iron roof of the houseboat, slapping into the surface of the river, drumming against the windows where he kept his little jars of nails and screws and hinges on the tiny kitchen windowsill—when he would hear Homer cough or sniff or mutter to himself. A zing of electric terror would erupt in his chest and he would glance around.

"Let's talk plans," Homer said eventually. Kradle waited until the big man was beside him. They had stopped in the shade of a rocky overhang.

"On the other side of these mountains is an air-field." Kradle pointed. "That's where we're headed."

"Why?"

Kradle thought about lying, but the seconds were pressing on and Homer's shockingly big hands were hanging there, and Kradle couldn't keep the words from tumbling out of his lips.

"Because I'm hopping a plane," he said.

"You've thought about this before." Homer gave a wry smile, waggled a finger at Kradle. "This is a great plan. How far to the field?"

"We'll take a break at sunset, try to catch a couple of hours' sleep," he said. His mouth was painfully dry. "Our priority has been getting out of sight and into the hills. But we don't want to stay here too long. The rocks will hold the heat of the day for a while, make it harder to track us with heat-seeking cameras. But when they cool we'll be easy to find. So by daybreak we want to be back in civilization."

Don't ask me, Kradle thought. *Don't ask me where we—*

"Where are we flying to?" Homer asked.

"*We're* not flying anywhere." Kradle straightened and looked Homer dead in the eyes. "We're going to split up."

"I don't think so." Homer gave a boy-next-door smile, dripping with sweetness. He gestured to the mountains. "This is the kind of plan that has taken awhile to think through. You've been lying in your cell, putting this together for months, maybe years. I want to be with the guy who has a plan, because I don't have a plan."

Kradle drew a long breath. "Maybe you should just come up with one of your own."

"You got a map in that bag? I bet you've got one." He pointed to the pillowcase hanging over Kradle's shoulder.

"No," Kradle said.

"But you've got water." Homer nodded to the bag. The big guy folded himself down like a tall clothes rack collapsing for storage under a bed, until he was sitting on a rock. "You were the guy who was smart enough to grab water before rushing out into the desert. I bet you there wasn't another man in E Block who grabbed water before heading out. I sure didn't."

Kradle felt another sharp prickle of energy in his chest, tight and hard. Homer was from E Block, but he wasn't from the row. There was only one other section in E Block besides death row, and that was the special housing unit. The SHU housed guys who were so violent they couldn't be moved without hand and leg irons, a shock belt, and a spit hood. Kradle had never seen the special housing unit, but he'd heard there were rarely any guys assigned to it at Pronghorn. They had more appropriate facilities for that kind of inmate on the other side of Vegas. Frankie Buchanan had gone to special housing only a week ago, after he lured an officer to the front of his cell and tried to spear him in the chest with a splinter of wood he'd broken off a chair in the visitors' center. Buchanan was gone now, shipped out to face a rape charge in Minnesota, Kradle had heard.

"Give me the water," Homer said.

Kradle handed over the water bottle. Homer sipped some and handed it back. Kradle thought he might vomit if he tried to swallow any, so he just held the bottle.

"We better stay hydrated," Homer mused.

Kradle looked at the mountains, thought about making a run for it. But he wanted to know what kind of beast he was dealing with before he annoyed that beast, and before he lost sight of it. You don't kick an alligator in the face and then leap into the water. He sank onto a rock and put the water bottle to his lips.

"I don't think I've seen you on the row," he said, forcing a sip.

"I'm new. Only a week in. Maybe that's why."

"What'd you do?"

"I ran over a cop." Homer rolled his eyes. "I wouldn't be on the row if it had just been some random dude. But I was in a car chase and they threw the road spikes out for me. I hit the cop when I swerved to try to avoid the spikes. It wasn't my fault. It was an accident."

Kradle nodded casually and crumbled a wad of dried sand in his fingers, but his mind was whirring. He'd heard that story. That was Frankie Buchanan's story. The guy had occupied the cell two down from Kradle's a few years earlier, and they'd exchanged origin stories, the way inmates did with anyone who lingered within earshot for a few months or more.

Kradle tried to tell himself that it was unlikely Homer had snatched the tale from Buchanan in the SHU and was now using it as a cover. More likely it was just a coincidence. It was a pretty common story. Kradle reminded himself that guys got into car chases. That cops threw out road spikes during those chases. That guys ran over cops. It happened. There was no reason to jump to conclusions. As long as Homer didn't say he was driving a stolen van filled with televisions, everything would be—

"See, I had all these flat-screen televisions," Homer said.

Kradle hung his head.

She walked into Kradle's cell and sat down on the rack, feeling the thin mattress compress and the steel bones of the bed dig into the backs of her thighs. Celine wondered where John Kradle was now, whether his sorry ass was riding in one of the cars stolen from the parking lot with a bunch of other scumbags, headed for Vegas, or if he was going to try to disappear into Utah or California. Celine knew the answer lay here, among his things, and she would do whatever she could to find that answer.

On the shelf by the desk, items were lined up in a single row. Envelopes organized into a cardboard shelving unit, a shaving mirror that reflected her worried, battered face, bottles of toiletries, and a stack of noodle packets a foot and a half high. Celine took the little handmade mail organizer and sat it in her lap. There were three sections labeled with marker. *Hate. Marriage. Lawyer.* She pulled out the papers in the thickest section, *Marriage,* and opened the first envelope. The writing was bulbous, juvenile, some of the ink pink and some of the i's dotted with little hearts.

Dear John,
I read about you in the Chicago Tribune. *I wanted to write and tell you that as soon as I saw your face in the picture, I felt a weird connection to you. My name is Debbie, and I think I can understand what you did.*

Celine's fingers gripped the paper unsteadily, as though they were numb. She skipped ahead through the letter.

Because if we got married, I could take care of you in there. I could send you commissary, books, whatever you want. I would understand you and come and visit you, and . . .

Celine tore the letter to shreds and threw the pieces on the ground. She took another letter from the stack and pulled it open. A picture of a tubby woman in a lime-green bikini fell on the floor at her feet. She flicked the folded piece of notebook paper hard, so that it snapped open.

Have you heard that song, "I Knew I Loved You Before I Met You"? It's by Savage Garden. I've included the lyrics on the second page. John, that's how I feel about you. Please write back so we . . .

Celine scrunched the letter into a ball and hurled it onto the floor. She shoved the organizer and the stacks of letters off her lap and onto the concrete. One letter remained on her lap, a small envelope slipped from the *Hate* folder. The paper was scrawled over with large, clumsy lettering in thick black marker.

You're a sick dirty fuck. Anyone who kills there own family has a special place in hell waitin for them. Kid killers are the worse kind of scum. Your gonna burn for eternity John Kradle. Fry fry fry. Scream scream scream.

Celine felt her heartbeat slow. She hadn't realized there were angry tears on her face until she heard a noise outside the cell and came back to herself, sitting there reading an inmate's mail. She swiped at her face and nose and went to the entrance, poked her head out.

"Hey," she called. The small, wiry man jolted at the sound of her voice. He was two cells down, looking at a notice on the wall, his hands clasped behind his back as if he were touring an art gallery. He pushed a pair of glasses up on his nose and adjusted the shirt of his uniform.

"Ma'am." He nodded.

"What are you doing here?"

"Oh, I, um . . ." He jerked a thumb behind him, but there was no one there. Celine and the man were alone on the row. Henderson had been taken to the infirmary and no other inmates under Celine's charge had been recovered yet. "Warden Slanter sent me just to, uh . . . You know. To check that everything is okay here."

Celine looked at the guy. There were prison tattoos crisscrossing his dark skin, the name *Kaylene* scrawled across his jugular. His guard's uniform had no name badge and was unbuttoned to the middle of his muscular chest. He was in his thirties, but looked slightly more worn than that. Celine sighed with exhaustion and put a hand on her baton.

"Put your hands on the wall, inmate," she said.

"Oh, damn." The guy slumped, dejected.

"You know you could get twenty-five years for impersonating a correctional officer." Celine took the cuffs off her belt as she walked toward the prisoner. "Where did you get the uniform?"

"When everybody ran out, a guard from my block left the door to the staff room open and I saw it hanging over a chair," the inmate said. "I think it's actually a lady's uniform."

"Well," Celine said, "there's going to be so much goddamn paperwork after today, and you've done such a terrible job of making like a guard anyhow, that I don't think I could bring myself to write this up."

"You're very kind, ma'am," the inmate said. He put his wrists out and Celine cuffed him.

"Who the hell are you?"

"I'm Walter Keeper. People call me ForKeeps, or just Keeps sometimes, if they're in a hurry." He brandished a tattoo on his wrist. 4KEEPZ.

"Where are you from?"

"Minimum." Keeps shrugged guiltily. "I'm scheduled for release tomorrow, so I wasn't going nowhere today. I was pretty tempted, though! I've been counting down the hours since last Wednesday. Got twenty-one hours to go. And that's not nothing."

"So to burn a few minutes you dressed up like a guard, thereby committing a felony, and came over here to death row?" Celine said. "You would have got less jail time for escaping than for—" She stopped, shook her head. Every now and then she found herself trying to explain to inmates the stupidity of their crimes, and had to remind herself it was a fruitless exercise. "Never mind."

"I just always wanted to see the row, that's all," Keeps reasoned. He looked around. "Figured it was the only chance I could get without killing somebody."

Celine smirked in spite of herself. She felt dried blood crackle at her temple.

"Well, this is it." She gestured to the corridor around her. "You had a good enough look?"

"Sure."

"Let's go, then." She took his arm. They walked down the hall, Keeps leaning forward and glancing into every cell as they went.

"Somebody pop you on the way out then, huh?" he asked.

"I got in a little tussle," Celine said. "I'm fine."

"You got all kinds of serial killers and shit up in here?"

"Not anymore."

"Man, this is some extraordinary business," Keeps said. He shook his head. "All those guys out there running around at the same time? I'm kind of glad I'm still in here where it's safe."

"The world is upside down today," Celine said.

"Inside out."

"Yeah, inside out."

"They'll be looking for an inside guy, right?"

Celine stopped walking. Keeps was peering into Henderson's cell, eyeing an unopened box of commissary sitting on the bunk.

"You know anything?"

"Nah, nah," Keeps said. "Just seems like something too big to organize from the outside, though. Too many chess pieces. You know what I'm saying?"

"Yeah." Celine nudged him on.

"Best way to catch a snoop is to send a snoop after him," Keeps said, sounding hopeful.

"Well, it won't be you. You'll be out of here legitimately in twenty hours and fifty-five minutes."

"Yeah, but I'm always looking for jail credit." Keeps

shrugged. "Might be able to use the brownie points the next time I'm in."

"The next ti—Keeps, most inmates don't make plans for the next time they'll be in prison while they're packing their things to leave."

"I'm not most inmates," he said. "I'm what you call a 'forward-thinking man.'"

"Yeah, well, you provide some evidence of your usefulness to me, and I'll provide some evidence of my usefulness to you," Celine said.

"Okay, okay, okay, okay." Keeps nodded enthusiastically. "I can do that. All right, uh . . ."

They walked out into the yard while Keeps thought, chewing on his lip and staring at the ground as it passed beneath his feet.

"Oh, okay." He straightened. "Your guys on the row. They got the same kind of lighting system we got over there in minimum?"

"What do you mean?"

"In the cells," he said. "Like, on the wall. There's a long, thin, gold light behind, like, cloudy kind of Perspex?"

"Yeah."

"You might want to look into that."

"We do a check of the lights every time we shake down the cells." Celine rolled her eyes. "That's not the kind of intel I'm after."

"Maybe you ought to look *around* the lights." Keeps lifted his cuffed hands and tapped his nose. "You feel me?"

"You'll have to be more specific."

"Oh, damn, woman." He gave a huge sigh. "I'll snitch, but I'm not gonna paint you a picture and put it in a pretty frame and hang it on the wall for you."

Celine gave a little laugh.

"Those lights," Keeps continued, "they're an up-grade. Used to be, back in the day, guys had those fluorescent tubes in their cells, up in the ceiling."

"I remember those."

"Yeah. But they weren't halogen, so they cost more to run. And also they did a bunch of studies about those fluorescent lights, how they're bad for you. They hum and blink and mess with your brain. The scientists, they found out that if guys have gold light instead of white light they'll read more at night. More reading means smarter, less depressed, less angry guys. When they put the halogen strips in, they say violence went down, like, twenty-five percent or some shit."

"How do you know all this?" Celine asked.

"I read in my bunk at night. The *Times*."

"Okay, Professor."

"So everybody's got a gold strip light above their bunk, right? But every time you add something into the prison, you weaken it. It's like if you . . . you bake a cake, and then you want to go and add something to the middle. Too bad. You got to cut the cake up. You got to bake stuff in for it to be right."

"You really like talking, huh."

"You told me to be more specific!"

"Find a middle ground," Celine said.

"Okay, okay. So when the contractors installed those lights, they were supposed to bury the wire in the concrete six inches back. That's the standard. But that's a lot of drilling, you know? Every cell in minimum, medium, maximum. That's hundreds of lights. Easier to just dig out a shallow channel, stick the wire in and smooth it over. So, take a look, and call me up if you find anything good."

"Okay," Celine said. "I'll call you up."

Celine walked Keeps back to minimum and locked him in a holding cell, then returned to the row. She went to John Kradle's cell and climbed onto his bunk again, standing and running her hands over the light set into the concrete wall.

Celine hadn't heard the light thing before, but she didn't dismiss it. Inmates had plenty of means of hiding things in their cells. They would fashion strings from strands of cotton taken from the bedding, attach them to watertight balloons made from commissary packaging, and float contraband items behind the U-bend in the toilet, retrieving the balloons on the string when they were needed. They would secret pieces of razor blades into the hems of their clothes or in the folds of their armpits and crotches, force tiny taped packages of drugs between the pages of their books, into cracks in the floor, into their anal cavities. Celine ran a hand over the wall beneath the light fixture, where she assumed the electrical wire was embedded. It was smooth, unbroken, uniform concrete.

She took a key from her belt and gouged the hard teeth across the surface of the wall. A tiny fleck of white appeared. Celine started digging around the fleck with the key. More white, fibrous material sprouted. She pulled the material away and broke it up in her fingers. Papier-mâché, probably constructed from wet toilet paper. It had been painted over with a murky gray dye, created, Celine guessed, from mop water or newspaper ink. Celine gouged out a section of the wall beneath the light until she could see the dull white plastic sheath in which the electrical cord that led to the light nestled in the concrete.

Lifting the cord carefully with her fingernail, she

exposed a tiny slip of paper. She pulled it out, unfolded it, and looked at the writing.

Wagon Circle 18 m NE (7 h)
Willie McCool 16 m S (6 h)
Brandon Butte 17 m ENE (8 h)

Again, Celine thought she knew what she was looking at. She only needed to confirm it. She made to jump down from the bunk but noticed another piece of paper poking out further down the electricity wire beneath the light. Celine dug it out, leaving shreds of papier-mâché concrete to tumble onto her feet and John Kradle's bed.

This little secret package was wrapped tightly in tape. She had to walk back to the control room, rummage through the drawer full of confiscated items, and find a sliver of razor blade to open it with. With painstaking care she unrolled an oval of newspaper as big as a thumbprint. It was a picture. The images were of two faces.

A woman and a teenage boy.

CHAPTER 7

It was the first sunset Kradle had seen in five years, and it was a thick, dusty, tomato red. He was too tired to make much of it, though. He watched for a while, thinking about the sunsets over New Iberia, which were purple. In a decade he hadn't been active outside his cell for more than an hour a day, and he figured he'd walked for seven straight hours through the desert and up Sheep Peak to where he sat now. He lay down in the dark of the shallow cave and listened to Homer easing his big body down a few feet away. Keeping his back to the man was a struggle. With every sound Kradle felt as though the killer was coming for him. When Homer spoke it sent bolts of pain up through the bottom of his feet, into his bones.

"What are you thinking about?" Homer asked.

"Louisiana," Kradle said. He was so exhausted that uttering more than a word at a time seemed like a full-body effort he couldn't yet muster. He needed to conserve his energy, stay awake longer than Homer, slip away when the other man fell asleep.

"Hot there."

"Uh."

"Hot in here, too."

"Yep," Kradle sighed, and blew sand from the rocky surface by his cheek. "It'll cool down."

"If it gets real cold we'll have to share body heat."

"We're not doing that."

"You from the South? I thought I recognized the accent."

"Uh-huh."

"You going back there?"

"Yeah," Kradle said. Just saying it out loud seemed to give strength to the dreams crowding at the corners of his vision. The gentle rocking of his houseboat as tiny waves reached it across the huge, watery planes, made by distant airboats going by; gator hunters. Kradle sometimes fancied he could hear the rhythmic knocking of a reptilian spine against the hull of his vessel as the creatures rose and kissed it while gliding underneath. He heard the hammering of the rain on the windows. The wind in the swamp trees. Froggers calling out to each other in the dark.

"I'm going to Mexico," Homer said from a million miles away.

"Hmm?"

"Police force down there is not like it is up here."

Kradle tried to answer but there was a wire around his throat. A belt. A band. A thick, and thickening, blockage. No air in, no air out. He bucked hard, his hands flying up, grabbing at the band. It wasn't a band but Homer's hands, both of them, the thumbs locked over his windpipe, fingers gripping around the back of his neck, squeezing. Kradle's eyes were already bulging from the pressure on his jugular. He flailed wildly. Homer lowered his body and sat on Kradle's hips. Kradle's heels gouged the rocky floor of the cave.

"I'm sorry," Homer said gently. "I have to do this."

The shrimp skidded into the room like a Maltese terrier running for the open door of an old woman's house, eyes big and full of dreams of murder. Trinity barely glanced at her. She was conducting, as she had been when she first encountered the woman, standing at the front of a room full of people, her arms held high, directing with skill and majesty. There were journalists from ten major stations, and their camera operators, filing into the small room off the chow hall. Trinity guessed it was a group meeting place for inmates. Lots of posters about alcoholism on the walls. Encouraging sentiments about taking it one day at a time, as if the morons who ended up here had enough working gray matter to delay gratification for an entire twenty-four-hour period. Addicts thought, and thereby predicted consequences, in fifteen-minute increments. Trinity knew this because she'd seen it— because she had three sisters who were all ice addicts and a brother dead in the ground, put there by Daniels, first name Jack.

"I know where he is," Celine said. "And I know where he's going."

"Who?" Trinity flapped her hand at a man who was trying to squeeze an additional mic into the huddle on the podium in front of her. "Back off, bozo. Can't you see this space is full?"

"John Kradle," Celine said.

"The wife-killer? Oh, please."

"This is a note I discovered in his cell." Celine un-

folded a tiny strip of paper. "These are airfields. Walking distances and times. He's going to jump a plane
back home to Mesquite. That's smart. If he flies, he'll
bypass all the road blocks. And look. Look." She
smoothed a fragment of what looked like gray newspaper on the papers lying on the podium.

"This is his wife and his son," Celine continued.
"He hasn't let go. He's going back there to—"

"You're standing on my foot," Trinity said. She
leaned in and spoke with her teeth locked. "And you're
yapping in my ear while I'm trying to brief the nation
on a crisis *you* took part in creating."

"But—"

Trinity brushed the fragment of whatever it was
off the papers before her, snatched a sheet of paper
from the stack and gave it to Celine. "You get up here
when I call you, you read these lines, and then you sit
back down and shut your trap."

"Listen, I want a team of—" Celine began.

"Ladies and gentlemen." Trinity smiled. All eyes and
cameras in the room swung to her. Bright white lights
warm on her features. She lifted her sharp chin, set her
shoulders back. "We're going to begin. My name is
Trinity Parker. I'm the United States Marshals Service
major case director for the State of Nevada. I'll be
outlining for you the current circumstances surrounding the breakout at Pronghorn Correctional Facility
this morning."

Trinity stood with her hands flat on the podium,
placed either side of her paperwork. Calmly and eloquently, she briefed the nation, probably the world, on
the case. She made eye contact with every camera at
least once. Took them through the response she had
coordinated. The roadblocks, grid searches, flyovers,

increased highway patrols, and doubled police man-power taking shape in Vegas.

"Volunteers are manning phones for tips and sightings," she said. "And I'm pleased to report that we have already recovered more than three dozen inmates, many of them medium and maximum security individuals hunted down by marshals and sheriffs. Inmates are *streaming* back into the facility by the minute. This situation is under control and will soon be completely neutralized."

She nodded to some nameless prison staffer standing in the corner by the projector, and a slide replaced the US Marshals' crest on the wall behind her. As she glanced around, she saw Celine Osbourne returning to the room from the chow hall.

"We have categorized our top-priority fugitives by their crimes." Trinity gestured to the four faces displayed on the slide above her. "These men, our Ace Card inmates, are all death row inmates. So, for that reason, I'm going to hand you over to Captain Celine Osbourne, supervisor of the condemned row section of this facility. Captain Osbourne?"

Trinity gestured, leveled her eyes at the woman. Celine walked up and took the podium. There was an audible ripple through the room, gasps and murmurs about her battered face.

"My name is Captain Celine Osbourne, and I am the supervisor of the condemned prisoners' row," Celine read from the pages she had been provided. "I am working with the US Marshals' department to recover inmates released from the facility this morning, having already single-handedly subdued and recontained a violent and highly dangerous inmate after he esca—Well, that's not exactly true . . ."

Celine looked up. Trinity, who had taken her place by the door, tried to communicate through her eyes all of her raw, hellcat-furious determination not to take even a teaspoon of shit from this woman in front of the world's media. It seemed to work. Celine went back to the paper. She read ahead for a moment.

Then shoved the paper aside.

"Let's get this done quickly," she said.

Trinity ground her teeth.

"This guy." Celine pointed at the wall above her, at the face of an elderly man with high, rigid cheekbones. "That's Walter John Marco. He's that kid-killer sicko from down Hackberry way. You remember that guy. Or maybe your parents remember. Anyway, the guy's eighty-one years old now. If anybody from the Marshals' office had asked me, I wouldn't have put him as Ace of Hearts. The guy can't open a can of tuna by himself and without his heart medication he'll keel over in, oh"—she glanced at her watch—"about eight hours' time."

There was a little titter of laughter throughout the room, cautious glances thrown Trinity's way. She gave a tight smile.

"These next two guys actually are pretty dangerous," Celine said, pointing. "Burke David Schmitz. The Mardi Gras Shooter. Opened up an AR-15 on crowds on the intersection of Loyola Avenue and Poydras Street in New Orleans in 2006, fled here to Nevada. Then you've got Abdul Ansar Hamsi. Failed Flamingo Hotel bomber. Plotted to blow up the casino back in 2015 when it was packed full for a World Poker Tournament. Would have killed hundreds if he'd wired the timing system on the bombs right. But terrorists aren't known for their intelligence."

Celine was working the room. The journalists were writing notes furiously, smiling all the way. Trinity couldn't believe it. She had initially been so stunned by the performance she didn't even consider putting an end to it. But she could see the shrimp was just getting started. Trinity started pushing through the crowd by the door, back toward the podium.

"Homer Carrington is the North Nevada Strangler." Celine pointed. "Now he is highly dangerous. Clever, deceptive. Comes off very friendly. He's been convicted of killing ten people, but I'd say he's got more under his belt that we don't know about." Celine glanced Trinity's way. "Homer is tricky. He made up a bunch of ruses to get his victims. Faked car trouble on the highway. Knocked on doors at night and asked to use the phone to report an accident. Pretended to have found an injured kitten in a back alley."

A cameraman stepped in front of Trinity, blocking her path. She poked him in a love handle.

"Move it. Coming through."

"Those are your Aces." Celine took a big piece of paper from her bra. She unfolded it in front of the crowd. "Now let me introduce the Joker card."

Blackness. Black creeping in from the edges of his vision, slowly consuming the red, the sweeping grip of unconsciousness taking hold over the pain. Homer's eyes were bearing down on Kradle, at once completely focused on him and distant, dreaming, surveying landscapes of pleasure as the pain shot through his victim's face. Just when John Kradle thought he was going to die, going to surrender to the blackness, Homer eased the pressure off his windpipe.

"Take a sip," the big man whispered. "That's it."

Kradle gasped a half-lungful of air, and then the band was tightened around his throat and he was kicking and clawing and struggling again, the pain somehow tenfold now that he had more air in his lungs.

"I've got to do this." Homer was speaking to him and yet at the same time not, mumbling to himself. "I'm so sorry. It's just something that I do sometimes. I can't help it."

Kradle tried to focus through the screaming panic in his mind. He knew another sip of air must be coming. Homer had prolonged the strangulation three times already. Kradle couldn't hold out forever. Homer bowed his head, eased the pressure off gently. Kradle forced himself to resist the urge to draw breath, to push breath out instead, against the will of every inch of his being.

"Listen—" Kradle squeaked.

Homer squeezed. Kradle struggled. He could feel the bigger man's cock through his jeans, pressed against his thigh. It was hard. Kradle scratched helplessly at his killer's hands.

The next sip came. Kradle sucked in the air and blew it straight back out with a word.

"Money!" Kradle yelped.

Homer's head twitched. For a full second, a period of time that echoed for a thousand years in Kradle's soul, Homer kept the pressure on. Then curiosity got the better of him, as Kradle hoped it would. The hands around his throat loosened completely.

Kradle rolled over, curled into a ball, coughed and coughed until he retched and emptied his stomach. He clung to the ground, gasping short, desperate breaths, his entire body shaking, head pulsing as blood rushed back into his brain.

"What money?" Homer said.

"I have money," Kradle managed, between long gasps for air. "Millions. I. Have. Millions."

Homer was on his knees only a foot or two away. Kradle wasn't safe yet. He was making his case. The big man would listen, and if he didn't convince him now that he was someone Homer should keep alive, Kradle knew the bone-chilling grasp of the other man's hands would come again before he could gather the strength to fight him off. He grabbed two handfuls of sand from the floor of the cave, but knew that even if Homer attacked him again and he managed to blind his attacker, he'd never outrun the guy. Not like this. Kradle had thirty seconds to come up with something. Something life-saving.

"I'm not a serial killer," Kradle said.

"Okay," Homer said slowly.

"I told you that to try to sound scary. I'm really a . . . I killed my wife and my kid."

Homer said nothing. He was watching, his hands on his knees, eyes wide.

"She found out that I . . ." Kradle sucked in air. "I was doing some work for the, uh . . . the mob. I had a stack of cash. A lot of cash. I'd walled it up in the garage at my home in Mesquite. She found out, and I killed her and the kid."

"Why did you—"

"It's a long story." Kradle held a hand up. "But the cash is still there. That's where I'm going. If you let me live, I'll give you half. You're going to need money. Think about it. Mexico. Freedom. Real freedom. How are you going to do that? You need money. You need me."

Homer was still as a stone, calculating, those big, deadly hands and long, thick fingers gripping his knees. Kradle couldn't look at them. Couldn't make eye contact while he tried to splutter a convincing stream of bullshit to his executioner as the guillotine blade inched down. Kradle couldn't tell if the story he'd grasped out of thin air, inspired by nothing more than having watched Martin Scorsese's *Goodfellas* on TV in his cell the night before, was doing the job. When Homer burst into tears, his confusion only deepened.

Kradle sat, rubbing his throat, watching the bigger man sob.

"I am so, so sorry," Homer managed.

"It's okay."

"No, it's not," Homer said. "I have this thing. I just . . . It comes over me. You could have died. I'm so sorry. There's no way I can tell you how sorry I am, buddy. Oh, man. I fucked up. Oh, man."

"Homer, it's fine. Let's forget about it."

"I've been doing it since I was a kid, hurting people like that." Homer sighed. "I knew it was wrong but I couldn't help it. I didn't know what I was doing. I blacked out. It's not my fault, really."

"I know," Kradle said carefully. "It's not your fault."

Homer dragged him into a hug. Kradle sat, rigid, his face crushed against the other man's warm chest, his stomach roiling and twisting, making audible gurgles of protest. Because he was under no illusion that Homer had been in anything other than full control throughout the strangulation. The big killer had been tasting every minute of Kradle's suffering, lapping it up. Kradle had seen it in his eyes, the way he set the pleasure aside deliberately at the mention of something possibly more gratifying: cash.

Kradle had known plenty of men like Homer in the can. Predatory pleasure-seekers. Homer was always on the lookout for something to be gained, and, luckily for Kradle, the thought of money had trumped the momentary physical pleasure of killing a stranger in a cave in the desert. Kradle got lucky. Homer was one of those very rare, very dangerous monsters who could forgo present physical satisfaction for future, less bodily satisfaction. Wait now, benefit later. Banking on Homer being a more sophisticated kind of psychopath than the average killer was the only thing that had saved John Kradle's life.

"I'm so sorry," Homer moaned. "Friends don't do that to each other!"

"Don't worry about it," Kradle managed. "Buddy."

They parted. Homer wiped his nose on his sleeve and dragged himself to his feet, grabbing the pillowcase that held all of Kradle's supplies and slinging it over his shoulder. "Guess we better go."

"Yeah." Kradle let Homer pull him up. "It's not far to the airfield."

They left the cave. Kradle saw a sliver of Homer's face in the moonlight, and noted there wasn't a single tear on his face.

CHAPTER 8

Lionel McCrabbin took the booth in the corner of the diner, his back to the wall by the bathrooms, because he'd read in novels about guys doing that so they could see any trouble approaching. He could hear the hand dryers in the restrooms, smell floor cleaner, and probably piss, if he tried. But a guy had to protect his family. His wife and daughter huddled into the bench across from him. He flagged down the waitress.

It was six hours since he'd watched the breakout on the computer monitor in his little office on Fremont Street. Night was crowding in. Outside the diner's grimy windows, in a lot jammed with cars sporting MAGA bumper stickers and dents from drunken side-swipes, his shiny Jaguar bulged with suitcases.

"How long do we have to stay here?" Deseree was watching the doors of the motel across the road, where groups of men in ball caps lingered, smoking and talking rapidly on burner phones. "This is so insane. We should have just stayed home."

"I've got thirteen former clients from Pronghorn," Lionel said, tapping the sheet of paper on the table before him with a sweaty finger. "Four of them are from maximum security. I'm talking about very, very bad guys, Des. Rapists. Murderers. I want the both of you to look at these photos. Look at the names. These are the guys we have to watch out for. If you see *any* of these men—"

"If you had only listened to me when you graduated law school, you wouldn't have rapists and murderers on your client list." Hannah took the paper and flicked it lazily, let her eyes wander over the faces there. "I wanted you to go into finance. How many embezzlers and inside traders do you see breaking out of prison and going to seek revenge on their former lawyers?"

"That's not helpful," Lionel snapped. The waitress came, and he struggled over the huge laminated menu, pointed to something. His collar was cutting into his throat. He unbuttoned it with difficulty.

"Daddy, this isn't right. Look at the place." Deseree was still focused on the motel, eyes narrowed. "We're going to get stabbed in our beds by drug dealers before any of your old clients have a chance to show up."

"I'll call the Monte Carlo." Hannah took out her cell phone. "Stanley will take care of us."

"Stanley the concierge is not taking care of you," Lionel said. "*I'm* taking care of you. We have to stay somewhere they wouldn't expect to find us." Lionel pushed down the hand holding her phone, trapping the device on the table. "I'm serious, girls. Okay? You know I always tell you not to worry. Well, now I'm saying it's time to worry. Worry hard. See this guy here? Ray Bakerfield?" Lionel tapped the paper. "I took a dive on that case, and he knew it. This guy went to prison so I could buy you that Cartier watch for our anniversary. If he finds me he's going to stick a hot poker up my ass, just like he did to his wife."

"Daddy!"

"Jesus, Lionel!"

"I'm not kidding." Lionel felt that his eyes were wide, bulging with terror, but he couldn't do anything about it. "We're in trouble here. But if we keep our heads down, play this smart, we'll be—"

He was going to say "fine." But Lionel McCrabbin had known his whole career never to say "fine," or even to plan to say it, because the second that cursed word came into his brain, the universe snuffled it out like a pig hunting around tree stumps for truffles; the slobbering, hungry, rabid, foaming universe then conspired to make life anything but. Just as his mouth went to form the word, the back door of the diner slammed open—the door just to the right of the men's room, down the short hall beside their booth—and the room was flooded with guys in prison denims. Lionel's heart sank. He watched some asshole in the booth by the front doors rise and hustle his family out in the seconds before the escapees took charge of the space.

"Nobody move! Nobody fucking move!"

One of the guys who passed Lionel and his family was carrying a huge silver revolver that still had a price tag hanging off it. He and Deseree and Hannah put their hands on the tabletop, as if they'd been robbed before, which of course they hadn't. Lionel swept the paper with the photographs onto the seat beside him with his thumb, then shifted over so that he was sitting on top of it.

"Wallets, phones, jewelry! Put 'em in the bags! Now, bitch! Now now now!"

"Oh, god." Hannah was frantically trying to work her Cartier watch off her wrist and into her bra before any of the guys came back. "Are they yours? Are any of these guys yours?"

Lionel felt his heartbeat throbbing in his ears. He looked at the men commanding the diner, crowding terrified patrons into their booths while a young, skinny guy held out a pillowcase for goods. A toddler in the next booth was red-faced and screaming. The robber by the counter was having trouble with the till, berating the waitress, slamming his gun on the top of the machine. It was all too much movement, too much noise. Lionel clutched at his throat and swiped at his sweat-matted hair.

"Uh, I-I-I don't know," he stammered. He looked again. "No. No. None of them are mine. They're too young. They're all too young. Just keep your heads down, girls. Keep your mouths shut. Do what they say."

"Yo, pig man." The skinny guy with the pillowcase was suddenly at their booth, panting behind a bandana that was tied around his nose and mouth. "Money. Now."

Lionel tossed his wallet and watch into the bag. Deseree threw in everything she had: necklace, purse, phone, even her Bishop Gorman class ring. Hannah threw in her phone and purse and looked the young man in the bandana right in the eyes.

"That's all I have," Hannah said.

Lionel shook his head. He couldn't help it. If she'd just listened to *him,* this time. If she'd just been quiet, like he said, maybe the man in the dusty, reeking prison denims wouldn't have looked over her curiously, spied the clasp of the watch poking out from between her expensive, too-widely-spaced breasts.

The guy reached for his wife's breasts. Lionel, in turn, reached for him, because he had no choice— because a guy had to protect his family. He put a hand out for the man's forearm, gripped it gently, uttered something pitiful, like "Please" or "Don't," but it was something. He did something.

There were men on him immediately, ripping him from the booth, slamming him into the stainless steel countertop, kicking him in the chest. The paper with the photographs fluttered into the fray slowly, artfully, like Forrest Gump's fucking feather, and someone snatched it up, and Lionel couldn't see for the red-hot pain clouding his vision.

"Yo, Bricks. Check this out, man."

"Oh, shit. Big Baby Ray is on here."

"You a cop, bro?"

Someone kicked Lionel in the balls. He couldn't speak.

"He's a lawyer!" Deseree was screaming. "Leave him alone! He's just a lawyer!"

Lionel felt the atmosphere change. Even the toddler had stopped screaming. He begged the universe to give him something. The sound of a siren. Commotion, trouble, at the other end of the diner. But it was all on him. He was in a silent bubble of doom, and nothing was going to get him out of it now.

"Dude . . . You Ray Bakerfield's deadbeat lawyer?" someone asked.

A spray of gunshots. Lionel curled into a ball, held his skull, braced every muscle in his body in anticipation. His teeth cracked and ground as he clenched his jaw. His eyes ached as he squeezed them shut. But when the firing stopped there was no pain. Only the thundering of footsteps.

Four of the robbers lay sprawled around him on the sticky linoleum floor of the deli. One of them had collapsed over the counter, legs death-twitching, making the tips of his rubber shoes squeak on the floor. Lionel watched as two guys, also in prison denims, marched into the diner from the parking lot, where they had opened fire through the big windows. The two new guys lowered their rifles, scooped up the guns and the bag of goodies from the bodies of their rivals, and walked out the back door into the street.

Celine held the picture of John Kradle aloft for the cameras. She flattened it against her chest, smoothed it out, held it up again, made sure everybody got a good look.

"We have reason to believe that John Kradle plans violence out there. He may be headed for Mesquite, his home town. Any information leading to the capture of this man will be greatly appreciated by law enforcement. Thanks very much."

She folded the paper and walked off the stage as the crowd erupted into questions. Celine expected Trinity Parker to follow her out into the hall, but she didn't expect the lanky, sharp-faced streak of a woman to grab her by the shoulder and shove her into the wall.

"What the hell is your problem?" Trinity was so mad she was spitting on Celine's face. "Are you mentally defective? You just completely hijacked the world's biggest manhunt."

"I'm having a busy day, aren't I?"

"Here's what you don't understand." Trinity glanced

down the hall. They were alone. She took a long breath, let it out slow. Then she sucker-punched Celine in the guts.

The smaller woman went down. Trinity crouched so that they were at eye level. "I'm in charge here. You desert people are simple. I get it. So I'm going to make it as plain for you as I can, okay? Listen carefully. *I. Am. In. Charge. Here.*"

"You need me," Celine said. Her words were coming out in strained groans. "You're not going to catch these guys without me."

"Right. So I need you to get that little hick brain of yours straight on how this works." Trinity tapped Celine's head with her knuckle, hard. "I choose the priority inmates. We don't redirect the public awareness away from the terrorists to chase after your small-fry targets. You want to catch Kradle, you do it on your own time."

Celine's face was burning with shame.

"Go home," Trinity said. "Get a couple of hours' rest. Come back with your head screwed on."

Celine listened to the footfall of Trinity's heels as she walked away.

CHAPTER 9

They waited at the edge of the airfield, crouched in the darkness. The heat of the day had dissipated as they left the mountains, diminishing to a bone-chilling cold, then warming again before long. They'd walked empty streets, crossed dusty fields, presenting a mild curiosity to horses standing at rotting, sunbaked fences. Kradle saw one person, who watched them through the windows of a little brick house, a hand clutched against a curtain. He was sure the news would be flooded with coverage of the breakout, and, in their prison denims, he and Homer would be an unnerving sight as they moved by. No opportunities to steal new clothes presented themselves. Homer saw a string of washing hanging on a line, but closer inspection revealed only babies' socks and ladies' underwear.

When they reached their destination, John Kradle and Homer Carrington crouched, watching the single squat white stucco building that represented the headquarters of the Wagon Circle airfield north of Las Vegas. The parking lot was empty, tumbleweeds shivering against the rusty wire that marked its perimeter.

"What are we going to do for a pilot?"

"We don't need a pilot. I can fly," Kradle said.

"Whoa. Really?"

"I did some odd jobs when I was a kid in Louisiana." Kradle rubbed his throat. It felt like it was full of sand and splinters of glass. "Crop dusting. I used to take my boss's plane to visit a girl in Pierre Par. And the mob, too. I, uh—I would fly cash down to Mexico now and then for the bosses."

"So what are we waiting for, then? Why don't we go in now while nobody's there?"

"Because we'll need someone to open the safe," Kradle said. "The keys to all the aircraft in the hangar will be in a safe in the office. It's not like stealing a car. Not after 9/11."

"Are you going to know how to fly these things?" Homer pointed to the hangar. "You've been in the can."

"Nothing much changes in small aircraft. The basics remain the same."

Homer sat back on his haunches. "John, you must be the coolest friend I've had in ten years."

"Is that how long you were in Pronghorn?"

"No. I told you, I've only been there a week." Homer scratched his brow to hide his eyes. "I ran over a cop."

"I don't think that's true, Homer." Kradle was speaking without meaning to. The words tumbled out of him. Maybe he was concussed from the shortage of oxygen to his brain. He knew he was poking a bear, and yet couldn't put the stick down.

"Are you calling me a liar?" Homer asked.

"You said you'd been hurting people like that since you were a kid," Kradle said, for some reason. "You almost killed me back there. I get the feeling . . ." He finally managed to shut off the words.

"You get the feeling that I'm a killer," Homer finished for him. "A real killer."

Kradle looked at him. Homer chewed his lips.

"Jesus, don't cry again," Kradle said.

"I can't help it. I feel bad. I'm not like you, John. When I've killed before, it wasn't for business." Homer put a hand on his heart, rubbed his sweat-stiff shirt as if he was soothing a pain. "They were all accidents, those people. I didn't know what I was doing, and then it was too late. I think it's because I started young, you know?" He sniffed. "I got into the habit. I got addicted. Then I couldn't stop doing it."

"How young are we talking?"

"Eight maybe?"

Kradle picked grass, tried to keep his features neutral.

"She was a girl who lived up the street," Homer said. "Carol? Carly? I think it was Carly. Doesn't matter. She had this pretty blue scarf with white polka dots. I used that."

"We can stop talking about this now."

"This is what people don't understand. Being an extreme empath, as I am," Homer continued, his hand on his chest, "every kill hurts me worse than anybody else. It's like, I have to be the one to feel everyone's suffering. Not only my victim's suffering but their parents' and their friends' and everybody around them. Because I did it. I'm at the center. It was me and the victim, and now it's just me left behind to take the brunt of what I did. So I've got to hurt for everybody. You know what I mean?"

"I do."

"And that's hard, you know?"

"So hard," Kradle agreed.

"Some people would call me brave just for bearing it," Homer said. He drew a long, shuddering breath, his gray eyes fixed on the building across the plain. The two men watched a car roll into the parking lot, the sound of the tires popping on the gravel reaching them where they hid.

"So we take out this guy, get the keys, and we're gone." Homer put out a fist. Kradle reluctantly bumped it with his own.

"Sounds like a plan," Kradle said. "But, look. Why don't you let me get the guy. I know what I'm looking for. You keep a lookout from the hangar."

Homer grinned and slapped Kradle's back, rising and jogging low across the perimeter in the direction of the hangars. Kradle watched the killer go, then ran off toward the car taking its place in the lot.

The guy was old. Small. The kind of man who tucked neatly into the passenger seat of light aircraft, who walked under wings to inspect rivets in ailerons without having to double over. The kind of man whose windpipe Homer Carrington would crush like a straw in his fist.

Kradle followed the old guy from his car to the building and stood in the shadows, waiting for him to unlock the door, thinking about how birdlike the people who hung around planes could be—like dog people who ended up looking like their pets, or subconsciously chose pets who looked like them, whatever the situation was. Kradle hadn't seen a dog in five years. Nervous thoughts like this fluttered through his tired brain as the man opened the door. Kradle stepped forward, tightly focused on his task and yet fighting the urge to be distracted, to not do the terrible, terrible thing he was about to do.

"Jesus!" The old man stepped back, spying Kradle's reflection in the glass door just as he pushed it open. He gave a startled laugh. "I didn't see you, I—"

"I'm sorry." Kradle grabbed a handful of the man's shirt. He realized with horror that the words that were coming out of him were the same ones Homer had spoken to him in the cave as his fingers wound around John's throat. "I'm really sorry. I've got to do this."

The guy went rigid. Kradle had seen people do that before. Freeze up. Lock down. He'd been in jail in Mesquite before he was sentenced, and some junkie psycho had taken offense to the way another inmate was looking at him across the shower room. He'd beaten the guy to death right there on the tiles, and the officer who had been allocated to the pod hadn't been ready for it. He'd been on the job for less than a month and had just frozen up and huddled into a corner of the room, watching the beating with eyes big, howling.

Kradle marched the airfield supervisor into the cluttered office behind the reception desk and sat him in a desk chair he found there.

"I'm not going to hurt you," Kradle said, knowing that these were the wrong words—the words robbers and killers spoke in movies before they shot you—but not knowing what else to say. "I just want the keys to a plane."

"Okay," the old guy said. "Okay. Okay. Okay."

He didn't do anything. Just sat there, staring at the floor, probably figuring Kradle might not kill him if he didn't look at his face. His fists were balled, clutched against his crotch. Head down. Arms locked in. True terror. The body protecting all its vital organs. Kradle didn't even have a weapon. He didn't need one. This guy had seen the news, had probably been glued to it.

"Open the safe and get me the keys."

"Okay," the man said.

"Get up. Do it."

"Okay." The guy finally moved, stiffly, as if he was wounded. "Please don't hurt me. I have a wife. Her name's Betty. I'm Roger, and—"

"I'm not going to hurt you. I don't want to know your name. This isn't . . . You don't have to convince me."

Kradle wanted to say so much more. That he didn't hurt people. That he'd never hurt anyone. That the whole goddamn reason he was standing there scaring the life out of an innocent stranger in an airfield in the middle of nowhere was *because* he'd never hurt anyone, and if he could just prove that he could go home. Not back to Mesquite, but all the way home, back to the little houseboat in the swamps, with the rain and the wild green avenues through the weeds, the huge blue skies hard as glass. Back before Christine, before Mason, before Audrey, before he stood over their bodies lying sprawled in blood on the floor of his home.

Focus, he told himself. *Focus.*

He switched on a small gray television set that sat on a desk at the side of the room as the shaking, panting old man unlocked the safe. When the screen awakened, he saw his own face. His eyes. A folded piece of paper. Celine Osbourne was showing his photograph, her mouth twisted and mean.

"*We have reason to believe that John Kradle plans violence out there . . .*"

"What the fuck?" Kradle breathed.

"Any information leading to the capture of this man . . ."

The old man was standing, holding a fistful of keys, looking at Kradle's image on the television set. Kradle took the keys from him and stuffed them into his pocket.

"You got a cell phone?" Kradle asked.

CHAPTER 10

Celine pushed open the door of the bar and found the timeless portal she'd been searching for. Here, it wasn't early, lightless morning. It wasn't Day Two of the worst thing that had happened in Celine's career. It was just a darkened bar, and inside she found about a dozen other Pronghorn employees taking advantage of the refuge from misery, where they could drink away their memories of the past twenty-four hours while the rest of the world headed to breakfast.

Celine took the stool next to Warden Grace Slanter and pulled it close to the bar. When the bartender brought her a glass of wine, Celine drew in a long, deep sip and felt microscopically relieved. Warden Slanter hardly acknowledged her presence. Grace's fingers were shaking as she pulled a cigarette from a cloudy brass container and stuck it between her lips. She took a matching brass lighter from her breast pocket and flipped the grinder a few times, unsuccessfully. Eventually the young bartender, a woman with a shaved skull tattooed all over with purple flowers, came and lit the warden's smoke with a match.

"I'm sixty-five," Grace said, as though they'd been talking for hours already. "That Trinity Parker woman didn't say it, but there's no denying it. That's old. But I'm not your average sixty-five-year-old. I can still put my ankles behind my head, same as I could when I was fifteen."

Celine choked on her wine. Grace didn't notice.

"But sixty-five is old in the public eye," she continued. "You get to my age, you're supposed to be raising grandchildren and pruning pimpernels."

"What?"

"It's a flower."

"I'm more of a cactus person."

"I'm old, I'm a woman, and I'm Haitian," Grace said. "So there are multiple groups of people out there relying on me to not look like the world's biggest fuckup at the end of all this. Parker was right about one thing: it's all on me. I want to bring some of those guys home and save face, and I also want to show up Ms. Thing for underestimating me."

"All right. Good." Celine took the piece of paper she'd confiscated from Kradle's cell and smoothed it out on the bar top. "We start here. I found this in John Kradle's cell this morning. These are airfields. I think—no, I'm certain Kradle would have spent the day walking to one of these."

"Wagon Circle." Grace put a finger on the paper. "We can drive there. Forty minutes, maybe."

"No point," Celine said. "We don't know if he's headed there, or if he's at Willie McCool or Brandon. He might have been and gone already, especially if he caught a ride. I looked at the CCTV. He left by the back, walking north, but that doesn't mean anything.

In any case, I know where he's going. He's going to Mesquite."

"Why?"

"These guys who kill their families, it's all about ego for them. He wants to go back to his own territory. Back to where the most meaningful thing he ever did in his whole miserable fucking life happened," Celine said. "There are plenty of targets for him there. The lawyer who represented him. His prosecutor. His in-laws. The neighbor and friends who testified in his trial. This is not over for Kradle."

"So what can we do?"

"I've called in the Mesquite cops," Celine said. "They're overrun, but they had a little time for me, being a fellow law enforcement officer. The chief said they're going to station some guys at a couple of the airfields nearby, wait for the plane to come in. I figure we go there once they've grabbed him, bring him home naked and hogtied to a pole like we're leading the village to a roast."

"Great image." Grace nodded, blew smoke across her whiskey glass and sipped it. The two women looked around the bar at tables of Pronghorn guards and other workers. Celine could feel the tension in the atmosphere. Even though there were officers in the dim, smoky room who had personally surrendered to the demands of the caller—Mike Genner from tower six playing pool by the men's room, Susan Besk tearing a coaster to shreds as she sat at the end of the bar—it was Grace who was getting the nasty sidelong glances. Grace's leg was jogging furiously, her knee knocking against the underside of the bar.

"So you're pretty sure Kradle was behind all this?" she asked Celine.

"What?" Celine looked at her boss. "No. I mean, that's obvious. It's got to be Schmitz or Hamsi, right? Only one of them would have the kind of resources to pull something like this off."

"Wait, so why the hell are we talking about this Kradle guy?" Grace gestured to the paper. "Who is he?"

"He's the family killer."

"Oh, lord no." Grace leaned back on her stool. "Celine, I'm talking about going for the organizer. The motherfucker who called me this morning. I want to get hold of him and the inmate he wanted released. I want to get them before Parker does."

"Yeah, sure. You want to go for the top dog. Undo it all. Be the redeemed hero."

"That's right." Grace slammed her empty glass down.

"So it's personal."

"It is."

"Well, if you want to work on that, we've got to work on this, too, goddamn it, or I'm out." She tapped the paper.

"Why?"

"You know why," Celine snapped.

Grace looked away. Celine saw something in her eyes, a subdued horror, that she'd witnessed in the eyes of just about everyone who had heard her story over the years. Pictures were swimming in Grace's mind. The bare imaginings possible for someone who had not experienced what Celine had.

"Because it's personal," Grace concluded.

The tattooed bartender topped up Celine's glass

with a splash of dark, cheap wine. A gnat almost immediately kamikazed into the glass. Celine fished it out and flicked it away.

"Okay. We've got to wait on Kradle," Grace said. "If you're right, he's in the air or soon to be so. So let's talk Hamsi and Schmitz."

Celine put her elbows on the bar and cradled her face in her hands. Her jaw ached from grinding her molars all day and night. Her mind wanted to turn toward home, to her shower, her bed. She turned it instead to Abdul Hamsi, the quiet, neat man who occupied the cell seven down from the control room on death row. She could see the bare shelf over the little iron desk, the legal papers stacked in a box under the bunk. He was the only inmate on Celine's row who hadn't decorated his cell with any photographs or pictures of people. John Kradle had been forbidden to keep images of his victims, but he'd at least propped a Christmas card from his lawyer above his bed: a picture of Conan O'Brien in a Santa suit.

"It's not Hamsi," Celine said finally.

"Why do you say that?"

"Because the guy's a loser." She blurted out the words, working on instinct, too tired to measure what she was saying. "His own lawyer thinks so."

Grace raised an eyebrow. "It's death row. Aren't they all losers?"

"Look, I approve the visitors for these guys, right?" Celine said. "Every inmate has a lawyer. Even the serial killers. Even the guys who are flat out of appeals. An inmate might sit on the row for fourteen years, and in that time he'll probably sue the prison a dozen times for being issued a crumbled cookie, or because he got a paper cut on prison stationery. I know Hamsi's lawyer. Known him for years," Celine said. "He's a guy named May. And he's *that* kind of lawyer, the one who'll take a child killer's claim for two hundred bucks' compensation because he cut his toe on a sharp tile in the shower room. He'll work the claim so he can get his ten percent."

"Okay," Grace said. She didn't sound convinced. "So May, a clear deadbeat, thinks Hamsi's a loser. How does that help us?"

"Because if Hamsi was an important ISIS terrorist, he'd have a good lawyer," Celine said. "His associates would have paid to rush through his appeals. He'd be suing the prison at every opportunity, trying to get himself moved somewhere cushy by being a nuisance. May or someone better would be there at the prison for him every day, seeing what he needs, passing messages."

"And May's not doing that?"

"No," Celine said. "May doesn't even answer Hamsi's calls."

"So ISIS or Al-Qaeda or whoever sent Hamsi out to bomb the Flamingo Casino has abandoned him?" Grace snorted. "Tragic."

"Maybe." Celine shrugged. "Or maybe they never sent him."

"I thought ISIS claimed responsibility for it, though," Grace said. She had taken out her phone and was tapping through internet search results for Hamsi. Celine glimpsed familiar images from the time of the failed bombing. Crowds evacuating the casino. People crying in the street. Duffel bags being approached by bomb specialists in huge, puffy green suits. "They said they wanted to kill infidels in a hotbed of gambling and debauchery. I remember. I'd been at the Flamingo the week before for a girls' weekend."

"I reckon they just claim responsibility for everything," Celine said. "Even for failed attacks. Any publicity is good publicity. They want you to think they can get that close to killing hundreds, even if their guy stumbled at the finish line. No—if I had to guess, based on how lonely Hamsi is, I'd say he was just a pathetic no-hoper who watched a few recruitment videos, read *Bomb Making for Dumbasses* and thought he'd give his life some meaning. Hamsi doesn't even order commissary. He eats the prison food. Most people wouldn't feed their dog that garbage."

"Hey"—Grace looked up from her drink—"I approved the winter menu myself."

"You tasted it, or you looked at a list on a piece of paper?"

Grace said nothing.

"Sorry, boss," Celine said. "One of the C Block lieutenants got drunk and ate a chunk of nutraloaf on a dare at the Christmas party last year. He found a whole human fingernail in it."

"Oh, Jesus." Grace covered her eyes. "This is all my fault."

"Oh, come on. The food's meant to be bad. It's prison, not the Ritz."

"It's not just that. It's the whole thing," Grace said. "I don't know who's in my prison. I don't know my family killers from my terrorists. I don't know what these guys are eating. What my staff are doing. What we're trained for and what we're not."

Two guards standing at the bar smirked, obviously eavesdropping. Celine glared back at them.

"You couldn't train anyone for what happened yesterday," she said loudly.

Grace held her head in her hands. "The past five years or so it's been all about numbers on paper. Inmates in and inmates out. Safety checks, dental programs, minimum staff to inmate ratios, goddamn waste disposal and energy incentives. I've got to keep the prison population above six hundred and six inmates at all times or I lose my laundry allowance. In February, I delayed a guy's release by a day so that two hundred other guys could have clean underpants that week."

Celine didn't know what to say, so she said nothing.

"He lost a day of his life because management were beating my ass down about the budget." Grace stared at herself in the mirror behind the bar. "I've thought about that guy maybe a dozen times since. I don't even remember his name. But I remember I cost him a day of his life."

Celine's phone buzzed in her pocket. She didn't recognize the number, figured it was probably a journalist. She tucked the phone away.

"Don't let it be Schmitz who's behind this," Grace said. She shook her head sadly. "I don't know everybody on the row, but I know that guy."

Celine pictured Schmitz the last time she had really looked at him; stopped to check all was well in his cell rather than just breezing by, trying to avoid him, the way a person does when they notice a spider in their bathroom but before they are prepared to do anything about it. She'd taken the late shift last night to cover for a staff member who needed to go home to be with a sick baby. She remembered she'd cautioned Kowalski about his television being too loud. Took a towel Kradle had hung over the middle bar on his cell door and threw it at him. Ten cells up the row, she'd passed Schmitz's cell. He'd been sitting on the end of his bed, staring at the floor, hands between his knees. The mass killer's close-cropped blond hair had been sparkling in the night lights in the corridor, as if he'd just rinsed his head in the sink. There had been a shoebox on the desk.

"He packed his things," Celine said.

"Hmm?" Grace looked to be on the edge of drunkenness, her eyes lazy and unfocused.

"Schmitz. He had a box on the desk last night when I saw him. He'd packed his things because he knew he was getting out the next morning," Celine said. "It was him."

Grace Slanter put her hands on the bar mat in front of her. "I know what I'm going to do," she said.

"What?"

"I'm going to get in my truck, go home, and get my rifle," she said. "I'm going to drive through the desert, around and around, night and day, until I find one of those fuckers. I don't need to go for the top dogs. I just need someone. Anyone. I'm going to find an inmate in the desert and drag him back to Pronghorn. Nothing short of me personally escorting a dangerous inmate back through the gates of Pronghorn is going to fix how the world sees me after all this."

"Please don't do that," Celine said. "You'll get a flat out there in the middle of nowhere. You'll run out of water and the buzzards will eat you."

"I'm doing it."

"This is not the Wild West. You are not a cowboy."

"I'll be whatever I want to be, pilgrim," Grace drawled.

Celine's phone buzzed again. She picked it up this time.

"Hello?"

"It's me," John Kradle said.

There was a long moment of silence on the line. Kradle watched the old airfield attendant watching him, sitting in the desk chair as footage of the mass breakout at Pronghorn played on the news on the little television set over his shoulder, and waited for Celine to gather herself. He heard the crack and tumble of billiard balls, voices murmuring, the music of a bar. Probably a twenty-four-hour place, he guessed. Then the grind of a door, and the background of the call went quiet.

"That's what you say to me?" Celine's voice burned like acid when she eventually spoke. Kradle imagined her standing outside a bar local to the prison, probably stuffed full of officers and other prison staff hiding from the press. "*It's me?* Like you're calling your fucking mama?"

"Celine, I need you to listen," Kradle said.

"No, *you* listen," she seethed. "And it's 'ma'am,' you inmate piece of trash. You better be calling me to tell me where the hell you are, because—"

"I'm out," Kradle said.

"I know you're goddamn out."

"Right," he said. "So I'm not an inmate anymore. I'll call you Celine. I'll call you Sugar. I'll call you Queen Hellbitch. I'll call you whatever I want!" He pointed to the television set, which was displaying her image yet again, standing before the press with the photograph. "I'm calling to ask you if you're out of your goddamn mind. I'm looking at you on a television screen right now, holding a picture of me."

"How the hell did you get this number?"

"You always divert the death row control center phone to your cell when there's a crisis," he said. "I must have heard you give out the number a hundred times over the past five years. I've had nothing to do but sit in that cage and listen. There's a whole bunch of stuff I know about you, Celine. I know where you live. I know you've got a new boyfriend named Jake."

"You stupid motherfu—"

"Listen!" he snapped. "Just listen to me. I know you've got a problem with me. But you can't send the entire country after me right now."

"Why in the hell not?"

"Because I need to prove my innocence."

She laughed, hard and angry. It was an ugly, hacking sound.

"Five years, and you've never said that in my presence," she said. "Not once."

"Would there have been any point?"

"No."

"Well, at least you're honest."

"I thought *you* were honest. I thought you were the only guy on the row who owned what he did," Celine said. "Man, I've been listening to stories from inmates about how they were set up or mistaken for someone else or just plain wrongfully convicted all my career. Never heard it from you, though. Now you're out and you're suddenly innocent? Oh, honey, spare me."

"Celine, I—"

"If there's one thing I know, John Kradle, it's killers," Celine said. "They've got a way about them, and you've got that way."

"Look at you. You think you're Nancy Grace or something. You're not Nancy Grace, Celine. You're just a glorified zookeeper from Bumfuck, Georgia."

"Just shut up."

"No, you shut up," Kradle said.

"No, you—"

"*Somebody killed my son!*" Kradle roared. The words shot out of him unexpectedly, as loud and sudden as they were vicious, and for a moment there was silence on the line. The hand that gripped the phone beside his ear was shaking. The man in front of him was cowering in his seat. Kradle sucked in a long breath, then let it out slow.

"Celine, I didn't kill my wife, or my son, or my wife's sister," he continued. "I came home from work that day and I found them all dead and the house on fire."

"Uh-huh," Celine said. She didn't sound sarcastic or mean. She just sounded as though she was listening. It gave him strength.

"Now that I've got a chance to find out who did it," Kradle continued, "I'm going to use it. You don't have to help me, but you do need to back off me. There are six hundred guys on the loose, and I'm the least dangerous of all of them. It would be real good for me if the authorities were tied up chasing those other guys so I can get my job done."

"Kradle," Celine said. "I'm not going to sit here and argue with you about what kind of monster you are."

"I'm not a monster. I'm innocent."

"Tell me where you are, and I will send the police to pick you up."

"You should know that I've got a very dangerous guy with me," Kradle said. The old airfield attendant sitting close by seemed startled by the words and glanced toward the windows, out into the dark. Kradle lifted a hand, made an "It's okay" gesture. He closed his eyes and pictured Celine on the other end of the call. "I can't let this guy out of my sight. He'll hurt someone the second he gets a chance. I'm going to try to set him up for capture when the time is right. That should show you I'm on the right side of this thing."

"Who is it?" Celine asked. "Who's with you?"

"A cold-as-ice, shitballs-crazy psychopath," Kradle said. "That's who."

"Which one?"

Kradle hung up. The old man was trembling gently in his seat.

"He's out there. He won't come in," Kradle said. "But just in case, is there anywhere you can hide?"

"The bathrooms, I guess," the old man said. Kradle walked him to the men's room off the side of the office and listened while he locked himself in. Then he jogged out into the darkness, found Homer waiting at the corner of the huge hangar, the roller door pushed open and the little aircraft waiting inside, silent and black-eyed like birds in their nests.

"We've gotta go," Kradle said. He fished a key out of the pile in his fist, matching a handwritten label on a yellow plastic tag with the tail numbers of a nearby Cessna. He pointed to the plane, and Homer gave him that gap-toothed grin.

"Coolest guy in the world," the serial killer said.

1999

She pinched the tobacco between her thumb and forefinger, flicked out the rolling paper with a little more flair than she probably needed to, and laid the little caterpillar of brown fibers down in its thin, dry bed. Three boys, all cousins of hers, crowded in to watch her lick and roll the cigarette. Celine put the smoke to her lips and lit up. Their eyes were big and wild with excitement. It was a thrilling display on many levels. They were all farm kids, and lighting a match for any reason in a barn full of hay was like flipping the bird to Jesus Christ.

"This is just a regular smoke," Celine explained coolly. "But you can put other stuff in, if you want."

"Like what?" Tommy asked.

"I don't know. Rosemary. Weed."

"You don't smoke weed," Samson sneered.

"Maybe I do, maybe I don't." Celine looked at the little brat and shrugged. "How would you know, you little peckerhead?"

"You haven't even smoked that yet." Samson

pointed at the cigarette blazing in her fingertips. "We haven't even seen you inhale. You're pretending."

Celine inhaled a lungful of smoke, let it trail out slowly for a while. When she got bored of that she blew a smoke ring. The boys cooed in admiration. They heard the last few steps of an adult crunching through the dry grass outside the barn and Celine did everything she could to hide the cigarette without looking panicked. The door flew open, and Grandpa Nick stood there in his gray coveralls, a big rifle hanging at his side.

Celine would wonder later whether she really saw him considering his next move as he looked over the three boys and the teenage girl huddled on the hay bales, or whether the tiny pause he gave in the doorway was something she had added to her recollection. Maybe he stood there for an eternity, his wide shoulders rimmed in red afternoon light. Or maybe he'd already decided how it would all go. Had known for months. Maybe he was already commanding her to go up to the house as his big, hard palm shoved open the door.

"Your mother wants you."

Celine grunted in derision as she slumped past him. Technically, she wasn't talking to Grandpa Nick. He'd been sour from the moment they arrived in their rickety van, her younger brothers tumbling out and running into the woods before they could be tasked with unloading any luggage. Grandpa Nick had barked at her for dragging her wheeled suitcase up the porch, letting it clunk loudly against the freshly varnished steps. When he got into his moods he trudged around snapping at people: a giant, swirling dark cloud that had terrified her as a small child and depressed her as a teenager. He was going to say something snide about everything she received for Christmas. She would have to kneel there under the tree and receive his commentary, box after box, on her pathetic obsession with technology and her narcissistic need for clothes. She was everything that he hated—a Walkman-toting, blue-haired, skimpily dressed back-talker who, if she didn't kill them all burning the barn down with a cigarette, would corrupt all the little males in the family with ideas about loose, smart-mouthed women with expensive taste. And there were a lot of little males to protect. Her two brothers, Paulie and Frankie, and Samson, Tommy, and Benjamin, her cousins.

Celine's Uncle Charlie had all the maturity of a fifteen-year-old. He was sitting on the back porch steps, reading the cartoon section of a newspaper in the sunshine, when she reached the house.

"You've gotta talk to the old man," Charlie said, without looking up.

"He's an asshole."

"Yeah, but Christmas dinner hasn't even begun yet," Charlie said. "Genny and your mother have only just started on the onions, which means we're about four hours out. Somebody will fight at dinner. You know they will."

Celine rolled her eyes and lit her cigarette again.

"So we gotta go in with a clean slate," Charlie continued. "We can't start the dinner fighting, or by the end it'll be war."

"You're just worried about yourself," Celine said. "Don't make like you're trying to look out for the family."

"Of course I'm worried about myself. I don't need

any awkwardness ruining my Christmas. I wait all year for fucking Christmas, and I just want to get through it without Nanna blubbering all over me."

Celine gestured toward the barn at the end of the long, dry field. "I'm seventeen. He can't talk to me as if I'm five."

"You're still pissed about the fence." Charlie glanced at the little picket fence by Celine's hip. Three Christmases earlier, Celine had decided she would surprise Grandpa Nick by painting the fence he'd just built around the driveway. He'd come home from the store and leaped from the truck, already blasting her. She hadn't primed the wood. She was using paint she'd found in the shed, and it was interior paint, water-based, when she should have used exterior oil. The drips and lumps she was leaving everywhere were going to ruin the look of the precise miter joints he'd cut. "I might as well have nailed the thing together from driftwood!" Celine had looked up to see the whole family assembled silently on the porch, an audience to her roasting. Nanna Betty had made Grandpa apologize in front of everyone at dinner that night. He'd sulked for three days afterward, until Celine's parents decided to leave.

"I'm not pissed about the fence," Celine lied. "It was years ago."

"You've got to go easy on Grandpa. He's upset about your father."

"Dad's not gonna die," Celine said. "He told everybody so. It's a slow-moving thing. It's going to eat up his liver one bite at a time, and maybe he'll need a transplant in, like, ten years or something. But it's not that bad. It's not cancer."

"If you had a kid you'd understand," Charlie said.

"Doesn't need to be cancer to get you upset." He beckoned for Celine's cigarette, glanced toward the house to make sure Aunty Genny wasn't watching.

Three gunshots. Sharp, propulsive cracks that rippled up the field and over the house like a wave. Celine and her uncle looked down toward the barn.

"They're shooting apples again."

"He's trying to run down that old rifle," Charlie agreed, drawing hard on her cigarette. "Nanna wants him to get rid of it, but it won't go for much, so he's having some fun. He's got rid of a lot of stuff the past few months. The shotguns and the musket are gone."

"Why?"

"Meh. Old people do that. They get rid of stuff."

"She better not get rid of any of her earrings," Celine said. "They're supposed to be mine."

More shots. They watched the barn, the gnats swirling in the light. The cows in the paddock by the barn were restless, trotting away from the noise, up the hill, toward the tree line.

"See, he always used to invite me to do that." Celine waved angrily at the barn. "I love shooting apples. He knows it. Fucking asshole."

Charlie shrugged, finished the cigarette. He got up and went inside. Celine was rolling another cigarette when her grandfather emerged from the distant barn door. She refused to meet his eyes as he walked toward her. She lit the cigarette and doused the match on her terrible paintwork on the picket fence.

"I want you in the house," Grandpa Nick said. He smelled of cordite and his silver hair was messed up. Celine waved her cigarette, clutched between two fingers.

"I'll finish this first," she said.

Grandpa Nick licked his dentures thoughtfully, watched the dogs in the field rushing to the barn to investigate the activity. He nodded, shouldered the rifle, a small smile on his lips. He'd made some decision.

"Suit yourself," he said, and went inside.

CHAPTER 11

John Kradle thought about killing. About whether Celine Osbourne really did know killers, whether she had spotted something in him in the half decade they'd spent together as jailer and captive that the jurors and judge had also seen. That the media had seen. That Christine's mother had seen as she stood spitting and crying with fury in the dock, reading her victim impact statement about losing two daughters and a grandson by his hand.

You've got that way, Celine had said.

Homer Carrington was asleep in the copilot seat of the Cessna as they rumbled and shook through the cold, hard sky over Nevada. The plane was a single-engine thing, tiny, designed for personal use, so small and rickety it wanted to yaw sideways through the sheets of air with Homer's substantial weight on one side. A bike with wings—something that could be brought down by an encounter with a large bird in the right circumstances. The sunrise was lighting the angles of Homer's placid, clumsily handsome face a searing orange. Kradle had made no call signs leaving Wagon Circle, no reports of his passage on the airwaves, so he had to keep his eyes locked on the unmoving brown horizon for other small aircraft approaching, unaware of his presence. But he could not stop glancing at the seatbelt buckle by Homer's hip, clicked into place, safe and secure.

Kradle had only to unbuckle the belt, reach across his passenger and unlatch the door, then tip the yoke and Homer would fall to his death.

Problem solved.

Logically, it made sense. Kradle couldn't do what he needed to do in Mesquite while dragging a serial killer along with him. Homer was distinct-looking, unpredictable, physically uncontrollable. Kradle might as well have been accompanied by a Siberian tiger. At any moment, Homer could see through the pathetic mob-money story and kill Kradle, or veer off to target an innocent bystander, and there would be little Kradle could do to stop him.

But pushing him out of the plane would mean killing him. It would mean being the executioner of another human being, bypassing the sentence that had been handed down to Homer to die by lethal injection in front of his victims' families after saying his final words to them. They wouldn't get to see justice done. He wouldn't get his last rites. And there was always the chance that Homer would fall on someone, or survive the fall somehow—or, worse, grab onto John, grip his way back into the plane and strangle him in his seat. Kradle glanced out his window at the earth passing below. Desert, cracked and ridged by sun and time and wind, the occasional town or snake of highway.

But it would be so easy, Kradle thought.

Three movements.

Buckle.

Door.

Yoke.

Kradle unbuckled Homer's seatbelt, just to see what it felt like. The killer stirred and stretched in his seat. "Are we there yet?"

"Ten minutes or so," Kradle said. "Get ready to run."

They approached the airfield from the south. Kradle saw it as a thin strip of blackness in the distance.

"How do we know they won't be waiting for us?" Homer asked. "Did you tell the guy at Wagon Circle where we were going?"

"Of course not," Kradle said. "But they'll know where I'm going. Little plane like this can only go so far without refueling, and I'll bet a good portion of inmates who go on the run head straight home. But there are a few airfields in Mesquite. They probably won't be manning every one. We'll take our chances."

"You've got this all worked out," Homer marveled. "I never spent a minute thinking about my escape plan."

Kradle had spent *every* minute thinking about it. It was all that kept him alive after the second year. That, the slow trudge of the appeals process, and trying to annoy Celine Osbourne in a new way every single day that she worked. He had tidbits of information he'd been able to gather that would aid his escape hidden all over his cell, and at night he fell asleep thinking about each one, making sure his plan was ready should the opportunity ever arise to use it. He had his lawyer smuggle tiny pieces of his plan to him once a week or so. The distances to airfields. The contact details of key people needed for his mission. Known locations for sleeping rough, where he might blend in with homeless men in Mesquite. Kradle knew the guy didn't really believe he'd ever escape. But he could see the little tidbits gave Kradle hope, and he needed a whole bunch of hope to keep filing applications, maybe for the next two and a half decades, before he ran out of appeals. Kradle built his escape plan because there was nothing else he could build on death row; because every day on the row was about being broken down so that when they took you to your death you were cowed, numb, submissive. Nobody wanted to see a grown man kicking and screaming and crying as they strapped him to the table. Not even the victims' families wanted that.

"What's wrong with you?" Homer asked. Kradle had to shake himself out of his dreams about escapes and executions.

"Huh?"

"Why'd you get into the mob?" he asked. "Like, have they done a diagnosis? Are you a 'natural born killer'?"

"Oh, uh." Kradle shifted uncomfortably in his seat. "They did a psych test on me to see if I was fit to stand trial. Didn't find anything."

"I love psych tests." Homer smiled. "They're so interesting. The last one I had, they asked, 'When you stand at the edge of a tall building or a cliff, do you think about jumping off?' I mean, what does that mean? What's the right answer?"

"Beats me," Kradle said.

Don't, Kradle told himself.

But then he did.

"What do you think's wrong with you?" Kradle asked.

"Look"—Homer shifted sideways a little, so that he was facing Kradle—"this is going to sound crazy."

"Lay it on me," Kradle sighed.

"When I was a kid I went camping with my dad a lot," Homer said. "We would go out into the desert, just him and me, get away from Mom and my sister. You know. Guy stuff. Anyway, one of these times, I woke up in the morning with this itch in my ear."

Kradle gripped the yoke in front of him, pursed his lips.

"So my dad looks in there," Homer said. "And what does he see? A black widow spider."

"Jesus."

"Yeah." Homer sat back in his seat. "I wanted him to get it out. I begged and begged him. But he said it was too dangerous. If he tried to grab it, it might turn around and bite me. I'd be dead inside of ten minutes. Plus, my dad was really good with animals. He would have wild birds, rabbits, foxes coming into our yard and eating out of his hand. So he tells me the spider in my ear canal is a good thing. He can control it. If I'm ever bad, he'll just tell it to bite me and that'll be it. Game over."

Kradle looked over at Homer. The bigger man was watching his eyes carefully.

"You serious?" Kradle asked.

"Yeah."

"And how old were you when he was telling you this?"

"I don't know. Eight? Nine? Doesn't matter. What matters is that it was true. He could control it. He had it under full control in a matter of days," Homer said. "Every time I was thinking about acting up, I'd feel this tickle in my ear, and I'd look over and my dad would be watching me. He'd tap his ear and I'd know to behave myself."

Kradle said nothing.

"Problem is, my dad *died* about five years later," Homer said. "Brain aneurism."

"So . . ." Kradle struggled.

"*So nobody's controlling the spider,*" Homer whispered.

"Haven't you had medical exams during your incarceration?" Kradle asked. "Hasn't anyone looked in your ear in all these years?"

"Oh, yeah." Homer waved dismissively. "Doctors have looked. They always say it's just dermatitis in there. They give me creams to put on it. I never do."

A shot of adrenaline hit Kradle's system as the radio in the console crackled.

"*This is Mesquite Municipal Airport, Mike-Foxtrot-Hotel. Aircraft on bearing oh-three-five call in, please.*"

"What's the plan? Are we literally just going to run?" Homer was gripping the frame of the door, watching the earth rise slowly beneath them.

"That woodland there, behind the airfield." Kradle pointed. "That's the highway just beyond it."

They aligned with the strip. Homer tugged on his seatbelt to tighten it, found it unbuckled. Kradle swallowed hard.

A dog.

A big brown-and-black creature rushed out of the grass at the edge of the woods, heading for the strip, barking at the plane. Kradle shifted upward in his seat as the flaps on the wings ground slowly down to ten degrees on either side of the fuselage. The wind roared as the drag increased. The dog got to the edge of the runway and barked soundlessly at them.

A man ran out of the woods to retrieve the animal. He was shrugging off a blue jacket with white lining, which he dropped in the grass. Kradle had seen those jackets before.

Kradle flicked the flaps off and tugged back on the yoke. The nose of the plane lifted, sinking his stomach. He held on as the g-force ripped through him. They turned away from the runway, only blue sky visible through the windshield.

"You see that?" Homer was twisted in his seat, looking back.

"The jacket." Kradle nodded. "It'll have *US Marshal* written on the back."

"Goddamn dog just saved our bacon."

"Yeah."

Kradle looked down as they turned. More marshals were walking out of the woods with dogs, the game over. He searched the land for a spot to put the aircraft down, but every street was littered with cars, the highway surprisingly busy with morning traffic.

"They might send jets after us," Homer said.

"This is not a movie," Kradle reminded him.

"Just put us in the desert," Homer said. "We need to get grounded, right now."

"We can't be out in the open," Kradle said.

He spied a field sectioned off with wire fences, surrounded by trees. Kradle turned the yoke in front of him. "Get ready."

The plane shuddered downward. The brown strip of dirt and gravel cleaved the entire garbage dump in two, like the trunk of a pale tree rimmed with branches that fed out into the piles of car bodies, broken and rusted appliances, twisted scrap metal lying like fields of thorny brambles. It was a rough landing. He consoled himself as the tires bounced twice on the earth that it had been two decades or more since he'd flown. The plane slowed, rattled violently, twisted sideways, and slammed into a pile of rubbish, the wing crumpling, the windows and windscreen blowing out. He pulled himself out of the craft as a bunch of refuse workers abandoned their truck nearby and started running toward them.

"Are you guys o—"

Kradle heard the men calling, but their voices drained away as he limped into the trash mounds, running awkwardly toward the fence line. Homer was ahead of him, leaping a washing machine like an Olympic hurdler, crashing through valleys of plastic bags, cardboard boxes, tin cans, corrugated iron sheeting. He slipped and stumbled on a flat stretch made from cardboard boxes and Kradle almost caught up to him. Something slashed at Kradle's thigh—a bent tube sticking out from the ruined body of a bicycle. Homer was halfway up the fence and waiting for him when Kradle heard the sirens on the highway in the distance.

CHAPTER 12

Celine walked into the break room, poured herself a black coffee, and stood watching the TV mounted above the staff bulletin board in the corner of the room as she drank it. Footage was playing of officers escorting inmates back into the prison through the huge gates, a symbolic gesture for the cameras, no doubt. There were few she recognized. She opened a tab on her cell phone and looked at the *New York Times* home page, which was keeping a tally of inmates escaped and inmates returned. So far there were 291 inmates returned to the facility of the 653 set free. Most had been rounded up on the roads to Vegas, Utah, or Arizona, in the desert, or in the houses most immediate to the prison—little farmhouses dotted throughout the desert wilds. With almost half of the inmates returned, Celine supposed she should be feeling pleased. But the *Times* was also reporting six common assaults, seventeen robberies, two hostage stand-offs, nine sexual assaults, and fifteen carjackings overnight. Two competing groups of criminals had engaged in a shootout in a diner in Meadows Village, leaving five escapees dead and patrons terrified. Not a single death row inmate had been recovered, unless Celine counted Willy Henderson, which she didn't, because the man had never left the building.

The *Times* had also managed to snag interviews with officers from Pronghorn about the moments after the hostage call began playing over the PA system.

I know how bad these guys are. I see what they do to each other. I know what they'll be wanting to do out there. But I also know my family was in danger, and there was nothing else I could do. I've got one daughter. You'd have done the same thing if it was you.

Everybody around me was releasing inmates. It didn't seem like my efforts would mean anything.

What if I kept the inmate back that they were looking for—the terrorists? What if he was in my cell block?

All the sources were anonymous. Celine couldn't understand that. Nobody who had willingly let inmates go from Pronghorn would be keeping their jobs. There would probably be a couple of spectacular firings, but most would be shipped out quietly over the next year or so, as officers were trained to replace them.

She checked her watch. At 6 A.M., inmates scheduled for release that day who had not participated in the breakout by leaving the general vicinity of the prison would be let out, having finished their sentences. That was unless the release schedule was delayed because of the breakout, and no one had told her. She imagined they would be driven into town and released in some inconspicuous backstreet so that the journalists waiting to interview them about their experience of the breakout would be left empty-handed.

Celine had never released an inmate in all her years on the row. This was where all hopes of walking free on the earth were abandoned.

She'd slept for an hour inside her car in the prison parking lot after leaving the bar. Dreams of her grandfather's farm and Kradle's words on the phone left her shaken and restless, the nap fitful and sweaty.

Somebody killed my son!

Kradle had said nothing about his wife or sister-in-law, Celine noted. But there were plenty of reasons for that. Family annihilators had strange ideas about their work, about the act of killing and the act of giving mercy. Maybe murdering his son had been so different an act from what Kradle did to his wife and sister-in-law that he just plain wanted to blame it on someone else. Celine didn't know. She tried not to rationalize the deeds of the men on the row. They didn't work with adult-level logic, were more like beastly children stomping on snails and then trying to talk their way out of being sent to their rooms.

"You stink," someone said.

Celine turned and looked Trinity Parker up and down. The US Marshal was immaculately dressed and smelled of perfume. Celine sipped her coffee.

"I said, you stink." Trinity wrinkled her nose. "I told you to go home, freshen up. What did you do instead?"

"I stayed here for a while," Celine said. "Checked some stuff off. Then I went driving around looking for inmates. Then I went to a bar. You want to know what I had for breakfast, too?"

"No. I want to know that you're ready to get to work."

"Is that what you call it? Work? Because being

physically assaulted is something I usually do in my spare time."

"I'm hearing your poor-man's Scott Peterson tried to land a plane in Mesquite early this morning, just like you told me he would," Trinity said.

"So I was right about that." Celine shrugged. "Any chance I might be right that he's got Schmitz with him?"

Celine had called Trinity as she stood outside the bar, told her about Kradle's claims to have a dangerous psychopath in his company. Trinity had hung up on her and failed to answer her text messages.

"You're not really naive enough to believe Kradle when he says he's got an important inmate he'll help you capture, are you?" Trinity gave her a sad look. "Come on. He wants something from you, and that's his only currency."

"Where's Kradle now?" Celine asked. "Did they catch him?"

"My guys are chasing him down as we speak."

Celine felt a cold shot of exhilaration pass through her.

"Moving on to things that are actually important," Trinity said. "Your instincts about Kradle and his movements were right. Maybe you are valuable to me. I want to use whatever intel you have to find Burke David Schmitz before he shoots up another mass gathering."

"Why would I help someone who popped me in the guts less than twenty-four hours ago?" Celine asked.

"You needed a smack to wake you up," Trinity said. "I was making a kind gesture, trying to communicate with you in your own language. People from your station in life only understand high-stakes situations through pain. You're like dogs. A dog barks too much, you don't plead with it. You smack it on the nose."

"My 'station in life'?"

"Farm people."

"Oh. I see." Celine nodded. "You did some creative googling in the night, did you?"

"Sure did," Trinity said. Celine bit her tongue so she wouldn't lash out, turned away, felt that old, hard, protective smile creep onto her face. She set her features and turned back.

"It was interesting reading," Trinity continued. "You've been through some stuff. I have a little more respect for you now. But don't get excited. It's microscopic."

"You don't want to go soft on me because of what happened to me," Celine said. "Turn your back on me and I'll bite you, just like any other dog would."

"So, let's try to make this as brief a liaison as possible," Trinity said. "We snag the Nazi, maybe round up your family killer on the way, and then we're done."

"Done," Celine confirmed.

Trinity offered her hand. Celine begrudgingly shook it.

Walter Keeper was standing at the counter in the administration office near F Block when Celine and Trinity arrived at the large, secure glass doors. He was wearing a white t-shirt and dusty, baggy jeans that hung precariously on the upper curve of his butt, the pockets bulging as he stuffed them with items handed to him through the screen over the counter—keys, wallet, phone, smokes, a little black book, and a huge black watch. Celine stopped Trinity outside, in the shadow of the chow hall. The two women heard a cheer and looked through the barred windows to see someone drawing a cross through the image of an inmate's face that was pinned to one of the partitions. Slowly, the wall of faces was becoming a wall of giant red crosses.

"This will probably be touch and go," Celine said. "Let me handle it."

"Come on."

"Some dogs are so used to getting smacked they don't even feel it anymore," Celine said. She went inside and stood, waiting, while Keeps signed his release forms.

"Oh, Death Row"—Keeps nodded to her—"you look at that light?"

"Yeah, and I found something," she said. "So I want you to come and tell me where else to look."

"Nah, man." Keeps smirked, handing the clipboard back across the counter. "That's a favor done. So you owe me a favor when I get back. I'm not spending my first minutes as a free citizen hangin' out with some screws inside Pronghorn. No offense. I'm getting on the release bus and heading into town so I can grab me a big, juicy burger and an ice-cold beer."

"I'll pay you."

"Lady, you couldn't afford ten seconds of my time in here beyond what the state sentenced me."

He walked out the back doors of the administration block. Celine followed. The gravel crunched beneath their feet. A pair of guards was marching a group of twelve inmates toward the yards.

"Have fun out there, Keeps!" an inmate called. "I sure did!"

Keeps waved.

"You got someone waiting for you on the other side?" Celine asked.

"Nah. I'm freestyling it."

"No family? No girlfriend?"

"Nope."

"So, what's the plan?"

"I told you, girl. Burger. Beer. In that order."

"Let me get this straight. You're going to use what cash you have in your wallet to get a burger and a beer, and then you're on your own. No accommodation. No job. No plans."

"People like me don't need a plan." Keeps pushed his glasses up onto his nose and grinned. "We hustle. We get lucky. Don't worry, pretty lady. I've done this a thousand times."

"How about this." Celine stopped him before he could reach the caged passage to the outer perimeter and, beyond it, the bus and the back gates of Pronghorn. "First, you stop with all the *pretty lady, girl, honey pie* bullshit. Then you give me twenty minutes of your precious time over on the row in exchange for these."

She pulled a set of keys out of her pocket, jangled them. Keeps spied the car key fob and frowned.

"What?"

"My car's out on the lot," Celine said. "Blue Caprice. I'll write down my address. You go get your burger and your beer then you can head to my place. Have a shower, watch some Netflix. Eat whatever you want from the fridge. And you can stay there for . . . let's say a week. Better than a dive hotel or a crowded shelter."

"Ma'am." Keeps shook his head, laughed, flashing

big white teeth. "You must be high as all fuck. You don't know me. What's say I don't go to your place and clean you out? Strip your car. Sell your stuff. What's say I don't have all my friends there waiting for you to come in the door so we can cornhole your silly ass? Oh, damn, you need to *not* be givin' the keys to your life to convicts you just met."

"I've got a feeling none of that is going to happen," Celine said. "Call me psychic."

"You just got a feeling says I'm all right? Just like that? You ain't looked at my rap sheet or nothing?"

"Nope. But I've been right before."

Keeps looked at her, at the caged path to the gate yard, at the keys in her palm. Celine got the sense that unexplained, unconditional trust wasn't something that he had seen often in his life. He took the keys reluctantly, with his thumb and forefinger, like someone gently picking up a stick of dynamite.

"Okay," he said. "The burger will keep, I guess."

CHAPTER 13

Kradle hadn't run in half a decade, but his body remembered. Somewhere deep inside him, that frantic, wild, powerful impulse to flee still lived, even though he hadn't traveled a distance of more than ten yards without chains on in all that time. There was a certain joy in it, a small flicker of happiness, his hips burning and legs reaching out and gripping the earth and pushing him forward, his lungs pumping in fresh, free air as the two men surged through the woods. But most of the experience was pure pain. The rocky earth jarred his bones. His heart struggled, hammering desperately in his chest, thrumming in his fingertips and toes. Hunger and dehydration left him wobbly, slow, his feet landing awkwardly between fallen branches or on rocks, trees appearing out of nowhere and crashing into his shoulders. Blood was pouring from the slash in his thigh. The sound of sirens pursued them for what seemed like an age, until they were both stumbling, an awkward half-jog, up an incline to a tree-lined peak.

They stopped and looked back. Maybe three miles

away they could barely make out the little ridges that signified the waste piles of the landfill, the brown strip of earth they'd landed on. There were red and blue lights. Kradle thought he heard the bark of dogs on the wind.

"We've got to get a car," Kradle said. "The dogs will get here before their handlers do, and they won't just want to pin us down."

"Don't worry," Homer said. "I'll handle this."

The earth on the other side of the hill was more lush, sheltered from the Nevada sun. Kradle's once-white prison sneakers, now caked in filth, sank in the soil and leaf litter. The sound of dogs barking came again, closer this time. A road appeared through the trees and Homer was out onto it before Kradle could stop him or ascertain some sense of his plan. He watched, appalled, as the serial killer sidestepped in front of a vehicle, which veered over the center line to avoid him. Kradle glanced back into the trees, thought again of bolting. But then he would be leaving anyone Homer managed to stop at the mercy of the monster. Whoever he met, whatever happened to them, would be a direct result of Kradle helping Homer out of the mountains.

Kradle approached the road, still dry-mouthed from the cold morning air and gasping, as a small yellow Kia pulled over and Homer gripped the edge of the passenger-side window when it reluctantly lowered two inches.

"Please help us!" Homer cried. "My friend and I— we were attacked!"

"What the hell happened?"

Kradle looked into the vehicle. A woman in her forties was leaning forward over the steering wheel to get a better look at them. She was wearing a bright-pink uniform of some restaurant or bar.

"We were hunting in the woods." Homer clutched at his shirt, pointed at the tree line, swallowed hard as he tried to regain his breath. "These guys came and beat us up. Oh, god. We're so lucky they didn't kill us. They wanted our clothes. They took our guns. They—I think they were inmates from Pronghorn!"

"Oh, Jesus." The woman gripped the wheel. Kradle could see her thinking about stepping on the gas. Through the dirt, sweat, and muck, she had just noticed the inmate number embroidered on Homer's shirt. She looked at Kradle's chest, at the blood-smeared denim and the number. Her eyes met his, as though she could hear the words he was screaming in his mind.

Drive, woman.

Just drive.

"I've got to . . ." She put the car into gear, shaking her head. "I can't . . ."

"It's okay." Homer put his hands up. "It's okay. You don't have to let us in. Just. Just get your cell phone. Just call 911. Please. Please do it now. Those guys are in there somewhere and they have our weapons and our clothes. We need the police to know we're not inmates in case they shoot at us, and if those guys come back . . . We need to tell someone before they . . . before they . . ."

"I saw some cops a few miles back." The woman glanced in her rearview. "We could . . . Maybe, uh . . ."

Kradle squeezed his fists, mouthed the words even though she wasn't looking at him.

Just. Drive.

"Cops. Where? This way?" Homer pointed. He

started moving and grabbed Kradle's arm. "Come on, man. We gotta get out of here before they come back. They'll kill us."

Kradle started following the big man, relief burning in his face.

His heart sank when the car reversed alongside them.

"Get in," the woman said. "I'll take you there."

Homer slid into the back seat. Kradle had no choice but to climb in beside him.

Inmates swaggered. All inmates. It was a primal thing, usually unconscious—a nervous, protective energy that made them want to present a dangerously casual facade to the predators around them. But Keeps put on a swagger as Celine led him back to Trinity that was unlike anything she had ever seen. It was that self-preservation bravado mixed with a new sense of self-importance. He was like the *Keep on Truckin'* guy on the best day of his life.

"What the hell is this?" Trinity sighed.

"This is our new inmate consultant," Celine said.

"Ex-inmate," Keeps corrected. "And, unluckily for you ladies, my services come at a premium today. It's a release-day charge of one hundred dollars per hour, starting twenty-four hours ago."

"What?" Celine blurted. "Why twenty-four hours ago?"

"That's when I started gathering intelligence on the breakout," Keeps said.

"Oh, please." Trinity started walking away.

"You're going to pay him." Celine caught up to her. "We need what he's got."

"We'll see about payment when we find out if what

he's got is any more than a penchant for criminal activity and a hard-on for pretty little blonde women with big sets of keys."

Celine dropped back and walked beside Keeps.

"Your fee was the use of my place and my car, Keeps," she said.

"Ma'am, that's a US Marshal right there," Keeps said. "You got any idea what her budget for this thing would be? Between the marshals, the FBI, the sheriffs—the president is gonna be raining money on this party like a world-class pimp. And the more money I make here, the faster I'll be out of your accommodation." He poked Celine in the shoulder.

They arrived on the row. Celine led them to Burke David Schmitz's cell, which had been ransacked by agents already—tagged, photographed, and bagged possessions were arranged in piles on all surfaces. The two women stood in the hall while Keeps took in the space. He turned in a circle, noted the scratch marks on the wall under the light where Celine had searched unsuccessfully for concealed items. They watched as he checked all the places Celine usually checked during a shakedown. The hems of the bedding and uniforms, which were folded and stacked neatly in unsealed paper evidence bags. The bolts and fixtures of the bed, shelf, toilet. Keeps stuck his hand down the toilet and fished around in the U-bend, peered down the drain of the tiny sink fixed into the cistern.

"This is hardly genius-level intel I'm seeing here." Trinity was leaning against the bars. "I've had my agents sweep the place like this already."

Keeps sat on the neatly made bed, bounced a little on the mattress. He picked up a small artwork someone had peeled from the wall—an eagle perched on a twisted branch. Celine had confiscated plenty of artworks from Schmitz in the years she had supervised the quiet, bookish inmate. He wasn't permitted to have images of Hitler or swastikas in his cell, which didn't stop him from painting them now and then. She couldn't remove his artistic privileges unless he committed an act of violence, but she always made sure to let Schmitz complete the artwork, put the fine, time-consuming finishing touches on it before she took it, scrunched it, and tossed it in the trash in front of him.

"Dude got some skills." Keeps waved the picture at the women. "For a Nazi asshole."

"This is not Art Appreciation 101," Trinity barked. "It's pretty clear Schmitz pulled off this thing. He's orchestrated one of the most deadly mass shootings *and* the biggest jailbreak in American history, so it stands to reason that whatever he's cooking up next is going to be distinctly unpleasant. Time is of the essence, inmate."

"Are you having a stressful morning?" Keeps patted the bed beside him. "You want to talk about it, pretty lady?"

Trinity licked her teeth so hard she made a loud clicking sound, then turned to Celine, the veins in her neck taut with fury.

"Get him out of here."

"Wait, wait, wait, wait." Keeps held a hand up. "I got something. I got something." He slapped the picture of the eagle. "It's right here." He came to the bars and showed them the image. "See this black?"

The women looked at the picture.

"That's contraband black," Keeps said.

"What are you talking about?" Celine sighed.

"This black paint here." He tapped the paper. "You can't get that color inside Pronghorn. Not through official channels, anyway."

Celine looked at Trinity. The woman was typing out a message on her phone.

"Two things we got a lot of over in minimum—wannabe rappers and artists. There's a lot of bad music, bad pictures." He handed the paper to Celine. "All the painters on my block got the same complaint. The black you get with the commissary paint kit ain't black enough. It's a very, very dark brown. That's a problem. You don't like the blue they got? That's okay. You can mix it. Change it. Make it lighter. Make it darker. Add yellow, make it greener. But you can't make black blacker, no matter how much you try. You want real black? You've got to smuggle it in, and if you consider yourself a real artist you need black-black, not brown-black."

"Right," Celine said. She was starting to feel the first tingles of excitement in her chest. "So someone was bringing in contraband paint to Schmitz."

"How does this help us?" Trinity didn't look up from her phone. "Could have been his lawyer or girlfriend or whatever smuggling it in. All that tells me is that your visitors' center is full of holes."

"Schmitz was Grade B. Non-contact," Celine said. "He only ever interacts with outsiders from behind bulletproof glass. So it wasn't one of his visitors." Her words were gaining momentum as she thought. "It was either another inmate, or it was an officer. And Schmitz hasn't had contact with any other inmates in the past three weeks." She pointed to the cells on either side of the one they stood before. "All the inmates take their yard time separately, so they don't interact in the halls, and these cells neighboring Schmitz's have been vacant. This guy on the left, he went to the infirmary a month ago. And this cell has been empty for three weeks because the sink's broken."

"So it was a guard," Trinity said. "A guard smuggled your Nazi inmate some paint."

"And if they were bringing him paint, what else were they bringing him?" Celine wondered. "And what were they taking out?"

Trinity looked at Keeps as though she was surveying an old car she wanted to buy cheap and run into the ground: a temporarily useful thing that she'd be embarrassed to be seen with. She started to walk off, talking over her shoulder as she went. "You might have been right about his usefulness," she said finally to Celine. "But don't get lost in your celebrations. They just lost your boyfriend in Mesquite."

"What?"

"He dumped the plane at a waste disposal site and disappeared." She waved her phone. "And, who knew? He did have someone with him. A big guy. Looked too tall to be Schmitz."

"I'm going," Celine said. She grabbed Keeps's arm. "You're coming with me."

Homer didn't wait to reveal himself to the woman. As soon as her foot hit the accelerator, he wound an arm around the back of her seat and hugged her throat to the headrest.

"Don't scream," he said.

Her hands came off the wheel and clawed at the

arm. The pressure wasn't much, Kradle could see, not enough to completely panic her so that she ran them off the road. But enough so that it was clear. All of it. That she'd just let two escaped convicts into her car. That she was completely at their mercy. That this morning had taken a turn so bad it might end up being the very last morning of her life.

Kradle saw the terror in her eyes in the rearview mirror. He gripped the seat beneath him to stop himself from attacking Homer where he sat.

"Keep driving," Homer said gently, his cheek pressed against the side of the driver's headrest, eyes on the road. He was focused. He'd done this before. "Hands on the wheel. Foot on the accelerator. Gentle. Gentle. That's it."

"Oh my god. Please, please, please."

"Take the next turn-off. And hand your phone to my friend here. Slowly."

The woman snatched the phone from the cluttered center console. Kradle took it from her shaking fingers.

"Find 'home,' John," Homer instructed.

Kradle did as he was told. The first suggested location in Google Maps was marked "Home."

"What's your name, honey?" Homer was stroking a loose curl at the nape of the driver's neck with his free hand, twirling it around his finger.

"Uh, uh, uh, uh, uh."

"Name."

"It's Shondra."

"Just drive home, Shondra. That's all you have to do."

"Okay. Okay. Please. Oh, god, please."

"Is there going to be anyone there waiting for us?" Homer asked.

"My—my boyfriend should have—what-what-what time is it?"

"We're going to have to kill anyone we find there, so think carefully," Homer said.

"He should be gone." Shondra gagged. "He starts at seven. Oh, shit. I'm gonna throw up."

"No, you're not."

"Ease up a bit," Kradle said. He had to unlock his jaw with difficulty. Force himself to pull at Homer's arm as if he were a friend, a co-conspirator, a non-threat, and not the secret, hateful, vengeful being he really was, his whole body pulsing with the desire to launch himself at the big man sitting beside him, to gouge at his eyes and mouth, bite and kick and punch and bring him to submission.

Homer sat back, his hand extended, resting on Shondra's shoulder. Controlling.

Shondra retched a few times. Her hands were making sweat marks on the steering wheel. Kradle leaned forward.

"No one's going to hurt you," he said. Out of the corner of his eye, he saw Homer smile. "Just keep breathing. Keep it together and you'll get through this."

Off the highway, into the manicured suburbs of Mesquite. Kradle didn't recognize the place the map told him was called Bunkerville, but this might have been any of the hundreds of suburban wildernesses his wife, Christine, had been called to over the years to eradicate poltergeists, angry spirits, or demons from pastel-colored houses behind picket fences. Stone-edged garden beds nestled under shade trees, cradling succulents and little pink flowers. He had followed her, the dutiful assistant and cameraman, into family homes like this in thirty states.

Shondra's house was baby blue with white shutters. Gray slate roof, mailbox with a red flag, a wooden sign on the porch that read LIVE, LAUGH, LOVE. Homer got out swiftly and pulled Shondra, whimpering, from the driver's seat, wrapping an arm around her shoulders.

Homer instructed her simply. The experienced killer pushed through the woman's terror with single words, probably knowing it was all she could handle right now.

"Quiet. Quiet. Keys. Door. Inside. Go."

Kradle followed them into a warm, cozy house. It was messy but not dirty. Empty coffee mugs on the sink. A towel hanging off a door. Open mail scattered on the dining room table.

"You got tape?" Homer asked.

"What?" Shondra choked.

"Tape. Duct tape. Tape for your wrists."

She couldn't answer. Kradle didn't blame her. He peeled off and went to the garage, found a roll of duct tape sitting on a shelf. Homer forced Shondra to the ground. She went down easily, shaking, then limp. The trousers of her waitress's uniform were wet.

Homer left her lying, bound and gagged with tape, on the kitchen floor, and came back to where Kradle stood in the entry hall. The big man's eyes were alive, his grin so wide Kradle could see his gums hugging his molars.

"Let's think what we need," Homer said. "Clothes. Food. A phone. I need to take a shower. We'll take the car. Drive to your old place. Get the cash."

"I need a computer," Kradle said. "And listen, it's not as easy as just driving home and picking up the money. The cops will be sitting on the house. Might be that I'll have to find an old buddy of mine, send him around there instead. Maybe tonight."

"All right." Homer rubbed his palms together, making a dry sound. "You gather all that stuff. I'm taking Shondra to the bedroom."

Kradle's stomach plummeted. As Homer moved, he forced himself to put a hand out, flat, against the killer's chest.

"Whoa, whoa, whoa," Kradle said. "How about me first, man?"

Homer's face twitched, awkward.

"Do you mind?" Kradle asked. "I mean, I know some guys aren't funny about stuff like that. But I am. I don't like anybody's leftovers. No offense."

"I could go first, then we put her in the shower." Homer gestured toward the back of the house, the bedrooms beyond, as cool and calm as a man talking about arrangements to borrow a car. "Then you go."

"I like to go first."

"So do I, and I caught her."

"Yeah, but you wouldn't have caught her without me. Your ass would probably still be wandering around the desert if I hadn't led you out of there. This is my payback," Kradle said.

Homer licked his lips. Kradle forced a pleasant smile.

"Okay." Homer shrugged. "Whatever you want, buddy. Just don't tire her out."

"You might think about taking that shower," Kradle ventured. "You smell like a dead dog. It would be nicer on her."

"Watch it." Homer elbowed him, hard, in the ribs.

Kradle's legs were numb as he walked into the kitchen and picked up Shondra from the tiles. The woman wriggled and screamed in his arms as he carried her to a bedroom and dropped her on the bed, slamming the door closed behind them.

CHAPTER 14

Keeps watched the desert roll by, one wrist on the top of the steering wheel, fingers resting on the dashboard. He slouched in the seat, eyelids low. Celine was gripping her jeans, sitting bolt upright, watching the mountains in the distance, which didn't seem to be getting any closer.

"Is this as fast as you can go?"

"This is as fast as I *wanna* go." Keeps glanced at her. "I ain't enthused about going any faster. I hate Mesquite. My ex-girlfriend is from Mesquite. She stole my CD player. The deal was I'd be chillin' in your hot tub, drinking your beer, while you stayed out searching for these losers, not driving you around. Do I look like Morgan Freeman to you?"

"I haven't slept in twenty-four hours. It's not safe for me to drive. And I don't have a hot tub."

"I'm pretty sure one was mentioned."

"Nope."

"Fuck my life." Keeps sighed, shook his head. "So, tell me again about this guy? He blew his wife away?"

"The wife was some kind of eccentric," Celine

said. "Christine Hammond. They met while she was in Louisiana, hunting ghosts. She was a paranormal investigator, I suppose you'd say."

"You're shittin' me."

"No shit. If you heard bumps in the night, she would roll in with her bag of tricks and work out what kind of bogeyman you were hosting. Splash some snake oil around, try to kick it out of your house."

"People can make a living doing that?" Keeps asked, smiling.

"I think it was Kradle who kept them afloat. He was a handyman. Builder. Plumber. Mechanic. Jack of all trades. Her family was wealthy but I don't think they supported her. Ghost hunting wasn't really in the family line," Celine said.

"You know all this how?"

"I looked real close at the case when we took him in five years ago."

"You do that with all the row guys?"

"Only the true assholes."

"So why'd he blast her?" Keeps asked. "The wife. Money troubles?"

"I think he just snapped," Celine said. "That's what they do, these family annihilators."

"Oh jeez, they have a term for it." Keeps laughed to himself.

"There's a pattern," Celine said. "The pressure builds and builds and builds, and they just snap and kill everyone. Financial pressure will do it. Maybe a sickness in the family or a recent loss. I think they were hard up for cash, but I also I think his relationship with her family wasn't great. And she had taken off from their marriage and gone missing for fifteen years."

"Fifteen *years*?"

"She walked out the day the baby was born," Celine said. "Left the hospital. Went into hiding. You're trying to tell me she felt safe with him?"

"Maybe she just didn't want to be a mom." Keeps shrugged. "Maybe it wasn't him."

"It was him, trust me."

"So why'd she come back, if she felt so unsafe?"

"I don't know. But she was back for less than three months before he killed her, and her sister, and the kid."

Keeps's mouth twisted, and stayed twisted. Celine sat watching it, waiting for it to untwist. It didn't.

"What?"

"I don't know." Keeps shrugged one shoulder again, the way he'd been doing for the whole conversation. Celine's blood was heating up, just watching that shoulder lift up and flop down, as if what they were talking about was no big deal. "Something ain't right."

"What ain't right?"

"The guy sounds like a pretty straight-up dude," Keeps said. "He builds things. Fixes things. Makes the money while she flutters around doing her ghosty-ghosty shit. Then she drops a baby on him and bounces out of town for fifteen years? Who raised the baby?"

"He did."

"Yeah, see?" Keeps clicked his tongue. "He didn't kill her. Kind of guy who would take a bitch back after all that wouldn't turn around three months later and kill her."

"Why don't you just trust me on this, okay?" Celine patted his shoulder. "I looked at the case. They found him standing on the lawn, soaked in the blood of all three victims, covered in gunshot residue and gasoline, watching the house burn to the ground." She straightened in her seat, but for some reason couldn't find the same level of comfort she'd had only minutes earlier. "I know John Kradle. He's not a nice guy."

Kradle tried to pin her down. It didn't work. He shoved the wriggling, screaming, kicking Shondra off the bed and onto the carpet, on her stomach, held her head down, and put his lips to her ear.

"Stop!" he rasped. "Stop, stop, stop! Listen to me! You've gotta listen!"

She stopped fighting and broke into furious sobs.

"I'm going to let you go," he said. He ripped off her shirt. The cheap restaurant uniform shirt gave way easily, the buttons popping, seams cracking as the stitches burst. It became a rag in his hands with one hard yank. "You have to do exactly as I say. Understand?"

Shondra's sobs ebbed slightly. They both listened, panting, as, at the front of the house, the pipes squeaked and water hit tiles.

"You're going to get up," Kradle said, ripping the tape from her wrists and ankles. "And you're going to hit me."

He climbed off her. Shondra scrambled backward into the side of the bed, reached for the tape around her mouth, found it hopelessly wound around her skull three or four times. Her cheeks bulged as she watched Kradle tug the clock radio from its socket in the wall behind the nightstand.

"Hit me with this." He handed it to her. "Then climb out the window and run for your fucking life."

He stood. Shondra got awkwardly to her feet. Her trousers were soaked in urine. Kradle could smell it. Her left breast had snuck sideways from her bra, the strap broken and the underwire cutting into the flesh of her ribs. He tried to take a step toward her but she backed away, almost fell on the bed.

"Hit me!" He gestured to his face. "Come on. Come *on!* We don't have time. You've got to do this. I can't do it myself!"

Shondra gathered up the cord of the clock radio, wouldn't meet his eyes with her own. Her whole body was shaking, a hard, bent, uncontrollable quivering.

"For fuck's sake," Kradle snarled. "Hit—"

The movement was too fast for him to follow. There was no build-up, no swing. She lashed out with the device from her center like a basketballer making a chest pass, the clock radio crunching into his temple as he tried to twist away. His knees hit the carpet, the room tilting.

"Okay." He gripped his face. "That was—"

She was on him. Beating down savagely with the device, knocking the radio on his forearms and elbows as he raised them to defend himself; her face turned away, swift, blind, brutal downward force. A second passed in which Kradle might have blacked out. He held on to the carpet as the room spun and dipped around him, and the woman named Shondra climbed through the bedroom window and disappeared.

Homer was there suddenly. Damp but dressed, lifting Kradle up by his arms and shaking him.

"What the fuck? What the fuck, man?"

"Oh! Whoa!" Kradle was suddenly awake, snapped

back into self-preservation mode. "She got me. She got me!"

"Get up." Homer wrenched him to his feet, pushed him toward the door. "Get packing."

1999

"Suit yourself."

Celine tried to grip on to those words as she hugged the cold, dry hardwood pillar in the crawlspace under the porch. She squeezed her eyes shut and tried to visualize her arms, hands, fingers folding around the two words, pulling the letters into her chest, clinging on. *Suit yourself. Suit yourself.* Because the teenager knew that if she didn't hang on to those words as if they were a rope dangling above a cavern, she would fall. The other words, the other sounds, would creep back to her. Sounds from an hour earlier, when her grandfather turned away from her and walked up the porch steps and into the house, brought his rifle down from his shoulder and aimed it.

"Jesus, Nick, what are you—"

Cha-chick. Boom.

"Oh my. Oh my. Oh my god. Oh oh oh—"

Cha-chick. Boom.

"Dad! Dad, stop! Dad!"

Cha-chick. Boom.

Cha-chick. Boom.

Celine gripped the pillar, hugged it with her knees, opened her eyes and looked across the dark space beneath the porch where she had hidden when the firing started. The dirt was lined with thin, gold pinstripes from the midday sun. She could see legs out there. Every time she opened her eyes there were more of them. Men going to the barn. Men assembling at the driveway fence. Men walking up the steps into the house.

She had seen two faces in all the time she crouched there, holding on to the porch pillar. The face of a police officer who bent and vomited into her grandmother's garden of purple petunias after returning from the barn. And the face of a paramedic who lay on his belly now, ten yards from her, his hand outstretched toward her.

"Celine," he'd been saying gently, over and over, "it's safe now. He's gone. We've got him. Okay? He's locked up. He can't hurt you. Celine, come toward me. Let me help you out of there."

Celine knew it wasn't safe. Her splintered, ticking, writhing mind knew that much. Her grandparents' neighbors were at the edge of the driveway, their dog going nuts, Michael staring at the dirt, Paula weeping madly, wringing her hair, recounting how she'd heard the shots and thought it was the boys fooling around. How she'd seen Nick's truck speeding away, the eerie feeling that gave her. How she'd gone over and seen Celine's father crawl out onto the porch and die on the steps. Celine listened as the shooting unfolded again over the telephone; a set of boots on the opposite side of the porch to the paramedic, walking back and forth, dropping a cigarette every now and then.

"He just walked into the station," the cop said,

"and put the rifle on the counter in front of the sergeant and said what he'd done, plain as that. That's what they're telling me. No, sir, I'm at the house. Oh, bad. Yeah. Yeah, bad. Seven, maybe eight. And five kids. He just went through and . . . one at a time. Everybody. Fucking everybody. Just . . . There's one left. A girl. Seventeen. She's under the porch. No. Nope. No. They're gonna give her a minute or two and then go in and pull her out, I think."

"Celine," the paramedic said. Celine squeezed her eyes shut and gripped the pillar tighter. She heard him shuffling forward on his belly in the dirt, coming into a crouch, crawling toward her. He was going to pull her out, like the cop on the phone said, and a piece of her mind was screaming with fury at that. At being pulled into the reality of it all before she was ready. Because, under the porch, it wasn't real. Above her head, above the creaking wooden boards, out there in the sunlight of the Georgia day, her little cousins were still playing in the barn, and her grandfather was rattling around the house somewhere, growling at people, and her mom and nanna and aunty were making salad. It was still just a day. Christmas Day.

CHAPTER 15

Old Axe had seen *The Wizard of Oz* plenty of times during his four decades staring at tiny, convex TV screens in prison cells at night. In his experience, most correctional facilities in Nevada had pretty shitty movie collections, county jails being the worst. Any violence had to be chopped out, so anything half decent, like murder mysteries, could lose twenty minutes or more. No boobs, no butts, no kids in swimsuits, either. You didn't have to chop anything out of *The Wizard of Oz* or *The Sound of Music* or *Willy Wonka and the Chocolate Factory*. Some of the kid-heavy films tended to rattle the fiddlers, but theirs was a quiet, harmless kind of unrest. *Oz* was a safe, universal prison classic.

Axe had been thinking about Dorothy stepping out of her black-and-white world and into that magical, shiny new place as he trundled through the desert sand toward the Joshua tree. The tree itself was taller than he'd anticipated, weird bristled fingers gripping a handful of blue sky. Worth the walk. He'd decided to keep wandering north, and stopped a few times to look at almost mystically beautiful rocks, cacti, scrubby plants. He halted at the sight of a spotted lizard, and put his hands in his pockets and watched it watching him for a while. Axe the alien on a new and pristine planet. He came across a Coke can shining like a diamond, its light drawing him from about half a mile away. The air tasted different and the world seemed unfathomably big.

One of those flying drone machines did buzz over his head just before nightfall, but it didn't descend to check him out or give him any orders. He let the breeze direct him, having no real intentions, feeling jubilant for the first time in a long time. He slept under the stars, woke under them, too. His ears kept presenting him with phantom sounds, the way that solid ground must lie to sailors for a week or so after a long stint at sea, he guessed. He heard someone call out his name and turned to find only emptiness behind him. He heard the peal of the chow bell and the clatter of feet on the steel steps outside his cell.

After a while, he hit an unlined road. He saw an animal, so pancaked and sunbaked he couldn't tell which was the head or tail, or what it had once been. He turned to his left, because the wind was going that way, and kept on.

When he heard the sound of a vehicle behind him, he figured it would be a prison van or sheriff or someone coming to take him back. He stopped, and the car pulled over, too far behind him to make any sense. Axe turned to look.

An RV was sitting on the shoulder, two women in the front seats, leaning together, talking. There were more people in the back. Axe waited. Nothing happened. The RV's engine hummed. The desert gaped.

In the distance, he could see something tracking across the sky—either a drone close by or a helicopter far away. Axe waited another moment or two, then turned and continued trundling. The RV came up and slowed alongside him.

He saw that the two young people in the front weren't women but long-haired men. Axe hadn't seen this kind of honey-brown suntanned faces, bleached eyelashes, and flowing, golden hair on men since the 1960s. He noticed surfboards on the top of the RV and clumps of sea grass in the wheel wells.

The vehicle stopped, and still nothing happened. He realized the kid closest to him, with his elbow hanging out the window, was listening to an argument in the cabin.

"Might be a crazy-ass serial killer or something!"

"Come on. Come on, Manny! Where's your sense of fuckin' adventure?"

"He's an old man. What's he gonna do?"

"If we leave him out here he'll probably die."

"There's only one of him and five of us."

"Dude." The sun-speckled kid in the window grinned at Axe. "Dude, hey. All this shit on the radio about a breakout. Is it true?"

Axe brushed dust off the chest of his prison denims, examined them.

"Seems like it," he said. They were the first words he'd uttered to someone outside a prison since before the man he was talking to was born.

"You, like"—the man paused to laugh at his own daring, or maybe at the absurdity of it all—"you want a ride with us?"

Axe thought about it. Sucked air down the sides of his teeth and examined the horizon. When he turned back, the window was crowded with young, apprehensive faces—curious, scared, excited, he didn't know.

"Guess so." Axe shrugged.

The young people looked at each other.

"Are you dangerous?" a girl asked from the back of the huddle.

Again, Axe thought about it. About the truth and how well it had served him in his life.

"Nope," he said.

The back door of the RV popped open. Axe went to it, climbed aboard with some difficulty. The air conditioning enveloped him, as did the scent of weed. He was standing in a cluttered kitchenette. Dirty plates. Wooden knife block on the counter, full of shiny blade handles. One of those flat-panel computers he'd seen on TV was lying on an armchair, its cover flipped open and screen blank.

"I can't believe we're doing this," someone giggled. Axe moved the computer carefully and sat down in the armchair. All the young people were grinning. The RV started up and rumbled back onto the road.

"You want a drink, old man?" a girl asked.

"Sure," Axe said.

When in Oz, he thought.

1999

He didn't believe in all the ghost stuff. But he showed up anyway. He figured that was what you did when you loved someone. You nodded and laughed and chipped in with a "She's right, you know. I've seen it!" occasionally. You held the camera steady and let her do her thing, and it wasn't as though she didn't do the same for him now and then, though it was usually a ladder she was holding, and his thing mostly ended up getting her crazy mad and covered in leaves or dirt. He sold the houseboat and made enough cash to buy a decent car, and they took her show on the road, answering emails that came through a webpage she'd been clever enough to cook up.

In Dallas, they exorcised a poltergeist from an old fishing trawler. In Long Beach, they shuffled a shadow walker out of a beachfront bar. In Chicago, they spent three days clearing an attic of a menacing presence that at first she thought was the ghost of a murdered girl, but turned out to be a demon masquerading as such while it built up its power reserves. Kradle thought Christine was taking the excitable young couple who were the owners of the attic for a ride. While Christine performed for the camera, got messages from the apparent demon in faux-Latin with her eyes rolled back in her head, he took a look at the roof joists and found some loose bolts, tightened them up on the sly. After all, he'd taken some people for rides in his life too, and these trust-fund kids seemed to get a kick out of all Christine's processes—the runes and gems she taped to the walls and the incantations she made them recite while on their knees in the middle of the living room rug. People shared the videos via the internet, and the call-outs went nuts. They spent weekends on yachts in Bermuda, talking to sea spirits, and a month in Jackson Hole, performing sage ceremonies on the log cabins of millionaires. He worked only so he could get sweaty now and then, so his hands didn't go all soft. Her money got so good they didn't know what to do with it.

So, they did with it what people usually do. They bought a house in northwest Mesquite, with a bullnose awning over a little tiled porch. They'd been in town trying to convince the ghost of an old Native American lady to cross over to the other side, and Christine liked the people and he liked the noticeboard at the supermarket covered in requests for handyman services. They spread expensive lawn all over the yard around a river-stone pool, real thick lawn that was totally impractical in the desert sun. She recruited all the neighbors as friends, because these were the kinds of people she liked to surround herself with— regulars, normies, average Joes—people who were so fascinated by her stories about ghosts and so charmed by her tasseled Miu Mius and eyeball-shaped earrings that they couldn't possibly talk about anything but her. They held backyard barbecues and she drank too much sauvignon blanc and started calling him her "rougarou," her swamp werewolf, scratching the back of his head with her nails, making the hair stick up. The way she told it, he was a backwater illiterate with yellow teeth and a beard when she found him, the Quasimodo of the bayou, a creature she alone had been clever enough to see could be taught to stand on its hind legs and wear shoes. John didn't mind her hamming up his story to make it seem as if she'd brought in a skinny street dog, tamed it, bathed it, taught it to bark on cue, and made a fine husband out of it. Christine needed people to like her, and the fact that his houseboat had been half-sunk with books when he met her wasn't as compelling a tale.

Everything was fine until that day in August. Sure, he'd caught a faraway look in her eye sometimes and knew in his heart she was dreaming of diagnosing screams at midnight in San Francisco or vibrations in the bathroom mirror in Tennessee. But she got by on her tarot readings, her $50 copy-and-paste email consults, her newsletter membership programs. Then one afternoon she came to him in the garage, where he was taking apart a microwave, and handed him a pregnancy test with two red lines on it. He smiled, and she burst into tears.

CHAPTER 16

It was clear from the contents of their haul how panicked they had been. On a picnic table that bore cigarette burns made by workers from the nearby packaging warehouse, Kradle dumped the trash bags of things they had taken from Shondra's house. Virgin River was a blinding strip of white through the long grass. He sorted through the items while Homer broke twigs.

The most important item, a laptop Kradle had grabbed from the living room, he set aside. He devoured three slices of white bread from the half-loaf Homer had nabbed from the kitchen, his heart still hammering as he ate. They'd managed to grab a Coke, a package of sliced ham, a jar of cookies, three candy bars, and a box of raw pasta in the way of food. Other supplies included two cell phones, a kitchen knife, and three dollars in cash. A hairbrush, a sock, a label maker, and a ball of twine had also come along for the journey in the trash bags, gathered up in the sheer madness of knowing Shondra was half-naked and screaming through her gag and running god-knows-where to get help.

"How the fuck did it happen?" Homer was shaking his head, his fist full of tiny twig pieces.

"You know how it happened." Kradle pushed open the laptop and sat down. "I ripped off her tape and she grabbed the clock radio from the nightstand, smacked me in the head with it. Jumped out the window. Simple as that."

"Why did you take her tape off?"

"I needed to so I could . . ." Kradle looked at the lake. "You know. God. Man, you're making me feel like an idiot here."

"You are an idiot," Homer said. Kradle watched him. There was a meanness in his eyes for a moment that made all the air leave Kradle's lungs and the fine hairs on his arms stand on end, his primal warning system kicking in. And then it was gone. The tiger in the tall grass just a trick of the light. "Sorry. Sorry. I shouldn't have said that, buddy. That wasn't right."

Kradle nodded, tried to look chastened.

"Women have got away from me before." Homer shrugged. "It happens."

They sorted through the clothes they had managed to snatch from the floor and closet. Two of the shirts were obviously Shondra's, and two must have belonged to the boyfriend. Kradle pulled on a blue T-shirt with a logo he didn't recognize, while Homer stretched a black Nevada Wolf Pack baseball jersey over his bulky frame. Disregarding the filthy jeans and shoes, they might have been two regular people standing by the water behind a warehouse.

"What's the computer for?" Homer asked.

"I've got to get numbers for my guys. Look up their details. See if I can call in some help."

"You didn't stay in touch while you were on the inside?"

"No," Kradle said.

"Why not?" Homer asked. Kradle rubbed his neck. "I thought you mob guys got an easy ride in prison. I thought you took care of each other."

Kradle tried a new strategy: ignoring the questions, rather than trying to provide answers for things he couldn't account for. Clam up. It had made the detectives go away for a while in the seventh or eighth hour of his questioning after Christine and Mason and Audrey were murdered. Homer wandered down to the water and Kradle started to breathe freely again.

He opened the Wi-Fi app on the computer, the way he'd seen his lawyer do in the Pronghorn visitors' center, and fished around for a free internet source. He found a signal coming from the packaging warehouse, clicked it and crossed his fingers. When the icon went green he opened a window and started googling.

A search on Homer Carrington brought up hundreds of articles about the breakout at Pronghorn. Kradle shifted the parameters to exclude links that had been posted within the past twenty-four hours. All the things he didn't want to see flooded onto the screen. Naked girls lying in desolate fields, their bodies looking strangely deflated and impossibly white in the flattened grass, faces turned toward grasping, lifeless hands. There was an image of a missing person poster, the young woman grinning at the camera. Big brown eyes. A Labrador puppy cradled in her arms. Crime scene photographs of a car abandoned mid-tire-change in a shopping mall parking lot, still up on the jack, the tire lying on its side. There was an old couple lying side by side on floral carpet, the coffee table knocked over, the front door of the house ajar. The most recent news article was a week old, headed ATTACK ON GUARD: NORTH NEVADA STRANGLER REHOUSED AT PRONGHORN. Kradle clicked. A CCTV still image of Homer in a prison hallway—not Pronghorn, somewhere older. The huge serial killer had his hands around the throat of a small, plump male guard. Kradle clicked out of the article, scrolled down, reading headlines.

NN STRANGLER HOMER CARRINGTON PLEADS INSANITY

CARRINGTON SENTENCED TO DEATH

CARRINGTON VICTIMS MAY BE DOZENS, EXPERT SAYS

CARRINGTON TRIPS TO MEXICO MAY REVEAL MORE VICTIMS

TWELVE-YEAR-OLD MISSING GIRL LINKED TO NN STRANGLER

Kradle knew he didn't have much time before the cell phone and laptop both became weapons against him. When Shondra found help, she would describe him and Homer to the police, and it wouldn't be long until someone somewhere decided they sounded just similar enough to two of the top-classified fugitives that they should prioritize tracking them down. He had minutes, not hours. He punched in a name that echoed loudly into the dark halls of his past.

Patrick Frapport.

Mentions of the detective online were scarce. No social media. Images of the heavyset, bald police officer were also rare. A blurry image of him receiving a medal from some police boss. A profile shot of him sitting in a courtroom, waiting to testify, the bulge under his chin tucked uncomfortably into the collar of his shirt, red raw from being recently shaved. Kradle read quickly over an article announcing Frapport's promotion in the *Mesquite Sun*, and clicked on a picture of the man and his slender wife, her the decidedly friendlier-looking of the two, with warm, rosy cheeks and a sharp brunette bob cut.

Shelley Frapport. Kradle clicked on her Instagram page. He knew Instagram only from television shows he'd watched inside prison, couldn't navigate the site for precious minutes, trying to figure how it worked. Unlike her husband, Shelley's online activities were full of breadcrumbs leading to her location. He recognized the caramel-leather-lined booths of Eden's Diner in one of the happy selfies of the woman, and noticed a slice of a public pool with a big yellow water slide in the background of another. He knew that pool, had taken Mason there when the boy was young for the birthday party of a school friend. For a moment Kradle was swamped with memories: standing with other dads in the shade of the kiosk, Mason tugging his arm, begging for candy money, a puddle of water pooling at his feet and his black hair plastered to his fleshy forehead. The pool and the diner put Shelley Frapport in the neighborhood of Beaver Dam. When Kradle clicked on the second-most-recent image he saw Shelley Frapport sitting on a porch swing. #afternoon #suburbanbliss #pinotgrigio. In the bottom right-hand corner of the screen, a little brass number was affixed to the front fence of the house. Number seven. Kradle stared hard at the image, trying to determine the angle of the sun, the style of house, anything that could provide a hint as to where it lay. In the background of the image, over Shelley's shoulder and past the side of the house, he thought he could see the top of a structure in the distance. A red and green water tower.

"My seatbelt was undone," Homer said.

Kradle looked up. The serial killer was standing just near him, the big knife from Shondra's kitchen clutched in his fist, the blade glinting in the light bouncing off the lake.

"What?"

"In the plane," Homer said. "I remember buckling it. I remember shoving the buckle closed, hearing it click, pulling on it to make sure it was tight. It stuck in my head because at the time I was thinking to myself, *What if this guy is lying? What if he can't fly?* But you weren't lying about being able to fly. You were lying about being my friend."

Kradle felt all the blood rush out of his head, face, neck, as if a plug had been pulled somewhere and all the life was draining downward at a dizzying speed. For a moment he just gripped the table and stared at the man holding the knife.

"There's no money, is there?" Homer asked.

"No," Kradle said.

"Because you're not a mob guy."

"No, I'm not."

"You let that woman get away, didn't you," Homer said. It wasn't a question. "And if you'd had the chance, you were going to push me out of that plane."

Kradle didn't answer. All his focus was on his body, his limbs, his breath, keeping the blood flowing, keeping his wits about him. But for all his focus, all his planning, he was tired, dehydrated, probably concussed, and half-crazed with terror that at any moment he was going to be seized again by any one of the half a dozen government agencies that were after him. The fear that he was going to wake up back in his cell on the row, staring into the deep dark forever, was suffocating. So when Homer lunged at him, Kradle dove sideways off the bench, staggered backward. But the big man's arm seemed to have infinite reach, and he wasn't fast enough to move out of that reach before it was coming forward, enveloping him, consuming him. That big arm that had swept around so many throats, those killer hands, those knuckles misshapen and scarred and scraped by fingernails trying to claw them away, including his own only hours ago. Kradle felt the blade slash through his arm as if it was butter.

"So, let me get this straight." Celine folded her arms. "You had a grab-all set up for Kradle, and a *dog* blew your cover?"

She stood in the parking lot of the Mesquite Police Department office, which seemed to have become a kind of field command center for fugitive-related activity. In the shade of a huge navy-blue US Marshals' intelligence van, Celine addressed an audience of four men—two sheriff's deputies and two marshals, who had reluctantly turned from their maps, laptops, charts, and radios to examine the two interlopers in their midst. Keeps was trying to disappear into a nearby bush, the recently released felon standing as close to it as he possibly could while sheltering a cigarette against the breeze.

"Sorry." The biggest marshal flicked his head at Celine. "Who are you again?"

"I'm Captain Celine Osbourne, death row supervisor from Pronghorn Correctional."

"So you're not a cop, a marshal, or a fed," the guy said. Celine didn't answer. "Captain Osbourne, we appreciate your interest in this matter. But my line to you is the same as it is to all civilians. We're doing the best we can to round up any fugitives who might come into town, but—"

"What's your name?"

"Lowakowski." The guy gave a heavy sigh, looked at his colleagues. *You hearing this?*

"Lowakowski," Celine said. "Those journalists over there by the vending machine just told me you had John Kradle in your hands and you fumbled it. I want to know what you have on his current location."

"Please step back, Captain Osbourne." Lowakowski put up a fleshy palm. "You're in an operational area here."

"The guy who was with him," Celine said, scrolling through apps on her phone to find her saved photos. She held up a picture of Burke David Schmitz. "Did he look like this?"

"I can't reveal—"

"Or this?" Celine held up a picture of Homer Carrington. The marshals glanced at the sheriffs. Celine nodded, then walked over to where Keeps was trying to turn himself inside out to avoid being looked at by the swarm of authorities.

"It's bad news," Celine said.

"Oh, excellent."

"Kradle has Homer Carrington with him."

"Who?"

"The North Nevada Strangler," Celine said.

"Okay, look," Keeps said. He took Celine's car keys out of her pocket. "This is where I bounce. All I wanted was a goddamn burger and a beer, and now somehow I'm miles from where I wanna be, chauffeuring your ass around while you chase Hannibal Lecter. I'm not going to end up in a hole in the ground putting lotion on myself. I'm done."

"If you've got such a big problem with being the driver, I'll drive," Celine said. "We'll drop by a gas station and I'll grab a Red Bull and you can get a beer and then you'll be halfway to—"

"No."

"Keeps, I need—"

"You need therapy," he said. He tapped his temple with his finger. "You need your head checked out, because you ain't a cop, okay? You don't fight crime. You don't solve mysteries. You don't hunt fugitives. You're a jailer, okay? Man, I've seen some egos on screws in my life, but this takes the cake."

"Egos?" Celine scoffed.

"Yeah," Keeps said. "You're acting as if this is all your doing. Like you let them out and you've got to get them back again. This. Ain't. About. You!"

Celine couldn't speak. She stared at her boots on the asphalt and felt far from home in an upside-down world.

"All I have been doing for the past fifteen years is keeping them boxed up, away from the world. Keeping people safe from them. This is me," she said. "This is who I am."

"No, it's not." Keeps eased smoke from between his lips.

Celine held up her phone. "You happen to notice how many people are *not* calling me on this thing?" she asked. "A normal person finds herself at the center of a history-making fuck-up at work, and she has all kinds of people calling her. Friends. Family. Why aren't people calling me and asking if I'm okay? What's happening. What I'm doing about it. If I need help."

"Because you don't have any friends or family."

"Why have I got a goddamn inmate I don't know from Adam helping me out on this thing?" She gestured to him.

"Because you promised me beer."

"Death row is what I've got, Keeps, and I'm just trying to get it back."

Keeps laughed, and a puff of smoke came out of his mouth and was snatched away by the breeze. "Look, I've heard guys talk like that on the inside. They spend so much time surrounded by prison walls they start to think that's all there is. You're just as institutionalized as I am."

"It's more than that," she began. But Celine didn't know how to tell him that driving home at night to her empty, immaculate house, knowing that all the men she was responsible for were locked away safely, was the warmest feeling in the world. That she liked to think that every minute, every hour they weren't on the street causing more pain to the people whose lives they had already devastated was due in part to her. That, somewhere out there, there were men and women and children going to bed safely because she spent her days checking green lights, turning keys in locks, punching codes into alarm systems, watching shadows of humans move about on security cameras. There were men on Celine's row who had climbed into the bedrooms of little girls in the dark hours and carried them away from their warm sheets, and their bones were still unlocated, their faces remembered only in photographs. There were men on her row who had wrung the life from desperate women working the streets, who had watched from the roadside as cars with whole families in them burned, who had fired shots on panicked crowds from on high, indiscriminately cutting down souls. And there was John Kradle, who had one day decided that his family didn't deserve to go on living.

Celine's phone rang and she grabbed at it. When she heard his voice on the line, her heart twisted in her chest.

Kradle stopped by the front of the warehouse and pulled his hand away from the wound in his arm. He couldn't tell how bad it was. It looked deep, black, wet. There were people running from the office at the back of the packaging warehouse, having spotted the fray from the windows that looked out over the water. They were rushing to assist the man lying by the picnic table, bleeding his life away. If he were a religious man, Kradle would have said a prayer for the warehouse worker who had been brave enough to come and intervene as Homer swung wildly at him with the kitchen knife. But Kradle wasn't the praying type. He could only hope the guy wasn't dead.

"Celine?"

"Oh my god." He heard her muffle the phone with her hand. "It's him."

"Listen to me," Kradle said. He limped across the warehouse parking lot between cars, heading for the road. "Homer Carrington just stabbed a guy behind the . . . the Resco Industries Packaging warehouse. It's near the river. He ran off, heading north."

"Who's the guy?"

"Some warehouse worker who tried to save me from Carrington."

"Is . . . is he dead?"

"I don't know."

"Stay there."

"I can't. You know I can't."

He heard her cover the phone again, shout the story to someone. He could only assume she was surrounded by other fugitive hunters. She would be in the midst of it all, trying to undo what she could of the breakout. Celine took everything personally. He heard a car door opening and closing, an engine starting.

"Celine? Celine?"

"I'm here."

"Homer and I carjacked and robbed a woman named Shondra." Kradle headed down an alleyway at the end of a strip mall, his bloodied shirt causing a couple with a dog to scurry away to safety. "I don't, uh . . . You'll find her. She escaped from us. We stole two cell phones from her house. This is one of them. Homer might have the other one. He took everything we had—the whole bag. He might . . . I don't know if the other phone works. It looked old. But you might be able to track him by it if he turns it on."

"Stay where you are, Kradle."

The alley opened into another strip mall. He spotted a secondhand clothing store with racks of coats hanging in the sunshine. When he spoke again he heard an echo, as though the phone was on speaker.

"I have to find the man who killed my son," Kradle said.

"Oh, Jesus," Celine sighed.

"Celine, I know your story," Kradle said.

"What?"

"I know what happened to you," Kradle said. He heard sirens. "My lawyer told me. He worked with your grandfather's lawyer over in Georgia way back when. I've known for years, Celine. Are you there? Are you listening?"

"You . . ." She was having trouble breathing. He heard her gasp, her breath hitch. "You never said anything. You never—"

"Listen, I get it." Kradle stopped and wiped sweat from his face. He was leaning against the window of a nail salon. A woman doing a pedicure just inside the window had stopped her work and was staring at him, open-mouthed. "What happened with your family . . . Of course you would hate someone convicted of a crime like mine. But I need you to take the emotion out of it now. I need you to put it aside. It didn't matter if you believed me when I was on the row, but it sure as hell matters now. You can help me. I know you can."

"I wouldn't help you if you were on fire, John Kradle," Celine said.

"Take an hour," Kradle said. "One hour. Just do me that much, please. Take an hour, look at my case. Have someone look at it with you, someone who isn't weighed down by the kind of history you've got. Your boyfriend or . . . someone. It doesn't matter. You'll see it if you open your eyes."

There was no answer. John Kradle dumped the phone in a trash can and limped down another alleyway, slid through a gap in a chain-link fence, and crossed the cracked concrete of an abandoned lot, passed threads of dry, brown grass hanging like hair over an old flight of steps. He found a park with a public bathroom and walked into the cool, dark brick building to rest.

CHAPTER 17

Trinity Parker sat down across from Lieutenant Joe Brassen and took a moment to stir her coffee. She had requested many things since she'd arrived at Pronghorn to handle the breakout. The partition walls with the faces of inmates. A quiet space with a sturdy chair where she could take briefings from her section chiefs, sit and map out her forty-eight-, seventy-two-, and ninety-six-hour plans, answer the odd phone call from Washington. Somewhere with a window, where she could look out over the press camped outside the gates. Truth was, she could have done without all those things. She wasn't prissy. Trinity had squatted in broken-down houses in Detroit while hunting fugitives, shitting in a bucket and living on candy bars and bottled water, cockroaches crawling up her ankles. But what she couldn't do without was strong, good-quality coffee, and at the thirty-hour mark a proper machine had arrived and the whole catastrophe had seemed impossibly easier to handle.

She put down her spoon and glanced at Brassen as

she lifted her cup. Trinity enjoyed dealing with people whose worlds were slowly crumbling. They were refreshing. Joe Brassen had to know he was on the verge of losing everything, of becoming one of the things he feared and dreaded most. An inmate. He was ripe for being taken advantage of. When someone is trapped in a grain silo, sinking desperately into the abyss with every movement, they'll take anything offered to pull them out. They'll grab at a red-hot poker. Trinity put her coffee down, smacked her lips, and flattened her hands on the table in front of her.

"Paint," she said.

"Huh?" Brassen gulped. He had been expecting a threat. A barrage of abuse. But not that word. Colors flushed through his face as he tried to find an emotion to center on. Trinity took her time.

"Black paint," Trinity said. "I know. I know. I could hardly believe it myself. But that's what will be your undoing. That's what will put you in a prison cell for the rest of your life. A three-dollar tube of acrylic paint, manufactured in China, imported to the US. 'Midnight True Black' is the shade. Number 4035."

"I don't know what you're talking about." Brassen smoothed back his thinning black hair, then pushed his glasses into place from where they had slipped down his nose on skin greased by sweat. "I want my lawyer."

"The minimum security guys were happy enough to talk about where they got their black paint," Trinity said. She sipped her coffee. "They're all snitches over in minimum. It's the same in every prison. They're in for short stints, so they don't have time to get used to bad conditions. They want to be comfortable. They all pointed to a guard named Maria Dresbone who was bringing in their contraband black paint."

"What the hell's that got to do with me?"

"Maria was harder to crack," Trinity said. "You correctional officers are somewhat more loyal to each other. Who among you hasn't snapped and slipped an elbow into an inmate's face, and relied on your colleagues to keep quiet about it? But she turned you in eventually. Maria told me that you supply her and three other guards with contraband items for inmates in minimum because you alone are able to get those items through security. Your girlfriend is the Entry B X-ray operator. She hasn't checked your backpack since you started dating six months ago."

Brassen stared at the ceiling of the office they occupied—some pencil-pusher's cluttered workspace inside the prison's administration block. There was a model truck on the edge of the desk, sitting by a framed photograph of a young girl. Trinity pushed the picture with her fingertip so that it was at a perfect forty-five-degree angle to the edge of the desk.

"The snitching inmates led me to Maria, and Maria led me to you," she said. "You work on death row. You're the only guy who could have got that paint to Schmitz. My agents found other contraband items in Schmitz's cell. His pillow isn't regulation, and there was a bottle of antibacterial nasal spray under his bed that wasn't on his list of approved meds."

"Lawyer," Brassen growled. It was the weak sound of a cornered animal, a hollow warning.

"If Burke David Schmitz kills again, and he will . . . ," Trinity began.

"I want my lawyer," Brassen said.

"You don't get a *fucking* lawyer," Trinity snarled, leaning forward in her chair. "Not here, not now, not until I decide you deserve one. I'm the person who decides everything you get from this moment onward, you gormless, knuckle-dragging sack of turds. You assisted a known neo-Nazi terrorist in escaping custody! You can sit here and tell me everything you know, or you can sit in a cell in Gitmo for the next three years while they burn out your eyeballs with strobe lights and blast the *Sesame Street* theme song until you chew your own tongue off."

Trinity leaned back in her chair and drained her coffee cup while Brassen stared at her, his eyes wide with visions crowding in of orange jumpsuits, hoods, electrodes. The images, Trinity knew, would be competing with hopeless dreams of safety, of his plywood trailer stuffed to bursting with cans of Bud and bags of Cheetos, a mixed-breed dog in there somewhere, probably something beefy, a pit bull or ridgeback with a big underbite of crooked teeth. It would sleep on his bed and be named something stupid: Blaze or Dagger or Harley. Trinity knew Brassen would choose the right path, choose the trailer and the dog over Gitmo and the orange jumpsuits and hoods. She just didn't know how long that was going to take. She put her feet up on the desk.

"I don't care about the paint and the pillows. I want to know what else you were bringing in for Schmitz."

Brassen looked at his hands on the edge of the table. The thumb of one hand was rubbing the knuckles of the other so vigorously that the skin was becoming pink and raw.

"Gun magazines," Brassen said. "Candy bars. Letters."

"Are you a neo-Nazi, Brassen?"

"No," the big man continued. "Not, like, uh . . . I mean, I don't like Black inmates. That's all. The Black inmates are worse than the white ones behavior-wise, and that's just plain old fact."

Trinity waited for Brassen to get uncomfortable and fill the silence. He did.

"Like, if you got a shank on the pod, you know it belongs to a Black inmate," Brassen said. "They get here, and it doesn't matter what crime they're coming in for. They weapon up straight away. I think it's just the violence in them. And that's my opinion." Brassen sniffed. "It's a free country, and I've got a right to my opinion."

Trinity stared at him.

"What, uh, what Schmitz did was terrible, though." Brassen cleared his throat loudly. "I mean, all those people down in New Orleans. The shooting. Nazi or not, you can't—"

"What did they offer you?" Trinity said. "And what did you bring?"

"Nothing. I don't—"

"What was in the letters you brought him?" Trinity said. "You mentioned letters. Stands to reason they would have contained communication Schmitz wanted to get past the censors. I assume you snooped."

"I didn't snoop. They told me not to."

"They told you not to, or they offered you money not to?"

Brassen wiped sweat from his neck with the collar of his shirt.

"Those letters will be gone," Trinity said. "Schmitz took a box of belongings with him when he escaped. I need something else."

Brassen gave a long, heavy sigh. "I want to make some kind of deal with you here."

"There's no deal. You give me what you have, and you hope that this time tomorrow somebody isn't waterboarding you," Trinity said. "In fact, I'll see to it that if you're waterboarded, it's a Black man who does it."

"You guys don't really do that kind of thing." Brassen ventured a small laugh.

Trinity said nothing.

"I let him use a cell phone," Brassen said.

Trinity sat forward. "Where's that phone now?"

"I was supposed to get it back from him. Yesterday morning. I never let him keep it because of the shakedowns. I'd give it to him and let him have it overnight. He must have taken it with him if it's not in his cell."

"Do you know who he was calling?"

"No."

"Do you remember where and when you bought the phone?"

"Yeah." Brassen nodded, took his own cell phone out of his pocket. "And I have the number saved, too. I put it into my phone in case I had a night off and I needed to tell Schmitz there was going to be a shakedown."

Trinity took Brassen's phone from him, sat with her feet on the desk and her elbow hanging off the side of her chair while she opened the device. On the wallpaper screen was a picture of a big, ugly dog sitting on the porch of a plywood trailer. She smiled to herself.

*　*　*

By the time Celine and Keeps arrived at the waterfront, the place was a swarm of people and vehicles, a concentrated hive of activity reminiscent of the chaos that had descended on Pronghorn after the breakout. It was early afternoon, the sun beginning to fall. Celine pressed forward through a group of people in gray coveralls with RESCO WAREHOUSE CREW embroidered on the breast pocket to find them clustered around a dead man lying twisted on the thin grass. She discerned from the sobbing account of a big man in a trucker cap that a couple of guys had been on their way to the picnic table from the warehouse for a smoke break, when they'd noticed two men getting into an argument. Whether Nugent, the skinny, bald man on the ground, saw that there was a knife in the fray before he ran forward to help was unclear.

"He just ran up there and the guy jammed the knife in his guts," the big man said. "Oh, Remy. Man, he's dead. He's dead."

Celine found herself being pushed back by the hands of a police officer. There were sirens on the wind, onlookers assembling in the warehouse parking lot, frowning, arms crossed, murmuring to each other the way that strangers will do when presented with a public spectacle of tragedy, sharing information, awe. Celine noticed a spot of blood in the grass at her feet. She let the cop push her back until she noticed another one, then turned and started following the dark splotches on the ground.

"Let's go, Celine." Keeps took her arm.

"He went this way." Celine pointed at the blood. "Come on. Come on."

"No, we're going."

"We can follow—"

"We're going!" Keeps barked. For an instant, Celine saw the inmate in him again. The prisoner defending himself against the other dangerous men stuffed behind the wire, bottled rage carefully pressurized and stored until it was needed. He pulled her out of the crowd and she tried to build her fury to match his, to fight him, to make him continue doing what she needed him to do. But she was so tired, and the night was not far away.

"You're exhausted." Keeps pointed at her chest, accusatory. He turned the finger on himself. "So am I. They're about to lock down this whole goddamn suburb to try to find those guys. I'm not spending my first night as a free man in Mesquite."

"We can just follow the trai—"

"What are you gonna do?" Keeps threw his hands up. "You're what—five foot nothin'? You're gonna chase down a pair of murderers and wrestle them to the ground yourself? Is that the plan? Because I sure ain't helping you. I don't like you enough to do what I'm *already* doing, let alone mess with some fugitive psychos."

"Keeps—"

"You might have been the big, tough officer with all the power over these guys while they were behind steel mesh and bulletproof glass, Celine. But right now you ain't nothin'."

Celine looked at the blood on the ground at her feet. Homer's blood, or Kradle's blood, or the blood of a murdered man, the first confirmed casualty of the men from her row. Her men. The ones she couldn't keep contained.

"Get in the car," Keeps said. "We're going home."

* * *

An hour and a half of heavy silence, the road roaring beneath them, the red sun creeping toward the rocky horizon through the windshield. When cars blasted past them, Celine saw one law enforcement vehicle after another—tan FBI vehicles and sheriffs' cruisers, the occasional border patrol car probably carrying officers who had been called in to assist. She slept thinly for a while, and switched wordlessly with Keeps at some unmarked point in their journey, the two passing each other at the back of the car in the warm, windy desert without meeting each other's eyes. He started texting someone maybe twenty minutes from home, and she wondered if he was trying to organize a pickup. It made her a little sad, but she didn't know why, exactly. She had lied, manipulated, and bullied him into helping her for an entire day with no tangible reward, on a mission that meant nothing to him. If he could beg his way onto someone's couch, away from her and her desperate, angry, stupid need to find John Kradle, then she believed wholeheartedly that he should.

He surprised her as she pulled onto her street, sitting up in his seat to examine the narrow Spanish-style homes drifting by, their stone-and-succulent gardens and darkened windows.

"So *is* there a boyfriend?" Keeps asked.

Celine laughed with surprise. "You heard Kradle say that?"

"I heard it. You got your phone turned all the way up."

"It's loud at Pronghorn. You can barely hear yourself think." She took her phone from the center console and tapped the button on the side to turn it down.

"So?" Keeps pushed.

Celine thought carefully about her answer. "Yeah," she said. "And he'll be pissed as all hell."

"Damn, man."

"And he's not warm and cuddly at the best of times."

They parked and walked up the drive. Celine tried not to think about the fact that if Keeps had heard John Kradle talk about her boyfriend on the phone, he'd also heard Kradle say that he knew what had *happened* to her. That word had cut through the line like a razor, slicing into her ear, into her brain, neatly parting sealed wounds and making blood run. She had heard it so much in the years after the massacre. How was she coping with what *happened*? Would she ever recover from what *happened*? It was as if a thunderclap had burst in the sky and snatched up with it every family member she had. It was a faceless *happening* that had moved through the house with the rifle that day, and not a man.

She punched a code into the panel inside the front door. Keeps stood on the stoop, looking into the eye of the doorbell camera.

"High security," he said.

"It's what I'm used to," Celine said. They went inside. There was a flapping sound, and she and Keeps stood in the spacious living room and watched as a heavy, brown tabby cat made its way toward them from the kitchen, trotting, head down with determination. The animal stopped at Celine's feet, looked up, and opened its mouth to let out a long, angry wail.

"Somebody's hungry," Keeps said.

"Like I said. Pissed as all hell." Celine picked up the cat. "Come on, Jake."

Celine went into the kitchen to feed the cat. She smiled as she thought about how Kradle must have overheard and misinterpreted a conversation between her and Jackson earlier that month about the "new man" in her life; the large, mean, wild cat she had befriended on her evening walk. *I'd seen him around the neighborhood before. He turned up again last night. I think we're going to make it a regular thing.*

Keeps followed her into the kitchen, smoothed a hand over the huge, bare marble surface of the kitchen island. She knew what he was seeing. That the house was enormous, that it was immaculate and loveless and cold as a tomb, that there wasn't a single photograph in the entire place—no happy-snaps of girls' getaways in Tijuana, no portraits of nieces and nephews in elf costumes from Christmases past. There was no sign of a human boyfriend. No cutesy notes about remembering to feed the cat or bring home milk, no calendar hanging on the wall, "Date night!" on a Wednesday, dinner and a movie and home by nine. Only Celine lived here. The house was a mistake she had made as a teenager in possession of three inherited estates. She figured she'd buy a big house on the other side of the country to the *happening*, one as far as possible from the seat of her memories, a place with high ceilings and a pool and a double garage, close to somewhere big and fun and filled with people, like Los Angeles or Vegas. She would fill the house with nice things, because she could afford it, and she thought things would make her happy. She couldn't have known back then that the bigger the house, the louder it yawned with emptiness.

"I don't have any burgers," Celine said as she scooped a tin of tuna into a bowl for the wailing, mewling, tail-flicking creature pawing at her ankles. "But I have beer."

"I ordered Uber Eats," Keeps said. He held up his phone. "It'll be here in ten. I got enough for the both of us."

"I'm not hungry." Celine tossed the tuna can into the trash. "Just put mine in the fridge."

"But—"

She waved as she walked to the bathroom.

An hour later, she had climbed up from where she sat on the floor of the shower, letting the hot water run over her face and neck and back as she stared down the drain into the darkness. She had pulled on sweats and a T-shirt, and walked into the living room, where she found the former inmate stretched out on the leather lounge, his body lit blue and green and red by flashing images on the enormous television screen. Jake was curled on Keeps's crotch, the cat's boxy head resting on the man's stomach. Celine stood examining the detritus of burger and fries wrappers on the coffee table, the empty beer bottles, letting her eyes wander briefly, indulgently, over Keeps's sleeping figure. The taut tendons in his tattooed hands and the rise and fall of his muscular chest under his singlet. Jake the cat hadn't let her pet him for two weeks, hadn't yet dared to venture onto her lap. The animal's tail was curled around Keeps's knee, twitching gently as the two rested.

"Oh, shit." Keeps jolted awake, bouncing Jake onto

the floor. "Woman, how long you been standing there like that?"

"Start a timer," Celine said, tossing her laptop over the back of the couch so that it landed on Keeps's flat stomach. "One hour. That's all I'm giving him."

CHAPTER 18

He wanted to stand in the woods, so they took him there. Burke asked them to pull over maybe ten minutes into the drive through the lush, dark woods, and he got out and walked to a spot just far enough from the roadside that he couldn't see the asphalt if he looked back. He had missed the color green inside Pronghorn. Not institution green—a milky, numb, plasticky paint color that was routinely slapped over everything that stayed still long enough. Psychology green. Neutral green. But the rich, vibrant green of sunlit leaves. He sat in the undergrowth and breathed the forest air.

If he'd asked, someone would have brought him a drink. A barrel-aged whiskey was what he wanted. They would do that, his handlers, rush into town while he sat there and scrounge up anything he desired. He could have women, food, clothes, guns—these were *his* days, his first free days, and he was going to enjoy them. Because he was a someone now. The Camp had promised that to him when they found him as a teen-ager in Massachusetts, lurking around the Columbine forums, a nobody. Burke had been *that* kid—the quiet, shy, monosyllabic "coaster" at the back of the classroom who the teacher only called on when there was a problem with the screen projector, the one who did the assigned task in the first ten minutes of class and then spent the rest of the time discussing third-shooter theories online with other mass-shooting followers.

He'd been searching around for raw footage from the Columbine library security cameras, rumored but not confirmed to exist, when another 4channer popped up in his messages. The lurkers online who still hero-worshipped Eric and Dylan, when so many younger people had moved on to your Elliot Rodger incel types, were the real diehards. Rodger and his contemporaries, the *Call of Duty* generation of shooters, were so focused on women that the media had a party every time one of them arose. The overbearing mother was pictured weeping on the front porch. The fat, nerdy, pimply friends described him as pussy-obsessed. Eric and Dylan, on the other hand, had a real cause. So the Camp watched patiently for lurkers like Burke, who came to the forums consistently, wanting to see the diaries, the autopsy reports, the unseen footage, wanting to discuss the theories, wanting to know why.

Burke's recruiter hadn't provided anything more than a gentle nudge into the online world of neo-Nazi groups and their plans for a race war, and Burke fell in love. He liked all the serial killer angles and the calls for disruption, chaos. Black-and-white photographs of a short, angry, determined Charles Manson, his beautiful, waif-like followers, his legions of admirers. Burke followed his recruiter's links into Timothy McVeigh's work in Oklahoma, and on and on it went, until Burke was lying in bed at night staring at the laptop until his eyes ached and teared with exhaustion, watching videos, reading manifestos, making notes.

After about a month, Burke's recruiter, Rauffs-Plan1, invited him to call him by his real name, Ken. He wanted to invite fifteen-year-old Burke to the Camp: a five-day retreat in the woods near Pelham for young people who he thought had potential. Potential for what, he didn't say. But the Camp had a legit-looking flyer he could present to his mom, listing all the activities she figured would be good outlets for the unexplained hostility he presented at home— wilderness survival, bushcraft, teamwork, fitness training. She didn't question why a kid who lived on energy drinks and Ruffles, who spent sixteen hours a day in front of a screen, wanted to go tramping around the woods. Burke went, and found everything he had been searching for in life there in the green, green wilds. When he'd returned home with a shaved head, a pleasant attitude, and a big hug, his mother hadn't queried him on a single thing he'd learned out in the mountains.

He'd completed some small tasks for the Camp over the years. Firebombings, scare raids, the supervision of a couple of drug shipments to bring in money for the organization. Always group work. The Mardi Gras shooting had been his own idea. He'd run it past his recruiter, who had sent it up the chain. He'd been given the green light. Burke didn't think they really believed he'd do it. He'd only been a part of the Camp for five years. He wasn't even a recruiter yet. This would bypass all that. He'd be a hero the likes of which the brotherhood had never seen.

The breakout had also been his idea. Initially the senior people in the Camp hadn't wanted to do it. Too risky. Too much exposure. Didn't Burke think that remaining behind bars as a martyr to the cause was better for them in the long run? Burke was a legendary figure. He got letters from potential recruits wanting to join the cause from all over the world. But when Burke had told them why he needed to be released, that he planned to unleash an operation he liked to think of as the Ignition, they'd been on board.

Now, the twenty-eight-year-old Burke rose to his feet, taking up a twig with him, and stood there testing it, not breaking it, as he listened to the sound of a nearby creek. Burke had thought about calling his mother over the years, trying to answer some of the questions she'd had for him after the shooting. Where had it all gone wrong? What could she have done to prevent it? Was it his father's death, or her being tied up all the time caring for his disabled sister, or bullies at school that made him do what he did? No. Those were all textbook explanations, gentle placations people developed for themselves about why *their* son or daughter would not wake up in the morning and do exactly what he did—take a rifle and a backpack and head down to New Orleans, fight his way through the jolly crowds to a roost above the avenue, then open fire and rain almighty hell on a bunch of Black people like a god stretching out his fiery hand.

In truth, Burke had been too young to really have been affected by his father dying. His mother got in the way of his activities, so he was grateful to Danielle for occupying her. And the kids at school mostly treated him like a sagging house plant—something a little depressing to stare at, best ignored. What had truly caused it all was a genetic quirk that made Burke intelligent enough and self-aware enough to see that America was suffering, and only brave individuals willing to set down their rightful, constitutional pursuit of happiness would be able to aid their country. Burke knew he could be "happy" getting an IT job at the local mall, working his way up to manager, pottering around in the garage attached to his rental condo diagnosing software upgrade problems in his spare time for grannies with too much cash. But he decided to trade in that happiness for three glorious, delirious, ecstatic moments of happiness made possible by the Camp and his devotion to it.

The moment he lined up his first victim at Mardi Gras and pulled the trigger, the swell of screams that erupted from the people below.

The moment the PA system at Pronghorn clicked on and he heard the phone call with Warden Slanter blast through the row, signifying the beginning of the breakout.

And the moment that would soon come, the Ignition that would spark the glorious war.

With his lungs full of inspiration, the thin, strong twig still in his hand, he wandered back to the van, where his handlers were waiting. These were the men and women who had conducted the Pronghorn breakout, pure-blood youths from all over the country. They were foot soldiers, like he had once been, people who could follow orders and intricate designs handed down from on high, like the Pronghorn plan, but who could be disposed of easily if they failed.

Like Charles Manson, the Camp's leaders knew that survival of the group meant sending in capable hands to do the dirty work while the brains of the operation stayed safe, to cook up new ideas for dominance should a plan go south. The Pronghorn plan had been a success. The Ignition would be, too. Burke would have to go into hiding for a while then. For some years, as the race war raged on, Burke's true genius and heroism would have to remain a secret. But when the white man triumphed, the full story would be told.

As Burke approached the van, the young woman sitting on the rear bumper shot to her feet, and the heavily muscled driver snapped to attention. Burke understood it was this guy—Henry, he thought his name was—who had figured out how to hack into the prison's PA system, transmit the call he made to Warden Slanter. Henry would probably get a commendation for his work. The shooter who had taken out the bus driver was the dull but pretty girl standing at the front of the vehicle, doing her best to finish a cigarette before Burke got back. She flicked the butt away and straightened, smiled. Silvia, he thought her name was.

"Better get him out," Burke said, nodding sternly to the back of the van. He hadn't offered a single shred of praise or admiration to his handlers since the breakout. Hadn't thanked them for their service, hadn't asked their names, just picked up that information as they spoke among themselves. Praise was poison, Burke believed. "I don't want to ride in the back with the smell of his piss. Make it quick."

The kids dragged the prisoner out of the van and threw him onto the asphalt at Burke's feet. Burke knew this guy's name for certain. Anthony Reiter had spat on Burke's shoes as the two passed one another in the visitors' center, one day maybe a month after Burke had arrived. Both of them had been cuffed and were being escorted by different sets of guards. *You ain't so tough now, huh, bitch? You punk-ass bitch!* The plan originally had been to secure any Black inmate from the rush outside the prison, but as Burke had climbed into the van in the Pronghorn parking lot, he'd noticed Reiter jogging by, testing the doors of cars, trying to find one that was unlocked. Burke stood over the inmate now and smiled as he writhed in pain on the roadside.

"Who's the bitch now?" Burke asked.

Axe had got his first hint that a cruiser was coming for him when his shadow against the side of the RV sharpened. The moonlight was pretty good, but the high beams of police cruisers could blast unabated for miles across the flat desert, and by the time the car was closing up on him, Axe could see individual whiskers in his stubble outlined as he turned his head. He closed the hood of the little camp barbecue he'd been cooking on, put the knife he'd used to cut the meat into the waistband of his jeans, and turned to show his face to the officers as the rocks at the side of the road popped and sputtered under their slowing tires.

The officers got out and put their guns on the rims of their car doors, the empty black eyes of their weapons watching Axe where he stood holding a pair of tongs and wearing an Iron Maiden T-shirt.

"Show us your hands!"

Axe showed them his hands.

"Drop it, whatever it is," the officer barked.

Axe dropped the tongs on the desert dirt.

They came for him, and the bigger one shoved him into the side of the van so that he bounced off the aluminum.

"Watch it, Roxley," the smaller one said. "Not too rough."

"What are you doing out here, old boy?"

"Barbecuing." Axe had shrugged. If being a long-term inmate, a "career criminal" as the occupation was known, had taught him anything, it was that the less a person offered in the way of information to screws, jacks, PIs, judges, or cops, the better things tended to turn out. The guy named Roxley shifted and shuffled around Axe and his barbecue before tugging open the door of the RV and looking in. Axe knew what he saw in there. Nothing. Prison life had made Axe very tidy indeed. The smell of washing detergent had replaced the smell of weed, and Axe had flipped the cover of the little panel computer shut and put it away in a cupboard with the phones and electronic watches and other technological things he'd found lying about.

Roxley, the big cop, came back to Axe and stood over him again. Axe stared at the guy's boots, the way he had at the boots of hundreds of correctional officers in his time, and waited.

"You just some old coot out here in the desert, alone, cooking a barbecue?"

"Seems like it." Axe shrugged again.

"And you didn't think to get the fuck out of here when a prison not fifty miles up the road got emptied this morning?"

Axe looked up briefly, made like he didn't understand. The smaller officer, whose name badge read NAWLET, was kicking stones.

"Just leave him, man," Nawlet said. "He's minding his business."

"What are you cookin'?" Roxley asked. "Where's your phone? Who else knows you're out here?"

"I got ID in the van," Axe said, gesturing to the door. "I can get it. Don't know nothin' about a prison, though."

Roxley was almost chest to chest with Axe. The old man could smell the young officer's breath coming down on the top of his head. He felt the whoosh of it on his brow, and then the stark absence of it as the cop lost interest, like a dog snuffling at a rat hole suddenly distracted by a noise behind him.

"Sir, it's not safe for you to be out here," Nawlet said. "We strongly suggest you take your vehicle into town and camp there for the night."

"Can't," Axe said. "I ran out of fuel. Was going to hitch into town in the morning, fill 'er up."

"Then get in the cruiser, for fuck's sake," Roxley snapped, his mind already on other things, on escaped inmates out there in the desert, calling to him, begging to be rounded up. "Sit in the back and shut the hell up."

Axe turned off the barbecue, didn't think it was smart to try to grab any belongings, not under the umbrella of the angry cop Roxley's impatience. He locked the RV, went to the cruiser, and climbed in behind Nawlet. The knife in Axe's jeans slid sideways along his thigh. He hitched it so that the handle was just poking out of the top of his pocket.

The car took off, rolling its high beams over the RV,

then the darkness of the desert air. Nawlet hung his hand backward over the seat, a shiny silver wrapper pinched between his thumb and forefinger.

"Gum?" he'd asked Axe.

"Sure," Axe said.

CHAPTER 19

They sat together at the eight-seater dining room table, a solid oak affair she had bought in an online auction that looked as if it was designed to host a Viking feast but had never hosted anyone but her. Keeps sucked the end of his beer and let it make a loud pop as he unsealed his lips from the bottle.

"We got one problem here," he said.

"What is it?" Celine asked.

"I don't know nothin' about investigating murders," he said.

"Well, neither do I."

"And I also don't see what this is going to achieve," he continued, opening his email account, the fingers of one hand dancing over the keys. Celine tried not to look, but she noticed he had plenty of emails from women. "I mean, what? You find out the guy is innocent and you're gonna stop chasing him?"

"I just need to know the truth about this, Keeps."

"You gonna turn around and *help* him?"

"Keeps, please."

"All right." He tore out a page of the notebook she

had brought to the table and took up the pen. "We're gonna do what I always do with my lawyer. We're gonna write down some stuff in a couple of lists, *Guilty* and *Not Guilty*."

"You do this with your lawyer?"

"Yeah." He smirked. "We look at what evidence we got, then we decide how we're gonna plead."

He folded the page in half lengthways, unfolded it again, drew a line down the crease, and labeled the columns.

"You have surprisingly delicate handwriting," Celine said.

"You're probably shocked someone with my record can write at all."

"I'm not," she said. "I've been looking through inmate mail for fifteen years. I've seen the best and the worst of the written word in there. What I am surprised by is the loop on that 'y.' Look at that. That's adorable."

"Stay focused. I'm tired. And we've got fifty-eight minutes on the timer."

Celine glanced at the numbers ticking down silently on her phone, felt a desire to crack more jokes, to draw the numbers further and further down, until she ran out of time to discover that she had been wrong about John Kradle for all these years. Because if she was wrong about him, that meant not only had her grandfather's actions on that fateful day taken away everyone she had ever loved, but she had also let him take something away from another human being. A man outside the family. It meant that the destruction hadn't stopped, hadn't been contained, when the firing ended on that day. The pain and the loss had in fact, through her own stubbornness and weakness and bias, her inability to shake off what had happened, stretched into the present moment. With as much courage as she could muster, she pulled the laptop toward her and followed a path she had trodden almost a decade earlier, into the online information regarding the Kradle Family murders.

The screen lit up with images of John Kradle, his tall, broad-shouldered son, Mason, and his petite, curvy wife, Christine. Kradle's other victim, the second to be shot dead in their house in Mesquite, only appeared in some of the images. The press liked to forget about the sister-in-law. The real horror and intrigue here was the suggestion of a ticking time bomb nestled in every family—the father who snaps, who comes home from work and cleans house, either to start afresh with a mistress or to go out himself in a blaze of glory. Celine scrolled through headlines.

MESQUITE FATHER SLAYS FAMILY.

LOVING HOME BLAZES AS KILLER FATHER WATCHES.

The infamous photograph of John Kradle appeared, a picture taken by a neighbor—Kradle stood on the lawn watching smoke billow into the sky from the upper windows of his house, hands by his sides, face expressionless. It was the picture that had made national and, briefly, international headlines. A father doing nothing to remedy the most terrible of actions, the slaughter of his loved ones.

"Guilty," Celine said. She was startled by the vitriol in her tone, so cleared her throat and tried to sound expressionless. "Put it in the guilty column. This, right here. He did nothing to fight the fire raging through the house, to go back in and try to get any of the members of his family out. He just stood on the lawn and watched the place burn with them inside. Everybody in the street saw him."

"Says here"—Keeps scrolled—"that physical evidence showed Kradle had just been in the house. That he was covered in his son's blood and there was soot in his clothes."

"Right," Celine said. "He went in, shot Christine and Audrey in the kitchen. They were standing in there having a glass of white wine. Then he went upstairs and shot Mason while the boy showered. Mason fought him, even with a bullet in his skull. The police know this because the shower screen was smashed. He had to shoot the boy in the head a second time to kill him. Kradle then poured gasoline all down the stairs, lit up the place, and walked out."

Keeps made notes in the *Guilty* column. Celine looked at the blank stretch of page that said *Not Guilty* in Keeps's glorious, curly, schoolgirl handwriting. Celine scrolled Google until she found a true-crime website that had a section on the Kradle Family murders. A signed copy of Kradle's statement in his chunky, windblown lettering loaded on the screen.

"*I walked in and found my wife and sister-in-law lying dead on the floor of the kitchen,*" Keeps read. "*I went upstairs and found Mason in the shower. I tried to pick him up, but he was gone. The house was getting smokier and I was worried I was going to get caught in the fire. I tried to drag Mason down the stairs, but—*"

"See?" Celine pointed at the screen. "Look at the language. *My wife and my sister-in-law.* He doesn't say their names."

"He says Mason's name," Keeps said.

"*I* was worried *I* was going to get caught in the fire. *I* went upstairs. *I* tried to pick him up," Celine said. "He's a narcissist. I've read about psychopaths, they—"

"How about we stop trying to read what we want to read into this," Keeps said. "You're just trying to see signs of guilt, and you can see them everywhere if you try. I can do the same thing in reverse. Look. Look, uh—" He pointed to the screen. "He says he knew Mason was gone. Like, he was dead. But then he says he tried to drag him down the stairs. That's a father trying to get his son's body out of the house even though he knows there's no point."

"I guess," Celine said.

"And all this *I*, *I*, *I* stuff," Keeps snorted. "Man, the dude is a tinkerer. He messes around with cars and wood and shit all day. He's not a poet. There might be fifteen ways to write a sentence, but *I did this* and *I did that* is just the plainest."

"So find me something to put in the Not Guilty column, then," Celine said.

Keeps clicked around the website. The timer told Celine they had thirty-five minutes left.

"What are you doing?"

"I'm looking for the experts." Keeps was scrolling through a scanned document that Celine could see was seven hundred and sixty pages long. "The DNA guys. Fingerprint guys. Blood guys. Bullet guys. Whatever. That's the sort of stuff we should be looking for here. The hard facts."

"What is this?"

"It's the trial transcript."

"It'll take longer than an hour to look through this," Celine said.

"They usually bring in the experts on day three of defense witnesses in a murder trial," Keeps said. "Two days to paint the picture, tell the story, get the emotions going before you bring in all the boring old guys with their graphs."

Celine tapped the table and shifted in her seat. Keeps sucked his beer dry.

"You know a fair bit about investigating murders for someone who doesn't know anything about investigating murders," Celine ventured.

"I know about trials," Keeps said. "I'm not a killer, in case you were wondering."

"Good to know. I figured as much, though, you coming from minimum."

"But you looked at my jacket, right?"

"No."

"You googled me."

"No."

"What?" Keeps turned and gawked at her. "You serious, girl?"

"I told you that already."

"Man." He shook his head. "You're some kind of fool."

"I told you, it's all about the feeling," Celine said. She nodded at the screen. "I'm making a point here. Kradle gave me that feeling as soon as I laid eyes on him. I knew he was bad. I got the feeling you're good, Keeps. I don't need to check up on that."

They sat in silence for a while, Keeps scrolling, not focusing on the words traversing the screen before him.

"I'm a con man."

"We really don't need to get into it."

"No, we should," Keeps said. "Even if it's just so

you get to know your feelings about people can be wrong sometimes. I'm a bad person. Real bad. But I seem good. I use the same skills you've seen in me, and I take them out there into the world to do my work of ripping people off. I notice details. I've got the gift of the gab. People underestimate me because of the tattoos and the baggy pants. Sometimes I wear corn-rows. That's my costume. That's my in. Some con men wear suits. I wear this. Kaylene? There is no Kaylene." He gestured to the tattoo on his neck. "It's an act. I show up looking like this, but I let people know I'm smart and they think: *Here he is, my diamond in the rough. All he needs is someone to trust him and give him some responsibility, and he'll be all polished up.*"

"That's not true," Celine said, smirking. "None of that is true."

"I'm sitting in your *dining room*." Keeps looked at her, his eyes wide. Celine glanced about them at the empty house, the gaping, dark rooms. A clock was ticking somewhere. A pipe groaned. Keeps's hand was resting gently on the keys of her laptop, where all her banking, email, and credit card details were auto-saved. Jake leaped from nowhere up into Keeps's lap, and he scratched the cat behind the ears.

"Maybe you've got a point," she said.

"Mmm-hmm."

"What kind of scams do you run?" Celine asked.

"It's not important."

"Come on. You started this. I'm curious now."

"I try to invent something new every time," he sighed, reading the screen, half paying attention to her. "I've done the traditional robocall scams and confidence games. You dig around on social media, find somebody whose kid is at summer camp. You call them up, tell them the kid's been in an accident, their insurance isn't covering the ambulance or whatever. They need to direct transfer some money to you via Western Union. Or maybe you find an old lady, an old veteran: you bug their house, bug their car, find out a bunch of stuff, worm your way in as someone from the energy company or someone from the bank. All that stuff gets very routine after a while. It's shooting fish in a barrel. You're just hanging around in nursing homes or sitting in front of a computer playing sound effects from YouTube in the background of calls. Sirens. Kids crying. People screaming."

Celine felt her stomach turning. She watched his eyes as he read, those expert fingers stroking the keys.

"Lately I've been into tools. I was in Pronghorn last year with this guy who's deep into wood. Like, real deep. He builds furniture out of crazy expensive wood from, like, Colombia or some shit. Anyway, I went to his workshop and found out he's got table saws in that place that are worth fifteen grand." Keeps smiled, remembering. "Fifteen grand! For a saw! So we knocked up this scam together. He made all these signs out of real nice wood that read DADDY'S WORKSHOP. We made a hundred of them. Advertised them on mommy'n'baby pages on Facebook. Whole bunch of wives bought them for their husbands for Father's Day. Then we looked at who bought them. Like, where do they live? What kind of space do they have on their property? What do they do for a living? That kind of thing. Once we figured out who was most likely to have expensive tools, we hit the road with the list of delivery addresses, and when—okay, look here."

He turned the laptop toward her. Celine was so lost

in her thoughts she had to shake herself to remember what they were doing.

"This guy here, the expert, guy named . . ." Keeps peered down his wire-framed glasses to read the name. "Dr. Martin Stinway. He's here talking about Kradle's shirt. Says he's some kind of micro-pattern-whatever analyst."

They read quietly together, Keeps scrolling as Celine tapped the edge of the laptop to tell him she was ready to turn the page.

"Stinway says gunshot residue on Kradle's shirt indicated he fired the gun that killed all three victims," Celine said.

"Right, so that's bullshit," Keeps said.

"How so?"

"Gunshot residue is the most junk science there is," Keeps said. "The FBI don't even use it no more. I know that because my lawyer won a major defense case with it. Guy had been sentenced to twenty-five to life, hanging on gunshot residue as the major piece of evidence that locked him up."

"But Kradle had the residue on his shirt," Celine said. "There's no mistaking it. Says so right here. Look. There are photos."

"Right." Keeps shrugged. "It was there. But how did it get there? Stinway says it was because he fired the gun. But the dude had been in the house. He admitted it. You fire a gun in a house, there'll be gunshot residue all over the place. It'll be on the floor, on the ceiling, hanging around in the air. It'll be on the victims. It'll also be on the cops who come into the house to check out what happened. They will have picked some up from touching their own weapons. Man, police stations are covered in that shit. Anybody who walks into a police station will come out with gunshot residue on them. The guy who my lawyer saved from the life sentence? The police sat him in the back of a squad car. There was GSR all over that thing. They did some tests and showed it."

"But I'm looking here." Celine was typing into the laptop. "This Dr. Martin Stinway guy has been doing this for thirty years. Look at all his college degrees. He'd know the difference."

"Would he, though?" Keeps said. "I mean, maybe you should ask him."

"It's three o'clock in the morning."

"So?"

Celine tapped the keys, scrolled. She left Dr. Martin Stinway's Wikipedia page and started down a list of newspaper articles.

"Oh, no," she said.

"What?" Keeps leaned over. Celine clicked the article and the screen was dominated by a huge headline.

RENOWNED SCIENTIST DISCREDITED IN SHOCK RULING

The timer went off on Celine's phone.

CHAPTER 20

Kradle could walk. He reminded himself that this was an achievement in itself. The streets of Mesquite were dark, the streetlights blurry and molten in his vision, and the cold breeze coming off the desert felt like cactus needles slicing at his neck and hands. But he had patched the hole in his body, kneeling in a godforsaken corner of a parking lot, using the sickly green light of an exit sign to stitch himself up. He had cash in his pocket and a destination in mind, and his limbs were still cooperating with him. All was not lost.

The encampment consumed the base of the highway overpass on both sides and was surprisingly loud. Rap music thumped from a long shanty at the center of the collection of dwellings, a lopsided headquarters made from blue tarps and sheets of plywood. It was bigger than Kradle had anticipated, but he remembered a documentary he'd watched about fentanyl and knew that smaller cities like Mesquite were having trouble with it. Tiny police forces, giant wildlands of desert in which to cook and mix and bag drugs in RVs and campers.

Kradle had never technically been homeless, but he knew from the tales of other inmates that many of the guys here probably had records, were on the run from the law, or were in active pursuit of criminal enterprises. And if he knew anything about cons and ex-cons, it was that they hated strangers encroaching on their space. He decided the best course of action, then, was to try to pick off a target from the edge of the herd. He approached a man who stood at the curb, smoking, the sharp angles of his face lit red by the burning end of his hand-rolled cigarette.

"Hey man, can I—"

"Fuck off, bro."

"Right." Kradle backed up, his hands out. "Right. No problem."

He received a few more "Fuck offs" for his trouble, approaching and finding men on the outer limits of the camp from the north and west. On his fourth attempt, he found an old man sitting on a wooden crate, staring at the lit screen of a cell phone.

Kradle forwent the greeting this time.

"I have money," he said, instead. It was the same thing that had saved his life only a day before, and it saved him again now. The old man looked up. One side of his face was webbed with burn scars, which took on hideous depths in the harsh, blue light.

"Whatchu want?"

"A place to sleep. Someone to keep lookout. Some new clothes. Food, if you've got it."

"You one of those Pronghorn creeps?" the scarred man asked.

"Yep."

"Well, you better have more cash than they'll give me as a reward for turning you in."

"You're not going to turn me in," Kradle said, and they both knew he was right, because bringing the law down on the camp for any reason would have the man blacklisted for life among the homeless community of Mesquite. And, chances were, he was probably wanted himself. The old man extracted himself from his little wooden seat with difficulty, and when he rose to full height he was a foot taller than Kradle, who stood slightly bent from his injuries. Kradle pulled out his bundle of cash, money he'd taken from Shondra, and handed over a couple of hundred-dollar notes to his new friend.

"Hey now." The old guy gave a hacking, wet laugh. "Anything else I can get you, master?"

"A cell phone, maybe."

"What's wrong with you?"

"I'm just tired."

"You need painkillers?"

"That would be nice," Kradle wheezed. The old man nodded and went away, and Kradle crawled into the little canvas tent that stood near them. It was black as pitch inside, smelled of sweat and mold and alcohol. He settled onto his stomach, felt objects beneath the thin blanket spread over the ground and spent a few minutes clearing them out of his way, identifying them by feel. A steel mug. A box of tissues. A tennis ball. A glass bottle.

He didn't realize he had fallen asleep until he was shocked awake by the feel of the side of the tent shifting against his hand. Someone was entering. He turned and saw the outline of something huge and hairy against the gloomy orange streetlight. The odor of dog enveloped him, chokingly strong.

"Oh, Jesus, Jesus!" Kradle pushed at the beast. "Hey! Get out! Get out!"

Laughter outside. The big dog lay down beside him with its back to him, hitting the ground with a heavy sigh and shuffling into place on the blanket.

"What the fuck, man?"

"You said watch out for the law. Didn't say nothin' about no dogs."

"Come on! Get it out of here!" Kradle groaned. But only more laughter answered him. The big animal was impervious to shoving, nudging, yanking by the thick, long hair of its neck. In the dark it felt like a shaggy bear, a mysterious collection of angles—elbows, hips, ribs under slabs of fur. The scarred man tossed a tiny baggie through the flap and Kradle examined it in the poor light, the sad little pill in the corner of the bag impossible to identify. Foolishly, he'd imagined the old man tossing him a box of Advil or something. The pill could have been anything, from ecstasy to fentanyl. Kradle threw it away and lay down beside the dog.

In time he reached out and touched the warm fur, sank his hand into it and felt the chest of the dog. Its heart was beating in there, ticking insistently. The bones rising and falling with gentle breath.

It had been half a decade since Kradle had given or received the touch of another living creature with any kind of genuine affection. He noticed every touch. He'd been medically examined at the prison, of course. He'd seen a dentist a few times. When he was removed from his cell for yard time, lawyer time, or to be let into the shower room, a guard, sometimes Celine Osbourne, took his elbow occasionally, as though there was any reason to run off when his wrists were cuffed and several yards of brick, concrete, steel, and iron stood between him and the free world. Once, a few years earlier, there had been an outbreak of hepatitis in the prison, and as an unexpected novelty, he and five other guys had been chucked together, uncuffed, in a cell while the row was disinfected. He'd shaken a hand, and punched a guy while trying to intervene when the inevitable scuffle broke out.

Now, he stroked the dog tentatively for a while, discovered and worked a bramble from its fur and flicked it away. Then he shuffled over and wrapped an arm around the beast, hugged it to him, buried his face in its fur, breathed in the smell of it. He squeezed it, and the dog gave a little groan that might have been irritation, but generally didn't object much to the hug.

Kradle lay there spooning the dog in the tent in the homeless camp, and he laughed quietly to himself at the furious stupidity of it all until sleep took him again.

CHAPTER 21

She'd been there the night of the bombing. Well, the bombing that was not. Becky Caryett knew that technically nobody had been injured when Abdul Ansar Hamsi walked into the Las Vegas Flamingo Casino six years earlier and deposited a bag of explosives right at the edge of the blackjack area. Nobody had been blown apart. Nobody had been incinerated alive. But, to Becky, it had happened, even if only in her daydreams, and its occurrence wasn't something she had been able to brush off in the half-decade since. In her mind, sometimes, while she stood there sweeping and pushing cards across the green felt mat before her, spouting rehearsed lines and giving half-smiles to the gamblers who came and went in the chairs, the bombing had actually happened. She stood there in her ridiculous flamingo-pink waistcoat, and Abdul Ansar Hamsi walked in, just like he did that night, a dusty gray ball cap hiding his eyes, a black T-shirt and jeans hugging his petite frame, his get-up as carefully designed in its casual, forgettable nature as military camouflage. He walked right up to the blackjack area, stood for a while, pleasantly and unobtrusively, with the duffel bag hanging from one hand, playing the newly arrived tourist musing on the idea of stopping for a few hands before he headed up to his room. Trying to decide if he felt lucky.

Just like she did that night, in her fantasies Becky locked eyes with Hamsi, and he returned her phoney smile, wandered over to where she was dealing out cards to a heavy, old white couple from Idaho wearing matching I HEART VEGAS shirts. Then he sidestepped and stood by the seat at the very edge of the table. He put his bag down right next to her. *Right at her side.* Maybe only two feet away. Practically touching her. At that moment, that fateful night, the wife from the Idaho couple decided to split her hand, and Becky got distracted, and Hamsi walked away. She didn't notice he'd left the bag. Not until a pit boss came over after a few minutes and asked what it was doing there, if it was hers.

In Becky's daydreams, the bomb went off at that moment. A colossal explosion erupted that consumed her first, of all the victims, a shocking white light billowing out, vaporizing the pit boss, the couple from Idaho, the rest of the blackjack area, eating up the poker tables and roulette station, taking out the third floor of the Flamingo in a single compressive boom. It crunched through structural-support beams as if they were sticks of Styrofoam. It collapsed the fourth and part of the fifth floor, leaving the huge building hollowed out like a lava cake and dripping concrete, electrical wires, plaster, brick, twisted steel, bodies. The blast killed hundreds of people, leaving dozens of others maimed and crawling, limping, dragging themselves through gagging smoke and roiling flames to try to find safety.

Technically, all that hadn't happened. But tonight it was happening as Becky arrived at her station and set up her decks. The table was cold—empty, unlucky, not warmed up yet by the presence of smiling, cheering people winning small bets in their losing battle against the house. Becky tried to push the visions away, called out a little invite to a couple walking by, another matching-shirt duo fresh off the plane from somewhere, bags in hand. *Try your hand, sir? Madam? Feeling lucky?* As the booms and crashes and screams played out silently in her mind, Becky swept her cards expertly over the table, fanning them, gathering them, shuffling them in a wide, horizontal stream from one hand to the other. Sometimes it was the hand tricks that brought bored patrons over from the nearby poker machines, following their desire to interact with a human being, who could do more than bleep and flash and sing robotic tunes. She played with her cards and wondered, as she had a million times already, why Hamsi had chosen her that night. If it was because she was a woman. If it was because she was Black. If it was because she was a casino worker. If it was because he'd spied the crucifix hanging around her throat.

When a man sat down at the table before her, rushing in and flopping down quickly, his pulled-low ball cap made Becky's heart leap into her throat.

"Hey, Beck," Elliot said.

"Oh my god." Becky dropped cards everywhere and stepped back, fanned her face, checked the blackjack stations around her. Everyone was distracted, warm tables full of happy players. "Elli, what the hell you doing here?"

"I need help."

Becky held her head. "Urgh. I knew this would happen. I saw the news yesterday and I said to myself, 'Becky, Elli ain't gonna make a run for it. Man's got eighteen months left on his sentence. He's gonna stay put. He's for sure not gonna come right into the goddamn Flamingo goddamn Casino in front of three hundred people and ask his ex-wife, of all the people in the world, for money. He's not that stupid.' And then I said to myself, 'Yes, Becky, he is.'"

"We're still technically married," Elliot said.

"You need to get your ass out of here." Becky scooped up the cards and dealt Elliot a hand, growling the words through her teeth. "They probably have cops watching me, waiting for you to show up."

"They don't." Elliot gathered his cards with his hairy hands. "They'll be saving those guys for the big fish. There are rapists and all kinds of punks on the loose."

"I wouldn't count on it. They did a special on the breakout on NBC last night. They said cops are gonna be sittin' on friends and relatives of inmates. They said half of the guys will run away, half of the guys will run home." She smirked. "I guess you were one of the dumb ones who ran home, huh?"

"Look. Hear me out. You can tell the bosses I threatened you." Elliot glanced sideways at the pit boss at the end of the row, who was watching a game with interest. "Tell them I showed you a knife, hell, I don't care. All you have to do is go use your swipe card to unlock that door over there. After that, it's all me."

They both turned and looked at the door to the back halls, manned by a security guard in a pink blazer. Between them and the guarded door, a bachelor party of young men with big hairstyles was laughing too hard, carrying plastic cocktail glasses shaped like cowboy boots.

"And then what?" Becky snorted. "You going to march in there and rob the vault? It's six levels underground, Elliot. There are about a hundred guys between you and it, and some of them have semi-automatics. Or so I hear—all that crazy shit starts at level minus two. I've never been down there and I wouldn't know how to—"

"I still love you, Becky."

"Oh, for the sake of all that is holy." She massaged her brow, pinched the bridge of her nose.

"Just go with me. Play along." Elliot reached for her hand. "We'll tell them you're my hostage."

"It's this table," Becky sighed. She smoothed the leather armrest of the table as though she was consoling an old, devastated friend. "This is a bad luck table. I never believed in them before, but I do now. I was standing right here when he came in. Hamsi. The bomber. He put the bag right there." She pointed to the colorful carpet. "I told myself I was going to go back to my table. I wasn't going to let him change a single thing about me. I like this damned table. I can watch the basketball from here. And then your sorry ass comes in and sits here and tells me this shit."

"Becky—"

"This ain't *Ocean's Eleven*." Becky shook her head. "You're not George Clooney. You got locked up in the first place for stealing a truck full of shaving cream,

Elliot. You gonna upgrade your criminal status from *shaving cream bandit* to *casino robber* and *international goddamn fugitive* just like that?"

"You're getting kind of loud." Elliot was rising to his feet.

"Do you have *any idea* how much I need this job?" Becky slammed her fist on the felt. A tiny old woman in a yellow dress, carrying a tray of casino chips in her withered hands, stopped a few feet out from Becky's table to listen. "You think I want to stand here all night on my aching feet, taking retirement funds from grandmas and grandpas who can't afford to eat in the downstairs bistro, and giving it to the assholes upstairs? You think I want to watch a guy blow his daughter's college fund on bad hands, just so I can hear he went and threw himself off the roof so he wouldn't have to call home and tell the wife? I need this job, Elliot, and you know why? Because your daughter needs pre-braces. Yeah, that's a thing. Not only do they have braces, they have *pre-braces* now, and your kid needs them because she got nasty, crooked teeth from your side of the family, and those pre-braces are even more expensive than—"

Becky stopped. Elliot was staring at her. The group of young men with cowboy-boot cocktails were all staring at her. The old woman with the chips was staring at her, and so was her pit boss, and the pit boss from the nearby roulette station, and a few patrons turned sideways in their swivel chairs at the poker machines, fingers resting on un-pressed buttons. But Becky was ignoring all of the attention she was receiving, because her own attention was focused on a man standing hesitantly at the edge of the next table.

Hamsi wasn't wearing a ball cap this time. He was

dressed in a white pressed shirt, gray trousers, prison sneakers, the security tag hanging from the sleeve of the shirt telling Becky he'd probably grabbed the outfit, sans the shoes, from a mannequin somewhere and bolted. He wasn't carrying a bag. He wasn't smiling. But, aside from all that, he was as pristinely, perfectly identical to her memory of him the night that he almost killed her as if he'd opened a door and stepped right out of her nightmares. Hamsi edged toward her table, all time and sound and movement standing still around the two of them, and Becky found herself stepping toward him, too, around the back of the table.

The failed terrorist and the casino dealer he'd tried to murder came together at the edge of the blackjack section, and Hamsi spoke first.

"You're here," Hamsi said. He gave a little laugh. "I can't believe it. I can't believe it. I just came here . . . I wanted to tell you that I'm sor—"

Becky Caryett had never punched anyone before. She'd never so much as hit a punching bag, a pillow, or a wall. She didn't like violence. Couldn't even stand to watch it on TV. But she delivered an uppercut to Hamsi's jaw that was so immaculately aligned and direct and powerful, using all the force of her shoulder, her neck, her rib cage, twisting and surging upward, that the man was unconscious even before his head snapped back, before his legs buckled and he slumped to the ground. She fancied she could feel through her knuckles the man's brain sloshing backward in his head and whumping against the inner surface of his skull, too fast for his neurons to handle.

Becky stepped back from the liquified figure on the floor that, only seconds before, had been an animated, talking, moving man, and she shook her hand loose, shooting Elliot a vicious glare of parting as her ex-husband dissolved into the press of people around them.

"Anybody else feeling lucky?" Becky asked the crowd.

CHAPTER 22

It was still dark when Kradle emerged from the tent with fresh clothes clinging to his reeking body. The dog exited beside him, shaking itself, and he got his first good look at it in the light of a Budweiser truck rolling under the overpass. It was big, black, pointy-nosed, and yellow-eyed.

"Here's your fee for last night." He handed some notes to the scarred man, who hadn't moved from his wooden crate. "And I'd like to buy this dog."

"Sure," the scarred man said, his hand still out.

"Fifty bucks cover it?"

"About right."

Kradle peeled off the notes and started handing them over, then held them back at the last second.

"It's your dog, isn't it?"

"No," the scarred man said, as if it was obvious.

"Well, whose dog is it?"

"Fucked if I know, man."

"Then why am I giving you the money?"

"Because you're the kind of idiot who would pay real-ass money for a stray dog any moron could grab off the street for free." The old man rocked back on his crate and laughed. "Look around, genius." Kradle did. There were dogs everywhere, pools of fur lying outside tents, silhouettes nosing around piles of trash, trotting through the camp with a sense of purpose.

"I'm just trying to do the right thing here," Kradle said.

"Yeah? Well fuck off out of my face then, and take your stupid dog with you."

They walked for an hour, side by side, Kradle saying nothing, the hood of the jacket the scarred man had given him pulled up around his face, the dog stopping now and then to piss on trees or stare back the way they had come, examining noises or smells on the wind. Once, Kradle spied a squad car doing slow laps of the silent streets. He ducked into a driveway to crouch in the moon-etched shadow of a trailer. The dog sat beside him, waiting. He didn't understand the beast's sudden loyalty, could only put the way it had rushed into the tent to lie beside him down as a resemblance to some past owner who had treated it well. Christine would have called the appearance of the dog a sign, an omen. She'd had all kinds of knowledge about mythology, about animals that showed up in the middle of fairy tales to guide lost wanderers through dark forests or give warnings about caves they were about to pass through. Kradle didn't know about anything like that. He just felt happy to have someone by his side. It had been strangely quiet and lonely in the hours since he and the serial killer parted ways.

He waited half a block down from 7 Solitaire Street, Beaver Dam, for what he guessed was an hour, looking for the telltale signs of surveillance: men sitting in parked cars, leaning on trees, watching from the windows of neighboring houses. He sniffed the air for cigarette smoke, leather, gun oil, fried food, strong deodorant—the kinds of smells he associated with law enforcement personnel—but found nothing but cold, clean desert breeze. Then the side door of number seven opened and a figure stepped out. Kradle grabbed the dog and moved forward.

He held the animal with two hands by a hank of its neck fur and shuffled in an awkward crouch toward the boy, who was locking the door behind him, a backpack hanging on one shoulder.

"Hey, kid," Kradle said.

"Whoa, shit! You scared me."

"Sorry, sorry." Kradle pretended to struggle with the dog, who was surprisingly placid, letting itself be manhandled by its new owner on the pavement without a shred of protest. "I just caught this dog. I saw it run out of a driveway down the street. Number twenty. It bolted right here. Can you give me a hand?"

"Oh, uh, yeah. Uh." The kid turned in a circle, bewildered, thinking, the way Kradle hoped he would. Ripe for instruction.

"You got a rope or something in there?"

"Sure," the kid said, and opened up the door. Kradle dropped the dog and followed the kid into the house, let the animal in behind him and then closed the door.

It did not escape Kradle that he had just used the kind of ruse Homer Carrington employed to stun and then corner his victims; that, as he deadbolted the door and sealed himself and the young man in the little kitchen, the boy was probably experiencing the same jolt of sudden, painful clarity that men and women had felt under the North Nevada Strangler's gaze. The kid turned toward him with a *What did I just do?* look on his face, the duped, the trusting, the naive, and Kradle felt bad for making the boy realize that everything he'd ever been told about strangers in vans with candy was bullshit. The real danger could come right to your house and cook up a pathetic story about a lost dog, and have you let them inside in ten seconds flat.

"Just stay calm," Kradle said. "I'm here to talk to your dad."

The kid was as tall as Mason had been, but not as broad or muscular. He was all sinew and veins, probably half the weight of the son Kradle had lost. Mason had died at a time when all the kids were shaving weird patterns into the backs of their heads and taking chunks out of their eyebrows with a razor, to look like rappers or fighters or something. This boy was long-haired and long-lashed, with lips so red he might have been wearing lipstick. But, aside from the physical differences, the boy and Kradle's son could have been brothers in their wide-eyed, eager, curious expressions, the look that said they knew they were in the best years of their lives and now was the time to notice everything, taste everything, be awake as long as they could every day, be ready for whatever the world threw at them. Spirit. Energy. Kradle felt tired just thinking about it.

"Tom? What happened? You forget your lunch?"

Shelley Frapport appeared in the doorway to the tidy kitchen in a pink fluffy robe, with a cat tucked under her arm like a football. The cat spotted Kradle's dog, struggled out of the woman's grasp and scrammed up the hall. Shelley took in the sight of Kradle, eased a long breath out of her lungs, and let her hands fall by her sides.

"I hoped you'd come," she said.

2000

Curses. Demons. Bad omens. Mason's birth was exactly as the pregnancy had been: a long and mildly hysterical affair infused with a kind of supernatural energy. From the beginning, when she learned of the baby growing inside her, Christine had begun to hear talk about the child's existence being much more than an accident brought about by a boozy Sunday afternoon barbecue and Christine forgetting to take her pill. Fast, dirty, half-hearted sex on the couch, Christine sprawled on a blanket on the living room floor watching *The Frances Falkner Show* long into the night, Kradle dozing beside her, lifting his head now and then to read the caption at the bottom of the screen with the show's subject. *Cheating Spouses Come Clean! I Married My Xbox! My Uncle is My Boyfriend!* Dread of the coming hangover and the roof-cleaning job Kradle had booked for the next morning, in the blazing sun. Christine's typical Sunday afternoon moroseness about the demise of her medium and ghost-hunting business, the soulless commercialism of people like John Edward and Allison DuBois.

No—to Christine, her pregnancy was an act of malignant forces so powerful and terrifying she dared not even talk about aborting the baby, because she feared upsetting further whatever cursed thing had made her pregnant in the first place. She spent the pregnancy reading runes, saying prayers, rubbing oils and herbs and ash and smelly lotions into her growing belly to try to remove the curse. Kradle mostly ignored all the weirdness, dismissing it as the anxiety of an expectant mother, and buried himself in his work so that they could have a nice little cash bundle to buy all the fluffy toys and stripy suits he noticed babies around town possessed.

Then, in early March, Christine sat bolt upright in bed and vomited up the roast lamb dinner they'd had that night, and he drove her to the hospital, calling her sister, Audrey, on the way.

In a dark, hot room, Kradle sat sweating in a plastic chair in the corner while his wife was exorcised of their infant son.

Audrey arrived at a respectable 11 A.M., wearing her court suit and talking on her flip phone all the way up the busy hall. She didn't get off the phone, even when Kradle leaned in and showed her the baby in his arms, gingerly pushing a fold of the blanket away to reveal the most beautiful face he'd ever laid eyes upon. Audrey wrinkled her nose and let her eyes flick to the ceiling.

"You can try to take it to the DA if you want, Georgia, but I'm telling you now you won't get any traction without Ferlich there."

Kradle followed when Audrey jerked her thumb toward the end of the hall. She carried on the phone call all the time as she made them coffee in the little maternity ward common room. He sat and marveled at his child and thought about creation and god and destiny and the universe, and Audrey tried to negotiate to get Ferlich, whoever he was, wherever he needed to be, then snapped the phone shut partway through her own sentence, having apparently given up.

"Idiots," she said, and leaned over, glancing again at her nephew.

"What do you think?"

"He's pretty fat."

"He is." Kradle laughed and wiped the tears that clung to his aching, exhausted eyes. "He's a big, healthy fellow."

"What's the name?"

"Mason."

"Urgh." Audrey smoothed out her skirt. "How obtusely masculine. As if people aren't going to know it's a boy from that Neanderthal brow."

"Christine wanted something that communicated the idea of stone, because the grinding of a stone in Wiccan mythology is—"

"John, spare me, please." Audrey held up a hand. "She's not here. We can avoid the idiotic blather about this kid and the mythological spiritual bullshit apparently infused with his being. If people ask you, just say you're a builder and you wanted something that sounded tough."

They sat, drinking their coffee from Styrofoam cups, Kradle setting his on the center of the table between sips, far away from the baby. Now and then, nurses in sickly pink scrubs came into the room to retrieve diapers or bottles from the cupboards lining the walls. The big baby with the heavy brow slept soundly in Kradle's arms, and Audrey leaned over to look occasionally but made no move to hold him.

"It's going to get worse from now on," Audrey said.

"What is?"

"The attention-seeking. Christine. All the mystical garbage. The drama. The ghosts and demons and crap. She's been cooking up reasons why she's special since she was a kid and she realized she didn't have the analytical mind to go into law like everybody else in the family. But guess what? When you have a baby you're not special anymore. The baby is special."

They both looked at the infant.

"Suddenly you're not a medium," Audrey said. "You're not a conduit. You're not a white witch. You're somebody's mom, and there isn't anything less unique in all the world. Everybody's got a mother somewhere."

"She'll be fine," Kradle said. "I like her attention-seeking. Gives me something to focus *my* attention on."

He didn't voice the rest of the thoughts that flooded his mind. That Christine mightn't have been the needy child that grew into a needy and praise-hungry adult if someone had bothered to look at her every now and then. If her parents had glanced up from their legal pads to watch her prancing around the living room at some point during their mutual race for district attorney. If someone had only listened to her fanciful tales instead of diagnosing them or relegating her to the kiddie corner at the charity balls and college fundraisers and gallery viewings her family frequented. He'd heard tales of a ten-year-old Audrey practically glued to her father's hip, trying to chip in to conversations about tax reform, while an eight-year-old Christine drew pagan symbols with the toe of her shoe in the dirt under her chair.

Audrey's phone rang and she took the call. Kradle stroked the single lock of blond hair sticking out of the top of his new son's head. He lost himself in thoughts of how to make Christine feel special again when she woke from the thick, open-mouthed slumber he'd left her in. Then he realized a nurse was tugging on his arm.

"Mr. Kradle?"

"Yes."

"Your wife just left."

CHAPTER 23

Bernie O'Leary had seen all kinds of things in his time manning the roadhouse on Cortez Gold Mine Road. There were few regular reasons a person would find themselves in Lander County at all. The bulk of his clientele was gold miners, the five regulars who stopped to sink a beer at the end of their shifts before heading up to their trailer homes on Battle Mountain or out on the plains. Those guys, only two of whom had ever shared their names with Bernie in the four years they'd been coming, were the predictable type. They came in and sat at the five deflated leather barstools at the counter in the otherwise featureless room, each guy to his regular stool, so that after a few years the seats had molded to each individual ass, and swapping places for whatever reason would have just been silly. Bernie figured that down in the mines it was dark and loud, and maybe nobody had ever bothered to introduce themselves or talk over the din on the first day down the shaft. Maybe, after eight hours below the earth's surface, not talking, not shaking hands, it seemed strange to introduce themselves in the elevator going back up, and after a while the awkward silence that settled around these men became acceptable, even natural. The five came in every day, sat down, drank their beers, and none of them ever lifted their eyes from the counter to exchange so much as a joke or a comment. Bernie had seen one nod to another once, when they announced Hillary had lost to Trump on the little television in the corner of the bar. But that was it. They all left at different times. Five in. Five out.

Aside from the five miners, Bernie had served a few geologists once. He'd listened with interest as they talked about Crescent Valley quartz deposits and fossils as he nailed fresh timber veneer around the windows of the trailer that served as the bar where the sun had baked it clean off. Some film people had come through the year before, scouting locations for a spaghetti Western, their trailer full of angry pampered horses huffing in the heat. Every few months there was an Area 51 pilgrim or two who came to Bernie's bar, having bought their share of rubber aliens and novelty T-shirts, and taken all the squinting selfies they wanted to take, before deciding to keep traveling north through the middle of the state to catalog what wasn't there.

Bernie didn't know what he was dealing with when the cop arrived. The guy didn't walk like a cop, didn't check his five and seven when he came in the door the way Bernie knew became natural to cops after they'd passed through enough unfamiliar thresholds and received a punch in the back of the head for their trouble. The old man's badge said NAWLET. He dusted his hands off and put them on the counter to balance himself while he climbed up onto Number

Three Miner's stool. Bernie leaned sideways and saw a police cruiser with a dent in the hood sitting at the pumps outside.

"You want a beer?" Bernie asked.

"Sure," the old guy said.

The daily silence of the miners had set Bernie up not to feel weird when a vacuum of wordlessness descended on the bar. Nevertheless, he felt weird for some reason now, handing the guy a Bud and trying to busy himself behind the counter. The old-timer's knuckles were bone-white on top from being skinned once too many times, and when Bernie rounded the counter to open a window and let some of the weirdness out, he saw the guy had one foot on the floor, as if he was ready to shift his weight onto it in the event he needed to get up suddenly.

Bernie slipped back behind the counter, just because he felt as if he should put something between the old cop and himself. He fooled with some glasses and a cloth, not really polishing them, keeping an eye on the old guy. The cop patted all his pockets, found a wallet eventually and opened it on the counter. Bernie watched as the man fumbled through it and seemed to find it empty. He extracted a credit card and examined it, tapped it on the counter a couple of times, thinking. Bernie found himself looking then at his own wallet, for some reason, which was sitting in a bowl by the register. Emu skin. A gift from his ex.

"How 'bout that breakout?" Bernie said, just to stop his ears from ringing in the quiet.

"Yeah," the old cop said. Bernie noticed he had to swallow a mouthful of beer he'd been holding in his cheeks, just swooshing it around his tongue like a fancy wine person.

"Were you there?"

"Why would I have been there?" the old guy asked.

"I thought you might have got called in, that's all," Bernie said. "Thing like that, I figure they'd call everybody in."

The old man sipped his beer again, held the liquid in his mouth while Bernie counted off seconds.

"Cruiser is shot," the old man said. He gestured to the door but didn't take his eyes off Bernie. "I hit a deer. Thought I'd come in and see if you knew your way around a vehicle. Help me figure out what's been knocked loose under the hood."

Bernie hesitated, tapped his knuckles on the bar. "I don't know nothin' about cars," he lied.

"Guess I'm stranded," the old man said.

"You could take my car," Bernie said. He put his keys on the counter.

"Then you'll be stuck here."

"I'll have a friend bring it back."

"Sounds inconvenient."

"It is." Bernie nodded. "But you're the law. You've gotta help the law."

The cop whose name badge read NAWLET took the keys and weighed them in his scarred hands.

He rose from his stool. Bernie stepped back and gripped the counter, and felt something like a cold hand release its grip from around his innards.

The old guy dressed as a cop walked to the door, stopped and turned back.

"One for the road?" he asked.

"Sure," Bernie relented, feeling a little as if he'd been unstrapped from the electric chair only to be asked if he wanted to sit back down and take a breather before he left the building. He turned and squatted and reached into the fridge, felt its soothing breeze against his sweat-damp cheeks.

When he rose again the old man was standing just near him, by the liquor cabinet, a hand's reach away.

2000

Celine had never been to a prison before, and it was prettier on the outside than she had imagined it would be. Where it stood on the hill, huge walls of smooth brick baked in the summer sun, cut by long geometric shadows made by iron gates, sheets of mesh, coils of wire. She stood in the parking lot and fingered the keys of the car that still smelled like her mother's perfume, her little brothers' farts, the occasional box of fried chicken her father used to sneak on the way home from work. They'd all been dead a year, and the smells and sounds of them lingered everywhere in her life. She heard her mother calling her name, and if she was distracted or tired she sometimes answered. She would feel the tug of a little boy's hand on her elbow, look down to find she was alone. Celine wanted there to be some stronger remnant of her lost family when she arrived outside Baldwin State Prison to visit her grandfather. But there was just the smell of them, and a familiar sense of impending doom as she prepared to face the old man, the same as it had been before the massacre.

A pretty woman in shiny black high heels met her at the admission checkpoint. Everyone Celine had dealt with since the killings had been young, pretty, cheerful—people possessed of the kind of limitless enthusiasm and delusional hope required to work with traumatized, "at risk" youths. The team who walked her through her deposition were a collection of grinning, laughing, toned and terrific types that looked as if they'd just stepped off a beach somewhere in Florida. The attorney that informed her that her grandfather had entered a guilty plea couldn't have been older than twenty-five. Celine followed the pretty blonde woman, whose name she had been too consumed with dread to grasp during the screening procedures, out of the building and down the caged walkway to the huge gates of the facility.

Passing through them, Celine felt a strange sense of calm envelop her, a bubble of numbness that wrapped around her limbs, distinctly at odds with what she was seeing. She put it down to some kind of trauma response, similar to that which had stripped her completely of emotions in the first days after the killing. She glided past fenced yards of orange-jumpsuit-wearing inmates, who hooted and hollered in her direction. Passed a pair of guards changing shifts with the watchtower staff, the two men loading and checking their rifles at the bottom of a concrete stairway. She was buzzed through five sets of big, clanging iron doors and down a tight hallway, past rows of empty windows with battered phone receivers mounted beside them. They arrived in a room with a steel table and two chairs bolted to the floor. Celine balked in the doorway like a wild horse being led into a truck.

"He's not coming in here with me," she said.

"No, no," the woman said, laughing. "No. You'll be behind glass. I thought you'd like a second to collect yourself."

"I'm collected," Celine said. "Just show me to him."

"Celine." The woman put a hand on Celine's arm. "You don't have to be brave all the time. I'm here with you. We'll take it slow. You can just sit here a moment and—"

"If I don't do this now, I'm going to lose it, okay?" Celine said through gritted teeth. She was so exhausted by speeches from the beautiful victim-liaison people about being "there" for her and her "bravery." Nobody was with her, not in this. And her survival for the 352 days since her family had been slaughtered was more a matter of anesthesia and habit than bravery, the unfeeling ability to follow directions and eat and sleep and move from one minute to the next without screaming.

She was escorted to one of the glass booths with a phone receiver, and the woman who was there for her went away. Celine didn't have to wait long before he was brought before her.

While movies and novels about prisons had prepared Celine for the smell of disinfectant, the cheap paint slapped over everything, the institutional coldness of the hallways, and the general grimness of the men she passed, nothing prepared her for seeing her grandfather the way that he was. He lowered himself onto the steel stool on the other side of the glass. He was exactly as he had been the last time Celine saw him, maybe a couple of pounds heavier. She had expected him to be as physically ravaged as she was by what had happened. For his cheeks and eyes to be sunken, his frame withered by neglect or abuse, perhaps months of sleepless nights thinking about what he had taken from the world. But he was as tanned as he had been by the farmyard sun, and his hair was thick and silver, and when he looked at her his gaze was bright and attentive but expressionless, like someone waiting for their name to be called at the DMV.

"Well?" he said after a while.

Celine opened her mouth to speak but couldn't find the words. She lowered her eyes and stared, her face burning, at the counter between them. The seconds ticked by. In the distant halls, men shouted and doors banged, an alarm started bleeping and was soon shut off. Celine tasted a sourness on her breath that made her think of rotting meat, and when she swallowed it was as if a rock was lodged in her throat.

"Why me?" she said finally.

Her grandfather laughed, a single bark, and shook his head.

"Of course." He nodded. "Not 'why.' But 'why me.'"

Celine was shaking in her chair, her fingers sliding in her own sweat as she gripped the edge of the table between them.

"Because of the damned fence," her grandfather said. "That's why."

Celine sucked air, tried to ease it out slowly.

"I had to look at that fence every day for three years, you know that?" he said. He leaned on an elbow, the phone clutched in his chained hands. When she glanced up now and then she saw that he was skewering her with his cold, blue eyes. "I had to remember what a shitshow you made of it. Not just the job itself. But me offering you any kind of basic advice about it and you losing your stupid little mind. What a performance you put on. Wow. Yeah. Because that's you. You've never been able to accept even so much as a shred of constructive criticism. You're perfect. You're fucking perfect, Celine, and Lord help anyone who tries to suggest differently. I mean, my god, child. If you're so perfect, how come you made such a hash of painting a goddamn fence?"

Celine found some words. Not many, but some.

"The . . . fence?"

"I mean, there was even dirt in the paint." Her grandfather snorted, shook his head. "You painted all the way down to the ground and flicked up the dirt, and just kept on painting over it. It looked like that expensive goddamn cookies-and-cream ice cream you insisted Nanna buy for the pancakes on Christmas morning."

He was carrying himself away now into the rageful memories. Celine saw a vein bulging from the skin of his temple, near where the receiver rested.

"Anyway," he said after a while, "I came up from the barn after I sent the boys on their way and I told you to get inside and you refused, standing there by that fence with your cigarette. With your fucking hip dropped and that bratty little pout. So I just thought, *You know what? Fine.*" He sat back and folded his arms. "Fine," he said again. "Suit yourself."

Celine snapped. She felt it as a physical break, a crunching of shards so hard and splintered with grief and fury that they sprayed out inside her, cut the underside of her skin to shreds. Her words sliced out of her, painful to form with her lips, her eyes burning as she banged the phone receiver on the glass with both fists.

"The fucking fence?" she roared. "You left me here to live with all this because of the fucking fence?"

"You and me, baby girl." Her grandfather shrugged. "We're in this together. Don't try to tell me you didn't ask for it."

Celine hardly heard his words. She was banging on the glass with her open palms, smashing it with her forearms and elbows, trying to get at him, trying to claw her way into the room with him. But then there were arms encircling her and pulling her away, voices cautioning her and commanding her, and for all her thrashing and twisting and screaming, nothing seemed to get through the glass protecting the old man as he sat, looking slightly amused, in his seat. Celine let the big female guard who held her carry her all the way back down the hall to the room with the steel table, and she sat there crying and clawing at her hair and face, trying to pull the words out of her brain even as she knew she would never be able to.

People came to the door, but the guard just waved them away. She sat near to Celine but did not touch her, twisting a little strand of hair at the bottom of her Afro hairstyle and staring at the corner of the ceiling. And, for the first time in a long time, Celine was glad for the silence of the other woman. For the fact that she wasn't smiling. That she wasn't talking about bravery or closure or justice. Her just being there, rather than talking loudly about how she was there, was a tiny comfort.

As her sobs subsided into helpless little hiccups, Celine distracted herself from the memories burning and staining their way into her brain by looking at the guard's uniform. The name badge that said WEBBER, and the shiny buckles, the equipment on her belt. She tried to memorize it all. To try to drive out the sound of the old man.

"You want to go home?" Webber asked eventually.

"Yeah."

"I'll walk you out the back way." Webber nodded toward the door. Celine got up and walked shakily, a few steps behind the broad-shouldered woman, her bones aching, feeling small and cold in the huge prison. They followed a convoluted path along shaded gravel walkways and empty, caged yards, buzzing through gates and doors, until the guard stopped by the entrance to a building and seemed to consider something.

She decided, and said, "Come with me." Celine followed. They emerged into a cell block. Celine was hit with the smell of men. The barred doors revealed small spaces crowded with personal belongings—posters, books, medicine bottles, clothes. In the tiny, boxy rooms, men sat quietly, one reading a book, one lying on his bunk, apparently asleep, one watching a small television set. The cells were like messy closets, with thin bunks rammed into one corner and a toilet squeezed into another.

"See this?" the guard named Webber said.

"Yeah?"

"This is death row," she said. "Small row, ours. We've only got seven guys. Your grandfather isn't here yet. He's still in processing. But he'll end up here, next week maybe."

Celine looked. In the cell nearest to her she could see a towel with brown stains on it hanging over the corner of a bed. The man who sat there was hunched over a little desk, staring at nothing, wringing his fingers and rocking gently. In another cell, a kid's drawing hung over a bed where an inmate lay with his arms behind his head, staring at the ceiling. The silence was icy.

Webber stepped back, and Celine followed, until they stood against the furthest wall from the cells, out of earshot of the men. Celine looked at the windows high above them and saw blocks of white sky cut with steel mesh.

"Let me tell you what I'm gonna do," Webber said. She pointed to a cell at the end of the row. "I'm gonna keep your grandfather in that cell there for the rest of his life."

Celine looked at the gray, striped mattress. The low ceiling. Nicks and scratches in the paintwork of the walls, some names and clumsy pictures.

"I'm going to make sure he doesn't get out." Webber was watching her eyes carefully. "Not soon. Not ever. This here? This is the little box he's going to get stuffed into. And he's going to scramble around in that box hour after hour, day after day, year after year, maybe until they take him out of there and kill him."

"You have to be his guard?" Celine asked.

"Me, and a couple of other guys." Webber nodded. "We keep them here until their time runs out. We make sure they live the life they're supposed to live. They don't get hugs or kisses. They don't get special food. They've got a menu they can order off from commissary, but there's nothing on there that would brighten up your day. Your grandfather has drunk his last glass of wine, girl. He's had his last good night's sleep. He's seen his last sunrise and his last sunset and his last tree. I don't know if he ever saw the ocean, but if he didn't, well, he's lost his chance. It's over for him."

Celine nodded.

"But none of that matters," Webber said. "What really matters is that now he can't hurt you anymore. He's going in the box, and he'll stay there, and he won't hurt anybody ever again."

Celine threw her arms around the woman. Webber stumbled a little, said "Whoa" and laughed, but Celine held on. Some of the inmates on the row were watching them. The guard's words had filled Celine with such happy, vicious, hateful emotion that she couldn't speak, could only hold the woman and watch the inmates and curse her grandfather with all her soul. She stared at the empty cell because she wanted to remember every inch of it, the smell of it and the shape of it, the hellish box into which he would be thrown and buried alive.

She walked out of the gates that day and unlocked her car, climbed in, and drove away without looking back at the prison reflecting the sunlight on the hill.

CHAPTER 24

When Celine woke up, Keeps was gone. One side of her face was aching from resting on her hands on the tabletop, her lower back yowling with pain as she straightened, stretched, tried to determine what had happened. The laptop and sheet of paper still lay beside her, and as she came to her senses she felt a wave of relief rush over her that the *Not Guilty* column still held only the name Dr. Martin Stinway. She recalled some half-hearted argument between her and Keeps about calling the specialist then and there to question him about Kradle's case, and Keeps fishing around on the internet, trying to hunt down contact details for the man. She must have drifted off.

The doorbell rang, and Celine realized the sound must have been what woke her. She walked numbly into the foyer and unlatched it, and it swung, hard, in her hand as Trinity Parker pushed it open, walking in as if she owned the place.

"Good," she said. "You're awake. Make me some coffee, will you? Please tell me you've got something better than instant. I'll get set up. You want me to call animal control while I'm at it?"

"Wha—" Celine shook her head. "Animal control?"

"There's an inmate swimming in your pool," Trinity quipped.

Celine returned to the dining room and looked through the glass doors. Keeps was hanging over the side of the pool, his elbows splayed on the tiles, looking at the desert plants in the manicured garden. Celine could see his bare feet gently paddling just under the surface of the water.

"Oh, Keeps," Celine said. "He's helping me with some—"

"I'm too busy for bullshit." Trinity held a hand up. "You want to bang an ex-con, go ahead. It's not my role to judge you. Not everybody's standards are as high as mine."

Celine sighed.

"Don't get me wrong. I understand the appeal," Trinity said. "The tattoos. The muscles. The danger. The deep-seated psychological need to rebel against your parents' dreams of you having missionary sex with a stockbroker once a month until he's too old to get it up anymore. What's he wearing? I assume he didn't bring his swimming trunks. Should we shift this meeting to the dining room so we can work with a view? Will that get you filled with vigor and verve?"

"Please stop talking."

"In all seriousness, you might want to look more carefully at that guy. He has rather a sketchy—"

"I know," Celine said. "I know."

"So, make the coffee then, Osbourne."

She did. Trinity sat at the kitchen island and opened her laptop. When Celine came to sit beside her there was a video set to play. She was watching CCTV camera footage from what looked like a large department store. The shadowy figure of a man limped onto the screen, powering up the aisle as fast as his wounded body could take him, snatching items off the shelves.

"Guess who?" Trinity said.

"John Kradle," Celine said.

"Clever boy, your *other* criminal beau," Trinity said, tapping the screen, following Kradle around the department store from video file to video file. "Most fugitives, if they get injured and need medical care, hit a pharmacy. Some will break into a veterinary clinic. Some go so far as to hold up a doctor. Not your guy. He broke into a Joanne's."

"Joanne's?"

"Craft supplies," Trinity said. "He took needles, wire, scissors, gauze, cotton balls. He went into the paint section and took some methylated spirits. Then he hit the manager's office and stole a cash box with four hundred dollars in it. Nobody responded to the alarm going off because it was a goddamn hobby craft store, and we've briefed all the sheriff's departments to be on alert for break-ins at doctors and vets."

"I thought you weren't interested in chasing John Kradle," Celine said. She watched Kradle limp down the hardware aisle and grab a hammer off the wall, probably for the cash box. "Especially since he and Homer Carrington have split."

"That's just the thing," Trinity said. "They haven't split."

Celine watched as Trinity pulled up a video of Kradle exiting the store through the rear fire doors. He disappeared off screen, carrying a plastic shopping bag of items. After a second or two, a dark shape materialized, seemingly from the shadows themselves. A big man stepped out from where he had been standing against the wall and turned, passing under the camera in pursuit of Kradle.

"Oh, shit," Celine said. A strange impulse pushed its way to the front of her mind, a tangle of emotions, the desire both to tell John Kradle he was being pursued and not to tell him—to both watch and intervene in his death. Trinity seemed to sense her conflict.

"I was in my kitchen once, and I looked out onto my lawn and saw the neighbor's parakeet had got loose from its cage." Trinity sat back, reflecting, smiling. "It was sitting there eating grass seeds. Then I noticed another neighbor's cat stalking it from my hedge. I felt the same thing you're feeling now, I suppose. The delicious, godly power of being able to stop death. Change fate. That wonderful curiosity that pulls you back before you can do so, that wants to witness things playing out in all their beautiful savagery."

"You really are incredibly full of yourself, aren't you?" Celine said.

"Should I tell you what I did?" Trinity asked.

"No." Celine sipped her coffee. "You should tell me why you're here, why you're giving me this lead on Kradle."

"Because I want something in return," Trinity said. "It's the only reason I do anything in life."

"Sounds about right."

"I want you and your delinquent squeeze to come and lean on Joe Brassen for me. I've managed to get a little traction with him by threatening to cut off his balls. But I've hit a wall. He'll sing for me but he won't dance, and I think you two could help."

"Joe Brassen!" Celine felt her mouth fall open. "He's not—"

"Oh, yes he is."

Celine rubbed her eyes. "Urgh, Jesus," she moaned. "It makes sense. He manages the prison baseball game. Not the team itself—he's not the coach—but he runs the event."

"Yeah, we already put the coach's head in a vise," Trinity said. "First guy we went to. He's clean."

"Brassen advertises the game in the staff rooms," Celine said. "He organizes catering. He would have been able to recruit personnel from all over the prison to be on the team, or at least invite their families to come watch."

"Is he a known white supremacist?"

"What? No!" Celine said. "You think I'd have a white supremacist on my staff?"

Trinity shrugged. "I think you'd have capable, punctual, and dedicated guys who can handle the most dangerous inmates in the prison on your staff. You'd look at their work performance and ignore their personal beliefs, because that's what you're like—all work and no personal life."

"I have a personal life," Celine said.

"Really?" Trinity glanced around. Celine refused to take her eyes from the woman's face.

"Let's just get going," Celine said.

"Before we do"—Trinity turned back to the laptop—"there's something else I want to show you."

She pulled up another CCTV file, this one attached to a news story. Celine watched people milling around the card tables in a casino. A woman in a frilly shirt and vest was shuffling cards for a guy in a ball cap.

Nothing looked out of the ordinary. Befuddled tourists sidestepped young men on a big night out.

Celine watched the card dealer leave the table, cross the floor, and walk up to a man in a white collared shirt, her fist already balled.

"Whoa!" Celine blurted as the punch played out. "Ho-ly cow!"

"Hell of a right arm." Trinity smiled.

"Is that—"

"Abdul Ansar Hamsi."

"Jesus. She's KO'ed him." Celine found herself smiling alongside her adversary.

"I want her," Trinity said. "I want to give her a counterterrorism job. First, I want to take her somewhere and feed her martinis and have her tell me all about her life. Then I want to give her a counterterrorism job."

"You'll have to fight talk show hosts for access to her for the next year and a half."

"Enough fun," Trinity said, slamming the computer closed. "We've got to roll."

Celine heard the glass doors slide open in the dining room, and wet footsteps on the hardwood floors.

"Yo, can I smell coffee?" Keeps yelled. "Where's mine?"

Keeps slid into the passenger seat and Celine climbed behind the wheel. They sat watching as Trinity Parker pulled away from the curb in her silver Mercedes and disappeared into the morning. Celine felt a strange, unspoken tension between her and Keeps, as though a line had been crossed, not when she recruited him as her fellow fugitive hunter but when she fell asleep in his presence. She imagined herself drifting off there beside him, and him wondering whether to disturb her, rouse her or try to move her, the self-professed con-man and criminal who had talked his way into her life now completely and truly alone with all of her world laid out in front of him. How vulnerable that made her.

Keeps took the lid off the reusable coffee cup she had filled for him and sipped the brew. He gave a small snort and she followed his eyes to the house across the road.

"What?"

"That outdoor setting there," Keeps said. "In the yard." Celine looked through an open gate and could see the outline of a six-seater wooden setting under a pergola.

"What about it?"

"That's a *Jacqueline* setting," Keeps said. "Six seater, solid oak with UV and water-resistant Texteline and cotton-blend cushions."

"You're an outdoor furniture connoisseur now?" Celine frowned.

"Yeah." Keeps sipped his coffee again, staring out the window. "I got that way. Used to be when I needed a quick buck I would slip into a nice neighborhood like this, have a look around, find a house with a big ole expensive outdoor setting in the yard. I'd hop the fence, take a picture of the furniture, put it on the internet at a ridiculously low price. You'd have people turning up within a half an hour with a trailer to haul it away."

"How much would you get for a setting like that?" Celine asked.

"It retails for about three grand," Keeps said. "You'd list it for four hundred. Get people climbing over the top of each other to get to you."

"Don't even have to break into the house," Celine said. Keeps didn't seem to register her tone.

"It's a good play." Keeps shrugged. "Not the best."

"What's your best?"

He thought for a moment.

"The Burn and Return." He gave a smile, remembering. "It's simple and it's fast. You can play it anywhere, and it doesn't require a huge set-up."

"How does it work?" Celine asked.

"You buy an electrical device—say, a waffle maker—from a department store. You don't spend much. Twenty bucks. You take it somewhere, set it on fire. When it's peak hour at the store, you bring it back and get hysterical with the manager that the thing almost burned your house down. You either demand a top-of-the-range, ultra-expensive replacement, which you then go and pawn, or you demand cash for your trouble."

"And you've done that?"

"Plenty of times. When I was young and stupid." Keeps nodded. "I'd use my girlfriend sometimes, maybe, if I had one. She's there screaming that she's going to sue the franchise, she's going to call CNN. If you can rope in somebody who's got a little kid, that ups the stakes. You put a bandage on the kid's arm and tell the manager your kid got burned. The manager doesn't check with the head office. You're causing a scene. The kid's crying. People are staring. He hurls money at you."

Celine sat for a while, her stomach shifting uncomfortably.

"Listen," she said eventually. "Now's the time to bounce if you want to bounce."

"I'll hang in for another day," Keeps sighed. "This game is a bit smarter than the old Burn and Return. I'm interested. And I need the cash."

"You think Trinity is really going to pay you a hundred bucks an hour for your services?"

"It's ninety now," he said. "I told you. A hundred was the release-day premium rate. And yes, I do. She'll give me the money or I'll take it."

Celine felt a tremor of uncertainty in her core and reminded herself that she really didn't know this man at all. She started the car and pulled out, and Keeps flicked on the radio.

"... *dinary tale of an encounter with two of the most wanted fugitives on the loose from Pronghorn Correctional Facility. The woman—*"

"Turn it up," Celine said.

"*—Shondra Aguirre, claims that the North Nevada Strangler, Homer Carrington, and family killer John Kradle abducted her when she stopped to assist them on the Route 15 highway in south Mesquite.*"

"That's your boy," Keeps said.

"*... of true terror and survival, with an unlikely twist: 'John Kradle let me go. He was going to hurt me, the big one, Carrington. The strangler. He was gonna rape me. I know it. I know it. But Kradle, he, like, set it up so I could get away. He made a show, like, 'Ahh, yeah, bro, I wanna go first,' and then he let me go out the back window of my house.'*"

"You want to put this in the *Not Guilty* column?" Keeps asked. "Or should we save it for the *Character Witnesses* column?"

"I don't know where to put it." Celine gripped the

wheel and tried to focus on the road. "I don't . . . I mean, we can't judge it. It's not relevant. And there's not enough information. I'm still undecided on Kradle, okay?"

Keeps took out his cell phone and began to dial.

"What are you doing?"

"Helping you decide," he said.

Celine drove. They had left the suburbs and turned onto the highway, heading toward Pronghorn, and as her speed rose so did a growing dread creeping like bile up her throat. She turned down the radio as Keeps's call connected.

"Ah, yes, hi. I'm calling to speak to Dr. Martin Stinway," Keeps said. His voice had changed. His words were clipped, thin, his jaw jutting forward as he snuggled back in his seat, eyes on the road ahead. "That's you? Excellent. Listen, this is Damien Koenig-Hadley calling. I'm an investigative journalist with the *New York Times*."

Celine widened her eyes, reached over and slapped his chest. Keeps didn't react.

"Yes, I know that, yes. It's only a couple of quotes that I'm after, or a *no comment*. Whichever you'd prefer. I'm working on a story about John Kradle, one of the escaped fugitives from Pronghorn Correctional Facility in Nevada, and the ongoing investigation into his case. You've been watching it all on the news, I presume?"

Keeps took the phone away from his ear and put the call on speaker. Celine heard the high, sharp voice of Dr. Stinway coming through the line.

"What investigation? What are you talking about?"

"Oh, well, I'm surprised you haven't been informed.

Perhaps the FBI hasn't got to you yet," Keeps said. He gestured for Celine to keep her eyes on the road.

"Son, I don't know what you're trying to tell me here," Dr. Stinway snapped.

"Let me explain," Keeps said. "My story about Kradle and the re-examination of his case has been cooking along for some time now, and with the breakout in the headlines, I've been approved for a massive feature. A source told me some months ago that agents from the Bureau were looking into the possibility that Kradle was framed for killing his family, that perhaps there had been some police involvement in that framing. Crooked cops tampering with evidence, trying to pin the murders on the husband."

Celine yanked the car to the side of the road. Keeps covered the receiver just in time to mask her growl. "This is not how—"

"Shhh!" he hissed.

"Are you still there?" Stinway said.

"Yes, I'm here. Sorry. I'm sharing my office today with another journalist who's also on a call." Keeps shot Celine a warning glare. "She's the loud, inconsiderate type but, you know, cutbacks in the media! What were you saying?"

"I was saying I don't know anything about a-a-a frame job." Stinway gave a hard, short sigh. "This is all news to me."

"So you recall the case and the evidence you gave in it?"

"Yeah," Stinway said. "I remember it well. And I'll tell you what I told John Kradle's lawyer: That I stand by any evidence I've ever given in any case of which I've ever been a part. I'm a scientist. We value truth above all things."

"You testified that a microfiber examination of Kradle's clothing definitively proved he and no one else committed the murders."

"Yes."

"That gunshot residue patterns indicated that he'd fired the weapon."

There was a pause. Celine wrung the steering wheel.

"Look, you can discount the gunshot residue stuff," Stinway said. "That doesn't hold up anymore."

"But you believed at the time that it did *hold up*, as you say?"

"It was . . ." Stinway sighed again, making the line rattle.

"The truth, above all else?"

"Yes," Stinway said. "Gunshot residue evidence was, at the time, undergoing some . . . some, uh, peer review. It was tricky. But if you did it right . . . Look, never mind. The truth has to take into account not only what I'm examining on my table but what the overall picture is. The evidence I had before me was . . . was part of the story. The overarching story. You understand? It's all part of a picture."

"What about the blood spatter? You said patterns indicated that Kradle had struggled with his son while the boy was still alive. That those patterns could not have been made after the fact—when, perhaps, Kradle found the bodies."

"Listen to me," Stinway said. "I'm a man of science."

"So you've said."

"And I'm not . . . I'm not the world's tallest man."

"The . . . world's tallest man?" Keeps frowned.

"Have you met the detective who worked on this case? Frapport? He's a big guy. He's a big, loud, intimidating guy. Full of confidence. Full of-of-of bluster. Okay? Imagine you're there and he comes in with a stack of notes—a binder, a big binder with pieces of paper sticking out of it and photographs and witness statements. He tells you he just wants your piece of the puzzle—of the picture—to match up to everything that's in this binder." Stinway cleared his throat. "This *huge* binder. You-you-you say you're going to look into it. And the next thing you know, he's calling you. Barking down the phone. Wanting to know if you've checked it out yet."

Celine rolled down her window. The desert air was cool, but it gave her no relief.

"So you're saying Detective Frapport intimidated you?" Keeps asked.

"No." Stinway gave a pause. "I mean. Some of the evidence . . . sometimes it's the kind of thing that can go one way or the other."

"It can?" Keeps asked.

"Sometimes you've got to make a ruling. Is it inconclusive, or is it positive? Maybe it's inconclusive on its own. We're talking about a couple of specks of blood on a shirt. But you have to interpret the evidence. And you have to consider what else you know about the case."

"What else did you know?"

"I knew that the father confessed."

Keeps reached over and slapped Celine's arm. She didn't move.

"The detective told you that John Kradle had confessed?" Keeps asked.

"Yes," Stinway said. "Detective Frapport said I wouldn't have to testify, because the guy had already confessed."

Keeps was tugging on Celine's arm. She brushed him off, her eyes locked on the horizon.

"What else did you know?" Keeps asked.

"Well, I knew there was an enormous goddamn binder full of evidence Frapport had collected which said he did it. Imagine you're there, and he's leaning on you to say the same—"

"He leaned on you?"

"No. I mean. He never said he—" Stinway made a sound, like a groan, an exhalation. Celine could almost see him leaning his forehead in his hand. "I can't have another scandal in the papers," Stinway said. "I can't have the FBI turning up on my doorstep. I mean, when it was the lawyer looking into it, I could blow it off. But I'm not . . . I can't be talking to the FBI and . . . Not now. I'm already on thin ice here."

"With your employer, you mean?" Keeps asked.

"No, with my wife." Stinway laughed sadly.

Keeps and Celine stared at the phone resting now in Keeps's lap, the green light indicating the call was on.

"It made sense that it was the husband," Stinway said. "It's always the husband. And my job is to look at the evidence and *make it make sense*."

"I've heard enough," Celine said. Keeps ended the call and the two sat quietly, the car engine ticking as it cooled down. "How did you know that would work?" she asked.

"People always talk to journalists," Keeps said. "Sometimes not right away. But eventually. They figure the story is going to get written one way or another, and this is their chance to put the record straight."

Celine nodded.

A sheriff's cruiser breezed past them on the road, heading for Pronghorn. Keeps started to speak again, but Celine held a hand up to silence him. She started the car and pulled out onto the road.

CHAPTER 25

Kradle tugged back the hood, certain that the light of the kitchen would reveal his true identity to Shelley Frapport and that some change would come over her. That she would cower and scream, twist away, that the numb terror that had infected the woman named Shondra would envelop her too, once she fully realized the situation she was in. But none of that happened. The boy named Tom took all of the shock into his thin frame instead, stepping back hard into the countertop and gripping it with his hands.

"Oh, wh-wh-whoa," he stammered. "Whoa. *Whoa!*"

"Tom." Shelley took the boy's arm. He grabbed her in response, his fingers buried deep in the fluffy fabric of her robe.

"Mom, Mom, that's—"

"John Kradle. I know."

"You *know*?" Tom said.

"Tom, it's okay." The woman smoothed her son's head. She had an eerie calm about her, as though she had been prepared for one of the nation's most wanted men to turn up in her kitchen. "Just sit down. Sit here."

She pointed to a chair at a small dining setting in the corner of the room. The boy didn't budge. His eyes were on Kradle, huge and quick, like those of a frightened bird. Kradle went and sat instead. He felt as if he was walking in a dream, and, if this was indeed some kind of hallucination, getting into a chair seemed like a good idea in case he started floating around the ceiling. Shelley went to the cupboard and took out a loaf of bread, opened the fridge and extracted a gallon of milk, and the man and the boy watched her from their separate strongholds in the small room. The black dog treated itself to a trotting tour around the dining room and, not finding the cat or anything else that interested it, came back and sat by Kradle's chair, eyes on the bread.

"You must be starving." Shelley selected a knife from a drawer. "Let me make you something, and then we can talk."

"I . . ." Kradle found himself looking at the boy, almost for help. "This is . . . You've been . . . ?"

"Expecting you." Shelley nodded. "Well. Not exactly expecting you. I thought it was a long, long shot that you'd make it all the way here. But I told the detectives assigned to the house that we were going away to stay with my sister in Minnesota. Just in case you did show up. I said we would be back once they gave us the all clear that you'd been captured."

"Mom." Tom was shivering from head to foot, still clutching the countertop as if floating around was also a concern to him. "What the *hell*?"

"Would you sit down, please?" Shelley pointed to the chair beside Kradle. Again, the kid didn't move.

"Is your husband here?" Kradle asked.

"He's dead."

Kradle felt a whump of pain, like a punch, to his chest. He gripped the fabric of his shirt and stared at the floor at his feet, bracing against the impact as the walls of his plan began to fall, one after the other.

"Patrick had a heart attack in the garage three years ago," Shelley continued. She put a peanut butter and jelly sandwich and a tall glass of milk down in front of Kradle. "I think he'd been trying to lift a tire. I found him. Luckily, it happened while Tom was away for the weekend. Probably the nicest thing Paddy ever did for this family."

"I'm calling 911," Tom announced.

Shelley walked over, confiscated the cell phone that the kid produced from his pocket, and pushed him toward the table where Kradle sat. Even in the chair, the boy was a half a foot taller than Kradle. The child and the fugitive sat face to face, both with their hands on the tabletop and their backs rigid, like poker-playing gunslingers about to draw over a fifth ace.

Shelley sank into the third and last chair at the table. She put Tom's cell phone down near his hand, the screen up, blank. The dog at Kradle's side started scratching its ribs with one back paw, its bony leg joint knocking rhythmically on the floor. It gave a dry kind of cough, as if it had a hairball, and then slid down into the sphinx position, and the room fell back into icy silence.

"Nobody's calling anyone," Shelley said. "Not until I explain."

Kradle stared at his sandwich. He wondered if he would be able to keep it down. His body was both raging at him to eat it and flooding his belly with nausea.

"I was going to divorce your father," Shelley said, taking her son's hand.

"What? When?" Tom shook his head sharply. His voice slowly rose to a yell. "What are you talking about? What divorce? *How is this relevant? There's a goddamn murderer in our kitchen!*"

"Don't lose your mind, Tom," Shelley cautioned.

"*I'm losing my mind!*" the kid yelled.

"He always says that." Shelley looked at Kradle knowingly. "Just listen, Tom. It'll all make sense."

The boy and Kradle locked eyes again. Kradle felt the sudden, strange urge to apologize for his smell. For the smell of the dog. His hands on the pale pine tabletop were filthy, the nails black.

"In 2015, I told Paddy I wanted a divorce," Shelley said. "Actually, I started raising the possibility about a year earlier. Paddy was working on a gangland shooting that was driving him nuts, and he was never home. You know these gang guys, they're up all night like cockroaches. Paddy started living their way, and he was always on the phone, trying to sort this guy from that guy. They all had nicknames. They all had records and pasts. He would come home for an hour to eat dinner and try to explain it all to me until I had a headache trying to figure out who Fisho was and who Nettles was and who stole whose girlfriend or corner or stash or whatever the hell. By the time Paddy was done it was as if he'd just vented and blasted steam all over me, and then he was out the door again before I could even say goodbye. I climbed into a cold bed every night for a year, and I just thought, *I don't want to do this anymore.*"

The boy burst into tears, then quickly tried to disguise the emotion behind his big, thin hands, wiping and rubbing, almost as if he was attempting to shove the emotion back into his face. Kradle kept his eyes on his sandwich.

"Maybe I should give you guys a minute," Kradle said.

"No." Shelley rubbed his arm, sending electric pulses deep into his bones. "Just listen. You need to hear this. It's maybe . . . It could be my fault you were put away."

Shelley Frapport drew a long breath and let it out slowly.

"Paddy came home for dinner, barging in like he always did, throwing his stuff on the floor in the doorway and sitting down at the table, ready to be served. And I just said it. I said, 'I want a divorce.' I told him I already had a lawyer." Shelley wrung her hands on the table, near Kradle's. "That was the day your family was killed, John."

Kradle listened to the rest, though he didn't need to. He could see it playing out in the room around him. The crying and raging and arguing, the desperately uttered promises, the young boy kneeling behind the door of his bedroom trying to make sense of all the tension in the air and how it weighed against his parents' constant reassurances that everything was normal and fine. Patrick Frapport, overweight, exhausted, mind-numbed and basically nocturnal, struggling through the daily jet lag of his previous gangland case and then being loaded with a triple homicide and a potential divorce just as he rose to come up for air. Kradle sat and imagined, perhaps in the very seat where Patrick had sat imagining, how the divorce would go. He saw the man pulling his books off the shelves in the living room, leaving hers oddly spaced among the fine dust, and loading the books into whatever would carry them, with the rest of his possessions, because getting boxes and packing tape would make it all too real. Carrying his stuff out to the car in laundry baskets and trash bags. Sniping with Shelley over who owed which utility bills, who should buy a new cutlery set. Moving into a loud, dirty motel where he could walk to work to save cash. He couldn't do it. It was undoable. The gangland trial and the Kradle Family killings and his divorce and his stomach ulcer and his alcohol problem and his un-tapped trauma and anger caused by too many years on the job was a mass of blackness that threatened to strangle him. So Paddy let something give. He did it to save his home life, because he knew that even if he put everything he had into his cases, they weren't go-ing to fuck him on his birthday, stroke his hair in the middle of the night after he came back from the bath-room, tell him he didn't look like a beached whale in his swimming trunks.

And Kradle's case was the easiest thing to let give, because it was obvious. The husband did it. The hus-band always does it.

"Things were okay for a while. Then, just before he died, I said it again," Shelley said. "I told him I wanted the divorce. Paddy had tried. He'd really tried. He was home every night and he was listening to me and . . . I just . . . My heart wasn't in it."

"And he told you then that he'd phoned it in on my case?" Kradle asked.

"Not in so many words," Shelley said. "He just said, 'I did really bad things for you. For us.' But I knew. I'd been married to that man for twenty years. When-ever someone would bring up the case, or they'd say something about it on the TV, he would shrivel up like a prune."

Kradle was afraid to ask his next question, so he just sat there with his eyes closed and the words on his lips, hoping and praying and willing the answer to be the one that he wanted. When he finally drew a breath he could taste the terror coating his tongue like acidic wax.

"Did you keep Paddy's case files after he died?" Kradle finally asked.

"The police came and took everything," Shelley said.

Kradle covered his face with his hands. He put his elbows on the table and willed himself not to scream.

"But I have something that might help," he heard Shelley say. Her chair squeaked on the floorboards as she rose. Kradle rubbed his eyes, clawed his fingers down the stubble on his ruddy cheeks, trying to push everything back in, the way he'd seen the kid do. He heard the black dog get up. When he looked over, it was sitting at the side door of the house, the one through which Kradle had come, its ears pricked and listening to something rustling out there in the morning light.

"Helping a fugitive is a crime," Tom said.

Kradle said nothing.

"I'm not going to let them arrest my mom," the boy continued. "Not for you. Not for anybody."

"It won't come to that. I'll be long gone before the police ever knew I was here."

The boy didn't look convinced.

"My son was about your age," Kradle said. "Someone came into our family home while I was out and shot him dead. My wife and her sister, too."

"So why'd they arrest you for it?"

"Because I was there," Kradle said. "Maybe only seconds after it happened. I went in and tried to save them but I was too late."

"If they locked you up for it, you must have done it," the boy said. "I mean, they . . . they have all kinds of stuff. Evidence and trials and stuff."

"I admire your unquestioning faith in the justice system," Kradle said. "I wish it was merited."

"All this stuff Mom's saying about Dad, it can't all be true. I was there too, you know. My dad was a good guy and he wouldn't send an innocent man to jail."

Kradle thought about telling the boy that it wasn't as cut and dried as that. That sometimes good people got tired, made mistakes, looked the other way, went into denial. Good people could convince themselves of bad things, sometimes. The boy was doing a pretty good job of it right now, trying to convince himself that his father hadn't sacrificed a human life to save his marriage. Kradle wanted to tell the boy that the easiest lies people told themselves were about the dead. But he didn't want to crush that lovely, naive spirit, something he hadn't encountered in many years.

"I mean, say there is some other guy who really did do it," the kid said. "What's your plan? You're going to find him?"

"Yes," Kradle said.

"And you're going to turn him in to the police?"

Kradle didn't answer.

"Why don't you just get, like, somebody else to do that? Like, your lawyer or whatever? Or a friend?"

"My lawyer has been working on my case for five

years," Kradle said. "But sometimes it takes extra-legal activities to get to the heart of the matter."

"Are you going to turn him in when you find him?" Tom asked again. Again, Kradle didn't answer. The boy snorted a derisive laugh. "See? You are a bad guy."

"I'm starting to get the feeling I can't win with you, kid," Kradle said.

Shelley Frapport came back into the room. She put a stack of papers onto the table and smoothed them out. "I dug these out of the basement yesterday," she said. "In case you came."

"I can't believe you did this." Tom shook his head, his mouth twisted and mean. "You called off protection on our house. You got these things ready. How did you know he was going to come here, trying to look for evidence? He, like, could have been on his way here to *kill* us. To get revenge on Dad."

"I have an enormous gun under the couch," Shelley said.

"You what?!"

"There's another one in the laundry." She nodded toward a door by the fridge.

"Are you freakin' kidding me?" the boy yelled.

"Your dad taught me to use them."

"What are these?" Kradle touched the papers before him.

"They're phone records," Shelley said. "Paddy and I were fighting like crazy over the bills in the months after he took your case, while I was working out if I still wanted to be with him or not. I kept these. I hoarded them up. Here."

Kradle looked at the pages, the highlighted and notated sections.

"This number." Shelley pointed to the account information panel at the top of one of the pages. "This was Paddy's work phone. I was always bugging him about getting the station to pay for the phone, the whole bill, but they wouldn't because he didn't use the phone completely for work stuff. I kept the papers because I wondered if my lawyer might want them. This is every phone call Paddy made and received in those months. Look at the date here."

She pointed. Kradle saw numbers that he'd seen a thousand times before, numbers that always made his heart seize.

"July eighth," Shelley said. "The day your family was killed. So from here down . . ." She stroked the list of figures. "Almost all of these calls will be related to your case."

They all leaned over and stared at the numbers.

"There might be leads in there." Shelley gestured wildly to the pages when Kradle didn't respond. "It . . . it has to help, right?"

Kradle folded the pages into a bundle and held them in his hands. He had traveled what seemed a million miles to this place, expecting so much. Expecting to grab the man who had put him away by the throat and wring the truth from him. Expecting to look at the files, the notebooks, the photographs and interview sheets relating to the murders of his family. Expecting to hear confessions, promises, revelations. But all he had were tales of a dead man and some phone records that sat so lightly and hopelessly in his hands.

That wasn't true. He also had a sandwich and a glass of milk.

Kradle nodded encouragingly to Shelley, ate half the sandwich, and gave the other half to the dog. Kradle was so hungry he didn't taste the sandwich, though he was aware in some deep, quiet corner of his mind that it was the first time he'd experienced peanut butter in half a decade. He stood and tucked the phone records into his back pocket.

It was then that he realized the boy's phone was no longer on the table where his mother had placed it. Kradle lifted his eyes from the empty space where it had been, lying face up, the screen blank, and saw the same cold blankness in the child's eyes.

"Sorry, dude." The boy shrugged. He took the phone out of his lap and put it back on the table.

Kradle heard the front door of the house being kicked in.

CHAPTER 26

"It was fifty thousand dollars," Brassen kept saying, hunched over the cinderblock and plywood coffee table dominating the living room in his trailer. "That's life-changing money!"

"Yeah, it's going to change your life, all right," Celine sighed. "It's going to change everything about your goddamn life."

She sat in the big, plush recliner chair opposite Brassen and held her head, just as he was doing, trying to accommodate the physical weight pounding in her brain with horror at the man's situation. Celine had hired Joe Brassen to work on death row exactly for the reasons Trinity assumed she had. Because he was punctual, efficient, methodical. Joe paid attention to detail, and detail was important, because the men they dealt with had little to no hope left in their lives. If anything slipped through, even so much as a smuggled shoelace or a single hoarded pill, it could mean an inmate was planning to take a life—either a guard's or his own.

She'd ignored Brassen's past—the unanswered

questions about his firing from the Las Vegas Police Department, the written cautions from his boss over in medium security about racist remarks—because all she cared about was his ability to keep the inmates and her colleagues alive.

Now he would be lost. He would end up an inmate, the only remaining question being where. The psychologically crushing monotony of protective segregation, a hothouse of corrupt cops, pedophiles, and child killers separated and locked away from the rest of the prison; or in general population, where his past as a prison guard would have him dead within the first month by shanking or stomping in the yard.

Celine was sitting across the shitty coffee table from a dead man who was breathing his last free air.

Trinity stood by the flyscreen door, refusing to touch anything in the cluttered trailer. Celine could see Keeps's silhouette on the porch, sitting and stroking Brassen's huge, hideous dog.

"Didn't it occur to you," Celine said, "that fifty grand was a hell of a lot of money just to let an inmate use a phone?"

Brassen shrugged. "You don't look a gift horse in the mouth. I figured he had a girlfriend and his Nazi pals were paying for them to talk. I didn't question it."

"You didn't question it because you're a Nazi," Trinity said distractedly, tapping away at her phone with one thumb. "You liked Schmitz. You liked what he stood for. And you liked his money."

"No," Brassen whined. "I'm not a Nazi. Celine, you can tell her. It's me, boss!" He tapped his chest. "It's *me*. Joe. You know me. I'm not into killing people."

"So long as you consider them 'people.'" Trinity smirked.

"Can you just let me do this?" Celine turned and glared at her. "What did you bring me in here for?"

Trinity shrugged and brushed invisible detritus from Brassen's trailer off her jeans. She wandered into the tiny kitchenette to ogle the filthy frying pans and takeout containers on the countertop, as if they were artifacts from a strange, forgotten civilization.

"Remember that camping trip to Big Bear?" Brassen's eyes were huge and pleading across the gloomy space, like those of a cornered deer. He gave a desperate laugh. "The team-building thing?"

"I remember you and Jackson having a grand old time getting drunk together, fishing in that creek. You remember Jackson? The guy whose wife and kid were almost taken out by a sniper because of you?"

Brassen eased a huge sigh.

"You don't need to remind me that you and I have a warm history, Brassen," Celine said. "I like you. I've always liked you. Somehow it got by me that you were a racist asshole deep down inside. I guess when people come into my life . . ."

Celine didn't continue the thought out loud. That when people came into her life that she liked or cared for, even just a little, she ignored everything unpalatable about them because she feared losing them so badly. She was too down about Brassen to think further about the string of cheating, gambling, idiotic, and emotionally abusive boyfriends her habit had brought into her life over the years. The convicted con-man currently sharing her home.

"Tell me what happened," Celine said. "How did all this start?"

"Look," Brassen sighed, "they didn't pick me because I'm, like, some kind of KKK guy. I don't attend meetings. I don't talk to them online. I'm not *one of them*. It just started with Schmitz wanting some stuff that other inmates were getting from me. Certain candy bars. He stopped me on the row and said he heard I got some Cashew Crush Bars for Donahue, and I said, yeah, did he want some? Ten bucks each. Then I started bringing him the paint for his artworks. Then, you know, he wanted a letter brought in from the outside. Wanted it to get past the mail room."

"Where did you have the letter sent?"

"My place." Brassen massaged his brow. "It didn't seem like such a huge leap, you know?"

Celine did know. She had heard the story a thousand times, of inmates securing small favors from guards that they later parlayed into bigger favors. One day an inmate was asking you for an extra napkin with their dinner tray, and a few months later you were letting them and another inmate have sex in a storeroom once a week on your watch. Celine had taken years of hurt from her colleagues for never allowing an inmate so much as an extra packet of sugar with his morning coffee ration.

"Did you ever have contact with anyone who worked for Schmitz in person?" Celine asked.

"No," Brassen said. "He'd ask for stuff, and I'd have somebody send it to my place. When he wanted the cell phone I went out and bought it from Walmart."

"And what about the baseball team?" Celine said. "How did that happen?"

"Schmitz just said he wanted certain people at the baseball game that day." Brassen swallowed hard. His eyes were glistening. "I figured he was organizing something inside the prison. Like, they were going to start a riot or something. Have key personnel all tied up seeing their families after the game so they could get it off to a good start."

"You were fine with them starting a goddamn riot at Pronghorn?" Celine barked.

"It was fifty grand!"

"Jesus, Joe!"

"Our riot procedure at Pronghorn is foolproof." Brassen wiped hard at his eyes. "It was going to be a storm in a teacup. As soon as they kicked off, we would knock 'em down, same as always."

"Somebody could have been hurt!"

"I need the money, Celine!" Brassen gestured to the walls around him. "Look at this goddamn place!"

Celine looked.

"My father died last year. Left me seventy thousand bucks." Brassen's lip was trembling. "I pissed it away into the slot machines in three weeks."

"Jesus."

"I got problems."

"No shit," Celine said.

"How could I have guessed what they were really going to do, huh?" Brassen said. "How could anybody have guessed that?"

"Do you have any idea what they're going to do now?"

"No."

"Nothing?" Celine insisted. "I mean, all those phone calls you facilitated. All those letters you delivered. You never saw or heard *anything* that would give you even a hint as to what they're going to do?"

Brassen shook his head helplessly. "I . . ." He swallowed hard. "The only thing I ever saw was some drawings."

"What drawings?"

"I don't know!" He shrugged. "Sketches. I saw them in a letter."

"When?"

"Maybe two weeks ago. I was standing outside Schmitz's cell. I gave him a letter, he opened it up and unfolded it, and I saw there was a sort of sketch in there. He saw me watching him and folded the paper back up again."

"What were the sketches of?"

"Boxes. Blocks. Lines."

"You're not helping me here, Joe."

"What do you want me to say? I saw a flash of shapes. That's it. It could have been anything," Brassen groaned. "It could have been the layout of Pronghorn. It could have been a map or . . . I don't know. I'm telling you, Celine, I don't know, I swear to god! Maybe you could put me under hypnosis, see if it's in my brain somewhere."

"Hypnosis is bullshit," Trinity said from the kitchen.

"Joe," Celine said. "You have to do what Trinity's asking you to do. You have to make contact with them somehow and tell them you need their help."

"If I make contact with these guys, they're going to laugh in my face," Brassen said. "It'll be completely obvious that the marshals are pushing me to get in touch so that they can hunt them down. They probably won't even answer."

"You have to try. You have no choice."

"What am I going to say?" Brassen spread his hands wide. "That you guys found out I'm the inside man and, what, I want to become one of them now? *Grab me a pointy hood in a large size, fellas! I'm all outta friends over here!*"

Celine caught Trinity's eye and nodded toward the porch. When they went outside, Celine saw that the big, ugly dog was lying on its back in the sunshine while Keeps rubbed its taut gray belly.

"He's right," she said. "He can't just call them up."

"Not literally," Trinity said. "We tried the number of the cell phone he gave Schmitz and, as expected, it's been dumped. No activity since the breakout. But there are ways we can get their attention. The FBI have been monitoring a bunch of websites known to recruit members of the Camp."

"The Camp?" Keeps asked.

"Schmitz's particular subgroup of unhinged losers," Trinity said. "They trawl the internet looking for angry, young, white male virgins everywhere you'd expect to find them. Sites related to mass shootings, revenge porn, serial killers. Stuff like that. They message potential members with pseudonyms and start filling their heads with junk about race wars and how that's going to make them kings of a new world."

"I get that," Keeps said.

"You do?" Trinity jutted her chin at him.

"I mean, I get the strategy." Keeps stood, making the dog groan with sadness that its belly rub was over. "You want to hook someone, you make them feel special. Make them feel seen. Like, you understand them and what they've been through, and the pain they're experiencing right now, and you offer them a safe place away from that pain. Because they're the chosen one. They deserve it. They're different. These groups are just finding directionless people and giving them a direction. Same things cults do."

Celine watched Keeps's eyes, which were blank and distant with thought.

"You gotta give Brassen what he wants," Keeps said quietly. "Make him feel special. Yeah, okay, you can keep threatening him with torture and life in prison or whatever. But if you make him feel like a hero, he'll work harder for you. And you gotta give these Nazi assholes something that they want, too, or they'll ignore him, just like he said."

"So what do they want?" Trinity said. "That they don't already have?"

"They want to know their plan is safe," Celine said. "Whatever it is. But that's the thing, we don't even know there is a plan. The whole breakout was staged to get Schmitz out of prison, but that doesn't necessarily mean they wanted him out so he could stage another shooting."

"We're *betting* they're going to stage another shooting," Trinity said. "It's almost Christmas. It's a good time for shooting people. So many gatherings."

Celine felt a ball of pain gather in her throat. Trinity flicked her eyes up from her phone briefly. "Oh," she said. "Whoops."

"What?" Keeps asked.

"Nothing," Celine said.

Keeps and Celine watched Trinity. She was leaning on the porch rail, her long-lashed, dark eyes cast down to her phone screen, casual and slightly bored, the way she always was, as if preventing mass death was just part of the job.

"If we know anything about terrorists like Schmitz, it's that they like momentum," Trinity said. "Once we announced to the press that we believed Schmitz was behind the whole thing, activity in the neo-Nazi on-line world went ballistic. The Camp and groups like it will be swarmed with recruits, and those recruits are going to become bored quickly if there isn't a fol-low-up event. Schmitz can't go into hiding in some farmhouse in rural Texas now. It would be cowardly. Their new members will want another demonstration of power."

"So how do we make Schmitz feel as if all that is under threat?" Celine said.

"Easy," Keeps said, smiling. "We pull a con, of course."

The shouting was so loud and frenzied that Kradle couldn't pick out individual words, but he knew what they were. He'd heard them dozens of times before, when shake teams busted into his cell for surprise searches, when officers responded to inmates getting violent or trying to trash their cells. *Get down. Get down. Get down on the ground. Hands on your head. Don't move.* He went down, as he was told, flatten-ing on the floor with his hands on the back of his head, fingers interlocked, the dive an almost automatic thing. His cheek hit the plastic seam between the floor-boards and the dining room carpet. Kradle felt the carpet against his temple and tried to think of the last time he'd touched carpet anywhere. He focused on the tiny loops of wool near his nose so his mind wouldn't tumble downward, as it wanted so desper-ately to do, into the black abyss of knowing that it was over.

It was all over.

A cuff snapped on his wrist.

"Shit," a voice above him hissed. "Shit. *Shit!* Reed, come here. Look. It's John fucking Kradle."

Kradle's wrist was dragged behind his back. Shelley and Tom were out of their seats, clutching each other.

"Oh, man! We gotta call for backup."

"No way. Let's get him back to the station ourselves. We're gonna be fucking her—"

Kradle felt the second cuff loop around his free wrist, and then the floor shuddered with a concussive boom.

Another boom as Kradle twisted to see what had caused the commotion.

His face was sprayed with dirt and blood. It was the smell that told him it was buckshot. He saw the second cop, Reed, fall against the table Tom and his mother were struggling to hide underneath, squeezing into the space like frightened mice. Reed had a huge hole in her chest.

Kradle tried to get up, but the cop who had pinned him had taken the second gunshot blast in the face and collapsed onto him, headless and dead as a stone.

Homer Carrington stood in the side doorway with a sawed-off shotgun hanging from one hand, assessing the damage through the gun smoke. He turned and looked at the spray of blood and brain matter on the wall beside Kradle's head.

"Stop yelling," Homer said, and Kradle realized that Shelley Frapport was screaming so hard her throat was grinding, making the sound like a high growl. Sounds were returning to his ringing ears. The black dog was guarding the couple under the table, barking at Homer, and Tom was shouting pleas, and Homer was raising the gun to blast the dog and the boy and his mother all at once.

That's when Kradle lost it.

He rose and smacked the barrel of the gun upward just as Homer pulled the trigger. The blast took out a massive chunk of ceiling, spewing dust all over the pair as they struggled for control of the weapon. Kradle had fought Homer once before. He knew his favorite move—that huge arm that came from outside his peripheral vision, sweeping toward him like a snake, trying to hook him into a deathly hug. Kradle let go of the gun, bowed, and slammed his shoulder into Homer's rib cage, sending the huge man backward into the kitchen counter. Kradle kept on, reaching for the gun with one hand, sweeping the counter for weapons with the other, pushing his body against Homer's chest, trying to avoid that big arm with its constrictive embrace or haymaker fist always threatening, always there, a yacht boom swinging in an unpredictable tide. Homer dropped the gun just as Kradle felt the smooth, wooden handle of a chef's knife in a block brush against his knuckles. Homer grabbed his whole face in one of his big palms, and Kradle's fingers barely grasped the knife. Homer pushed with that gigantic hand, and Kradle's whole head snapped back and he fell against the floor, tucking the knife against his body just in time for Homer to fall on it.

The serial killer wrapped two hands around Kradle's throat. Kradle remembered the cave, the sick, detached look in the other man's eyes, the feel of his body above him, and all the vicarious horror the weight and smell of him brought—of young women struggling under his grip, scratching helplessly at the air, inches from his smiling face. But this time was different. Homer had a knife handle sticking out of his chest, and his hands were weak and growing weaker, and Kradle could just repress the animalistic urge to buck and jolt and twist under the crushing pressure of those hands so he could see the darkness crowding into Homer's vision.

"You were supposed to be my friend," Homer yelled, defiant, trying to load the pressure back on, his thumbs pinching down against Kradle's windpipe like a clamp.

Kradle surged upward, flipped Homer's weight, took the knife out and shoved it immediately back in.

"I was never your friend, you idiot!" he snarled. He couldn't believe the words as they came out of him, that he was having this conversation with a man as he murdered him. That it had come to this; to convincing a psychopath that he wasn't the victim, that his life was being taken not due to betrayal by a loyal companion but as a reaction to him killing two innocent police officers only seconds earlier, and as a denial of him taking further lives. It wasn't personal. It was for the greater good. Kradle let out a hard, exhausted, angry laugh, just one, and then stabbed Homer in the heart a third time.

Homer grabbed Kradle's wrists, blood-soaked and warm, and Kradle expected some further admonishment of his performance as a fugitive compadre, but only dark blood poured from the corner of Homer's mouth as he tried to speak. Kradle heard sirens in the street. Tom and Shelley Frapport were holding each other under the table, their heads tucked together, their bodies racking with frightened sobs.

Kradle was looking at them when he heard the ratcheting sound of his loose handcuff as it closed on Homer's wrist. The killer let the cuff go, smiled, and then died, chained to his betrayer.

CHAPTER 27

Reiter had got himself into some fixes in his life, but nothing like this. The trouble for him had traditionally come from women, and part of that was his fault, he was man enough to admit. He liked women who answered back. Women who fought and challenged him. He liked to go into a bar and tell a woman her shoes looked stupid with her outfit and see what her reaction was, and the woman who threw a drink in his face was usually the one he took home. It was like finding a wild horse that bucked and yanked and kicked, and grinding it down and down until it was tame, until it came trotting up for the bridle happily, as if being a kept beast was all it had ever wanted out of life. Other men liked to shower women with gifts when they were courting. Call them up. Leave them messages. Take them places and open doors for them. Reiter liked the rage he saw in a woman's eyes when he let a door slam in her face, or when he threw the dinner she'd cooked on the floor. He liked to play games. Throw gas on fire.

And then, after a while, the reactions softened and

the rage subsided, and the women learned all his moves and started ducking his swings. Reiter usually got bored then and shuffled the women on. A smooth ride wasn't his desired mode of transportation. And he should have guessed that enough years messing around with wild women was going to get him kicked in the jaw some time or another.

But this. This was something else entirely.

Reiter sat against the wall in the van with his wrists chained to a bolt in the floor and wondered if what was being done to him was just. Because Reiter was under no illusion that Burke David Schmitz had brought him along for the ride simply because of the spitting incident on death row. He'd seen the raw amusement in the white boy's big, blue eyes as the spittle landed on his prison-issue white sneaker, the look that said, *Just you wait.* He saw it again after Reiter ran with the crowd out of the gates of Pronghorn, through the shadows in the back of the van, two big, blue eyes full of amusement. *You waited. Now your time has come,* they said. But Reiter believed in fate, and this wasn't supposed to be his fate. He'd ended up on the row for trying to tame the wrong woman, pushing her too hard one night after a few too many cheap tequilas and accidentally crushing her skull against a concrete step in the backyard. But to end up in the middle of a plan like this, just for spitting on the shoes of a Nazi asshole, seemed like getting slapped in the mouth for telling the truth.

And that was exactly the attitude he took to Schmitz when he was hauled out of the van and brought into the house. He tried to look around as the young men dragged him across the short distance between the van and the front door, but someone smacked the back of his skull, so he kept his eyes on the gravel, the wood, the thin, dusty carpet. When he looked up and saw Schmitz standing there, freshly showered and rubbing his short blond hair with a towel, Reiter winced as the tape was pulled off his lips, and then blurted the words the first chance he got.

"This ain't fair."

Schmitz laughed, and having heard their leader laugh, all the cronies did too.

"It ain't clever, neither," Reiter said.

"It's not?" Schmitz asked.

"It's not," Reiter said. "See, I know what the plan is here."

"Okay." Schmitz took a beer that someone handed to him and twisted the top in his fleshy palm. He took a chug and said *Ahh* in the way Reiter had always hated people doing, then said, "Enlighten me."

"You gonna do another shooting," Reiter said. "Like the New Orleans thing. Open up on a crowd of innocent people. Only this time, you're going to try the other route. You're going to kill a bunch of whites, frame a Black man for it, try to start your big, stupid race war that way."

Schmitz gave a delighted laugh, looked around the group sitting on the busted, tattered furniture or leaning in the corners of the room.

"Has somebody been chatting to this guy?" Schmitz asked.

"I had a KKK guy for a cellmate in 2011," Reiter said. "I know all your schemes. You think one of these days you're going to shoot or blow up or gas enough people that you'll kick off a big man-on-man battle and, at the end of it all, you guys will be able to establish your . . . your *new world order*, or whatever you like to call it."

"This is amazing." A skinny girl, standing in the doorway to what looked like an old kitchen, laughed. "He's taking us to school."

"I am. I am taking you to school," Reiter sneered. "So listen up, bitch. Learn something. You think you got this all worked out. That if you keep yanking and yanking on that cord, eventually the lawn mower is going to start up. You think you're going to kill somebody from one side, and the other side's going to retaliate. A shooting sparks a riot. A riot sparks a crackdown. A crackdown gets some fool killed in custody, which sparks another riot. Places get looted. People get beaten, raped, killed. It all gets filmed, and it all gets shared around. There's turmoil in other countries. Enough sparks, you got a big-ass fire."

The group nodded along.

"And then, at the end of it all, when the military and the police can't get everybody to calm down, they'll be looking for someone else to lead. And there you are. Burke David Schmitz. President of the New World Order."

Burke smiled.

"Well, here's the problem, assholes," Reiter said. "Your New Orleans thing didn't work. And this here ain't going to work either."

"Why not?" Schmitz sipped and *ahh*ed again.

"Because you got the wrong patsy," Reiter said. "I'm not a mass shooter. I'm just some small-time guy from Mesquite killed his girlfriend by accident and landed on the row for it. I didn't even graduate high school. Before I got locked up I used to deliver linen for restaurants. Nobody's going to believe I did all this."

"You're underestimating yourself," Schmitz said. "You don't have to graduate high school to know the world needs to change, and that we have the power, and the duty, to change it now. Some of the greatest men in the history of this country were everymen, just like you and me."

Schmitz drew a breath, preparing to carry on his history lesson. Then the enthusiasm for it seemed to leave him. His shoulders relaxed with the ease of someone realizing their efforts weren't worth the trouble.

"I can understand your anxiety about having a meaningful death," Schmitz said. "I had the same concern. I would have martyred myself at the scene on Dumaire Street if I had known for certain that what I had done that night would have the impact that I'd hoped it would."

Reiter looked around. All the Nazi losers were listening to their leader with fixed eyes and shallow breaths, quiet children. He felt sick.

"And I haven't failed," he said. "I—"

"No, you haven't, that's the last thing you've done," a guy behind Reiter gasped. Reiter looked over his shoulder at the paunch-bellied, red-headed guy with a lightning strike brand just visible above the collar of his shirt. Lightning Strike didn't seem game to go on. Schmitz looked torn between annoyance at being interrupted and gratitude at the encouragement.

"I have been able to inspire others," Schmitz continued cautiously. "Recruit a new generation of soldiers. But this will be bigger. And I assure you, this is going to make its mark. *Your* actions will make their mark."

Lightning Strike and a small woman standing with him high-fived.

"Your role in this won't be mistaken," Schmitz said, looking Reiter over. "We're planning on making things as convincing as we can. We think your body, left at the scene, with a self-inflicted gunshot wound to the head is going to get some people nodding along. We think a manifesto, handwritten by you, mailed to the *New York Times* on the evening of the massacre, is going to sew things up very neatly."

"You kidding me?" Reiter snorted. "How the hell you going to get me to hand-write anything? You give me a pencil and I'll stab you in the eye with it, you stupid motherfucker."

"I really doubt that," Schmitz said. He nodded at one of the men in the room, a lean, tattooed guy with jet-black hair and a goatee. The goateed guy took a pair of pliers out of his left back pocket and a pencil out of the right. Reiter gripped the chain between his wrists and looked at the faces around him, trying to find a friendly eye among them, but all he could see was the bored gazes of cats trying to think of new ways to play with their trapped mouse.

"Which is it?" Schmitz asked Reiter. "The pencil or the pliers?"

For a few seconds of sheer, electric panic, Kradle simply tugged on the chain connecting him to the dead man. He pushed his cuff against his wrist with all his might, grabbed Homer's and did the same. He got up, yanked hard, felt the impossible weight of the killer's body anchor him to the kitchen floor. The sirens in the street were getting louder. He heard people yelling.

His senses came to him in a painful whump, knocking clarity into his brain. This was his second chance. Two police officers had died trying to contain him, and he was still free. If he was captured now, all that lay ahead was the story that had been written for him; of a quiet death behind a sheet of one-way glass, maybe with Christine and Audrey's parents watching, crying, whispering abuse from the darkened viewing room. John Kradle wanted to die where he had been happiest—under a Louisiana sunset on the swamps. He leaped onto the body of the officer who had restrained him and started fishing in the pockets of his shirt and trousers, his shaking fingers pulling at pouches on his belt.

He heard a noise, looked over, and found Shelley Frapport was desperately searching the body of the officer named Reed. The black dog was dancing around madly, trying to console the boy under the table, trying to attack the fallen body of Reed, grabbing her sleeve and tugging, letting go, the animal utterly confused by the situation and which people belonged to which team. It realized its only known friend, Kradle, was searching for something and decided to help, snuffling and pawing at the pockets Kradle searched, trying to nose the man out of the way.

"There's no key!" Kradle cried.

Shelley was shaking her head madly. "It's not here either."

Kradle made a decision. He wrenched the knife out of Homer's chest. It came out slickly, soundlessly, trailing blood. Kradle wiped it on his jeans.

Shelley looked at the knife and nodded her understanding. "I'll try to hold them off. You head out the back. Take the car. The keys are hanging on the hook by the door. It's parked in the alley."

"Take the kid," Kradle said. Shelley gathered up her bug-eyed, trembling son and all but dragged him out of the room. The sirens were deafening now. Kradle took Homer's still warm hand in his, gritted his teeth, and set the blade to his unfeeling skin.

The last time Old Axe had been inside Whisky a Go Go on Sunset Boulevard, he'd been twenty-eight years old, sporting a nose ring and wearing a necktie he'd swiped from his father's dresser drawer tied around his forehead to keep his long hair back. The Whisk wasn't a place he'd tended to go—he was more of a Pandora's Box man when he wanted a crowd, but he'd followed the horde down to the rock club when he heard there was a protest kicking off. A young Axe had liked a protest, and at that time in his life there had been many, and he had known from the heat of that afternoon that this would be a goody. People jostling together, chest to back, hips to butts, yelling and spitting and rushing the police. Sweat. It had made him feel as if he were part of a living organism: a hot-blooded snake coiling and striking, and he was a guy who didn't feel part of things very often. He remembered that night the upset had been about curfews at the Whisk or something like that. All he could remember now was that he'd taken an egg from a carton a guy was carrying around, hurled it and hit a line cop right in the face, and a guy wearing pigtails, with SLUT! painted across his bare chest, had burst out laughing at the accuracy of his shot. He was thinking about that guy now as he put a shoulder into the door of the club, a heavy thing that got stuck in the heat from too many layers of black paint over the years.

It was cool inside, and nothing but the structure of the place seemed the same to Axe. There was the old scaffolding the dancers and bands had been forced to scale above the writhing masses, and the big dusty lights hanging precariously from rusty framework above that. The floor was still tacky, but where it met the bar it was littered with used electronic cigarettes and not the stubs of hand-rolled joints and peanut shells like he remembered. He didn't recognize the names of any of the bands that were going to perform there over the coming weeks, and half of the signed posters hanging in frames behind the bar were mysteries to him, too.

He put his policeman's cap on the bar and pulled himself onto a stool. Midday. The Whisk was quiet. The bartender, who was probably born about half a century after the Whisky a Go Go opened its doors, came and looked at the badge on Axe's shirt.

"Nawlet," she read.

"Yep," Axe lied.

"Should you be drinkin' in uniform, Officer Nawlet?" she asked.

"All I want is a Coke," Axe reasoned.

The girl made him the drink and put a lemon slice in it, for some reason, and a fancy coaster under it. Axe opened his emu-skin wallet and pulled a note from a thick stack, paid her. He was following this girl with his eyes while she was stacking glasses on a high shelf when the older couple walked in and set their bags on the floor.

He was tall, gray-haired, pear-shaped, and she was

his short carbon-copy in chinos and sneakers. Sensible haircuts that fit nicely under sunhats. They clambered onto the stools two down from Axe, and he admired the gold-rimmed reading glasses the guy had hanging from a chain around his neck. Axe had been wearing tamper-proof plastic reading glasses at Pronghorn for some years, and his record for days between the prison issuing him a new pair and somebody chewing on them or sitting on them and snapping them in half just for the hell of it was only about two and a half weeks.

Axe felt a little tingle of energy in his bones when the couple started speaking in German. He'd taken some German classes as a young man, when he was locked up for the first time, and as he listened some ancient, creaky door of his brain popped open and began interpreting the sounds.

"All right, let's take stock for a moment. Did you give the hotel key back or did I?"

"I did."

"And where's my puffer?"

"In your pocket, there."

"I've got my passport . . ."

Axe glanced over, saw the guy slap a blood-colored booklet with gold lettering on the bar top, flip it over as though he wanted to check it wasn't a forgery, then slip it back into a kind of cash-hiding fanny pack strapped to his waist under his T-shirt. The German lady was patting the pockets of her chinos, searching the zippered pockets of a similar nervous-tourist-style cash belt.

"It's . . . ," she murmured, trailing off.

"Where is it?" the guy demanded. "Did you leave it in the room?"

"I brought it from the room. I know I did. It was the first thing I packed!"

"Well, where is it?"

"I, uh . . ." The woman's face was flushing pink.

"Jutta, don't tell me you've lost it. We—we have half an hour until we have to leave!"

The couple started attacking their bags, ripping open zippers and making Velcro flaps roar. Axe sipped his drink. It was while he was turning back to the bar that he saw the door to the Whisky a Go Go shunt open again, a guy muscling a crate of wine bottles through. He noticed a shape in the light reflecting off the shiny floor and put his drink down, turned around, and looked behind him.

"Ent . . . ," Axe said clumsily. The German couple kept searching their bags. Axe thought for a moment.

"Entschuldigung?" he said. *Excuse me?*

They looked up. Axe nodded to the doorway, the passport on the floor.

The German man strode over and snatched up the passport.

"Oh, thank god, thank god." He shoved the passport at his wife. "Thank god. Thank you, Officer."

Axe shrugged, turned back to the bar.

"No, really." The German man came over. "You have helped avoid certain disaster."

"Es ist in ordnung," Axe said. *It's okay.*

The big German smiled. Axe saw crooked teeth, a bit like his own.

The German man switched to English, clapped Axe on the shoulder. "May we buy you a drink?"

Axe thought about it.

"Sure," he said.

CHAPTER 28

Celine was sitting with her feet in the water, staring at the shards of afternoon light flickering against the sides of the pool, when she felt the soft trace of a tail running up the back of her arm. Jake the cat wandered by her, the perhaps accidental tail-flick his only acknowledgment of her presence, and took his place at the head of the pool like a swimmer warming himself up for the first plunge. She'd heard some cats simply preferred men, but the fact hadn't taken away the sting of jealousy when she and Keeps arrived home and the beast greeted him by headbutting his shin, purring heavily.

Keeps slid open the dining room doors and wandered out, barefoot, watching the screen of a phone Trinity had given him. Celine had her own new device that mirrored one given to Brassen. While the traitorous guard languished in his isolated cell at Pronghorn, he would be tasked with monitoring the chatlines connected to sites owned and run by the Camp, waiting for a response to his message about needing to talk. She, Keeps, Trinity, and Brassen were all logged in to the message boards under the same account. If any messages came through, they would all see the exchange at once.

Celine hadn't waited around at Brassen's trailer to watch the man being escorted again into custody. She thought letting him go back to his home, to taste and smell his former life while knowing that every part of it had been destroyed, was a cruel trick by Trinity. She'd let the man wander in the tomb of his past. Celine didn't envy the night that lay ahead for her former friend and colleague. He would be lying on an inmate bunk, listening to the sounds of the prison around him, familiar sounds made somehow horrifyingly new and foreign, awakened from fitful dozes now and then by Trinity asking questions. Celine guessed she wouldn't let Brassen sleep too long at any point, just for the pleasure of tormenting him.

Back at Pronghorn, Celine, Keeps, and Trinity had taken a table in the chow hall to plot their strategy with Brassen. Celine had scanned the printed faces of the inmates pinned to the petitions, a sea of scowls, many of them slashed with red marker. In the hours she sat there, only once had a woman in a sheriff's deputy uniform walked up triumphantly and crossed off a face, causing a little tired cheer from others in the room. Celine knew that, like her, the men and women who had joined in the recovery effort could be presented with an almost complete wall of red-crossed faces, but while the really dangerous ones were still out there, there would be no cause to celebrate. One rapist running free because of her inability to keep him contained was too many for Celine. One child molester. One spree killer. She wouldn't feel safe or satisfied until they had all been put back where they belonged.

She wore the unease now as she sat with her feet in the pool. "It's been hours," Celine said to Keeps. "Anything on the line?"

"Not so much as a nibble." Keeps sat down beside her and slipped his feet into the water. Celine tapped the phone next to her, which was open to the message board where Brassen had left his note. *Need to talk. Situation changed. Urgent.*

Keeps put down the phone he had been monitoring and took up his own device, flipping open the screen cover and hitting a news app.

"You seen what your boy got up to today?" he asked.

"What? No. I got distracted. Why?"

"Check this out," Keeps said.

He opened an article. The header image was of John Kradle's and Homer Carrington's mugshots superimposed over a small blue house in a narrow street that was crowded with police cars and mobs of gawkers behind a police cordon.

THREE DEAD IN POLICE SHOOT-OUT WITH TOP FUGITIVES.

Celine snatched the phone away. She felt Keeps's eyes on her.

"*The department stated that Kradle killed Carrington after the wanted serial killer murdered two as-yet-unidentified Mesquite Police officers at a suburban house in Beaver Dam,*" Celine read. "*Police said that body-cam footage from one of the fallen officers appears to show Kradle intervening when Carrington tried to turn his gun on two residents of the property—*"

"He's looking like a solid guy," Keeps said. "While he's on the lam, anyway. First he lets that abducted lady go. Now he's diving in front of bullets to save women and children."

Celine held up a hand. "I'm not trying to find out what kind of guy he is now. I'm trying to find out what kind of guy he was when his family was killed."

"When are you gonna tell me why you care so much?"

"Because me and this guy, we've had a . . . a thing, for the past five years," Celine said. "Just about from the first day he arrived at Pronghorn, Kradle has been . . . in my head. You know?"

"No, I don't know."

"Like . . ." Celine struggled. "Okay, so I wasn't very nice to him when he arrived. The moment he got there. I . . . I didn't give him the best greeting."

"In what way?"

Celine tapped her knees.

"I knew he was coming," she said. "I'd been following the case on the TV and I was disgusted, just like everyone was, I suppose. I was almost happy he got sent to Pronghorn. I made sure he got the worst cell. The worst mattress. I held back his dinner until it was stone cold, and I held back his commissary papers so he couldn't order so much as a razor for three weeks. All that was before he even slept the night."

She let her mind go back, just for a moment, saw him being led in on that morning. She remembered being shocked at his bruised eye, his nose still pumping blood, the limp. She didn't bother asking who had done whatever had been done to him. Child-killers either got a pummeling for their crimes in county jail or they got a rough ride between prisons from vengeful transport guards. She'd seen it many times. Celine remembered standing outside Kradle's cell while he sat numbly on the mattress, staring at nothing.

"I asked him if he needed to go to the infirmary," Celine said. "He said no. I kept needling him. Saying, like, 'If you have internal bleeding and I come down the row in the morning and find you dead, that's a problem. That's *my* problem. So do you need to go to the infirmary or not?' He kept saying no, no, no. And maybe, you know . . . Maybe I should have realized this was a bad time for him. He'd just got to the place where he was going to rot for the rest of his life. He's just been introduced to the walls. The four walls."

Keeps nodded knowingly.

"So what happened?"

"I pushed him over the edge and he snapped," Celine said. "He leaped up and hit the bars at a hundred miles an hour and tried to grab me. It was what I wanted. I stuck him in the hole for a couple of days. From then it was, like, *on*. It was on between us. He came up from the hole with this mean look in his eyes. It said *I'm going to get you*. And I gave him that look right back."

"And did he get you?" Keeps said.

"Oh, yeah," Celine said. "Not right away. Nothing big. He just watched for a while. And before long he found something. He found out I hate it when people cluck."

"When they *cluck*?"

Celine flicked her tongue off the roof of her mouth, making a hollow *cluck* sound.

"Why do you hate that?" Keeps laughed.

"Because it's annoying!"

"Okay."

"He sends a kite down the row asking inmates to do it while I'm around," Celine said. "Like, he actually gives out commissary as payment for people to do it."

"That's hilarious."

"Everywhere I go it's like, *CLUCK!*" Celine said. "I'm putting my stuff in the control room and I hear *CLUCK!* I'm going to the bathroom and someone out in the hall goes *CLUCK!* I'm doing my rounds and all the inmates are going *CLUCK! CLUCK! CLUCK!*"

"I like his game."

"He started everybody drinking from their mugs backward." Celine shook her head ruefully. "Gripping the cup with the handle turned toward you."

"So, like, the handle is under your mouth?" Keeps asked.

"Yes."

"You hate that?"

"Yes."

"Why?"

"Because it's not—that's not how you do it."

"Ha. I love it."

"It's got a handle for a reason! Use the handle!"

"I need to remember some of this stuff."

"One time," Celine said, "I was walking past his cell and he just said, 'Thirty days.' I said, 'Thirty days to what?' He just shrugged. So, next day, I'm coming past and he says, 'Twenty-nine days.'"

"A countdown," Keeps said. "Interesting."

"Yeah, interesting," Celine said. "So I really ask him what he's counting down to. I'm dead serious. He won't budge. By the time it gets to twenty-seven days, I say, 'All right, I've had enough of this.' I pull him from the cell, sit him down, do a formal questioning. I write a report for the warden. I brief all the staff. By twenty-one days, other inmates are in on it. And there are hours and minutes attached now. Like, there are nineteen days, seven hours, and forty-one minutes left."

Keeps sat laughing quietly to himself.

"So I do another formal questioning," Celine sighed. "I issue an official warning. I read him all the prison regulations about violence toward staff, breakout attempts, riots. I tried to write him up for threatening staff, get him sent to Special Handling, but the warden says it's just a countdown, it's not a threat—we don't know what he's counting down to. I'm up all night looking at calendars, astrological signs, looking at his case. When was his kid's birthday? When was his wife's birthday? What time of day did they die? The numbers keep coming down and down and down, and in the last three days I'm just . . . I'm pulling my hair out."

Keeps was laughing harder now.

"On the day the countdown was supposed to end I finally convinced the warden to put the prison into Code Orange. I organized a raid team to get all suited up and stand outside Kradle's cell. I'm standing there, too, with a fucking helmet on. I'm a mess. I look at my watch and my whole arm is shaking."

Keeps grinned. Celine glared at him.

"It was nothing," Keeps said.

"It was nothing," Celine confirmed.

"Funny motherfucker," Keeps said.

"It was about as funny as a brick to the face."

"You ever do anything back to mess with his head?" Keeps asked.

"Oh, yeah," Celine said. "Of course. I did everything I could think of. I put sand in his coffee. I sent him to the infirmary with a request for a brain scan. On the request form I wrote, 'Appears to be a moron.' I know he hates spiders, so every couple of months I hide a tarantula in his cell somewhere, or I at least give him the impression that I have."

"Where the hell do you get a tarantula?"

"It's Nevada. You can get them at any pet store." Celine kicked her feet in the water. "They're not expensive."

Keeps kicked his feet beside hers. "You know, I didn't ask you why you care so much about this Kradle guy being guilty. I said, *When are you gonna tell me why you care so much*."

Celine froze.

"How did you . . ."

"I have my sources."

Celine looked away, shook her head. She took a long time finding the words.

"You change your name," she said. "You move to the other side of the country. You don't tell a living soul. And still, every man and his dog knows your secret."

"Any of the guards at Pronghorn know?"

"Maybe." She shrugged, the anger making her shoulders hot and tight. "Probably. Seems like all the inmates do. Warden Slanter knows, and her predecessor Wilke knew. He hired me. He had to know. But my personnel file is supposed to be confidential."

She felt tears behind her eyes, found herself putting on that hard smile to make them stop. Minutes passed in which they sat and watched the water.

"It's fucked up, man," Keeps said. "It's just about the most fucked up thing I ever heard."

"You're telling me."

"Is he still alive? Your grandfather?"

"No," Celine said. "I visited him once when he was in prison. Never again after that. He asked his lawyer to ask me to come to the execution, so I said no. I just sent a note back saying, *I'm not coming.* That was it. He killed himself three days later."

"Jesus."

They fell into silence. Celine knew more questions were coming. All her muscles were hard, bracing for blows.

"Were you not there that day, or . . . ?"

"I was there," Celine said. "Everybody was there. He spared me."

"Why? Were you the favorite?"

Celine looked away, swallowing a sob, which passed like glass down her throat. "No," she managed. "I wasn't the favorite, Keeps."

"I'm sorry. I should keep my questions to myself."

"I'm not that person," Celine insisted. "I'm not what happened to me."

"And a part of not being that person is not letting it cloud your judgment," Keeps said.

"Right." Celine looked at him. "Exactly."

Keeps touched her hand with his, just barely, the knuckle of his pinky brushing against hers, and Celine felt a rush of warmth immediately doused with a torrent of ice.

His words returned to her from outside Brassen's trailer.

You want to hook someone, you make them feel special.

Make them feel seen.

Like you understand them and what they've been through.

The phones bleeped, an unfamiliar tone, and Celine looked at hers at the same time that Keeps looked at his. A red bubble had appeared on one of the messenger apps. Celine opened it. At the top of the screen was Brassen's message.

Brass_on: Need to talk. Situation changed. Urgent.

Underneath it, a new line of text had appeared.

Addam123: Situation changed?

"Addam123," Keeps read.

"Trinity will be cross-checking people named Addam who are known members of the Camp." Celine shrugged. "But it's probably just a pseudonym."

They waited, watching their screens.

Brass_on: I want more money.

"He's going in too hard." Keeps eased air through his teeth. "This is not what we talked about at all. This is not making them feel as if he knows their plan, as if he's a threat. This isn't the script."

"Trinity must not be with him," Celine said. "She must not be there to coach him."

"Or maybe she is," Keeps said. "Woman's pretty direct."

"He's typing."

They watched the screens. Jake the cat had wandered over to Keeps's side and was trying to muscle his way onto his lap. Celine sighed.

Addam123: Fuck off, man. You got paid.

Brass_on: It wasn't enough. The marshals are grilling everybody at Pronghorn. They know there was someone inside and it's only a matter of time before they get around to me.

Addam123: So run.

Brass_on: I need money to run. 50k isn't enough. I'll need to start a whole new life.

Addam123: Your problem, not ours. You served your purpose.

Brass_on: But it IS your problem. I know more about your plan than you think I do. If they decide to snatch me up I will talk.

Addam123: What do you know?

Celine realized she was gripping the phone with all her strength when her knuckles started to throb. Her fingers were sliding on the case with sweat. This was the moment. The con. The bluff. Brassen needed to do the impossible: to convey a poker champion's confidence in his hand without the aid of face-to-face acting. The flicker of a smile, the straightening of his back, the idle shuffle of cards. Every typed word was critical. The seconds that passed while he figured out what to say. Too long a response time and he would seem uncertain. Too quick and it would all seem too rehearsed. Celine saw the words appear on the screen and reminded herself to breathe.

Brass_on: I have copies of the drawings.

"He made the play," Keeps said, his voice tight.

"This is it," Celine said. "This is all we've got."

"It isn't much," Keeps said. "But, hey, I've worked with less."

They watched for the bubble that indicated Addam123 was typing. It didn't come. After a minute or two they saw the bubble appear on Brass_on's side of the screen.

Brass_on: This is a risk-free venture for you. I'm proposing you put a bag of cash in a locker or under a tree, or goddamn anywhere, I don't care. Just drop the money and get out of there, then tell me where it is and I'll go get it. Another 50k. Pretty cheap to buy my silence.

They waited.

Addam123: We don't work with cash. You know that.

"Oh, god," Celine said. "They're calling it. They're calling the bluff."

"Just hang on."

Brass_on: Bitcoin is too risky for me right now. There's a trail. It's got to be cash.

Silence. Celine chewed her lip.

Addam123: We'll be in touch.

"You think they'll go for it?" Celine asked.

"They have to," Keeps said. "It's all we've got. They *have* to."

Jake had settled into Keeps's lap and was curled into a thick ball, vibrating with purrs, his front paws tucked beneath his bulk. The tabby's auburn mottles were flaming in the sun. Celine met eyes with the creature and the cat gave her a mean glare.

"A match made in heaven," Celine said. Keeps stroked the animal's back, running his fingers down to the tail.

"This is trust," Keeps said. "I move my legs? Splash. Boy's in the pool." He smiled. "It's all about trust," he continued. "How fast you can get it."

Celine's phone rang. She picked it up.

"Me again," Kradle said.

CHAPTER 29

John Kradle shut the driver's-side door of Shelley Frapport's car after the black dog leaped out. He knew from one of the probably hundreds of crime novels he'd read in his cell on death row that burning the vehicle wasn't a good idea. That it would only draw attention, bring looky-loos and cops, and the car would be identified pretty quickly anyway. The smartest move was to leave it in a bad neighborhood and hope it was stolen or stripped before the police located it.

He pulled his hoodie up, took out the phone he'd snatched from the Frapports' kitchen table, and dialed Celine. Kradle knew it would only be a matter of time before, in all the chaos of the scene at the Frapport residence, somebody noticed the boy's phone was missing. It felt as though, in the hours since he had left Pronghorn, a dozen tools of sanity and survival had slipped through his fingers. This would just be another of them. He had slid the knife with which he had killed Homer Carrington into his back pocket, and a pistol taken from one of the dead officers into his waistband. In the pocket of his hoodie he clutched dearly to the phone records Shelley had given him. The handcuffs were also there, one shackle still closed on his wrist, the other closed on nothing and sticky with blood. He watched the dog trotting faithfully beside him as he walked the streets north of the River- side district and wondered whether the beast was just another comfort, a survival tool, that would eventu- ally be tugged away from him.

Celine gave a kind of huff he couldn't interpret when she heard his voice on the line.

"You again," she confirmed.

"So, I just sawed off a dead serial killer's thumb with a kitchen knife. How was your day?"

"What? Why? Urgh. Never mind. My day was tir- ing," she said. "I was up all night trying to figure out the truth about you."

"You mean 'How wrong you are about me'?"

"Oh, I'm not wrong about *you*," she said. "I know you're an A-grade jerk. Everybody knows that."

Kradle found himself smiling, despite everything. There was silence on the line for a moment and the smile faded.

"But your crime," Celine said. "Maybe . . . maybe there's something there."

"A 'shadow of doubt,' even?"

"Something," Celine said. "I spoke to Dr. Martin Stinway."

"How?" Kradle rounded a corner, tucked his head low against his chin as he passed a group of teen- agers. When he snuck a sideways glance he realized they were all staring at their phone screens, oblivious to him. "How did you talk to Dr. Stinway? He's been stonewalling my lawyer for years."

"We pretended to be from the *Times*."

"What?"

"People always talk to journalists. Or so I'm told."

"That's good. I might use that," Kradle said. "Who's 'we'?"

"You said to find someone impartial. Give it an hour. So I did."

"My man Jake."

"Jake is a cat, Kradle."

Kradle thought for a moment. "Oh." He laughed. "Ohhh!"

"Yeah."

"So what did you find out?"

"I found out there was a confession."

Kradle stopped walking so suddenly his sneakers skidded on the cracked concrete. "I never . . ." He could barely form words. The fury clamped down hard and fast around his throat like a manacle. He put a hand on a fence for support. "I have never, *ever*—"

"You never confessed," Celine said. "I know."

Kradle was trembling with rage. The dog stood watching him, alert, ready to fight again.

"Frapport said that?"

"Yeah, to Stinway."

Kradle couldn't speak.

"If you'd confessed, it would have come up at the trial," Celine said. "It would have been in the media. They'd have recorded it. I mean, they recorded all your interrogations. Why not that? And why not have you sign a sworn confession?"

Kradle stood and shook and said nothing.

"No mention of it," Celine continued. "Except by Stinway, on the phone to us."

"Frapport told Stinway I'd confessed so he would

fall into line on the forensic stuff," Kradle finally growled.

"Maybe," Celine said.

"I've just seen Frapport's wife," Kradle said. "She thinks he phoned it in on my case. Actually, she's so certain about it she let me into the house and sat me at a table with her son. She thinks her husband played quick and dirty, pinning the murders on me so he could spend his time at home trying to save his marriage."

"Well, I don't know anything about that." Celine sounded distant, as if she was pulling the phone away from her mouth.

"But you're still in?" Kradle said.

"I'm still in," Celine said. "The Stinway stuff, it's dodgy. I'm not all the way to believing you're innocent, but I'm some of the way to believing something fishy went on with your case. And I want to know where that goes."

"Because you're personally invested." Kradle felt the corner of his mouth twitch with a dark smile.

"Personally invested?" Celine asked.

"Yeah."

"Maybe."

"You're obsessed with me."

"Oh, Jesus." The phone crackled as she huffed. "Look, I know you're not real smart, so I'm going to say this slowly. *You need to hand yourself in, before somebody shoots you.* We can get Stinway and Frapport's wife to say what they know. It might get you a new trial, at least."

"Sure. Sounds great. I'll just do another ten years on the row waiting for it to go through the courts."

"Urgh, Kradle—"

"Celine, you're wasting your breath."

"I know," she said. "I know."

"I'm going to send you pictures of some documents," he said. "Phone records. This is every number Patrick Frapport dialed in the months after my family was killed. It might help us. You start at the bottom, I'll start at the top."

Kradle pulled the phone away from his ear, looked at the numbers ticking by as the call ran on. Precious, dangerous minutes.

"I've got to dump the phone after that."

"How am I supposed to—"

"I'll call you," he said. He hung up.

Kradle stopped in the street and looked around. There were people at a nearby bus stop. An old woman, two more teenagers, a stringy guy with a ball cap pulled low. All of them were watching their phone screens, heads bowed as though in prayer. Kradle crouched and spread the sheets of paper from his pocket on the sidewalk. He photographed the pages with the phone, spent some precious moments fiddling with the message functions on the device, trying to understand how to send the images to Celine's mobile. In the seconds he paused there, swiping and tapping, she didn't attempt to call him back. Kradle told himself that didn't mean she was going to stop helping him. That she wasn't lying when she said she wanted to know the truth.

That's why he'd chosen her. Because she had to know the truth about a crime like his.

The phone made a whoosh sound as the pictures flew away to their destination. He popped the phone open with his bloody fingernails, took out the SIM card, and tossed it over a chain-link fence. The phone he dumped down a storm water drain. He glanced at the people at the bus stop as he passed, but none of them looked up.

Celine looked at the phone screen, watched it go dark in her fingers, the call ended. Keeps was standing at the fence, watching the red desert sunset. Celine imagined that, all over Nevada, criminals she knew were feeling the effects of their incarceration through their bodies, and this would be the time their institutionalized brains told them they were hungry for dinner. Even as a correctional officer, Celine reacted to sounds—the ringing of a certain type of bell, the blaring of a horn, the snap of heavy switches—and she felt tired, hungry, alert, or relaxed in response, as if chemicals had been dumped into her system, powerless to resist the prison routine. Keeps turned and walked toward her and she felt her stomach lurch, her fingers restless, remembering the touch of his hand against hers.

"He's sending pictures. Phone records," she said. She looked at the device in her hand. "He sounded tired and weird."

"Well, he just killed a dude." Keeps shrugged. "If you believe his story, he's never done that before."

"I don't know what I believe anymore," she said. Keeps's hand was just by hers again, and Celine felt as though her very skin was alive with desire, tingling and singing, sensations rushing up her arms, anticipating a touch that had not yet and might not ever happen. "Everything is inside out."

He touched her cheek, lifted her face, and he was kissing her, and Celine heard a clear voice in her mind telling her that he was taking advantage of what she had just said. That he knew her brain was spinning and now was the moment to strike. But she also didn't care. Celine grabbed his hips and dragged him to her and she felt so good with his hands around her head, cradled, kissed, wanted, that by the time the sun gave its last flicker of light she was following him back into the house with her hand in his.

The phone woke her. She jolted in the sheets, reached out, felt the hard curve of his arm. He was lying turned away from her. Something about that—about reaching to hold his hand or put her hand on his heart or to roll toward him and kiss him and instead feeling his hard shoulder blade, his cold back—made her snap into consciousness with terror.

She didn't recognize the number. Celine realized she wanted it to be John Kradle. When it wasn't his voice, she felt the air go out of her, and that made no sense at all. Nothing made sense. She went into the kitchen and gripped the bench, just to get some idea of time and space and reality.

"Ms. Osbourne?"

"Yes."

"My name is Diana Fry. I'm calling from the Bank of America anti-fraud squad in regards to some suspicious activity we have noticed on one of your accounts. Could I please confirm some details with you?"

Celine felt her mouth go dry. She worked quickly through the identity confirmation questions, staring back at the door to the hall, to the bedroom, where Keeps lay sleeping.

"What kind of activity are we talking about?" she asked.

"It's what we call a 'test payment,'" the woman said. "A small amount was transferred from your Maxi

Saver account to an account located in Kuala Lumpur. That amount is reading seven dollars and twenty-five cents in US dollars. You didn't purchase anything online for that amount recently?"

"No." Celine felt her back teeth lock together. "I didn't."

"Sometimes these scammers will push the boundaries, try to transfer a small, inconspicuous amount to see what the security is like on your accounts. If the payment is successful and you don't challenge it, that gives them the opportunity to make a bigger transfer. Then they'll go for a larger amount," the woman said. "We'll shut everything down and ask you to come in to a branch and confirm your identity as soon as possible, ma'am, so that we can reset everything. Is that okay?"

"No problem," Celine said. "I'll get it done."

She hung up and put the phone on the counter before she could be asked to complete a customer service survey. In the bedroom, she heard Keeps call her name. She rubbed her face with her hands and tried to focus on keeping her expression neutral, even in the dark.

2000

He considered himself a terrible father to an infant.

It began on the first day, as he carried the baby, squalling and mewling against his chest, from maternity ward to hospital administration, from hospital administration to the security department, from the security department back to the maternity ward, where police were waiting to ask him questions about where Christine had gone and why. On his son's first day on the earth, Kradle sat by his wife's empty hospital bed, joggling and shushing the fleshy pink bundle, trying to figure out why he kept spitting out the nib of the bottle while officers gazed upon him with their soul-destroying eyes. Half his brain wondered in terror at the spots and blushes of color in his newborn's face, at the rise and fall of his chest and the restless movement of his eyes beneath the lids, while the other half struggled to convince the officers that he didn't know why Christine had run away from him. Why she would climb out of her hospital bed, pull clothes onto her birth-ravaged body, and walk out into the sunshine of the day without saying a word to anyone, without even taking her bag with her. Kradle told himself that this was one of her dramas, her "attention-seeking episodes," and she would be back within hours or days, ready to help him figure out how the hell to get the baby to stop screaming and what he was supposed to dress the child in and whether or not he was going to accidentally—terror of all terrors—do something to cause little Mason to die in his sleep.

But she was not back within hours or days.

And she was not back within a month.

There was a flurry of help in the beginning. Friends, quiet and strangely watchful, dropped around to show him how to change a diaper and how to burp the baby and how to figure out if Mason was cold or hot or hungry. The police came, and there were interviews and updates on the search for Christine. The cab company connected to the car she hailed from the hospital parking lot knew she'd been dropped in downtown LA, and that was all. Kradle's household was a flurry of noise and activity.

Christine's parents visited the baby, and there were weighty questions delivered in deceptively casual voices as they stood in the darkness over Mason's crib. Had Christine been depressed during the pregnancy? Had he shouted at her? Had he "lost his cool"? Had either of them been seeing someone else? Kradle kept it together, because where he came from men were hard and didn't go to pieces when a woman walked out on them, or a baby shit through his diaper all over a car seat. But when the house was empty and the baby was asleep, Kradle would go out across the back porch and down into the blackness of the furthest corner of

the yard and sit on the grass under the stars and cry
out of sheer confusion.

The help died away. His friends couldn't figure out
why, if Kradle was the guy they'd all thought he was,
Christine would bail on him and go into hiding. Running off was one thing, but completely disappearing
was another. Christine's parents stopped answering
his calls, and the police answered every fifth or sixth.
They let him know they'd inquired unsuccessfully after Christine with an encampment of artists in Detroit
after hearing a rumor that she was there. They chased
similar rumors of her as far as Nova Scotia.

For two years, he leaped at every phone call. When
there came a knock at the door, his scalp tingled.
Sometimes when he was standing in the kitchen in the
blue-lit morning, stirring hot water into semolina, or
scrubbing food stains out of tiny shirts in the laundry
room, he thought he smelled her shampoo or saw her
standing there out of the corner of his eye.

When Mason was two years old, Kradle was bent
over a garden bed outside a house in East Mesquite,
digging irrigation into the soil. The boy toddled across
the lawn, crouched beside him, and grabbed a handful
of the soil in his meaty fist. Kradle watched as the kid
leaned back and threw it so that it scattered against
the side of the house. Kradle laughed and the boy,
cheered on by his father's amusement, laughed too.
Kradle handed the child a little trowel he had tucked
into his back pocket, and the boy plopped onto his
butt on the dirt and started digging.

That's when Kradle realized he could not only
keep the boy alive. He could also teach him things.

He taught the boy to throw his handfuls of dirt into

a plastic bucket, and then to lever them in awkwardly with the trowel, and by the time the kid was three he could be set to digging in one spot so Kradle could plant flowering ground cover in commercial parks in Mesquite. Kradle taught the kid to lay mulch, to water, to weed, to prune, and by the time the boy was ready for kindergarten he could hammer a nail and paint a semi-decent undercoat. Kradle trusted him with a handsaw by the time he was seven, and a nail gun by the time he was eight, and when he was ten the kid was taking all the measurements for the porches, garden sheds, picnic tables, and Adirondack chairs Kradle found himself building for strangers who called him up from his ads in the paper. Mason and Kradle lay together on shady concrete under old cars, changing oil filters and replacing gaskets, and they crawled into steamy ceilings, gloved up and sneezing in the dust, to catch families of possums.

Mason had been big when he was born. Boxy-headed, heavy-browed, with roly-poly arms and jiggling thighs and cheeks that bobbed as he rode in the carrier in the car. And he remained big, towering over the other kids at school, busting seams in the shoulders of his shirts, wearing and then growing out of Kradle's boots before he had entered puberty. While he'd been slightly caveman-esque as an infant, his awkwardly oversized features began to make sense in grade school and then smoothed out and arranged themselves in a way that made women turn their heads in the street by the time he hit his midteens. Kradle came around the side of a house on a property maintenance job one day and found the woman who had hired him and her friend sitting on the porch, drinking iced tea and admiring his child, who was bent over, clearing the pool filter of leaves with his oven-mitt hands.

"Your buddy." The younger of the two women nodded toward Mason. "Is he single?"

"He's fourteen," Kradle replied.

The woman choked on her drink and fell silent.

It was a December morning, before sunrise, when Kradle roused the boy, like he usually did. He walked into Mason's room and tugged on the toe of the foot that the boy always hung over the side of the bed during his sleep, regardless of the weather. The boy let out a big sigh and buried his head beneath his pillow, thereby completing a father-son ritual that had been in place since the child was big enough to move from a crib to a bed.

"What is it?" the boy asked as Kradle headed for the kitchen.

"Turf."

"It's too cold to grow turf!"

"Yeah. That's what I told him."

Kradle handed the kid a mug of tea when he finally reported for duty, and then sat down to drink his own coffee in the light from the oven rangehood. Mason was a kid who wielded an axe like a lumberjack, stuck his arm fearlessly down rat and snake holes, and could carry six rolls of buffalo grass under one arm, but he liked to start his day with English breakfast tea and comic books at the kitchen table, for reasons Kradle didn't understand or question. The two sat wordlessly together for a while until Kradle decided he would go ready the truck. He opened the front door of the house just as Christine was raising her hand to knock on it.

For a full five seconds, maybe more, Kradle didn't

recognize her. Her hair was streaked with white in the front and her skin was tanned coconut brown and she was dressed all in black—wispy, wavy, layered sort of stuff that she and other people who believed in fairy magic always wore, but black, which had never been her thing. He stood in the doorway, his brain telling him that something was deeply amiss here but being coy on what it was, and she took a deep breath and held it, waiting for his response to her presence. And then it all came back to his under-caffeinated brain in one compulsive blast—the baby, the blood, the lost hours being questioned by police, the crying, the dark, unsleeping hours, the pointless phone calls—and he knew that Christine had returned and was standing on his porch, and the very fact of it froze each of his limbs in place and arrested the words he'd dreamed of saying so many, many times.

She was the one to speak first.

"John," she said. "Hi."

Kradle wet his lips and tried to speak, but he felt the floor vibrate beneath his feet with Mason's heavy step, and he turned to put a hand on the boy's chest only a second or two before he could reach the door.

"Whoa. Whoa. Just back it up a bit, buddy."

"I gotta get my—"

"You've gotta get nothing." Kradle pushed the boy away. "Go away. Go to the yard. Wait there. Just do it."

Kradle had said "Just do it" plenty of times in the boy's life. Mason knew what it meant. It meant put that thing down, or hand me that tool, or stand back, or go away, and do it right now or one of us will get hurt. Kradle was already hurt, and all he knew was that he needed to stop that hurt spreading, so he said

"Just do it" and watched his son walk quickly but uncertainly back down the hall. He stepped out onto the porch and pulled the door closed. He faced Christine in the growing light of day, after wondering for a decade and a half if she was even alive.

"Was that him?" Christine asked.

"Yeah," Kradle said.

She didn't say anything else. Her silence made the words, gentler words he'd planned and practiced, dissolve in his mind, so that what came out was a vicious, white-hot hiss.

"Where the fuck did you go?"

She seemed shocked. The shock, the silence, wasn't helping. He walked to the end of the porch, telling himself not to scream that she hadn't tottered off to the local mall for an hour without leaving him a note on the fridge. That she had completely missed the childhood of a young man so strong and brave and handsome and smart and funny Kradle could hardly comprehend it; not just missed that childhood but actively avoided it. Dismissed it. Discarded it. That she had made him feel like a failure and look like an abuser and act like a madman over the years, and he was so mad his eyeballs felt as though they were on fire.

"I went to Tibet," she said finally.

"Of course you did." Kradle almost laughed. He cracked his knuckles and kept his eyes on the grass. He counted his breaths. "Of course you did."

He let her speak. She said some things about needing to find her essence, to discover her spirit, to communicate with the earth and the sky, to drink mountain snow and consult ancient beings, and for once Kradle didn't give her his attention. He listened instead for sounds of the boy in the house, creeping up to the door to eavesdrop, of which there were none. Then he straightened his cap and put a hand on the doorknob, and she took a step forward as if he was going to invite her in, and he almost laughed again at the idea that she thought she deserved that. When he didn't budge she stepped back again.

"I want to see him," she said.

"Well, if you want to do that, you'll have to do a lot more talking," Kradle said. "And not here, either. I'll meet you tomorrow at the diner. Eight. I've gotta go. We've got a job."

He went inside, into the empty hall, and shut the door.

CHAPTER 30

It was the neon blue that pulled him in. Kradle saw the tech store from the end of the street, a glowing artificial sapphire wedged in a tiara of white-lit stores. On the right of it sat a pet supply store, on the left a massage parlor and a deep, narrow place that sold socks for fifty cents a pair and big novelty sunglasses inset with plastic rhinestones. He stood for a while on the sidewalk, looking through the windows of the tech store at shelves crammed with devices he didn't recognize in white boxes and shrink-wrapped plastic. Everything seemed to come with some sort of garden-themed name. There were buds, pods, seeds, stems. When he walked inside the store with the dog, a buzzer announced their presence. It was the same kind of buzzer used at Pronghorn to indicate that the door to the shower room had been unlocked. For a moment he reeled, trying to get a grip on where he was, the young man at the counter ignoring him completely as he pushed aside lank black hair to read his phone. Kradle tugged up the hood of the sweatshirt he'd stolen from a clothesline, found it tighter around his head than the last one.

"I've got a question," Kradle said.

"Shoot," the kid said, reaching for a huge lime-green can of soda without lifting his eyes from the screen.

"Is there a way I can make phone calls from a phone without the device being traceable?"

He was expecting an upward glance. A quizzical frown. A flat-screen TV mounted on the wall was playing footage of the breakout, now and then flashing on his mugshot in the collection of carded fugitives. MOST DANGEROUS flashed on the screen as the mugshots were shown—Burke first, then himself. He remembered having that picture taken. How weird it was, the instinct to smile when it was the last thing in the world he wanted to do. Carrington's mugshot didn't appear on the screen. Kradle guessed that his death would be public knowledge by now.

The kid flicked a hand at a rack of black phones sitting in little plastic stands.

"Buy a basic burner," the kid said. "Download an onion router to hide your IP and use an app to make the calls. Switch or Neevo or one of those. Something with end-to-end encryption."

"Man, you're speaking Greek to me," Kradle said.

"I'm not Greek, I'm Korean." The guy finally looked up. He had some kind of piercing at the corner of his eye, set into the skin. The neon blue light from the front of the store was bouncing off it, making it look like the point of a laser. Kradle saw no recognition in his face. He took some bills out of his pocket and lay them on the counter.

"Can you set up all that stuff for me? Just make it so I'm using the right programs."

"Programs." The kid smirked. He took the bills and slipped them into the cash register sitting on the glass. Kradle wandered the store while the young man unboxed a phone. He kept one eye on the store clerk and the other on the television screen. Soon he recognized the porch of Shelley Frapport's house on the late news, the lanky figure of Tom Frapport huddled in a crowd watching a stretcher being lifted down the stairs. A huge shape encased in a black body bag. Homer, or maybe the male cop, the one who had held Kradle down. He realized he'd never learned the guy's name. The scrolling text under the news anchors said something about the announcement of rewards for the capture of inmates from Pronghorn, but Kradle saw nothing about how much that reward was, or how a person qualified for it.

The kid whistled after ten minutes and Kradle went to the counter.

"Okay." The clerk leaned lazily on the glass, pointing at the phone screen. "You open this guy up. Type in the number you want to dial here. Press the green button and you're good to go."

"Thanks," Kradle said. He reached for the phone, tried to take it, but the kid held on. Kradle looked at his eyes, followed their gaze to the handcuff dangling from his wrist.

Kradle saw the nose of the revolver emerge from behind the glass. He could do nothing but watch as the kid lifted it, extended it, and pointed it right at his face with the confidence of someone who had grabbed that same gun from its holster under the counter and aimed it at three or four scumbags a month who were trying to rip him off for burner phones. Kradle looked at the gun, looked at the kid, looked at his own hand

and the kid's hand both still gripping the phone. Finally, he looked at the dog, sitting by his side, watching the whole exchange with the tired skepticism of an animal who had already run for its life once in the past few hours and didn't feel particularly enthused about doing it again.

On the screen above the store clerk's head, Kradle's face was showing again.

MOST DANGEROUS.

"You one of the big ones or the little ones?" the kid asked.

"What do you mean?"

"There's a million bucks going for each of the big fugitives," the kid said. The piercing at the corner of his eye lifted as he smiled. "And ten grand for everybody else. Please tell me you're one of the big ones."

"I'm neither," Kradle ventured. "I'm just a guy with a broken phone who thought he'd try some kinky sex games with his girlfriend and ended up losing the handcuff key down a drain. Now I've got to call a locksmith before I'm forced to turn up at work like this in the morning."

"Good story. I like it. You come up with that just now?"

"Yeah," Kradle said.

"Fast on your feet."

"Desperate times."

"So, if your story's true, what's the phone got to be untraceable for?"

"I don't know," Kradle said. "I'll come up with something soon as you take this big-ass gun out of my face."

The kid pulled back the hammer on the gun. Kradle

watched the cylinder rotate, loading the bullet into the chamber about eight inches from his nose.

"Let's talk about this," Kradle said.

"What makes you think I want to talk?" the guy asked. Didn't wait for an answer. "Let go of the phone and put your hands on your head."

"You haven't hit the button yet," Kradle said.

"What?"

"The panic button under the counter. The one that calls the police. You haven't hit it. So I assume you want to talk."

"I haven't hit the button yet because I've got one hand on this gun and one hand on the phone. Let go of the phone and I'll hit the buzzer."

"You're not delaying the arrival of the cops because you want to hold on to a twenty-dollar piece-of-shit burner phone," Kradle said. "I'm guessing you're do-ing it because there are things in the store you don't necessarily want the cops looking at."

"Okay, fine," the kid said. "You got me." He let go of the phone. Kradle pocketed it. "Here's the plan. You're going to get down on the floor, nice and slow. I'm going to cuff you all the way up and we're going to walk down to our sister store on the next block."

"Who's going to lock up this store while you're tak-ing me to the next store?" Kradle asked. The guy's face twitched. Kradle felt a surge of hope and leaped at it. "Police!" he yelled.

"Shh!" the kid snarled. "Shut your fucking—"

"Police!" Kradle yelled again. "Everybody get on the ground! This is a raid! Come out with your hands up!"

The dog at Kradle's side caught the fever of the

game and started barking loudly, the noise ear-splitting in the tiny store.

"Daeshim?" An elderly lady's voice came from upstairs. The kid yelled a string of words in Korean. Kradle assumed he was telling the old woman to stay where she was, that it was not the police, that everything was fine, but Kradle could hear boards creaking over his head, a thump like a book hitting the floor.

"Police! Put the gun down! Put the gun down!" Kradle bellowed.

"Shut up!" Daeshim yelled.

"Go ahead," Kradle said to him. "Shoot me. Shoot me. Blow my brains out in front of your grandma just as she gets to the bottom of the stairs."

Don't shoot me, Kradle thought. *Please don't shoot me.*

"Daeshim? What's happening down there?"

"Go back upstairs!" Daeshim yelled. The gun was shaking in the kid's hand, wavering between Kradle's nose and his left eye. Kradle was waiting for it, watching for it, and as the footsteps down the creaky stairs on the other side of the wall behind the counter became louder, it came. Daeshim turned his head to look for the arrival of the woman. Kradle grabbed the gun with one hand, pushed it sideways, twisted it out of the kid's grip. He used the other hand to shove the kid so that he fell into a rack of buds and stems and pods or whatever the hell they were against the back wall of the store.

Kradle caught a glimpse of the old woman peering timidly out from the doorway, reflected in the glass doors, as he burst out into the street.

*   *   *

Kenny Mystical was overconfident. His momma had been saying it since he was a child. She'd drive him to the local hospital with a broken forearm or a twisted ankle or a fractured skull and tell the nurse behind the counter, who she knew by name, that he'd got overconfident again. That little Kenny had decided, without a shred of credible evidence, that he had the engineering know-how to construct workable wings out of PVC piping and cardboard, and had tried to fly from the roof of the garage to a tree in their backyard, only to land spectacularly on a stack of wrought-iron yard furniture. In high school he had got overconfident about the looks he was receiving from Gretchen Cubby across the science lab and challenged her boyfriend Herb Mirouse to a fight for her devotion, only to have the much larger boy put his head through the glass doors of a cabinet full of frog skeletons. An excess of confidence kept Kenny warm on the streets of Los Angeles for twenty-six years while he pursued Hollywood stardom, until a casting agent told him he was too old and his paunch too prominent for him to be hired anymore as one of the henchmen, security guards, butlers, angry villagers, and Egyptian slaves he was accustomed to portraying on screen.

It took confidence for Kenny to pick himself up from that, brush himself off and pack his car for the long and humiliating drive back to Texas to begin again in his hometown of Rockwall. He only got as far as Vegas before he had an idea.

The new girl was staring at Kenny's framed pictures of his Hollywood days as he locked the register and put the day's takings into his briefcase. It had been a three-wedding day, which was about standard for the end of the year, but Kenny was beat. He took off the shiny, jet-black Elvis wig he'd been wearing all day and slipped it onto a Styrofoam head behind the counter just as the new girl got to the picture of him, midtwenties and oiled and shirtless for his role as a dead gladiator being consumed by a lion.

"Is that a real lion?" she asked, as he crossed the shop toward her. Kenny had a new girl in the shop about every three months, and every single one of them asked if the lion in the picture was real. His endless renditions of "Love Me Tender" for awkwardly giggling tourists, up to eight pairs of them in a single day, would drive the girl away before long. The itchy wigs, the leering drunks, the crushing monotony of the ceremonies would get to her, and the chapel that had probably seemed kitschy and cute when she arrived looking for casual work would become a hellish place of creaky floorboards, thin carpet, dusty plastic flowers, and chipping candy-pink paint before long. But, for now, she was under his spell, and Kenny was confident that he'd bed her before her first week was through, with the help of his wall of silver-screen memories.

"It's real," he said. "Friendly beast, actually. I've worked with lions a few times, and they can be a bit unpredictable."

"Wow."

"Did you see this one? This is me in *Cleopatra*."

"Whoa, with Elizabeth Taylor?"

"No! How old do you think I am? It was an independent remake."

"Oh."

"And look at this. This is me auditioning for *Mission: Impossible*."

"Amazing!" She clapped, bouncing her platinum-blonde Marilyn wig. "What part did you play? Did you meet Tom Cruise?"

"Uh, we better lock up." Kenny flipped one of her synthetic curls and turned away. "And remember not to wear the wig home this time." She giggled and took it off, set it on the wig stand beside his behind the counter. She paused, smoothing the bangs on the inky-black Morticia Addams wig beside it.

"You going to be okay?"

Kenny laughed.

"I'm fine." He waved her off. Gave her his best Johnny Depp "*Fuggedaboudit!*"

The door shut behind her. He was alone.

The girl's words were a worrying reminder. Kenny had indeed forgotten about Ira Kingsley and the break-out, the reason he had shut the store before sunset the past couple of nights and walked out either with the new girl at his side or his phone in his hand, 911 already dialed. The day's events—the happy Australian couple who slow-danced to "Can't Help Falling in Love," and the stonkingly drunk ladies who'd signed their marriage certificate while he crooned "Always on My Mind"—had taken his mind off the danger. Love, even when it was $500 a pop, gimmicky, plastic-wrapped love under fluorescent lights, shot for novelty cardboard frames that would only go in a box somewhere back home, was distracting. Now Kenny faced walking to his car in the dark of the Nevada night, knowing Ira Kingsley, the man who had tried to murder him, was out there somewhere.

Kenny drew a deep breath, held it, and pushed open the door.

He didn't even get one foot out onto the concrete.

Ira was there in the dark. He pushed a woman wearing a stretchy yellow tracksuit into the shop in front of him. It was all so perfectly in keeping with Kenny's nightmares that he stood dumbly in the hall, watching with his hands by his sides while Ira shoved the woman to the floor and locked the door, the knife poking from his hand, long and silver and cleaner than the one he'd used to stab Kenny ten years earlier. Kenny stared in wonderment as his night-time imaginings played out right in front of him, and asked himself why, if he'd known so plainly that Ira would come back for him, he'd allowed himself to be cornered alone and defenseless like this.

The answer was simple. Overconfidence.

"You," Kenny managed to say.

"Yeah." Ira grinned, showing those little, beady teeth under his mustache that Kenny remembered like it was only yesterday he'd seen them for the first time. "You remember me, don't you, Kenny?"

The woman on the ground was sobbing. Kenny could see as she rolled onto her side, struggling to sit with her hands tied with wire behind her back, that her belly was swollen with pregnancy.

"Oh, god," Kenny said.

"You don't even look surprised," Ira said.

"I'm not."

"Then you should know why I'm here," Ira said triumphantly, lifting his skinny arms, the knife glinting in the light of the studio lamps. "We're gonna do this, finally. We're gonna do it right."

"Please, help me," the woman moaned. "Please don't let him hurt my baby."

"Who is this?" Kenny asked.

"Don't you recognize her?" Ira said. He crouched

on the threadbare carpet and yanked the lady's hair, showed Kenny a face he didn't remember. "It's Marissa. Look. It's Marissa. You remember her, right? She married some asshole who designs playgrounds and preschools and let him knock her up. But it's her, and she's here, right back where it all started. And you're gonna marry us, Kenny, like you should have done the first time. Get your fucking wig on. We don't have a lot of time."

Kenny didn't remember Marissa. He remembered Ira, the stupid mustache, the playful mood he'd been in on the day he and the woman now bound on the floor had come in to be wed in the chapel. He remembered ribbing Ira about the French tickler, getting a shark-eyed glare at the counter, deciding that was going to be his thing for this couple. It was supposed to be funny. Supposed to be a gag. He was going to incorporate it throughout the ceremony, hopefully get snickers of delight, the way he did when he sang *"Oh let me be, your cream éclair"* to French couples, or *"Don't you, step on my veal ragu"* to Italians. But he was only three jokes in, and the couple hadn't yet decided if they wanted Hawaiian Elvis or Rhinestone Elvis, when Ira shoved the butterfly knife into his belly and Kenny knew he'd stepped over the mark with this one.

Kenny pulled his wig off the Styrofoam head, held it like a hairy hat in his hands, and went to Marissa, whom Ira was trying to heft into a folding chair.

"It's okay, honey," Kenny said. "We're going to be okay."

"All you had to do was sing a couple of fucking songs," Ira said. "Get away from her. Get away. Stand over there on the stage. Over there. Behind the microphone. Yeah, look at you. Kenny Mystical. Master showman. A couple of songs, some vows, a certificate. That's all you had to do. And you go running your goddamn mouth. Trying to be funny. You ruined everything, you fat piece of shit, and I've waited ten fucking years to come back and put everything right."

"Tell me what you want me to do," Kenny said.

"You know what to do!" Ira snapped. "You do this every day! Sing two songs. Do the ceremony. Sing another song. I paid my money ten years ago, and I want what I goddamn paid for. You're gonna marry Marissa and me, right here, and I get the twenty-four-photograph package with the bonus DVD. Then you're gonna die, you motherless fuck."

"Okay. Okay. Okay. We can do this. You, uh . . . you just gotta pick the songs," Kenny said. "That's part of the deal. There's a list, there, on the wall."

Ira stood looking at the laminated list, clutching Marissa's arm as she hunched in the seat. The man's eyes lingered over the traditional favorites. "Love Me Tender," the well-used favorite, sat at number one. Kenny let his eyes drift down the list, his brain seeking a distraction from the terror in his gut, and when he landed at number thirty-one his lips twitched with electric anticipation.

He told himself not to. Then he found he couldn't resist.

"Can I make a suggestion?" he ventured.

Ira looked at him.

"'Jailhouse Rock'?" Kenny shrugged.

Ira launched himself at the stage.

CHAPTER 31

Celine put her feet up on the dashboard of her car and leaned back in the passenger seat, resting her morning coffee on her stomach. Outside, her garage was unlit, but she could make out the edges of boxes that had stood against the wall since she moved in, taped and labeled in handwriting she didn't recognize. One of the social workers, she guessed. There were ten boxes of her family's belongings from her grandfather's house, all that was left after the massacre. The rest had been destroyed on her request—anything that belonged to Nick, and anything that was even slightly damaged in the event. A single speck of someone's blood or a fresh nick in the paintwork that could conceivably have come from a bullet, and Celine instructed that the item be incinerated. In the decades since, she had not regretted her decision or ventured into the boxes.

With the phone against her ear, waiting for the line to connect, she wondered if she ever would.

"Hello?"

"Hello," Celine said. "My name is Anita Fulton. I'm calling from the features desk at the *LA Times*."

"The *LA Times*!" the voice said. "Jeez!"

"We're running a story on the Kradle Family murders, in connection with John Kradle, the escaped inmate from Pronghorn Correctional Facility," Celine said. "I wonder if I could speak to you for a few moments."

"Well, I don't know why you'd want to talk to us," the man said. She heard shuffling on the other end of the line. "We don't know anything."

"Perhaps." Celine chewed her lip. "Could I just confirm the spelling of your name, sir? Is it with an 'e'?"

"It's Aaron Scott," the man said. "There's no 'e' in it at all."

Celine cleared her throat. "Oh, uh, you never know." She wrote the name next to the phone number on the sheet of paper beside her. She had made five calls already that morning, working up the list Kradle had given her. "So you remember the murders, Mr. Scott?"

"How could I forget? I'm one of the guys who called 911. I smelled the smoke from my backyard."

"Right, because you lived next door," Celine said.

"Across the street. John Kradle built the deck around my pool. It's still here. Sturdy as anything. If you want pictures for the article, I can send them to you."

Celine heard the man's voice drop to a whisper. "*It's the* LA Times*!*"

"I'm just trying to confirm what you told the police back when the crimes were committed," Celine said. "I've got your statement here." She shuffled the pages of phone records.

"I never made a formal statement," Aaron said.

"I mean, uh, the police report. The report the detective wrote that, uh, detailed what you said."

"Well, it can't say much. That detective guy never even came to the house. He just called. Must have been two minutes he was on the line."

Celine glanced at the pages. "Three minutes thirty," she said.

"What?"

"The report says some"—Celine squeezed her eyes shut, struggled—"interesting things. Would you mind retelling me what you told the detective? Just so I can see if you remember anything new that isn't already here."

"Well, all I told the guy is that John Kradle was innocent," Aaron said. "I believed it then and I believe it now."

"You do?"

"Yeah. We would go around there for barbecues sometimes. Great guy. One time my car wouldn't start—me and my wife were supposed to fly to Florida—he drove us all the way to the airport, and when we got home two weeks later he'd fixed the car. Didn't even charge us! Cracked radiator head, it was. Oh, crap. *Hang on a sec. Hang on!* Oh, god. Look, my wife wants to speak to you. She wan—"

"Hello," a new voice said. "This is Lydia Scott. Wife of Aaron Scott. Former neighbor of John Kradle and the Kradle family."

"Okay." Celine eased a sigh.

"We believe John Kradle is innocent."

"I know, Mrs. Scott. Your husband was just saying so," Celine said.

"I'd like to make it known officially, in an official

sense, that if John Kradle turned up here in the middle of the night looking for shelter from the police, I would give it to him. And I don't care who knows it."

"That's really nice, Mrs. Scott, but I'm looking for details," Celine said. "For the article."

"What kind of details?"

"Something that tells me Kradle is innocent. Something a bit more substantial than the fact that he drove you to the airport once and the guy grilled a mean steak."

"Well, that's all we know," Lydia huffed.

"The murder weapon was found at the scene of the crime," Celine said. "It was too badly burned to be identifiable. Did you ever see guns at the Kradle house?"

"Certainly not."

"What about that day?" Celine said. "He's supposed to have returned from a job only minutes after the gunshots were heard. If that story is correct, he must have missed being killed himself by only seconds. Did you see him driving around the neighborhood that afternoon?"

"No."

"Ever see him fight with Christine? Or his son?"

"That man was as gentle as a lamb," Lydia said. "And very tolerant. We knew the family well, even before Christine did her disappearing act. She was what you'd call an eccentric. But not a genuine one, either. The kind who wants to be *thought of* as eccentric. She would get drunk at the barbecues and start talking about spirits and auras and all kinds of junk. Reading people's heads. It was embarrassing."

"Kradle didn't mind all the theatrics?"

"He laughed it off. He was a plain kind of guy.

Real. Reliable. Solid. Like a house brick," Lydia said. "Some people are fairy princesses, and some people are just house bricks. And two of the same in a relationship gets a bit tiresome, I think."

"Okay," Celine said. "What about after Christine left?"

"Oh, he handled that with so much dignity," Lydia sighed. "He raised that boy really well. I'd see them at the local hardware store together sometimes, buying supplies. I'm ashamed to say I hid once or twice so as not to run into them. The whole thing was just so strange. I didn't know what to say about her running off on him like that. I mean, what do you say?"

"I don't know," Celine admitted.

"Whatever happened in that house that day, it's got to do with her," Lydia said. "I can tell you that much. Christine was trouble. She was always talking about evil, and what happened was evil. I say she brought it home with her. That's my take on it all."

"Okay," Celine said. "Look, Mrs. Scott, I have to go."

"Will you use that quote, about the fairies and the bricks?" Lydia asked. "I think it's quite clever. I just came up with it."

Celine hung up and crossed the Scotts off her list. The car door popped open and Keeps, wearing only boxer shorts, slipped into the driver's seat, slung a wrist over the steering wheel.

"The king is dead," Keeps said.

"What's that mean?"

"It means somebody stabbed Elvis Presley dead last night in Vegas," Keeps said. "He's left the building."

"That'll have them crying in the chapel."

"You ever hear of an inmate named Ira Kingsley?"

"I have, actually." Celine's eyes widened as she realized. "I knew Ira back when I worked over in medium. Oh, no. He—"

"He did it." Keeps nodded. "He always said if he ever got out he was gonna go back there and make the guy perform the whole thing again. The Elvis wedding. Make him apologize about the mustache thing."

"It was a pretty stupid mustache," Celine said. "I'm with Elvis. That was too much mustache for just one face."

"Yeah, well, now Ira's dead too."

"Elvis kill him?"

"No. The woman broke her binds and ran away, got help. Police came and shot Ira."

Celine sighed. She hadn't had enough coffee to deal with everything she was being exposed to this morning: death, evil, innocent incarcerated men, celebrity impersonations. When Keeps reached over and stroked her knee she closed her eyes and tried to access the warmth and anticipation she'd felt only hours earlier. But all she felt was dread.

"What are you doing sitting here in the car?" he asked.

"I didn't want to wake you. I've been making calls from Kradle's list." She opened her eyes and showed him the pages. "I've spoken to two sets of neighbors, the owner of a gun shop, and a couple who had Christine clear their shed of a malevolent spirit about a month before the murders."

"And what did they say?"

"The neighbors and the couple said Christine was a weirdo and Kradle was the long-suffering but gentle husband." Celine heard the exhaustion in her own voice. "The gun shop owner says he never sold a gun to John Kradle. And he said Detective Frapport never asked about anybody else. It was just, 'Did you sell this guy a gun?' and showing a picture of Kradle."

"So Frapport had his tunnel vision on."

"Yes."

"Let me have a look at the other gun stores around," Keeps said, and took her phone from the dashboard. Celine felt her hands stiffen in her lap.

"Huh. A passcode," Keeps said.

"Oh, yeah." She took the phone and typed in the numbers as casually as she could, then offered the device back. Keeps didn't take it.

"There wasn't a passcode on your phone last night," Keeps said. Celine didn't answer. He continued, his face unreadable. "I know, because I used it to order dinner."

"My phone prompted me to add one," Celine lied. "I thought it was probably good practice."

"Your phone just randomly prompted you to add one?" Keeps asked.

"Yeah."

"Did you add one to your laptop, too?"

"No."

"So if I go in there and try to use your laptop right now, it won't ask me for a password." Keeps pointed to the door ahead of them through the windshield. Celine felt her neck burning, threatening sweat. They sat in silence for a while.

"What the hell happened?" Keeps turned to her.

"I was scammed."

"What?"

"The bank called me last night to tell me I'd been scammed. A test payment to Kuala Lumpur."

"And you . . ." Keeps struggled to form the words.

A tight, unfriendly smile played about his lips. He touched his chest. "Whoa. Whoa, now. You think *I'm* the one—"

"No, no, no."

"Oh, this is amazing." He laughed, slumped back in his seat. "This is *amazing*."

Celine stared at the dashboard, chewing her lip. That old, protective smile wanted to rise to her lips, but she forbade it. She felt angry, and she deserved the anger, and she wanted to feel it transform her face into an ugly mask.

"Is it really *that* amazing?" she asked suddenly. "You're in my life for what, two days? And suddenly I get scammed? I've never been scammed before. Why should it happen now? You scam people *for a living*, Keeps. It's *what you do*."

Jake the cat wandered alongside the car, from the rear to the front. Celine spotted his tail in the side mirror. The animal leaped soundlessly onto the hood, sat and watched them through the glass, seemingly aware of the tension and curious at its source.

"You know," Keeps said carefully, "I think this is just about this Kradle guy."

"Oh, come on."

"You're starting to believe he might be all right," Keeps said. "And if he's all right, that means you don't know your bad eggs from your good ones. And maybe you never have."

Celine listened. She knew the words were true. That she was starting to believe that John Kradle might have been a good man all along, and that the same cursed blindness that had prevented her from seeing her grandfather as a potential killer had blinded her to his goodness. Was she still blind? Was the same man who had held her and stroked her and gasped in her ear in the dark the night before—who had led her to break every rule she'd ever made about men who she'd kept behind bars—a man who wanted to hurt her?

Keeps opened the driver's-side door and slipped out. He scratched Jake's ear briefly as he headed back into the house. Celine didn't leave the car until she heard the front door of the house slam behind him.

CHAPTER 32

Trinity Parker was walking out of the small office outside the front gates of Pronghorn as Celine arrived in her car. The US Marshal had a tactical vest strapped to her chest, black jeans and black combat gloves pulled on, a black cap securing her dark hair. Celine saw for the first time the Trinity Parker she must have known was underneath the managerial facade the whole time, the one who went out into the wilds and hunted men for a living. She opened the door and made to get out of her car, but Trinity waved her back into the vehicle and came around to the passenger side. Celine noticed that, in the corner of the parking lot, a crew of maybe twenty men in the same tactical gear as Trinity were assembling near two big black vans.

"I'll ride with you," Trinity said as she slipped into the vehicle. "I don't like to head out to a mission with the men. Gives them the idea you're one of them. And there's always someone who starts nervously farting."

"We're going on a mission?"

"We have the pick-up details for Brassen's money,"

Trinity said. "What did you think, I was calling you in so we could head to a salon and get our nails done?"

"The message just said *Come to Pronghorn*," Celine said. "You know, part of effective personnel management is telling everyone what's going on."

"Here's what's going on. We got a message this morning, at five, from someone on the other side. They've left a duffel bag of cash for Brassen at the Rancho Salvaje Wildlife Park outside Coyote Springs."

"A wildlife park?" Celine pulled out of the parking lot, heading into the desert.

"Makes sense. We've scoped out the venue. Great place for a sniper to set up shop. The park is in a valley. Lots of rocky hills around, just like Pronghorn. And by this time of day the place will be flooded with early visitors, trying to beat the Christmas rush. Children, families, park workers."

"Well, we have to shut the place down," Celine said.

"Not a chance," Trinity said.

"You can't carry out an operation like this with hundreds of innocent bystanders in the crosshairs," Celine said.

"Are you telling me how to do my job?" Trinity smirked. "Please, carry on. I didn't know you'd brought down extremely dangerous terrorist organizations before."

Celine sighed.

"The park has to run as normal," Trinity said. "If we shut it down, the first thing that will happen is that angry families will take to social media to complain, and the gig will be up that we're helping Brassen. We're going to fill the area around the lockers where the bag is with agents dressed as civilians, and we'll siphon any real civilians who come through the gates away from the danger zone. There won't be park visitors or staff within five hundred yards of the drop point. That's the best we can do."

"Sounds terrible," Celine said. "Go on."

"We need the contact from the Camp to believe Brassen is on his own, and scared. Best-case scenario is that the target will be lying in wait somewhere near the bag so that he can take Brassen out in close quarters. Shoot him, or stab him maybe." Trinity leaned back in her seat and put a big boot up on the dashboard. "We should be able to spot that. Anyone hanging around the danger zone who's not a part of my team will likely be involved, so we'll just grab him. The second-best-case scenario is the target from the Camp tries to pick off Brassen from afar with a sniper, like they did with the bus driver. If that happens, we'll have to try to scoop him up with the outer cordon crew. That'll be harder. It's a big area."

"What if Burke's guy really has just dropped the bag for him to pick up?" Celine asked. "And they trust Brassen to take the money and keep his mouth shut?"

"That's the worst-case scenario," Trinity said.

The two women rode in silence for a while, the flat earth stretching wide and featureless all around them.

"I just noticed that your buddy isn't here." Trinity glanced into the back seat. "Lover's tiff?"

"We're not lovers."

"That hickey on your neck tells me otherwise."

Celine grabbed the rearview mirror and turned it toward her, tugged down the collar of her T-shirt. "What hickey? There's no hickey."

"No," Trinity said. "But now I know everything I need to know."

Celine felt a rush of anger billow up inside her, a painful swelling under her ribs.

"Like I said," Trinity continued. She was tapping away at her phone. "I understand the temptation. Point is, you can get confused by criminals. Especially when they're out there blending in with everybody else like foxes among the dogs. Best thing to do is just stick to your job, Osbourne. Your job is to put them where they've been deemed to go. In a cell or in the ground. You're not a judge, or a jury, or a detective."

Celine moved as though through a dream, parking the car in a crowded lot under a big sign directing patrons toward the ticket booths. Trinity pulled a jacket over her vest and zipped it to the neck, stuffed her hands in her pockets and nodded toward the side entrance to the park. Celine didn't see the huge black vans or the rest of the team until she found herself wandering the concrete back halls of the park with Trinity and a very nervous man in a navy-blue suit. They passed one-way viewing windows that looked into lush green enclosures, the windows passing by so quickly that Celine didn't catch a glimpse of any animals. It struck her how like the prison the zoo was, with its swipe-card security doors, motion-sensor cameras, and iron gates. There was a smell here, more fetid and primal than the one at Pronghorn, but not by much.

While Trinity and the park manager walked ahead, Celine suddenly looked back and found the tactical team walking behind her, more joining the convoy from side halls as they moved along.

"I don't understand why we weren't given more notice about this," the park manager was saying. "My park is full of customers. I've got more than a hundred staff on duty today."

"Yeah, and I need those staff to keep doing what they're doing, diverting civilians away from the section I indicated on the map I sent you," Trinity said. "How's that going?"

"Well, I'm losing a lot of merchandise sales," the manager said. "If I'd had more of a briefing—"

"I don't give people notice, Mr. Eprice." Trinity stopped and put her hand on the guy's shoulder. "What I do is more like a blitzkrieg. I can't have a hundred park employees, all with cell phones, assembling in a boardroom with coffee and cookies while I lay out the plan with a PowerPoint presentation. There's no rehearsal dinner. We're at the wedding and it's time for the vows."

"What do I do?" Mr. Eprice glanced at Celine, the only other person not in tactical gear, but she could only offer him a small smile of mutual confusion.

"Go have a coffee and a cookie somewhere. We'll make sure we clean up after we're done." Trinity nodded to two of her team members, who grabbed the park manager and ushered him away. A person dressed in a huge, fluffy zebra costume stepped into the hall from what looked like a staff cafeteria, turned this way and that, surveying the scene, and then backed into the room again and closed the door.

They stopped at a small room full of computers, monitors. Celine noted there was a station of monitors for "enclosures," one for "transit," and one for "retail." Trinity went to the "retail" monitors and stood watching. Celine came up beside her.

"These are civilians," Trinity said, pointing to the screen. Celine saw a bank of turnstiles and ticket booths. She watched as a family paid for entry into the park, pushed through the turnstiles and were immediately intercepted by a man dressed as a tiger who gestured wildly to a place off screen, bouncing on his tiptoes.

"Where is he taking them?"

"He's not taking them, he's luring them." Trinity gave a small smile. "We're giving away cuddly toys, T-shirts, and ball caps. Nobody says no to a free ball cap. Once the tourists are through the giveaway area they're forced down a long path toward the elephant enclosure, which takes them to the complete opposite side of the park."

"It's working," Celine conceded, watching a couple with a baby being diverted sideways from the area immediately outside the ticket gates. "But what if some of the Camp's people try to walk through there and your staff direct them away?"

"I have a feeling they won't let themselves be lured with the promise of free gifts." Trinity smiled. "Come on. We haven't got much time," Trinity said to Celine, beckoning. Two female tactical team members followed close behind them as they took a set of stairs. They emerged into an empty building, a large, sprawling affair with boarded-up windows and display cabinets shrouded in white sheets. Trinity led them to a bare room on the second floor with a balcony that overlooked a sunny square. Celine peered down toward the intersection of wide, clean streets between the buildings.

"What is this place?" she asked.

"Used to be the reptile and insect house." Trinity was peering through a shutter at the people below. "They're turning it into a restaurant, I think."

"Where's Brassen?"

Trinity nodded. Celine came to the shutters, looked out over a large paved intersection between storefronts of gift shops and restaurants. Looking to the left of the square, she could just make out the entry turnstiles in the distance. She watched as another costumed mascot scooped up a family for free gifts, while a solitary man bypassed the crowds and made his own way down the avenue toward the square. She realized as he neared that it was Brassen, walking uncertainly, head down, hands in his pockets.

"The bag, we're told, is in locker twenty-three," Trinity said. Celine followed her gaze. Across the square, under a long green awning festooned with fake tropical plants, a wall of lockers stood. Celine could barely read the big sign displaying the rental prices. She watched a couple in T-shirts and ball caps wander past the lockers and stop by a glass-walled enclosure that held fairy penguins flapping and waddling on white sand. The woman posed by the glass as her partner snapped a picture with his phone.

"These are all your people?" Celine asked.

Trinity nodded.

Brassen stood nervously outside the gift shop windows, pretending to be fascinated by a postcard stand. Trinity lifted a radio off her belt and gave some commands to her team, checked on the assembly of the inner and outer cordons. Celine only had eyes for her former colleague. Even from a distance, Joe Brassen looked thin and wan compared to his usually plump, sunburned self. It was impossible that he had lost a substantial amount of weight in the days since he had been exposed, but something had loosened inside him, deflated, sagged. He wandered the front of the gift shop and then crossed to a cotton candy stand, watching a man in a pink hat fiddling with the dispenser.

"Teams Alpha, Bravo, and Charlie, you're all checked in," Trinity said. "Command team is good to go. Brassen, you can approach the lockers."

Celine saw Brassen jolt at the sound of his name. He wiped his nose and mouth, a clumsy cover as he spoke into what she guessed was a collar microphone.

"I . . . I can't. I can't do this. I feel sick."

"He looks like shit," Celine said. "He's a sitting duck out there and he knows it. You can't make him do this."

"You're right, I can't," Trinity said. "But he wants to be able to tell a judge he put his life on the line to redeem himself after helping Burke break out of Pronghorn. It might be the difference between a life sentence and twenty-five years."

"I can't do this," Brassen repeated.

"He wants to back out," Celine said. "You have to let him."

Trinity nodded to one of the women positioned by the window, who took a radio out of a pouch on her thigh and tossed it at Celine. "He just needs encouragement. Your time to shine, Osbourne. Do your thing."

"That's why I'm here? You want me to talk him into it?"

"You did all right the first time."

"Look, you're asking me to walk him into the danger zone," Celine scoffed. "He could have a sniper lining him up as we speak. Any of those people down there could be about to—"

"He's wearing a vest," Trinity said. "And I've got five men down there within a stone's throw of where he's standing. See there?" She pointed. "In the gift shop window? That's one of my guys. I've got two guys up there, behind that screen. One guy there at the cotton candy stand. One guy over there. If anyone attacks Brassen, they'll rush to his aid."

"What if the sniper—"

"Heel, little doggy," Trinity snarled. "Just fucking heel, and do what you're told. You remember what it felt like the last time I gave you a smack for messing me around?"

"Yes," Celine groaned.

"So, take the radio and get your friend into line before I shoot him myself."

Celine snatched the radio. Her lip twitched with the urge to cry or smile, she wasn't sure.

"Brassen, it's Celine," she said.

"Celine?"

She saw Brassen turn and look around the square.

"You're safe, Joe," Celine said. Her throat felt hoarse. "I'm here with Trinity's team. They've got everything under control. Just do what they're telling you to do."

"I don't want to die, Celine." Brassen wiped his brow. Celine bet he was drenched in sweat. "I shouldn't have . . . I know I shouldn't have done this. But I . . . I just . . . I'll do the time in prison. I'll do it. I-I-I just don't want to die out here."

"Command, we got a possible target," a voice on the radio said.

Trinity shoved Celine aside, looked toward the ticket booths. A tall, thin man in a heavy green jacket was shaking his head in refusal at a costumed parrot trying to lure him toward the free gifts.

"This might be one of the Camp's guys," Trinity

said to Celine. "We need to get Brassen to pick up the bag." She held the radio to her mouth. "Alpha team, cover the possible target. Don't let him come any further down the avenue."

Celine watched as a pair of women in colorful uniforms rushed out of a restaurant with a tray of food to intercept the thin man. He stopped and started picking from their sample tray.

"Celine?" Brassen called. "Can you tell them? I want to back off."

"It's too late for the ballad of the condemned," Trinity growled in Celine's ear. "Tell him to go to the locker and, while he's at it, stop looking around everywhere like a fucking moron. He's going to blow our cover."

"Just go to the locker, Brassen," Celine said. "You're safe. Just go."

"What if it's a bomb?" Brassen said. "We-we don't know that it's not a goddamn hand grenade tied to the inside of the locker door."

"He's got a point," Celine said. "He might open that locker and blow up the entire building. What exactly do you know about what's in that locker?"

Trinity gave a hard, rueful laugh.

"What we know, *Captain*," she sneered, "is that at seven twenty-five p.m., just before the park closed last night, someone in a cap, gloves, and jeans paid cash at the ticket booths, came in, and deposited a duffel bag in locker twenty-three. We have CCTV footage of the drop. The guy walked in, shoved the bag into the locker, slammed the door shut, and locked it at the pay station. He didn't rig it as a trap. We know that from the footage. From the length of time he spent standing in front of the locker."

"That's some pretty good footage," Celine said. "Was it very clear that he—"

Celine noticed Trinity's right hand curling into a fist.

"Okay, okay." She put a hand up, pressed the button on her radio. "Joe, we know the locker isn't rigged."

"W-what if it's remote detonated? What if the bag's rigged?" Brassen said. "For when I open it."

"You're not going to open it, genius!" Trinity shouted into her radio. "Go to the locker, get the bag, turn, and walk out of the park. That's all you have to do. Now do it!"

Brassen stood frozen. Celine put the radio to her lips.

"You're safe," she said again. "Joe, you can do this."

Celine watched as Joe Brassen turned from the cotton candy stand and started moving across the square like a man walking on a tightrope above a pit of fire. For years, it seemed, he walked. One foot in front of the other.

"I'm gonna have a heart attack," he said. Celine watched him reaching for the keypad on the front of the locker. His breath rattled on the line. "I can't breathe."

Celine looked around the square. There were three people outside the gift shop—one perusing postcards, one talking on a cell phone, one fiddling with the lid of a water bottle. The thin man seemed to be flirting with the waitresses. In the seconds that had passed, two more people had refused the free gifts blockade and were walking down the avenue, one holding a phone to her ear, stopping by the gift shop to peruse the items there, the other heading for the toilets just inside the gates.

Brassen opened the locker. Celine held her breath.

He took down the black duffel bag. Celine saw the weight of the items inside the bag shift as it came off the shelf, sliding downward beneath the thin fabric. Brassen gripped the straps of the bag, weighed it a little in his fist, then turned toward the building from which Celine watched him.

"Okay." She heard his wet, rattling breath. "Okay. I'm okay. I'm okay. I'm okay."

"Turn and walk out of the park," Trinity said. "Alpha team, move out. Delta, get ready in the parking lot."

Brassen turned toward the ticket booths at the front of the park. Celine watched him emerge from the shade of the awning that covered the wall of lockers. It seemed as if the sun hit his face like a punch. His mouth twisted, one hand rising and gripping at his chest. Brassen dropped the bag and went down on his knees, flopping on his front in the sun.

CHAPTER 33

A tearing. That's what it felt like. Pieces coming apart. Skin ripping, blood oozing, warm and delicious. She felt it all over her body. Kerry Monahan pressed the phone too hard against her ear, standing outside the Rancho Salvaje gift shop, watching the man with the bag go down. She was wild-eyed, being torn apart by competing desires: wanting to stay and watch the man die, and wanting to get out of there, to pull her focus away from what she was seeing and concentrate on what she was hearing on the phone. The voice of Burke David Schmitz. The boss. The others had told her that he would personally call to listen in on the assassination, but Kerry hadn't believed it until the phone started ringing in her pocket. She was just a kid from Michigan with big ideas about how the world should work. About self-awareness, and genetics, and peace. Now she was a killer, and the master of all killers was talking to her, of all people, telling her she was doing a good job.

She was a soldier. A warrior.

"They're rushing in to help," Kerry said. Her chest

felt tight, hard, only small amounts of air getting in and out, the adrenaline zapping and tingling in her veins. "Jesus. They're everywhere. There are people coming from everywhere."

She backed up a little as men and women in tactical gear seemed to materialize from the very air, rushing in to assist the man who'd taken the bag from the locker. People she had thought were other park visitors were rushing over, too. A pair of waitresses dropped a tray and turned and ran, while the customer they'd been giving samples to stood staring at the fray.

"Do not get snatched up," Burke insisted.

"I won't. I won't."

"He's definitely down?" Burke said on the phone.

"Oh, yeah, he's down."

"Good," the boss said. "Good work. Get out of there. Call when you're clear."

The line went dead. Kerry felt herself sucked back into the present moment. The man on the ground. The woman with the black cap shaking him, yelling at him, dragging him up while others tried to push him down. They seemed like they were going to try to resuscitate him. Like they thought it was a heart attack. Kerry shifted her feet and turned to walk away, but then she saw one of the tactical squad going for the bag, the bare hand reaching for the handles, the exposed skin slipping around the fabric, and she had to stay and watch her second ever kill.

The effect of the poison on this man was almost instant. He clutched at his throat, gagged, coughed white foam onto his chest. Kerry was shivering with excitement. The first one hadn't foamed at the mouth. She wondered why the effect was different, supposed everybody took the chemical differently. The man went down. Finally, they were coming to their senses, realizing what was happening. Pushing each other away from the bag, fumbling, yelling. Kerry really had to go now. Had to force herself. She gripped her way along a railing and pushed toward the ticket booths. She treated herself to one last backward glance at the scene she had created.

That's when she locked eyes with the short blonde woman.

She was not part of the tactical team, but was dressed in jeans and a T-shirt. Kerry hadn't noticed her in the square while she waited for the man to pick up the bag. Perhaps she had burst out of a shop or emerged from one of the roads into the square at the sight of the chaos. Kerry told herself she was okay. She had time. She walked to the ticket booths and put a hand on a turnstile.

Something made her look back again. She saw the blonde woman had started to run toward her.

Celine saw it in her eyes. The excitement. She'd seen it in the eyes of inmates before, a kind of primal ferocity that was the closest thing, she was certain, to the hunter inside every human being. The thing that liked the sight of blood and gore and death. A fight would erupt in the cell block, and while the faces of some men showed shock, horror, fear, there were some whose eyes glowed with adrenaline.

She was kneeling by Brassen in the center of the square, which was crowded now with members of Trinity's team, including the marshal herself, who stood directing her personnel to secure the area, grab the three civilians who had made it down the avenue, and drag Brassen to safety. That's when Celine looked up and saw the girl by the gift shop.

Wild eyes. Her mouth taut, face hard, thoughts obviously whizzing through her brain. The eyes were recording everything, gathering up pleasurable memories of Brassen and the male agent's deaths. Then the girl looked at Celine, and knew she had been made.

She ran.

"She's there! She's there!" Celine shouted.

She got up and sprinted after the girl.

The first indication that Celine wasn't alone was a boot scraping against the back of her shoe as she ran. Celine glanced over her shoulder and saw Trinity so close behind her she could feel her body heat. Celine burst through the turnstiles after the reedy, thin teenager, who had slipped through the hands of the team members posing as ticket sellers as if she were made of smoke. She was now halfway across the parking lot. Trinity and Celine ran side by side, feet pounding on the asphalt, their breaths in unison.

They slid seamlessly into single file, sprinting between cars, a side mirror bashing against Celine's arm as she turned into an aisle, following the bobbing shape of the girl's head.

"She's going for the trees!" Celine called. Trinity surged ahead of her, shoving her out of the way. Celine skidded to a halt at the sight of the black pistol rising in Trinity's hands.

Two blasts. The girl stumbled and pressed on.

"No! Stop!" Celine grabbed at Trinity, catching her jacket briefly as she took off again. "She's a kid!"

"She's a killer," Trinity huffed. Celine felt the ground beneath her feet rise, becoming concrete, then

dirt, then grass. The woods swallowed them. Trinity
kneeled and lined up another shot, and Celine rushed
past her, unable to slow herself. She heard the crack
of the gun and watched the girl tumble onto the
ground in front of her.

"Oh, god! Oh god! Oh god!" Celine scrambled to
the kid's side and threw herself on her warm, writhing figure. "Don't kill her! Trinity, please!"

"Get off, idiot." Trinity grabbed Celine's shoulder
and shoved her aside. The girl was flushed pink and
gasping for air, blood smeared on her pale, freckled
face. Celine watched as Trinity climbed on top of the
girl, straddling her.

"What's the target?" Trinity said. "Tell me now before I put another bullet in you."

"I don't know. I don't know. I don't—"

Trinity pushed the girl's wrist against the earth,
pressed her gun into the center of her palm.

"Trinity, please!" Celine begged.

"I'm not taking you into custody, little girl." Trinity
grabbed the teenager by the throat to silence her cries.
"I'm not spending another two days rattling around
a stinking prison, bouncing threats and promises off
another halfwitted piece of redneck trash. You tell me
now what Schmitz's target is, or I'll put a hole in your
hand."

"I can't!" the girl screamed. "I don't know—"

A gunshot. It was loud, thunderous, echoing. It
rolled over Celine like a wave, thumping in her chest,
pulsing in her eardrums. Trinity slumped sideways off
the girl and fell near Celine's legs. Celine wiped blood
out of her eyes, gripped her way toward the girl as the
second shot came whizzing past her, sputtering dirt
and grass.

She gathered the shaking girl under her arm and dragged her to a small tree, which exploded almost instantly, shorn in half by another shot. Celine used the cover of the falling branches to run with the girl to a different tree, then another, away from where she guessed the sniper was. As the trees began to thin before them, a huge black tactical van skidded to a halt at the edge of the shade, and Celine shoved the girl through the door just as it slid open.

The firing had stopped.

She sank to the carpeted floor, gripping the girl, the two of them still screaming as the van pulled away.

2015

He'd calmed down a little by the time they met at the table in the very back corner of Ballie's Diner. It was the place they'd used to go to when they first moved to Mesquite, when they had grown tired of living on the road, chasing ghosts and cramming themselves into tiny, moldy motel showers. Kradle arrived first, looked at the menu, which still served the blueberry pancakes she used to order before she disappeared from his life to find herself in Tibet. It was about the only thing that remained the same. The new owner had painted the place, ripped out the shelves Kradle had installed above the cash register for the last owner, added a gelato freezer. Christine appeared in the doorway twenty-five minutes late and stood there for a moment, just looking at him across the restaurant, half-seeming as if she was going to step back out into the street and disappear again for another decade and a half without explanation.

When she finally slid into the booth, Kradle nodded to the waitress. He expected Christine to order coffee with room for milk, the way she always had, but she ordered chai tea instead with a side of hot water, in case it came too strong, he guessed.

He leaned back in his chair and drank his coffee, and waited for her to say sorry for running off on him. He'd run their conversation at the door of their house through his mind a hundred times during the night, and was sure she hadn't said sorry yet. She'd said hi. She'd told him she went to Tibet. She'd asked to see their son. But she didn't say sorry, and she wasn't saying sorry now, and Kradle took a long breath because he could feel the tips of his ears getting hot again, and he knew what that meant.

"He looked handsome," Christine said. "From what I could see."

"He is handsome," Kradle agreed. "And he's smart. And he's funny. He's so funny he brings me to tears sometimes."

"I bet."

"He was a funny kid. A trickster." His words were coming out angry, as if he felt he had something to prove. "He used to put things in my shoes before he left for school—buttons, paperclips, notes, a whole banana one time. He sings all the time. On the worksite. At home. In the shower. He never shuts up. We don't own a radio for work. Don't need one. The kid knows the words to every song he's ever heard, from show tunes to heavy metal. The past week it's been all Etta James. Beats me why that is. It's not my kind of stuff."

Christine laughed.

"You've missed all that," Kradle said, his face stiff.

Christine's smile disappeared slowly.

"You missed him learning to walk." Kradle lifted his cup to drink his coffee, realized his hand was shaking.

He put it back down. "You missed all the hard stuff. I was terrified when he was little. There was nobody to help me. I didn't know anything about babies. One time he just stopped eating for a week and a half. All I could get into him was cheese. Just cheese. That's it."

"John—" Christine began.

"No, let me talk," he said. "When he was nine he read a magazine about UFOs and lost his goddamn mind about it. He was up screaming in the middle of the night that they were going to come abduct us and experiment on us. When he was twelve, he fell in love with his math teacher. I'm talking real love. I found a note in his room proposing marriage to her."

Christine sipped her chai.

"Right now he's all torn up about this terrorism stuff." Kradle waved at the next table, where a newspaper lay face up by an empty plate. A picture of Abdul Hamsi, the failed Flamingo Casino bomber, dominated the cover. "I can't stop him watching the news."

"What did you do about the woman?" Christine asked.

"What woman?"

"The teacher."

"Oh." Kradle put his arms on the table, looked at the holes in the wall above the register where his shelves had once been. "Uh. Well, I sat him down and told him he had the wrong idea. That he was just a little boy and she was a grown adult and they weren't going to run off together and get married."

Christine listened.

"And I started bringing women around the house," Kradle said. The flicker of emotion in Christine's eyes gave him a mean little thrill. "I figured he didn't have enough women in his life if he was getting the idea that his math teacher was in love with him because she'd had a few friendly conversations with him in the schoolyard. So, after that, when I had a girl on the go I would bring her to the house, let her meet him, hang around him a little. Show him that just because a lady's talking to you, doesn't mean she's in love with you."

"Did you have many 'girls on the go'?" Christine asked. "After I left?"

"Are you really asking me what my dating life was like after you disappeared on me and our newborn child?"

"I guess." Christine stared into her cup.

"It was clear to me after about—oh, I don't know—three *years*, that you weren't coming back. I got lonely."

"I get that," she said.

"You didn't even leave me a note," Kradle continued. "The police thought I must have abused you. People around here thought I abused you. I don't . . . Urgh. I don't even know what to say to you."

"Well, you're saying plenty."

"I thought about having you declared dead."

"Why?"

"So I could get a divorce." He shrugged. "So I could sell the house. So I could have a memorial. Some fucking closure."

"I'd have liked to have seen that. My own memorial."

"Oh, I bet you would."

"I wasn't dead," Christine said. Her smile twisted something in his chest, made him snap.

"You don't seem to understand the fact that I *didn't*

know that!" he growled. The waitress looked over from behind the counter, worried. "Do you know what it's like to wonder if your wife is dead?"

"No, John, I don't. Of course I don't."

"Where the fuck did you go?"

"I told you, Tibet."

"No. I mean, that day."

She told him about the frantic moments after he'd left the room with their child, pretending to sleep while he closed the door and then slipping out of the bed and grabbing her wallet from the hospital bag. He sat and watched her face, listening to the story as it rambled on. The group of hippies she found herself with in Vegas, their rusty campervan where she slept during the journey to Los Angeles. Slumming with street people in Santa Monica. Hitchhiking to Oregon. Picking strawberries and living in a barn, deciding to travel with a group of young poets to Vietnam, then China.

"Was it me?" Kradle asked when she ran out of words.

"No," Christine said. "It was the baby."

"What about him?"

"His spirit," Christine said. "I felt it, when he was inside me. He might be all right now, but back then he was a dark spirit destined for pain and sadness."

"You can say something normal about it, you know," Kradle said. "You don't have to couch it in all that weird stuff. You can say 'I was depressed' or 'I was scared.' Maybe you never wanted a baby. Or maybe you thought you did and then changed your mind. Maybe you were ashamed of that, or terrified of telling me. Maybe me being so excited about the baby intimidated you or—"

"It was none of those things," Christine said.

"Well, what was it then?"

"It was his spirit."

Kradle put his hands on the table, stared at them, and felt a wave of relief roll over him. A part of him had known, in all the years that Christine had been missing, that she had left simply because she was broken. That even if an explanation ever came, it wouldn't be rational or healing to him. Whether Audrey had been right, and it was a flair for the dramatic and a need for attention that had driven her away, or whether it was because of any of the reasons he had just given her, Kradle knew then that the only person in the relationship who could sew up what had been ripped apart was him. She wasn't going to say sorry. She wasn't going to make it all better. He had to do that for himself. He also knew that, faced with the challenge of it, he could do it. If he could raise a boy like Mason, he could eventually be all right with what Christine had done to him.

But he had to say it. For Mason.

"There's nothing wrong with that kid," Kradle said, stabbing the table with one finger to the beat of his words. "He's a glorious child. Was then. Is now."

Christine sat in silence, her tattooed hands cupped around her chai, and Kradle thought how old she looked. How beaten down by the foreign winds that had carried her around the earth from place to place, anywhere but where he was.

"*The Frances Falkner Show* is coming to town," Christine said suddenly.

"Don't tell me you came back here just for that."

"No." Christine looked wounded. "It was time. It was just time to come home. But I also noticed, after

I got back, that she's going to be here in a month's time."

Kradle nodded, knowing the discussion of her actions was over for now, but not really wanting to talk about anything else.

"So?" Christine asked.

"So what?"

"Do you want to go?"

"Are you kidding me?" Kradle's mouth ached with a tight smile. "No, Christine, I don't want to go to *The Frances Falkner Show* with you. That's your thing."

"I was thinking if you said no, I'd ask Audrey," Christine said.

"Have you spoken to Audrey at all in the past fifteen years?" Kradle asked.

"No," Christine said.

"So, you're just . . . You're just going to call her and say, 'Hello, I'm back. Do you want to go to a taping of *The Frances Falkner Show* with me?'" Kradle's smile loosened.

"Well, yes, something like that." Christine sipped her chai.

Kradle waited for more. There was none. He felt a laugh burst out of him.

"Can I listen in?" he asked.

CHAPTER 34

The dog woke him, snuffling in his ear, a cold, wet nose that jolted him out of a thin slumber. Kradle's mind reeled through snapshots of the past twenty-four hours—the Frapport house, the car, the kid with the gun in the technology store, the mad sprint into the street and away from the scene. He'd found a bike leaning against a fence and taken it, pedaled until the scenery around him changed, becoming warehouses and garages, chain-link fences and unpaved streets. The dog, which had trotted faithfully by his side when he started riding, began to hang back before long, its pink tongue foamy and wagging between loose jaws. Kradle had stopped in the shadows behind a quiet warehouse, sunk down into the dirt, and taken out the phone and list of numbers, ready to dial.

Then he'd fallen asleep. At some point he must have slipped down onto his side, worrying the beast, who nudged at his neck and chin now, trying to rouse him.

"I'm all right," he told the dog, looping an arm around its neck. "I'm okay. I'm just tired."

His charge revived, the dog wandered off to find

water or food, Kradle supposed. He knew he needed some sustenance himself, but that was a concern for another time. The numbers, and then answers, were waiting. With the sun creeping toward his sneakers, splayed on the gravel, he started to dial.

"Hello?"

"Hello." Kradle cleared his throat. "This is . . . My name is, uh, John. John . . . Sky."

"What?" the voice asked.

"I'm from the *New York Times*."

"No thanks. I read the *Post*."

The line clicked. Kradle looked at the phone in his hand, blinked, and decided he would circle back to the number he had just tried. He shook his head awake and dialed the next number on the line.

"Hello?"

"This is James Mackley," Kradle said. "I'm a journalist calling from the *New York Times* with some important questions for you."

"What?" The voice was female, husky, vaguely familiar. Kradle felt the hairs rise on the back of his neck.

"I'm looking into the breakout at Pronghorn," Kradle said. "Some of the more infamous prisoners who are on the loose. We're doing a . . . a profile. I understand you were questioned about John Kradle. About those murders."

"Oh, jeez, I sure was." The woman laughed. "And I had plenty to say, all right."

"Can I just confirm who I'm talking to?"

"My name's Jasmine O'Talley."

Kradle thought. Remembered. Swallowed wrong and coughed.

"How'd you get my number?" Jasmine asked.

"We have our sources," Kradle wheezed. "You . . . uh. The detective on the Kradle case called you, didn't he? Back in 2015? You spoke for . . . seventeen and a half minutes?"

"Well, I don't know how you know all that stuff, but yeah." Jasmine sniffed. "I can't remember how long we talked. But he called me. Asked me if John Kradle was a nice guy or not."

"And what did you say?" Kradle's face burned.

"I said he was a real piece of shit," Jasmine said.

"Oh. Wow."

"I said he probably murdered his wife, for sure," Jasmine sneered. "He was a cold, callous jerk and probably a psycho-maniac. And the guy snored like a train. Not that it's relevant, I guess."

"It's not."

"Like sleeping beside a goddamn chainsaw factory."

"Jasmine, I think that's all I have for you," Kradle said. "Thank you for answering my questions."

"I hope the police catch his ass and put him back in jail where he belongs," Jasmine said.

"Is . . ." Kradle licked his teeth. Decided he couldn't help himself. "Is it possible your low opinion of the man may be just because he never called you back?" Kradle said.

"What?"

"You went on three dates. He took you to that nice steakhouse. And then he never called you again. You ran into him at the grocery store that time and it was weird."

"How do you . . ." The line was silent for a moment. "*John?*"

Kradle hung up quickly. The dog was back, sitting

upright at his side, staring at him with its big brown eyes, judging.

"Sometimes you just . . . ," he began. "Never mind. You're a dog."

Kradle dialed. He spoke to three neighbors, two gun store owners, the owner of a hardware store he had frequented at the time of the murders. He looked at the list of numbers and saw that most of the calls were outgoing. Then he noticed an incoming call that was very short, fifteen seconds. A short call back, forty-five seconds. Another short call incoming. The caller and Frapport were playing phone tag. When they finally connected, they spoke for only three minutes. Kradle called the number.

"In Focus Studios."

Kradle opened his mouth to speak, then paused, thinking.

"Hello?"

"Yes, hello," Kradle said. "Sorry, who is this?"

"This is In Focus Studios."

"What's In Focus Studios?" Kradle asked.

"We're a production company. How may I direct your call?"

"I don't know," Kradle answered. He struggled to his feet, feeling weirdly lightheaded. It was exhaustion, hunger, low blood sugar, burnout. But also something else. A sense that he had just taken some kind of important step toward his goal, without any basis for knowing why or how. "I'm, um. I'm calling from the *New York Times*."

"Oh . . . kaaay?" the woman said. She sounded young, bored. Kradle could hear something tapping rapidly, a pen on a table, maybe. "So what can I do for you today, sir?"

"Let me level with you here," Kradle said. "I've got a list of numbers that I'm dialing. They're connected to a murder I'm writing a story about."

"A murder?" the girl snorted. "Whoa. Well, this just got a bit more interesting. And creepy."

"Yeah, it is creepy," Kradle said. "It's a creepy story. Guy murdered his whole family. I'm trying to get to the bottom of what happened."

"Is this a joke?"

"No."

"What did you say your name was?"

"John . . ." He shook his head helplessly and looked around. "Uh. Dog."

"John Dog?"

"With two Gs."

"Mr. Dogg, I don't know if—"

"Look, I'm a researcher, and I've got this number. Someone at your studio called a detective connected to a murder case back in 2015, and I'm trying to find out who that person was."

"Well, what department did they call from?" the girl asked. "What extension?"

"I don't know. This number."

"This is the front desk."

"So who worked on the front desk in 2015?" Kradle asked.

"Dude, I don't know."

"Could you find out?"

"Maybe." A frustrated sigh. The novelty of the call was wearing off and becoming hard work. Kradle felt his throat tightening with desperation. "Urgh, I'd have to look it up. And I don't know if I can tell you that. It's, like, private, probably. Confidential information."

"What does your studio do?" Kradle asked.

"TV shows," the girl said. "We're the home of *NDN News*—the voice of Nevada!"

"What else?"

"*Ready, Set, Clean*," the girl said. "*Paulie the Pawn-King, Trailer Park Wars, The Frances Falkner Show, The—*"

"*The Frances Falkner Show*?" Kradle said.

"Yeah. Look, can you hang on?"

Kradle's mind was racing. It made sense that Detective Frapport would think to speak to the producers of *The Frances Falkner Show*. Christine had attended a taping two months before she was murdered. What didn't make sense was Frapport actually doing it. Almost all the calls Kradle had made so far were to people Detective Frapport had selected because they knew Kradle. They were his neighbors, local businesspeople who he bought from, clients he had serviced. Frapport was tunnel-visioned, bent on proving Kradle was the killer, without seeking to examine any other suspects. The *Frances Falkner* producers didn't know Kradle, and had never met him. Christine had attended the show by herself after he and Audrey refused to go with her.

And *the show* had called *Frapport*. Kradle looked at the list of numbers, checked and rechecked. Yes, the first contact made between Frapport's number and the studio was incoming, not outgoing. After they'd chased each other back and forth, the detective and whoever called from In Focus Studios had spoken for only three minutes. Whatever the issue had been, it seemed Frapport had shut it down fairly quickly. Kradle ran his finger up and down the list of numbers, trying to find any calls to or from an extension at In

'ocus Studios other than the number he was now on
old with.

A voice came back on the line. It was not the bored
irl from the front desk but a high, male voice that
vas thick with disapproval. Kradle thought he noted a
outhern accent, something familiar, from his corner
of the world. Maybe Carolina.

"Are you there?"

"Yes," Kradle said.

"In Focus Studios has no comment to make on any-
hing related to the Pronghorn breakout," the voice
aid. "And we'll ask you please not to call here again."

"Can I maybe—" Kradle started, but the line went
dead. His stomach growled, half with hunger, half
with a physical acknowledgment that he was getting
raction, the instinct that he was on the right path.

He sat again against the wall, put a hand on his heart
and found it hammering. He went to the internet app
on the phone and opened it up, tapped through to
YouTube, and started searching. There were weekly
episodes of *The Frances Falkner Show* dating back to
1996. He scrolled them, trying to think which week
Christine must have attended the show.

He closed his eyes. It had been a month after she
returned. He saw the little motel room she was stay-
ng in down by the river, her backpack slumped in
he corner by the bathroom, festooned with badges,
patches, ribbons, and other keepsakes from her travels. He remembered going there to pick her up, to take
her to a park to meet Mason for the first time. How
awkward it all was—the smell of her body in the motel room, his bizarre nervousness that something intimate might happen between them, then the big green

park sprawling around them, Mason sitting upright at the picnic table with his hands between his knees, the way he'd sat in countless doctors' offices as a little boy waiting for check-ups and vaccinations. It had been three weeks after that that Kradle stopped going with them to their meetings, stopped trying to explain to Mason why his mother was back, why she'd even gone away. Maybe a week after that, Kradle had let her come around the house for the first time. Maybe another week before Audrey had come to the house to meet her, and Kradle had gone to work, leaving the three of them alone.

He remembered the boiling tension as Audrey and Christine talked on the back porch. Kradle making use of himself in the kitchen, lying on the floor fixing a leak under the sink, hearing mention of France Falkner through the parted back doors.

"Don't tell me you came all the way back here finally to go to that fucking show!" Audrey had screeched.

Kradle remembered smiling in the dark, surrounded by cleaning bottles and the smell of dampness, the heaviness of the wrench in his hand.

He opened his eyes now as the phone buzzed in his lap. A message. He opened it. The number was unfamiliar, not one he had dialed, not one he recognized from the list.

Will talk about Kradle murders in person only.

Kradle tried to answer, feeling sick with exhilaration. His fingers were trembling so bad he had to type the word out in full twice.

Where?

The phone buzzed. An address in Vegas. Kradle gave a sharp sigh of disappointment.

You will have to come to Mesquite, he typed.

I'll be at that address at midnight. You're not there, don't talk.

Who is this? Kradle typed. He waited for an answer. None came. He called Celine. She didn't answer either. He called four more times. The dog sank down beside him in the gravel and put its head on his thigh. A little sunshine had leaked into the desolate, empty corner of the world where they sat, and it was picking up lashes of chocolate brown in the animal's fur. Kradle smoothed the creature's head as the phone rang and rang.

It was dark by the time Celine arrived in her driveway, which seemed to have doubled in length while she was away. Though she had checked her phone, and none of the media coverage of the incident at Rancho Salvaje Wildlife Park had mentioned her by name, her neighbors seemed to know she had danced closely with death. Across the street, she spied a couple she had never spoken to huddled in their doorway, openly watching her wave off the cab that had driven her home. As she turned to shut the front door behind her, she saw a man standing on the corner with an impatient little dog, looking toward her property. Celine had never interacted with any of her neighbors. There seemed no point. She was never home long enough to make meaningful connections with them, to share stories on front lawns, to borrow tools, to remark at kids learning to ride bikes on the sidewalk. Celine's life was at Pronghorn. It felt like years since she had walked its halls, and she yearned for the clanging of doors and sounding of alarms as she closed the door and flicked the deadbolt.

Her phone was jammed with missed call notifications and unread messages, all of which she had ignored as she sat in an isolation room at the Mesa View Regional Hospital. She had been escorted there by members of Trinity's team after being rescued from the woods. She had lain on the bed in the room, listened to the noises out in the hall—people talking, walking, rolling gurneys. Sounds of life. No one seemed to know what to do with her, uninjured yet numbed with trauma, sectioned off from the world in her little room, awaiting instructions and avoiding the press. Celine supposed she was not a high priority. There would be the teenage girl to question. Brassen's body and the body of the fallen tactical team member to deal with. Another US Marshal would need to be assigned as head of the Pronghorn inmate recovery effort. Celine didn't care. She put her head on the pillow and let her phone buzz and buzz and buzz. When someone came for her, she asked them if Trinity Parker was dead. The man, who she'd never seen before, said that was classified information. Celine gave up and went home.

On the cab ride home she learned of the death of "a second US marshal" at the Rancho Salvaje Wildlife Park. She thought about Trinity's body slumping to the ground, how the fall had made her seem like a rag doll when only seconds before she had been a powerful beast terrorizing the girl on the ground.

Celine sank now onto her couch. Jake the cat came and tried to breeze past her, offering no more than his usual tail flick against the back of her arm as consolation. She grabbed the cat by the hind legs as it reached the end of the couch and dragged it back to her, where it struggled, yowling with horror.

"I don't care." Celine hugged the animal to her. "I don't care. I need this right now. I need this."

She hugged the cat until the yowling turned to growling, her chin buried in the fur at the top of its head. When she let it go, the animal sprinted away, claws skittering for traction on the floor.

Celine opened her phone and looked at the notifications. There were sixteen calls from a number she didn't recognize, and a bunch of text messages.

Need your help. K.

Please please please answer.

It's JK. Pick up.

Have got something major and need to be in Vegas by midnight. Can't get there. Need you to go.

Trying to get out of Mesquite. Road blocks. Will keep trying.

CELINE WHERE R U?

There was only one missed call from Keeps's number. And a single message.

Talk 2 me.

Celine opened his number, let her thumb hover over the call button. Then she closed the message, went back to Kradle's messages, and dialed him.

"Oh, thank god," he said when she answered. "Listen, I—"

"No, you listen," Celine seethed. "I killed someone today."

Celine waited. Kradle didn't speak. She heard cars passing in the background of his call. Wind rattling through the line. A dog barking. The wilds of the fugitive life. She didn't realize how close to tears she was until she tried to speak again.

"I talked a guy to his death," Celine said. "He was scared. He . . . He didn't want to do it. He trusted me.

And I walked him right into it. I said it was safe and I knew it wasn't. And then . . . And-and then we ran and someone was shooting at us, and Trinity . . ."

"Celine?"

"Three people died in front of me, Kradle."

"Celine," Kradle said. "You're okay. You're okay. You're okay."

His voice was gentle. Warm. She'd never heard it that way, and it pulled her out of the long descent into misery. For most of the time she had known him, Celine had listened to John Kradle's prison voice. The voice that had to be strong, unflinching, confident, because prison was a place where the slightest waver could indicate to a nearby predator—whether staff or inmate—that a person was vulnerable. She'd heard John Kradle's mocking voice. She'd heard him challenging, taunting, raging, but she had never heard him comforting, and for a moment she had to stop and check the number she had dialed to make sure there was no mistake.

"Seriously, though," Kradle said after a time. "When you're finished feeling sorry for yourself, I need your help."

"You are such a dick!"

"I am a dick," he agreed. "But listen." He explained the call to In Focus Studios, the messages that came from the unknown number, the address in Vegas. Celine held her head and felt the weight of the day crush her spirit, and with it the very last remnants of who she was before the breakout, of the woman with the keys, the rules, the rock-solid sense of who was good and who was bad and what that meant for her.

"I can't believe I'm going to say this," she said when he was done talking.

"What?" Kradle asked.

Celine drew a deep breath, let it out slowly.

"Tell me where you are," she said. "I'm going to come and pick you up."

CHAPTER 35

For four days, Randy Derlick had been stationed a
the desert roadblock closest to Las Vegas from th
south: a small, slapped-together job that had bee
set up at short notice and never strengthened. H
guessed that the brains running the Pronghorn recov
ery effort probably had minimum quotas in place fo
roadblocks and the people staffing them. Most polic
ing, he had discovered in his nine months on the jol
was about meeting certain numbers. The setup of fiv
checkpoints was probably more about keeping to
number written in a handbook about prison break
outs somewhere, and less about the chances of actu
ally catching an inmate. An escapee from Pronghor
would have to get through four other roadblocks t
get to where the twenty-one-year-old probationar
police officer stood now on the asphalt, and that
if they were coming from the south, having loope
around the city for some obscure reason before decid
ing to head in. If they made it past Randy and hi
fellow officers, it would be another couple of miles be

fore they saw the barest hint of pink neon lighting, cheap hookers, and palm trees.

So for four days, Randy had done nothing but wave cars, vans, trucks, motorcycles, and every other known type of vehicle into the bay by the side of the road and search fruitlessly for escaped prisoners. As the days wore on, his hopes of finding a real-life fugitive stowed away in someone's trunk or pretzeled into a box in the back of a cargo truck were dwindling, and his irritation with tourists from the West Coast was increasing. There was only so many times a guy could hear, "How 'bout that breakout, huh? Catch any bad guys yet?" before he wanted to blow out his own or somebody else's brains. The one highlight from his searches was the RVs full of sorority girls heading into the city of sin for Christmas fun. On day two, a blonde with big tits had run a hand up the inside of his thigh as he bent over a huge cooler searching for stowaways. While it had been a cheap thrill, all it left him with was a hankering for vodka pre-mixers on ice and a hard-on that wouldn't quit for the rest of the day.

If he enjoyed anything about standing in the desert sun, sweating into his jockey shorts and staring at the unchanging rocky horizon, it was shooting the breeze, or lack thereof, with his teammates. Somehow, the last-ditch roadblock between Pronghorn and Vegas had ended up being staffed entirely by rookies, none of whom Randy had ever met before. Vinnie from Enterprise District, Tuko from Paradise South, and Randy from Silverado Ranch bonded over their frustrated desire to find anything interesting in a car headed for the great gambling city behind them. And when

Tuko nabbed a bag of weed from a car on day two and smoked it in the cruiser, and Vinnie suggested a rotation of afternoon naps in the shade on day two, Randy knew he was with a good crew.

The van appeared on the distant horizon just as Tuko's phone bleeped in his pocket. The young officer was leaning on the road partition, his arms folded, his aviator sunglasses like devil eyes, colored sunset red. The text message and the van were the first things to happen in forty minutes, so Randy felt a little buzz of excitement in his chest. He watched the speck in the distance become a watery ball, then sprout two black tire legs as the van grew closer.

"Aw, shit."

"What is it?" Randy glanced over.

"My buddy," Tuko groaned. "He's on a checkpoint in the north. They just caught an inmate."

"You serious?" Vinnie was sitting nearby in the driver's seat of the cruiser, with the window rolled down and his elbow on the sill. "God*damn* it."

"Anybody good?" Randy asked.

"Nah," Tuko sighed. "Some medium security guy. Smash'n'grab robber. Found him curled up under a blanket in the back seat."

"Criminal genius."

"This is such bullshit." Vinnie thumped the steering wheel. "I just want one inmate. I don't even care if he's minimum. He could be a tax evader. A fucking DUI dirtbag. I just want to bring *somebody* in."

"Not me," Randy said.

"Huh?"

"I don't want just anybody," Randy said. "I want someone with money. Somebody who's gonna slide me a tasty bite so I'll let them through the roadblock."

"Oh, yeah." Tuko smiled. "Like a, like a . . . bank robber. He just hit a place in some shitty town down in Mexico, and now he's all cashed up. He wants to get to Vegas for a big score, so he slides us ten grand each to say we never saw him come through here."

"Or a rich guy." Randy lit a cigarette, his eyes on the approaching van. "He's been locked up in Pronghorn for ten years for trying to kill his wife. Now he's out and he wants to finish the job. So he transfers a million bucks each to our bank accounts." He grinned. "We take off into the sunset. Rich-ass motherfuckers."

"You two ought to write a screenplay," Vinnie yawned.

"It could happen." Tuko shrugged.

"Yeah." Randy nodded at the van. "This van right here might be full of the big four ace cards. Hamsi driving. Carrington riding shotgun. Marco taking a nap in the back . . ."

"Schmitz hanging on underneath the van like Pacino in *Cape Fear*." Tuko laughed, holding up his hands like they were claws.

"They got Hamsi already," Vinnie said. "And Carrington's dead. Marco never left Pronghorn. He's a million years old. They found him in the prison infirmary, taking a nap. Don't you guys watch the news?" He shook his head. "And it was DeNiro in *Cape Fear*, for Chrissake."

"I love that movie," Randy said. He took a few steps toward the van as it slowed for the last hundred yards, and held up a hand to halt it. Two young women in the front seats: tattoos, glasses, college types, probably. Feminists. Randy went to the driver's side and Tuko headed for the passenger side.

"Ladies," Randy said as the driver rolled down

her window. Randy heard Beyoncé on the radio and smelled pomegranates. Disappointment flooded him. "What you got in the back?"

"Tampons."

"*Tampons*?" Tuko said from where he crouched at the passenger-side wheel, shining a flashlight beneath the van for signs of Max Cady–type characters.

"We're from an organization in South LA called Debbie's Dignity. You've probably heard of us. We supply care packages for homeless women in Los Angeles." The girl tossed a little pink backpack through the window at Randy. He unzipped it and glanced in. Womanly things. Bottles, packages, baggies.

"So now you're spreading the hobo-love in Vegas, are you?" Randy said.

"We've had a surplus of stock. Christmas givers. People have been very charitable."

"Uh-huh," he said. He reached through the window to hand the bag back. 'Tis the season, all right."

The passenger leaned over to take the bag from Randy. Her paisley top slid up her forearm, exposing a tattoo of a rope swirling in and out of itself as it wound around her arm.

Randy felt all the hairs on his arms rise.

"Interesting tattoo you have there," he said as she settled back in her seat. He said it just to see her reaction. The girl glanced at her sleeve, tugged it down.

"Oh, yeah. Stupid."

"What's it mean?" Randy leaned his forearms on the windowsill.

"Togetherness," the girl said. "Like, uh, loyalty. Being bound together with someone."

"Oh, really?" Randy said.

"They're all good." Tuko came to Randy's side. "Ladies, you can shoot through."

Randy stepped back. Then something pushed him forward again, an urge that seemed to come from nowhere. It made him shove a hand into the windowsill again just as the van lurched forward.

"Do you ever get any shit for it?" Randy asked.

"What?" the passenger said.

"Your partner said we could go." The driver glared at Randy.

"Just hold on. I want to know if you ever get any shit for it," Randy said. He turned to Tuko. "She's got a rope tattoo."

"So?" Tuko frowned.

"So sometimes people interpret tattoos in different ways." Randy shrugged. "My dad was a tattoo artist. He had a shop back home. In Texas. I've seen tattoos like that. The rope with the swirls going in and out."

"I have too," Tuko said. "The hipsters are getting all kinds of weird tattoos. Arrows and ropes and swallows. It's, like, symbolism and shit."

"What's going on?" Vinnie had appeared out of nowhere, his hands in his pockets. Tuko and Randy backed off from the van. As they assembled a few yards away, it seemed to Randy that night had slammed down on them like a cupped hand. The horizon was gone. Dust swirled in the air, gold and thick as smoke in the van's headlights.

"Something doesn't feel right here," he said.

"It's a fucking tattoo." Tuko rolled his eyes. "Jeez. She also has a dolphin tattoo on her neck. You see that one?"

"No."

"He was like this yesterday about the guy with the beard."

"It looked like a fake beard!" Randy said.

"It was very thick," Vinnie conceded.

"Listen"—Randy huffed an excited breath—"we're supposed to be on the lookout for skinheads, right? Skinheads love rope tattoos. I've seen dozens of them in my dad's shop. Nooses and swirly ropes. Ropes spelling out letters. It's a thing from a book that they like. The, uh . . . *The Day of the Ropes*."

"You're thinking of *The Day of the Jackal*," Vinnie said.

"No, I'm not."

"They're not skinheads," Tuko said. "They're feminists."

"When I said something about the tattoo," Randy said, "she pulled her shirt down, not up. It's not a hipster tattoo." He waited. The guys weren't reacting. "I just—"

"You're bored, Randy," Tuko said. "If you want to strip a vehicle, let's wait for something fun. You want to get knee-deep in tampons and Vagisil? Because I don't."

"Look." Vinnie put his hands up in surrender. "Let's just go back, we'll quickly open the van and we can—"

Thumping. That's what the gunfire sounded like. Randy's mind told him an old generator had started up behind him, and the rapid thumping was its engine turning over, coughing to life. But he felt the thumping through his center, three hard knocks against his back, and the big black bowl of the Nevada sky whipped downward from above him as he arched and hit the ground. He rolled, saw another staccato blast of white light as the shooter rounded the back of the van and sprayed the three officers again. Randy felt Tuko against his legs, fallen sideways, already dead. He heard Vinnie give a wet cough from somewhere to his right. Randy reached for the gun on his hip, but the driver of the van was standing over him now, and she kicked his wrist away.

And then Randy saw a man whose face he had spent hours memorizing. Burke David Schmitz walked up and stood over him with the AR-15 still clutched in his hands, his finger on the trigger guard. The crew from the van talked, their voices barely reaching Randy as he lay dying at their feet.

"One more roadblock," Burke said. He let out a long, disappointed sigh. "We were so close."

"Sorry, Burke," the woman with the rope tattoo said. "I'll go get the shovel."

"Hurry up," Burke said. "I'm hungry."

Randy reached up, tried to say something to them all, but all he got for his efforts was them staring down at him as Burke lined up the barrel of the gun against Randy's forehead.

CHAPTER 36

Celine parked the car on a side road leading to the ballpark and looked around. There was no game, though the street seemed to tell the story of a recent celebration, the asphalt festooned with French fries and take-out containers. She sat with the phone in her lap, watching a rat inspecting the contents of a brown paper bag, the thrumming of a nearby club leaking into the brick walls around her, making it sound as though she was waiting in the artery of a great living being. She counted down ten minutes on her phone, then got out, looked up the alley toward the stadium entrance, then back the way she had come, to the main street. A night jogger passed and was gone before Celine could really focus on her. With her nerves making her scalp itch, she dropped her keys and her phone on the driver's seat and raised her hands in the air.

"Would you just get in the damned car!" she yelled. "I haven't got all night!"

John Kradle emerged from his hiding place: a stairwell above a dumpster twenty or more yards down the alley. A large black dog trotted out from behind the dumpster itself. The dog walked up and, without acknowledging Celine at all, leaped in the open driver's-side door, crossed to the front passenger seat, and sat down.

Kradle glanced nervously behind him as he approached. In the thin light Celine saw that he sported thick gray stubble. His hoodie was bloodstained and there was dirt on the knees of his jeans. A dirty hand with blackened fingernails rose and swiped nervously at his face.

"This isn't a trap," Celine said.

"If you say so."

"You look terrible. I've watched *The Fugitive* a thousand times," she said. "Great movie. Harrison Ford looks immaculate throughout, even after he jumps off the dam. Look at you. Four days in Mesquite and you're an island castaway."

Kradle seemed distracted, didn't take the bait. Celine chewed her lip. It was her nerves making her babble, the blaring alarm bells ringing in her head at the very sight of inmate number 1707, one of her men, walking and talking in the free world, wearing civilian clothes, going to the passenger side of her car. She was walking in a nightmare. She slid into the car as Kradle shooed the dog into the back seat and sat down.

"Did you bring the key?" he asked.

She opened the glove compartment and took out a handcuff key. He lifted the wrist that had the cuff connected to it. Celine looked at the swinging, empty cuff that was covered with blood.

"Oh," she said. "That's why you . . ."

"The thumb."

"Don't say it." She held her throat.

"Why I cut off Homer's thumb? He shackled himself to me."

"Are you deaf? I said don't say it."

"Harder to cut off a thumb than you might think," Kradle mused. "Lots of connecting tissue. Sinew. Veins. Tendons."

"Stop!"

Kradle laughed as he uncuffed himself, pocketed the cuffs and key. They sat in silence for a moment.

"This is weird," he said.

"Sure is."

"I've never seen you in civilian clothes."

"Likewise."

"This is your car." He ran a hand over the dashboard. "I'm in Captain Osbourne's car."

"It's my neighbor's car. I borrowed it. Mine's in the parking lot of a wildlife park. But let's not talk about that, either," Celine said. She started the engine. "The less we put into words what I'm doing, the better I'll feel about it."

"You mean, assisting a fugitive?"

"Yes. It's a felony, but I'm sure you knew that. Five years in federal prison and a hefty fine. Certainly the loss of my job, my credibility, and probably my sanity. The worst thing that can happen to a prison guard is finding yourself on the other side of the bars."

"You're doing a lot of talking for someone who says they don't want to talk," Kradle said.

"Right."

"Did you bring food?"

"At your feet," she said, and pointed. Kradle picked up the bag and pulled out a McDonald's burger, unwrapped it with shaking hands.

"Oh, god," he moaned. Celine cringed as she drove,

listening to his munching and moaning. "Oh, god. Ohhhhh god. Oh god. Oh god."

"There's a loudly orgasming fugitive in my car," Celine sighed. "So what's with the dog?"

"Just someone I met on my travels who recognized how great it is to be on the John Kradle train. Like you," he said through a mouthful of burger. He handed the dog a chunk of bun.

"Don't do that."

"He's hungry."

"What kind of person spends five years in prison and four days on the lam waiting to have their first taste of takeout, and then shares that takeout with a dog?"

"This guy."

"Talk to me about this message," Celine said.

He opened his phone, looked at the message. "*Will only talk about Kradle murders in person.*"

"No indication who it's from?"

"No."

"But you think it's someone from In Focus Studios?"

"Yeah."

"What even is *The Frances Falkner Show*?" Celine asked.

"You've never seen it?"

"I've heard of it, but I haven't paid much attention to what it actually is."

"It's trash TV." Kradle pulled up his hood as they stopped at a traffic light. People passed on the crosswalk before them, oblivious to his presence. "It's in the *Jerry Springer, Ricki Lake, Jenny Jones* kind of category."

"Oh."

"Christine never missed it. And she would watch the reruns. Sometimes she would search for the people who had appeared in certain episodes online, try to find out what had happened in their lives after the show, how they dealt with the problems they'd presented to Frances."

"She sounds like a very serious fan," Celine said.

"She was. She liked drama. Her favorite shows were all about people yelling at each other. Devastating secrets revealed, betrayals, back-stabbings, scandals."

"And you weren't into that?"

"No." He smiled. "Christine and I were very different people. She was sort of . . . dramatic. Theatrical. You know me. I'm a bit more simple."

Celine shifted uncomfortably in her seat. His words rattled in her brain. *You know me.* She had indeed spoken to John Kradle almost every day for the past five years. She had passed his cell and seen him sleeping, eating, crying, bouncing off the walls with boredom bordering on madness. It made her uncomfortable now, how well she knew, and also didn't know, him. The very sound of him breathing in the seat beside her seemed familiar, but she couldn't say yet, one way or another, whether she believed he had killed innocent people.

"So people come on the show to reveal secrets?" she asked, trying to focus.

"Sometimes," Kradle said. "I managed to track down the episode where she attended the taping. I've watched the footage. The subject was *My Psycho Father Doesn't Know I'm Gay!*"

"Seriously?" Celine said. "In 2015?"

"They've cleaned up their act lately, but not by much." Kradle was fishing around in a box of fries, shoving some in his face and handing others over his shoulder to the dog. "On this episode, a bunch of people come out on the show to their crazy dads. There's a woman who reveals she's a lesbian to her father, who's a welder. Pretty tough dude. There's a lot of build-up to suggest he's going to lose his shit, but he doesn't. It's kind of cute. There are other less gentle reactions. Some people throw chairs."

"You watched the episode in full?"

"Yeah."

"And you saw her in the audience?"

"I did."

"Anything happen?"

"No." Kradle drew a long breath, shrugged helplessly. "She sits in the audience, claps and cheers when everybody else claps and cheers. There's an empty seat next to her. She bought two tickets but couldn't find anybody to go with her."

"Why didn't you go with her?" Celine asked.

"The show is not my thing. They basically just get people on camera and pay them to be publicly humiliated. And, aside from that, I was angry with her," Kradle said, like it was the most obvious thing in the world. The silence swelled, and enveloped the car. With no food left, the dog sank across the back seat of the car and blew out a huge sigh, smacked its lips.

"I've never denied the fact that when Christine returned, I was mad as hell," Kradle said.

"What happened that day?" Celine asked.

Kradle smoothed the knees of his jeans and watched the town rolling by, becoming suburbs stretching toward the desert.

"Christine and Mason were at the house," Kradle said. "I went on a job by myself. The plan was that

I'd be home by four o'clock. Audrey was going to be there already. We were all going to have dinner together. I kept meeting Christine for meals—first in a diner, then at the house, thinking eventually it would get easier. When you're eating you don't have to talk the whole time, and you've got something to look at. Your food."

"Okay."

"Tensions were high." Kradle nestled back in the seat beside Celine, covered a yawn. "Audrey never liked me. I think she figured I was a meathead, and nothing I ever did around her challenged that theory. And all the time Christine was gone, we didn't speak. She didn't offer any help. So that was weird. What's worse is that Christine was trying to build something with Mason, but it wasn't really working. She was trying to slap a Band-Aid over a wound that was going to take a lifetime to heal, if it ever healed at all. About two o'clock that day I got a call from the kid saying Christine had bought him a bubble machine."

"A bubble machine?"

"Yeah," Kradle sighed. "It's like this: When Mason was a boy, a toddler, I bought him a bubble-making machine. It was this little box you poured dish soap into that spewed out thousands and thousands of bubbles. He went mad for it. Running all around the yard, squealing and laughing and trying to catch the bubbles."

"Okay."

"I told Christine that at one of our meetings," Kradle said. "So she goes and buys him a bubble machine. She presented it to him at the house, poured the dish soap in, and set it off in the yard. Well, it did what it was supposed to do. It spewed out all the bubbles. But the kid is fifteen now. Who buys a teenager a bubble machine? Mason found the entire thing incredibly forced."

"She was trying to re-create a magical moment," Celine said.

Kradle nodded. "Exactly."

"And it didn't work."

"No," he said. "It was wildly off target with him. He froze up and didn't know what to say. Christine got upset that Mason wasn't getting into the moment, and Mason got upset that Christine was upset. They both called me, angry. And I sided with him."

Celine said nothing.

"Imagine this. I'm underneath some old lady's house, trying to fix some creaky floorboards. I got dirt in my eyes and I'm drenched in sweat and I'm fielding calls and texts about this bubble machine." Kradle heaved a sigh. "I just snapped. I told Christine she was being a spoiled little princess. Mason rejected her and her little bubble machine performance. Rightfully so. He's fifteen, not five. And you know what? She needed to taste a little rejection. It was her getting exactly what she deserved."

Celine swallowed. She turned onto the highway.

"What?" Kradle said eventually.

"You know how all this sounds, right?" Celine said. "*I was angry. I just snapped. Christine was getting exactly what she deserved.*"

"Yes, I do," Kradle said. "I know how bad it sounds, because I said all those things in my initial interviews, before I'd called in a lawyer, and then they were all played back to the entire courtroom. But I'm saying them again to you now because they're the truth. And you want the truth, right?"

"Right," Celine said, and she meant it. They fell silent, and the highway stretched ahead of them, a long, dark path that sliced the earth in half, forming two identical black slabs of desert. Celine thought about the truth—how precious it was, how she had never really received it. Because while she had sat as a teenager and listened to her grandfather tell her that he'd spared her life because of a fence, and psychologists had told her over the years that he'd murdered her family because he was a narcissistic sociopath, Celine knew she still didn't have the truth of the matter. She would never know what those moments had been like when her grandfather made the decision to kill everyone. She imagined him sitting in his chair in the den and sipping wine and watching her little brothers playing with their trucks on the carpet. Him musing about his plan and deciding that they must be included. Had it been a moment like that, months or years before the murders? An otherwise ordinary evening filled with dark thoughts? Or had something shifted on the morning of the event? Had one last domino finally fallen? Had he gone down to the barn to shoot apples with the boys and relented to a sudden urge? She imagined him taking his gun from the cabinet, checking it, loading it, heading down the hill. Passing Nanna in the kitchen. Her father in the den. She didn't know if he had said anything to anybody at the house before he left to kill the children. Whether there'd been some kind of cryptic goodbye that alerted no one to the danger that was approaching, yet satisfied some sick desire inside him to have the final word.

As her thoughts turned darker and darker, Celine glanced over and realized John Kradle was asleep with his head against the window and his hands in his lap.

If he was innocent, Celine thought, then he still had a chance to get that truth. To find whoever had done to him the worst thing a human could do, and ask him why. Celine might never have been able to understand the pain that had been such a large part of her life since she was child, the pain that had formed and deformed her as an adult. But John Kradle had a shot. And she was helping him. There was no denying it. He was in her car now, and her hands were on the wheel, and before them stretched the road that would take him to her house, to a plan, maybe to his freedom. Celine felt an aching in her chest, a joyful, shimmering kind of pain, relief and excitement at the idea of seeing the truth uncovered through the fight of another person. It wouldn't be the same as having it for herself, but it was something.

She wiped at a tear. Carefully, silently, she reached over and took Kradle's hand. It was warm and hard in hers.

And then it moved.

"Whoa." Kradle stirred. "What are you doing?"

"Nothing." Celine snatched her hand back. "Nothing."

"Were you . . . trying to hold hands with me?"

"No."

"You were."

"I was having a moment." Celine sighed. "Just . . . Just shut up."

"That was so awkward."

"Go back to sleep."

"I would, but I'm afraid you'll hug me or something."

Celine gripped the wheel, shook her head, her cheeks flaming.

"God," she said. "I hate you so much."

Celine was pulling into her garage when Kradle roused in the seat beside her, giving a full body stretch and scratching at his scalp and stubble the way she had seen him do inside Pronghorn. He snapped to attention as the walls of the garage enveloped the car, turning and watching the automatic door close behind them.

"I told you, this isn't a trap," Celine said.

They had stopped twice on the road from Mesquite, Celine talking her way through searches at roadblocks with her prison ID while Kradle lay curled in the trunk of the car. Between the roadblocks, the inmate had slept soundly with his head against the window.

They went inside, Jake the cat trotting to meet them at the door to the garage and arching into a defensive position at the sight of the dog.

"It's okay." Celine put a hand out. "It's fine, we just—"

Jake lifted wild yellow eyes with huge pupils to Celine, the glare of the betrayed, and darted away.

"Of course." Celine let her hands fall. "Because it's my fault you brought a dog."

"He'll get over it," Kradle said.

While Kradle showered, Celine went to the couch and opened her phone. Another message from Keeps sat on the screen.

I'm not a bad guy, Celine, it read. *And I like you.*

She swiped the message away, turned on her TV, and connected the phone to the big screen in front of her. She opened YouTube and searched *Frances Falkner Psycho Father Gay*.

Celine recognized Frances Falkner in the thumbnail image of the first video that came up. The petite brunette appeared on the screen wearing a turquoise pants suit and holding a microphone. Behind her stood a crowd, clapping and chanting her name, breaking into cheers as a guitar riff closed off the show's opening credits. The camera swirled in to focus on Falkner from above the stage, leaving glimpses of the studio setup—hot lights in the rafters, a security crew guarding the edges of the brick room.

"Wow! Wow!" Frances flipped her hair, adjusted the question cards pinned between her fingers and the mic. "Thanks very much. Thank you. Good crowd. Back at ya, everybody! Have a seat! Have a seat!"

Celine cringed, slipping off her shoes and putting her sock-covered feet on the coffee table.

"Today my guests are here to reveal intimate details of their private sexual lives to people they love the most." Falkner grinned at the camera over the microphone and raised a coy brow. "They say their families won't accept them for who they are in the bedroom, and they're here to tell them that ain't right!"

"*That ain't right!*" the crowd cheered.

"We're gonna find out what happens when deeply held prejudices clash with family loyalties." Falkner smiled. "Let's start with our first guest!"

The crowd erupted into cheers. Celine watched a young Asian woman dressed in gray work coveralls walk out onto a stage and take a seat in one of two empty, plush pink armchairs.

"Please meet Tammy," Falkner said as the camera

cut back to her standing among the crowd. "Tammy says she and her father have been working together at his welding business since she was a kid. But Tammy wants her father to know it's not men who make her sparks fly. Tammy, tell us all about it!"

"Oh, Jesus." Celine slumped back on the couch.

By the time Kradle appeared at the end of the couch, Celine had watched the welder's daughter confess to her father about her girlfriend and the other women she had dated. She listened to the audience coo over their hug, and scream with delight as the next guest, a male flight attendant, revealed to his police officer brother that he was gay, only to have the brother pick up a chair and hurl it across the stage at him. Kradle's hair was wet, and he was wearing the clothes Celine had picked up from Walmart on her way to Mesquite. He was drying his ears with the corner of Celine's favorite towel.

"I haven't smelled this good in years," he said, bending to sniff his armpit.

"Did you use my toothbrush?" Celine grimaced.

"Was there something else I was supposed to use?"

Celine closed her eyes. "Note to self: Burn all belongings."

He sat and they watched a teenage boy tell his mother he was having a secret love affair with his first cousin.

"This show is terrible," he said.

"Yeah. But it's probably not the worst thing out there."

"Hmm."

"Where's Christine?" Celine asked, handing Kradle the remote. He watched the screen carefully for a while, then paused the clip. He walked to the screen and pointed to a blurry image of a plump woman sitting three rows from the back of the studio. An empty gray chair sat beside her.

"Right there."

"Okay."

They watched the show in full. At the end, while credits slid slowly across the bottom half of the screen, members of the audience stood and asked questions or made comments about the guests, who were all assembled on the stage in pink chairs.

"Does Christine make a comment?" Celine asked.

"No," Kradle said.

They watched a woman in a red dress stand and take the mic from Frances.

"I just wanna say y'all need to have your heads checked." The woman cast a finger over the people on the stage. "What you're doin' is against God's word, and—"

The audience exploded with jeers.

"And it's Adam and Eve, not Adam and—"

The camera panned over the people in pink chairs on the stage. Some of the guests were nodding. Others were calling back insults. The welder reached over and hugged his daughter into his side.

"Well, I feel stupider," Celine said as the In Focus Studios logo flashed onscreen. She looked over. Kradle was asleep with his head hanging against the back of the couch, his mouth open. As she watched, he drew a snoring breath. Celine guessed it would take some time to recover from the fugitive life. She opened her phone to disconnect it from the television and paused with her finger above the episode she had just played.

The length of the video was displayed on the

thumbnail. It read 33 minutes and 3 seconds. As she glanced down the list of videos, she read the numbers indicating the length of the other episodes.

44 minutes, 19 seconds.

46 minutes, 3 seconds.

41 minutes, 20 seconds.

Celine scrolled. There were no other episodes of *The Frances Falkner Show* from season eight that were under forty minutes. She went back to her initial search, opened a collection of videos marked season five, and scrolled through the running time of the videos. As her excitement built, she reached over and slapped Kradle in the chest with the back of her hand.

"Something's been cut out," she said.

"Hmm?"

"Of the episode. A segment's been cut out."

"Trade you," Kradle murmured, turning his head away. "Five sachets of coffee."

Celine got up and pushed Kradle sideways on the couch until he lay down, then lifted his legs onto the seat.

"Don't get too comfortable," she said. "We leave in an hour."

"Hmm."

She went into the bedroom and flicked on the ensuite light, throwing light on her bed, where two figures curled side by side. Jake made a small, round ball near the pillow on the left side of the bed. The black dog made a bigger ball of fur on the right side.

CHAPTER 37

Burke David Schmitz took his blue snow cone from the food truck vendor and made his way through the crowd to the edge of the rink. On the ice, there seemed to be three types of people skating: confident zoomers, who twirled and skidded and danced around the inner circle; semi-confident skaters, who shuffled awkwardly in a wider circle around the blue-lit rink, now and then slipping and thumping dramatically onto the hard, white surface; and an outer ring of newcomers to the sport, who gripped and giggled their way around the edge of the rink, gloved hands trembling as they slid along a surface painted with colorful snowflakes. Schmitz pulled the edges of his hoodie up around his face, adjusted the fake glasses on the bridge of his nose and scanned the crowd. Mostly white faces. The following morning, Christmas morning, there would probably be a good mixture of races in attendance, but what mattered would be the colors of the targets as they lined up on the big stage at the far end of the rink. For now, the stage was empty. A sound technician was fiddling with a microphone mounted behind a podium. Burke looked at the huge Christmas tree dominating the left side of the stage, twinkling with fiber-optic stars transitioning between pink, purple, and blue.

Burke looked at the ice in front of him and thought about a mixed crowd of people, rubbing shoulders, exchanging smiles, some of them running into each other, gripping each other's arms, tumbling to the ice. He thought about the ice itself, a huge, circular slab sitting like a jewel in the middle of the desert, exactly where it didn't belong.

Beyond the rink, the Planet Hollywood Resort hugged the park in which the rink lay, at the center of a makeshift winter wonderland. The hotel was a huge black mass in a sea of buildings lit with hundreds of gold windows, strips of flashing globes, upturned golden cones of light from inground lights. Along the front of the building, painted wooden panels were hung with signs detailing the building's renovation timeline.

Burke stood licking his blue snow cone, running his eyes along the wall that sectioned off the front of the hotel. It was ten feet tall, windowless, seamless, a perfect barrier that at that moment stopped civilians interfering with the construction site that lay beyond it, but on Christmas Day would prevent panicked, screaming civilians from escaping that way.

Burke could just see the faint traces of #VegasStrong tags that had been painted on the panels back in 2017. Like the memory of Stephen Paddock's massacre, the tags had been exposed to time and had lost their strength. Rain, the searing Nevada sun, splatters of dirt and paint, and the coming in contact with the shoulders of passers-by had taken the edge off the lettering, but Burke knew that the ink would be layers deep under the surface, seeped there, immoveable.

What he would do on Christmas Day wasn't just going to deeply stain the memories of men, women, and children in Nevada. It would not be rubbed down and faded by time. What he would do would blast right through the world, splinter it, shatter it, crush some of it to dust. Because Burke was not some lunatic with no discernible motivation cutting through young lives at a concert. He was a soldier with a specific target, a strategic intent, a master plan.

On the ice, a family with two little blonde girls were shuffling haltingly along the middle circle, grinning and holding hands. Burke turned, put an elbow on the edge of the rink, and watched. The family was heading for the stage, the Christmas tree, and, beyond it, a line of trucks backed bumper to bumper containing equipment for the Christmas Day extravaganza on the ice. Burke turned again and surveyed the third wall that corralled the ice rink, a second row of wide, high trucks, these painted bright colors and hung with signs. The food trucks were giving off a mixture of enticing smells, the strongest of which was the Mexican truck, which had just put on a fresh batch of ground beef. Burke locked eyes with the woman behind the counter of the snow cone truck, who was squeezing red food coloring out of a ketchup bottle onto a dome of ice in a pointed cone. The woman raised the cone in a small salute, and Burke nodded back. From where he stood he could see the sleeve of her shirt slide back down over the rope tattoo on her forearm.

He turned back to the ice. The family with the little girls had stopped to rest against the barrier. Burke heard Christmas carols on the wind and smiled.

CHAPTER 38

An hour's solid rest on the couch, and the snippets of sleep he had snuck in the car, had filled Kradle with a disproportionate amount of energy. The shower, the fresh clothes, and the first substantial meal he'd had since the breakout had probably also helped. He sat in the passenger seat of the car, itching to get going, while Celine readied herself inside the house, now and then passing the door to the garage, a dog or cat following close behind. He honked the horn a couple of times and she leaned into the doorway and flipped him the bird before disappearing again.

By the time they were pulling out onto the street, his heart was hammering in his chest and his fingers were dancing on his knees.

"Would you chill?" Celine asked. "You're making me nervous."

"You should be nervous. You're driving a wanted man to a secret meeting with a mystery person in the middle of the night."

"Stop."

"Pretty ballsy stuff."

"Yeah, well." Celine shrugged one shoulder. "I'm a pretty ballsy chick."

"I haven't said thanks yet."

"Any time is good!"

"Thank you," Kradle said. "Although, now that I say it, it doesn't seem like enough."

"It's not."

"I appreciate it," he said. "After everything you've been through."

"Kradle, I don't want to talk about that with you. At all. Not ever."

"I'm not talking about what happened to your family. I'm talking about what I put you through at Pronghorn."

"You think you're the most problematic inmate I've ever had?" She rolled her eyes.

"I do."

"Well, you're not."

"What about the countdown?" He was smiling. "What about the Valentine's Day cards I sent you from Satan? What about Fingernail Jesus?"

"Urgh, Fingernail Jesus," Celine groaned, remembering the six-month period when Kradle had refused to shave, have a haircut, or trim his fingernails. He had ended up a taloned, Christ-like figure who preached nonsensical commandments at passing officers.

They drove toward Vegas. Through five checkpoints, Celine showed her ID, smiled and joked with the checkpoint police officers about being the angry Pronghorn correctional officer who introduced the world to the five most wanted men from the breakout. A young officer took a selfie with her at the third checkpoint. At the fifth, on the crest of a hill looking down toward the valley where the great shimmering city lay, the tone was more solemn.

"They got no word from them at all?" she heard one officer ask another.

"Nothin'," the officer responded. He was a young man, looking at his phone. "The cruiser is gone. The barricades are gone. It's as if they just bailed out. I'm calling Tuko but he won't pick up."

Celine stopped behind a Costco just inside the city limits and let Kradle out of the trunk. They followed Route 95 through a block of shopping malls north of Summerlin, the blazing white lights of Target, Walmart, and the little chain restaurants that clustered at their base making the highway seem lit almost by daylight. Kradle watched the stores pass as if he were a kid at the aquarium. They stopped at an intersection and saw a family wheeling a huge flat-screen TV across the six lanes of the highway in a shopping cart. Kradle glanced at the clock set into the dashboard.

"Must have been a sale," Celine said.

Kradle shrugged. "Hey, you want to go to Walmart at midnight? Go to Walmart at midnight. Go to a bar. Go to the beach. If you're free to do it, do it."

"I guess you'd come away from death row with that kind of attitude," Celine said.

"I used to go on little mental journeys if I woke up in the middle of the night in my cell," Kradle said. "Drive down the highway, stop at a gas station, look through the aisles. Pick up a Coke and a burrito, maybe."

Celine drove through the intersection. "You nervous?" she asked.

"A little," he said. "More . . . More excited. I've wanted an answer for so long."

"What are you going to do? When this is over?" Celine watched the road, the streetlamps crawling overhead. She couldn't deny the jealousy that was making her throat ache, that Kradle had a chance of not only learning the truth about his family's murders, but of going back to something that resembled the life he had once lived. There was no place Celine could go where she could be who she had been—the teenager, the daughter and sister and niece and cousin, the naive kid filled with hope and dreams about her future. She realized before long that she had got so caught up in imagining Kradle back in the swamps on his houseboat that she had not heard him say that was his plan. In fact, he had not said anything at all.

Celine fidgeted in her seat.

"Because, I mean, when we . . . you know," she said. "When we catch whoever did this to your family, we'll bring him to justice. You'll be found innocent and set free."

Again, Kradle didn't answer.

"That's the plan," Celine said slowly, firmly. "To find him and bring him in."

"Here it is." Kradle pointed.

They pulled alongside the parking lot of the Everpalm Motel, at the corner of an intersection. Celine felt her jaw aching with tension.

"Don't go in," Kradle said. "Pull in here and we'll watch."

Celine turned left instead of right and parked in the lot outside the Best Western across the street from the Everpalm, and the two watched from between rows of short palm trees bordering the road. There were only three cars at the Everpalm. Celine could see no one hanging around the edges of the lot, no one watching from the laundromat next door or from the Chili's restaurant on the other side of the street from the squat blue building.

"Text him," Celine said. "Tell him to come out and wave."

Kradle did. As they watched, the door to room three opened and a man stepped out, dressed in jeans and a pinstriped business shirt. He looked up and down the road, waved, and pushed the door open fully with his boot. Kradle leaned forward and squinted at the doorway.

"Recognize him?" Celine asked.

"No."

"Maybe I should go first," she said.

Kradle nodded.

Celine got out, crossed the highway, and went to the door. The man was sitting now on the edge of the faded floral coverlet on one of two single beds in the room. He swiped a hand nervously over his long nose and chin and gestured to the bathroom.

"You can check," he said. "It's just me."

Celine went in and checked. A tiny bathroom that smelled of mold. A plywood closet, empty but for laundry bags and empty hangers. Nothing under the beds but dust. She walked to the doorway and waved.

"You have a friend with you?" the man asked.

"'Friend' is a strong word," Celine said.

John Kradle walked into the room and shut the door behind him, pulling down his hood as he did so.

"Oh, *shit*!" The man got up and backed into the dresser, rattling the fingerprint-spotted mirror.

"Calm down," Celine said. "He's fine. You're safe. It's him you've been texting."

"*You* called the studio?" The man pointed at Kradle.

"I did," Kradle said. "I'm not from the *New York Times*."

"Yeah! Ha! No kiddin'!" the man said. "I agreed to meet a journalist here, not a fucking escaped prisoner. I could—I could get arrested for this!"

"Right," Celine said. "So let's get this over with quickly. The longer we all sit here wailing about what we're doing, the more likely it is that we'll get caught doing it. You're from In Focus Studios?"

"Yes."

"What's your name?" Kradle asked.

"Never mind." The man put a long-fingered hand up as though to hide his face. He sank to the edge of the bed again. "Let me just tell you what I know so I can get out of here."

Celine sat on the edge of the opposite bed, next to Kradle.

"I was . . . an employee at In Focus back in 2015," the man said. His eyes were searching the patchy carpet, his mind sifting through what he could and couldn't say. "I worked on the front desk during the day. That was my regular job. But I was also interning on *The Frances Falkner Show* two days a week. I ended up giving up the internship. It wasn't paid, and my interest in television—"

"You're babbling," Celine said.

"Okay, okay, sorry. Point is, I worked on the show, and I worked on the desk. The episode your wife attended, Mr. Kradle—I was there when they filmed that."

"*My Psycho Father Doesn't Know I'm Gay?*" Kradle said.

"Right." The man nodded. "We had guests bring a loved one on the show and come out to them. I was in charge of a lot of the arrangements for the family members. Booking flights, organizing hotel rooms, catering, that kind of thing."

The man fidgeted with the cuff of his shirt, glancing now and then at Kradle.

"The episode that aired on TV had four sets of guests," the man said. "But there were actually five."

"I knew it," Celine gasped.

"We were well ahead on filming the program," the man said. "Three or four months. So when what happened *happened*, we deleted the footage of the extra guests and your wife's comment. A shortened version of the episode went to air. And after that—"

"You're getting ahead of yourself," Kradle said. "What happened on the show? Who was the guest?"

The man rubbed his hands together as if they were cold.

"The guy's name was Mullins," he said. "Gary Mullins. Military guy. His son Brady wrote to the show after we put a call-out online. He said he was gay, and his dad didn't know, and the guy was going to blow his stack big time when he found out. It was exactly the type of letter we were looking for. Most of the time we wanted to set up the show with one guest who was probably going to react well to the secret—whatever it was—and one guest who we could guarantee was going to react badly, and a couple who could go either way. We had a pregnancy-reveal show once where all the reactions were cute and the ratings tanked. We needed at least one explosion."

"So how did Gary react to the son's news?" Celine asked.

"On camera, he was bad," the man said. "I don't mean, like, he blew his stack, as his son predicted he would. As we hoped he would. I mean he was bad for TV. He . . . he just went icy. Kind of weird. He froze, I think. I've seen it before. People get this fake, hard kind of smile. We call it the lizard smile."

"The lizard smile?"

"Yeah. They smile and they don't say much."

"You do that." Kradle turned to Celine. "When you're cornered."

"It's like a defense mechanism," she agreed.

"It was a disappointing segment," the man continued. "But that's reality TV for you. The director told Frances to cut it short and move on."

"So Christine asked the guy a question at the end of the show?" Kradle said. "When people from the audience stand up and take the mic?"

"She made a comment about Mullins."

"What did she say?" Celine asked.

"I can't even remember. I . . . I have a USB with the full episode on it with me. She just said something about fathers and sons, or sons needing love or something."

"So what the hell makes you think this Gary Mullins guy murdered my family? Because this all seems pretty thin to me," Kradle said. Celine looked over. Kradle's neck was taut, his jaw muscles flexing. "If there's nothing else—"

"Just hold on," the man said. "I'm getting there. A week after we finished taping the show, Gary Mullins called the front desk. He said he wanted to know the name of the woman with the long brown and gray hair and tattoos, who made the comment at the end of the show. He sounded mad. Not screaming mad, but, like, cold. I said I couldn't tell him. And I got this . . . this feeling."

Celine watched Kradle. His eyes were locked on the man sitting on the bed before him.

"What kind of feeling?" Kradle asked.

"As if it wasn't over."

Kradle nodded.

"Then a couple of days later, he calls again," the man said. "Only this time he's pretending it isn't him. He's pretending to be someone from ticketing. He wants the address of one of the guests, because he says she's requested a refund and he doesn't know where to send it to. He knew her name by then. Christine Kradle."

"And you knew the caller was Gary Mullins?" Celine asked.

"I knew." The man nodded. "And I knew all that stuff about the ticket refund was bullshit. I managed refunds and bookings at the front desk."

"So what did you do?" Celine asked.

"Well, I was so creeped out that I called and checked on the son, Brady. I had all his details from having organized his appearance on the show. He said he hadn't seen his father since the taping. His boyfriend had picked him up and they'd flown back to San Francisco. They hadn't spoken at all. I kind of got the feeling Brady was really just in it for the ten thousand bucks we paid him to appear."

"Did you tell the show's producers?" Kradle asked. "About the phone calls?"

"Sure did," the man said. "They blew it off. It wasn't even the weirdest thing a guest had ever done after the show. We had this one woman who came on the show to reveal to her husband that she was dating his brother, and—"

"Stay focused. What happened after the murders?" Kradle snapped.

The man shifted uncomfortably. "I went right back to the producers. I told them we needed to go to the police about this. That it might be a . . . a lead. Someone calls trying to hunt the lady down, and then she's killed? I mean, come on!"

"Yeah," Kradle said. The malice in his voice was thickening. "Come on."

"They told me to shut my mouth about it," the man said. "They cut the segment and your wife's comment. I was the only person in the studio that seemed to think it was a big deal. People were telling me I was trying to cook the Kradle Family murders up as a *Jenny Jones* thing."

"A *Jenny Jones* thing?" Celine asked.

"*The Jenny Jones Show* was a *Frances Falkner Show* predecessor back in the nineties," the man said. "A couple of weeks after a taping, one of the guests blew his friend's brains out with a shotgun in the doorway of his home for embarrassing him on the show. They canceled the show and the guy's family sued for twenty-nine million dollars."

"And your producers didn't want *The Frances Falkner Show* ending up the same way," Kradle said.

"They said I was being crazy. But, yeah"—the man shrugged—"I knew that was why they were doing it. A lawsuit like that would shut down the show and tie everyone up in court for five years."

"So that was it? You just dropped it?" Celine asked.

"No," the man said. "I went ahead and called the

detective on the case on my lunch hour when the place was quiet. When he finally called me back, he told me they already had a suspect locked in for the murders and it wasn't our guy."

Kradle's lip was twitching hard. He stood so fast the man in the striped shirt cowered back from him.

"Give me the USB." Kradle put a palm out. The man grabbed a backpack that was sitting at the head of the bed and extracted a thumb drive from it. Kradle took the drive, walked stiffly to the door of the motel room, and was out of it and halfway across the parking lot before Celine could catch up to him.

"Hey." She grabbed his shoulder. They stopped beside a row of bike racks under a bright street lamp. "Let's stay calm. We're making progress. We have a lead now. Let's go back to my place. We'll call the police and tell them what we know, go from there."

"Good plan." Kradle nodded. His fury was slowly dying, his face softening. "Give me the car keys. I need to drive. I can't sit around doing nothing any longer. I'm too itchy."

Celine handed him the car keys. He took them, grabbed her wrist, and snapped a handcuff to it, yanked the other cuff to the bike rack and clicked it closed.

"What? No!" Celine grabbed at Kradle as he pulled away. "You mother*fucker!*"

"Little trick someone taught me recently," Kradle said. "I'm sorry, Celine. I'm really, really sorry." He turned and threw the handcuff key with all his might toward the hotel, then jogged away, across the highway to the car parked at the Best Western. Celine roared after him, but he didn't look back.

CHAPTER 39

Both the cat and the dog were behind the door when Kradle entered the house. He ignored them, heading for the laptop on the dining room table. He opened it, flipped the machine, and looked for the USB port. There was none. Helplessly, he swiped a finger over the mousepad and the screen came to life, an empty box requesting a password.

Kradle groaned, then spied the television and went there. While he fiddled around at the back of the machine, the dog and cat assembled on the rug, watchful, curious. Kradle found a place for the drive and stood between the animals, the remote in his hand. All three of them watched as the video file opened and began to play.

Frances Falkner in her turquoise pants suit. The gawdy set with the plush pink armchairs and low-hanging spot lamps, the rock music. Kradle scrolled through the video, watched people hug, cry, writhe in the chairs. He stopped the video when a man he didn't recognize walked onto the screen: a tall, stubbled young man with an immaculate jet-black quiff.

He sat in the pink chair and grinned at the crowd, tugging at the chest of a thick black knitted sweater.

"Audience, meet our next guest." The video cut back to Frances, who was wandering the aisles of the audience casually. "Brady says his dad, Gary, is an ex-Marine who doesn't approve of his career in graphic design or his ownership of a cavoodle, Sparkles. But Gary's really going to lose it when he learns his son has been keeping a deep dark secret from him since he was thirteen years old. Welcome to the show, Brady!"

The audience cheered. Brady waved and grinned.

"Thanks, Frances! I've always wanted to be on your show! I'm a huge fan!"

"Oh, stop it, you." Frances flapped a hand at the stage. "First off, tell me what the heck a cavoodle is. Sounds like a type of pasta."

The audience giggled. A picture of the Cavalier King Charles spaniel cross miniature poodle flashed on the screen above the stage, and the audience cooed as one. Brady explained the curly brown puppy's heritage.

"She's my little baby." Brady smiled.

"And your dad doesn't like her?" Frances gave a quizzical frown. "How could you not like her? Look at her! She's a peach! That ain't right!"

"*That ain't right!*" the audience cheered.

"I know, I know. He says she's a glorified cat."

"But there's a lot more about you that doesn't rub with your father's way of life, isn't there, Brady?" Frances said.

"He doesn't know . . . ," Brady paused for effect, looking at the audience with a coy grin. "I've been dating guys since I was about thirteen years old."

The audience erupted. Kradle fast-forwarded. Brady

and Frances jittered and jostled as they presumably discussed Brady's childhood, his father's prejudices. Kradle hit play as Frances swept an arm toward the side of the stage.

". . . bring him out!"

A taller, thicker version of Brady walked stiffly onto the stage. Gary Mullins was suntanned and heavy-jawed, with the kind of ropy forearms and wide knuckles reserved for men who had never hired another man to fix or clean or kill or carry anything for them in their entire lives. He took a seat next to Brady and gave the boy a kind of smile that was laden with hidden meaning. With dark, uncertain meaning.

Kradle had to remind himself to breathe.

"Welcome to the show, Gary." Frances beamed.

"Thank you."

"Or, should I say, Sergeant Major Mullins?"

"Gary is fine."

"Your son Brady invited you to the show a couple of weeks ago, didn't he? He told you the studio put a call out for veterans and their children to come on the show to celebrate Memorial Day."

"Right." Gary nodded. Kradle watched the older, bigger Mullins gripping his knees, his eyes locked on his son, the younger man twitching and shifting in his seat, leaning as far away from his father as the seat would allow. Frances left space for Gary to elaborate on his journey toward coming on the show, on the delicious misapprehension he had about the show's purpose and subject. He did not. A couple of awkward beats passed in which Kradle could hear individual voices in the crowd calling out taunts or encouragements, he couldn't tell.

"So, uh"—Frances shuffled her question cards—so, why don't you tell us about your son, Gary?"

"He's a good kid." Gary gave an exaggerated nod. His head was turned toward his son, eyes locked on his face, which was turned toward the audience. "Yep. Never had a problem with him."

The audience tittered, gave a rumble of anticipation.

"Why don't you look up here, Gary?" Frances said.

"Oh, sorry."

"Over here."

"Right. I got you."

"Is there anything your son could ever do that would make you—"

Kradle hit the fast-forward button. His stomach was roiling with vicarious terror and humiliation. Brady did his big reveal and his father's smile stiffened even further, so that Kradle could see the molars at the corners of his mouth and the veins in his temples. Then the big man hunched forward in his chair, his elbows on his knees, his face turned toward his son, and the grimace was hidden from the camera, which Kradle knew was exactly what the show's directors didn't want. They wanted to see and smell and taste the humiliation. Before he knew it, the segment was over. Kradle kept rolling through the tape until he got to the audience questions at the end and, his skin tingling with excitement, he watched his murdered wife rise from her chair as Frances approached her with the microphone.

"Frances, oh." Christine clasped her hands around the mic as soon as the host was within reach, her hands around Frances's hands, the two of them gripping the device like it was a torch. "I'm just so in love

with you and this show. I've been a diehard France.
Falkner fan forever."

"Thank you, thank you." Frances winced. "Do you
have a question for our guests?"

"Look." Christine turned to the stage. "I just want
to say, you guys all need to get back to the love. It'
all about love, people. These are your kids. I'm a par
ent to a beautiful, beautiful boy, and I've always tried
to raise him to believe in—"

Kradle felt his mouth twist. He gripped the remote
in his fist.

"—people being who they are. I'm just so proud o
him."

The audience cheered. The camera panned across the
guests, resting on Brady and Gary Mullins at the very
edge of the stage. Brady was staring at his fingernails
Gary was expressionless, rigid. Kradle thought Chris
tine's time with the mic must be over, and felt a chil
rush through him as the camera turned back to her.

"I happen to be a medium," Christine continued.

"A medium?" Frances was trying to extract her
hands from Christine's. "Really?"

"Yes, and I'm feeling an incredible pull toward you
on the end of the row. Mr. Mullins."

The camera cut to Mullins and his son. The father'
mouth was a toothy grimace.

"There are dark energies clustered around you."
The camera cut to Christine as she waved an illustra-
tive hand. "Spirits that have passed and have been
disturbed from their slumber, brought back to wake-
fulness, by your refusal to accept your son."

"Jesus, Christine," Kradle breathed.

"Is your mother still with us, Mr. Mullins?" Christine asked.

"I think we better move on," Frances said. The
owd was beginning to jeer again, sensing Christine's
tent to hog the mic for as long as Frances would al-
w it. As the camera panned away, following Frances
she left Christine's side, Kradle saw his murdered
ife yell out toward the stage.

"She wants you to love him!" Christine called.

Kradle ran through the rest of the tape but saw
othing he wanted to examine further. He stepped
ound the television and extracted the USB, then
illed his phone out of his pocket and searched for
rady Mullins, San Francisco.

With his heart pumping, throbbing in his fingers, he
pped open a stylish website advertising "corporate
set design," whatever the hell that was. He scrolled
itil he found a phone number, then dialed.

"He—hello?"

"Brady Mullins?"

"Jesus, who is this? Wha—what time is it?"

"Is this Brady Mullins?" Kradle insisted.

"Yes, yes, yes, wha—"

"My name is . . . Terry Sellers. I'm a paramedic."

Kradle heard blankets rustling. A muffled voice in
e background of the line.

"What's going on?" Brady asked.

"Your father has just been in a car accident."

"Oh . . . whoa. Whoa. Where? Is . . . Is he okay?"

"He's okay," Kradle said. "He's going to be fine.
ut he's in and out of consciousness. Took a bit of a
nock to the head. He's saying he has some . . . some
iedication at home that he needs. Do you know any-
ing about that?"

"Um." Brady heaved a sigh. "Oh, god. We, uh. To
e honest with you, we don't really talk."

"Okay." Kradle squeezed his eyes shut.

"I mean, he had high blood pressure. Back when . . . He's always had high blood pressure."

"We need to know exactly what medications he on," Kradle said. "Could you give us his address? We send someone out to his home to see what's there."

"Isn't his address in his wallet?" Brady asked.

Kradle's stomach sank. He took the phone awa from his ear, hovered his thumb over the red butto to end the call.

"The wallet is . . . uh, it's not here. I'm not seein it. It's probably back at the crash site."

"Seventeen Cloudrock Court, MacDonald Ranch, Brady said.

Kradle's heart swelled in his chest.

"Just outside Vegas . . . ," Kradle said.

"Yeah," Brady said. "Let me get a pen. Whic hosp—"

Kradle hung up. He went to the front door an opened it. The dog and cat watched him go.

Kradle paused before he swung the door closed. H looked at the dog, at its huge, earnest eyes, and when he spoke he heard that his voice had lost all warmtl and humanity, all soul. It was almost robotic.

It was the voice of a man with only one purpose.

"I won't be back," he told the dog, and shut th door.

CHAPTER 40

eline watched the black Lexus pull into the lot, driv-
ıg diagonally across the empty parking spaces toward
er at a leisurely pace. When Keeps finally pulled to a
op, the headlights of the car were pointed directly
: Celine, illuminating her like a hog with its hoof
ıared in a trap. He had a delicious smile on his lips
s he popped open the door, rounded the hood, and
ıt on it, folding his arms.

"Okay, okay," Celine said. "Drink it in."

Keeps looked at the motel nearby, cold and quiet,
ıe red neon sign painting the sidewalk pink. The door
ɔ number three was closed. Celine had considered
ılling out to the man she and Kradle had met in the
ɔom after Kradle chained her to the bike rack, but
ıeer embarrassment had caused her to stand in front
f her cuffed wrist and wave with her other hand as
ɛ too fled the scene. Calling the police was out of
ıe question. The last thing Celine wanted to do was
nswer queries from authorities about how she had
ɔund herself attached by a bloody handcuff to a bike
ıck in the parking lot of a dingy hotel at one o'clock

in the morning. She knew what an incident like tha
meant. It meant police reports. Interviews. Waitin
rooms. A glance at her personal records. A raised eye
brow. Whispers.

Keeps lit a cigarette and blew the smoke over hi
shoulder, looking her up and down.

"You arrived fast," Celine said.

"I happened to be nearby."

"I'd ask how a man who had nothing to his nam
a couple of days ago is now driving a Lexus," Celin
said. "But you're the guy who can turn a twenty-dolla
waffle maker into five hundred bucks, so . . ."

Keeps didn't answer. Didn't smile.

"He threw the key that way." Celine pointed at th
motel. "I heard it bounce."

"I didn't come here to let you out." Keeps smirkec

"What?"

"I came here to see you chained up. Not every da
you get to see that. Pronghorn guard locked down lik
an inmate, stuck in one place, watching the world tic
by. This is a real hoot."

Celine felt her mouth fall open. Every limb seeme
to be growing numb, one after the other, so that sh
felt she wanted to slip awkwardly to the ground.

"I was always going to scam you, Celine," Keep
said.

"*What?*"

"Come on." Keeps lifted his hands. "It's what I dc
I *told* you that's what I do. I *showed* you it's what
do!"

Celine bent in two and stared at the concrete at he
feet.

"I am going to *murder* you," she growled.

"I don't know why you're so angry. This is you

his is all you." Keeps gestured to her with his ciga-
ette. "You let me into your house. You let me into
our bed. You opened your world to me. We both
now you were trying to test the limits, see if your ra-
ar was working. Whether you knew good from bad.
Well, you were wrong about me, Celine. I had it in for
ou from the very beginning. So, now you have what
ou wanted. You know at least some of your instincts
ren't good."

"You sent that payment from my account," Celine
aid.

"Actually, no." Keeps shook his head. "No. That's
tupid. That's the short game. I didn't have to go to
our house to access your bank account. Come on.
And why the hell would I send the money to Kuala
Lumpur? You ever *been* to Kuala Lumpur?"

"No."

"Don't. Stay home. Save yourself the trouble."

"You wanted me for the long game," Celine concluded.

"The long game." Keeps nodded. "The big payday.
was going to make you love me. I was going to see
how long it would take for you to give me the house,
he car, the jewelry, the bank account. Didn't take you
ong to give me your body. I figured by the end of the
month I could ha—"

He had stood and wandered within striking dis-
ance. Celine lunged, got the edge of his sleeve and
nothing else.

"Shhh, shhh," Keeps said. "You're making a scene."

Celine gave a hard smile that cracked into a vicious
augh.

"What's so funny?"

"I'm just thinking," she said. "About the next time

you wind up in Pronghorn. Having John Kradle on my row was just training. I'm going to have myself put on whatever cell block you're assigned to and I'm going to make your life a nightmare. You will *beg* to be put in the hole, you slimy son of a bitch."

"Not this time." Keeps tapped his temple. "I told you. It's the big payday. And when you get one of those you move on, somewhere far, far away, where nobody knows your tricks yet."

Celine exhaled hard. "Kradle."

"Yup. The million-dollar man," Keeps said. "You brought him to my attention."

"I won't tell you where he's going," Celine said. "Not in a lifetime."

"I don't need you to," Keeps said, and Celine realized why he had come for her so fast after she sent the message asking for help. Because he had been nearby, just like he said, following the tracker he'd probably placed on her phone, probably the first time she brought him into her house. The bug he'd told her he used to scam old people, to decipher key parts of their lives he could use to convince them he was trustworthy.

"I told you I was a bad man, Celine," Keeps said.

"Yeah, well." Celine gave a miserable sigh. "I guess I should have trusted myself. At least that time, anyway."

He reached for her, and she took advantage of the slip, grabbed his wrist and yanked him toward her. But with her other wrist chained, there wasn't much she could do. Keeps laughed and pushed her off. He was gone into the night before she could get her phone out of her pocket.

* * *

He could see Gary Mullins. For five years, John Kradle had lay on his bunk in his cell at Pronghorn and stared at the scratches in the paintwork on the ceiling and imagined a faceless figure murdering his family. But now that figure had a shape. He had a name. Kradle gripped the steering wheel and watched the white lines passing on the road in front of him while, in his mind, Gary Mullins walked down the side of the house in Mesquite where he and his son had lived.

Kradle watched him round the corner of the yard, stepping over the bike Mason always dumped on its side at the end of the porch, sliding open the unlocked glass door to the living room. He saw Gary stop as he heard Christine and Audrey arguing in the kitchen. Audrey pouring wine and admonishing Christine for trying to make her fourth phone call to Kradle about the bubble-machine fiasco. Audrey telling her sister she would have to suck it up, stop being a spoiled brat, accept the fact that she had fucked off on her family and they hadn't thrown a parade when she returned like she'd expected. Kradle saw Gary Mullins walking in from the living room with the rifle raised. Cutting the two women down where they stood. He saw Mullins lift his head as Mason called out from the upstairs bathroom, wanting to know what the noise was, the water still running. Mullins standing there, trying to decide if he was going to leave a witness or not.

Kradle saw his son murdered where he stood in the shower, the glass door pulled open, the blast, the shattered tiles. Kradle didn't know if he'd uttered a single word. Sometimes, in his musings, Mason did cry out. Sometimes it was all so fast there was only the sound of the gunshot. He saw Mullins pouring gasoline in a straight line from the garage, where he found it, to the glass back doors. The fire licking the walls. Kradle saw a stronger, healthier, more fresh-faced version of himself opening the front door and stopping dead at the sight of the strip of fire working its way up the living room walls, already billowing against the ceiling in the kitchen. He saw his body snap out of shock and into action as he heard a groan from upstairs. Running past the flames, feeling their mighty heat against his cheek as he swung around the banister, finding Mason half in, half out of the shower. He saw himself gathering his dying son up in his arms.

The rage had been something Kradle kept tightly leashed at Pronghorn. Whenever he felt it burbling up his throat or pulsing behind his eyeballs he'd always talked it down, strapped it in tight, a twisting and groaning and snarling thing that was always waiting for an opportunity to burst free. Waiting for a weak moment. The right provocation. Eventually, the rage had exhausted itself and fallen asleep. As he'd walked through the desert, run through the forest, then walked the streets as an escaped man, the rage had started to stir. It had begun to break its binds in the motel room when, for the first time, he heard the name of the man who had ruined his life.

And now the rage was free.

It was wielding Kradle's body like a precise weapon, every muscle zinging with tension, every movement sharp, silent, fast.

The phone on the seat next to him buzzed. He looked over and saw Celine's name on the screen. Ignored it.

His intention had been to blast through any roadblock that he encountered on the way out of Vegas city proper, but all he found were abandoned wooden barriers standing like restful horses by the side of the road, flashing orange lamps making geometric shadows on the sand. It occurred to him for the first time that he hadn't seen any roadblocks on the way from the motel back to Celine's house. They had all fallen, disappeared into nothing.

The unexpected ease with which he headed toward his fate continued. Christine would have called it that. Fate. Destiny. He drove through empty streets off the highway, past a gas station with a big blue Bud Light bottle resting on the awning above the pumps. A police cruiser sitting behind a billboard advertising home insurance took no notice of him. It was as if he had frozen time. He turned into a sprawling estate of manicured houses. Wide lawns without fences, plastic Christmas reindeer grazing over rock gardens full of cactuses. Before sunrise, Christmas morning—a time that had been filled with joyful anticipation back in the days when Kradle had a child and the boy was small and excitable. The memories seemed too distant, and yet at the same time perfectly reachable. He could hear socks on the stairs. Whispers, giggles. Time ticking down. Kradle's jaw was grinding as he turned onto Cloudrock Court and stopped the car outside number seventeen.

The house was unremarkable. A modern Spanish-style villa identical to two others Kradle had noticed in the street. Beyond the property, a shallow valley stretched toward a ridge of rocky hills. Kradle supposed that Gary Mullins could probably sit on the back porch at sunset with a Coors and watch coyotes emerging from their dens to hunt jackrabbits.

He crossed the driveway, past the sensible Buick with the yellow-and-red VETERAN bumper sticker, and found the side gate of the house unlocked, bags of potting mix stacked by a rack of garden tools. He was walking in Gary Mullins's footsteps now. The killer trembling with dark anticipation, sliding open the unlocked glass door, walking into the house. His senses were alive, sucking in the smell of hand soap in a dispenser shaped like a chicken on the edge of the spotless sink. The big kitchen windows looked out over the porch, the desert beyond, framed by curtains with bright yellow lemons on them. Kradle could see the sharp outlines of a framed cross-stitch hanging on the wall of the living room. BLESS THIS MESS. He turned and walked past a portrait of Gary Mullins in uniform, turned three-quarters to the camera, a classic textured gray backdrop.

Kradle pushed open the bedroom door. One lump in the bed, turned away from him, buzz-cut gray hair on a white pillow. A full glass of water on the nightstand. On the other nightstand, an empty glass. Kradle walked to the head of the bed and lifted his pistol, nudged Gary Mullins in the back of the skull with it.

The man rolled over fast and looked up at him in the dark.

"Get up," Kradle said.

CHAPTER 41

"Settle a bet for me," the officer said. The handcuff key looked comically small in his huge fingers as he took Celine's wrist in his hand. He jerked his head toward a troop of officers standing around a nearby cruiser, drinking coffee from the local Dunkies. "You that Pronghorn guard who was on TV?"

"No," Celine said.

"You sure look like—"

"Can we just do this, please?"

The car smelled like every police cruiser Celine had ever been in. Of fried food and sweat. She slumped against the greasy window while the officers said long goodbyes to the others, and then watched the parking lot slide out of view, the words catching in her chest as she spoke them.

"Please take me to your captain," she said.

"Why?" the officer riding shotgun asked.

"Because I have to make a report," Celine said. "About a possible murder that's about to happen. That may already have happened."

"*How* possible is the murder?" The driver wiped his

nose on the back of his hand. "Because we're pretty overrun as it is, lady."

"Just take me there, please," Celine groaned.

"I'm afraid we can't. We got instructions to drop you off on the corner of Beatie and Ellett," the cop said. "Probably be somebody there who can take your report."

"Huh?"

"The call was from on high," the driver said. "That's all I know."

Celine was too exhausted, too furious, to play further guessing games with the officers. She waited, and, in time, the cruiser pulled up at an intersection outside a game fishing supply store. Celine walked to the silver Mercedes that was pointed out to her and opened the passenger-side door.

"Whoooooa!" she moaned as she slid into the passenger seat.

"Whoa what?" Trinity asked.

"I thought you were dead!" Celine's voice was higher, more hysterical, than she intended. "That's what!"

"Oh, please." Trinity rolled her eyes. "It'll take more than a gunshot to the neck to kill me. My people are indestructible. After the nuclear apocalypse it'll be cockroaches and a bunch of Parkers who crawl out of the rubble."

Celine sat staring at the other woman as she pulled the car onto the road and drove. Her entire neck and left shoulder were strapped tightly in gauze that was speckled in parts with blood. She had two black eyes, exposed stitches in her chin, and dried blood in the hair that was visible under her black cap.

"You got shot in the neck in the forest!" Celine screeched. "What the hell are you doing here?"

"Please adjust your volume," Trinity said. "You're at a nine. I need you at a two. And it was shrapnel. The bullet must have hit a tree and shattered, and I got a piece of it in my neck. What's more bothersome is the rock I must have smashed into when my head hit the ground. Raging headache. Bad, bad. So there it is! I'm disgruntled but alive. Get over it. I am."

Celine sat back in her seat.

"And, alas, while I'm still kicking in bodily form, my term as director of the Pronghorn breakout is officially over," Trinity continued. "As soon as someone prescribes you Vicodin, you become operationally ineffective, apparently, whether you actually take the drug or not. It's an inconvenience we will have to overcome, and quickly, before word of my usurping spreads. At the moment I'm hoping we can still get in to see Kerry Monahan at the Mesa View Regional Hospital."

"Who?"

"The girl you saved." Trinity glanced over. "The little red-haired redneck who killed your friend Brassen."

"I can't get into that right now," Celine said. "I've got to stop Kradle."

"Stop him from doing what?"

"From killing the man who killed his family," Celine said. "We know the guy's name. Or, at least, we have a very good suspect. Kradle is on his way to—"

"Save it." Trinity held up a hand.

"No, I can't *save it*," Celine yelled. "It would take you five minutes to get someone out to this guy's address to watch for Kradle. It's a human life we're talking about here."

"Take my phone," Trinity said. She tapped the enclosed compartment in the center console between them. "Text whatever information you have to a number saved as GS in the contacts list."

"Who's GS?" Celine asked.

"Just send the text." Trinity waved, bored. "I guarantee you, the Kradle thing will be met with the swiftest possible response."

Celine grabbed the phone and typed out a text about Gary Mullins, John Kradle, and the revenge mission she believed he was on. She didn't know where Mullins lived, how Kradle planned to get to him, or whether she was already too late to save the killer's life. When it was done she gripped her seatbelt and watched the horizon beginning to glow with approaching dawn.

"Why me?" Celine asked.

"Why you?"

"Yeah," Celine said. "You wake up in a hospital, discharge yourself, find out you've lost your job, decide you're going to keep going after Schmitz anyway—"

"You don't decide a thing like that, Osbourne." Trinity smiled to herself. "It's either in you or it isn't."

"Your remarkable self-sacrifice and humility aside"—Celine rolled her eyes—"the next move is to come and find me, of all people?"

"I like you, Osbourne," Trinity said. "Is that what you want me to say? It isn't true. But I'll say it if it means you'll be quiet."

"How did you know I was there?"

"I happened to be trying to recruit the chief of police to help me continue my crusade to find Schmitz," Trinity said, "when I heard a very interesting report on his radio. A short-ass white woman was handcuffed to a bike rack outside a crappy hotel on the outskirts of Vegas. A bystander witnessed an African

American man pull up in a black Lexus, and, while the bystander thought the guy was there to rescue her, he seemed to taunt her and leave her there."

Celine waited, feeling tired.

"Seemed like a familiar scenario to me." Trinity smiled. "I thought—could it possibly be?"

"You knew Keeps was bad," Celine said. "You tried to warn me."

"You thought you were dealing with a cute little conman," Trinity said. "But that guy's got missing people all around him. Ladies with deep pockets who went out on yachts and never came back."

"He's not . . . ," Celine said. "He's not a killer . . . ?"

"Like I said. Nothing confirmed. There are just unanswered questions. Blank spaces." Trinity shrugged. "That's what you get with confidence men. Part of the picture. Never all of it."

Celine looked at her hands sitting folded in her lap.

"What are we going to do to Kerry Monahan that hasn't been done to her already?" Celine asked. "You threatened to shoot the girl in the hand, Trinity, and she gave up nothing."

"She'll talk for us," Trinity said. "Don't worry."

"Why?"

"Because we're going to pull a con." Trinity smiled, exposing a chipped front tooth. "Of course."

CHAPTER 42

Mistakes happened in war, Silvia reminded herself. Battles were full of failures, overestimations, accidents. It was human nature, especially in the face of a prolonged engagement—that exhaustion caused by nervousness and eagerness for triumph made soldiers, even highly trained soldiers, stumble. She leaned on the counter of the snow cone food truck and watched the first tendrils of Christmas morning light creeping along the windows of the empty Planet Hollywood hotel across the ice rink.

For a few hours, the radio at her elbow by the syrup pumps had been playing reports of the discovery of the bodies of the three police officers they had murdered at the last roadblock into Vegas. The cleanup after the shooting had been a real rush job. There hadn't been time to bury the bodies. The earth was too hard, too dry. She and Clara and Willis and Burke had driven the bodies and the two cruisers out onto the plains, found a crevice, and rolled the cars in. But the second cruiser had hit a rock shelf and wedged itself half in, half out of the hole, the rear bumper visible for miles around. Burke had taken it all pretty well. He was focused on the plan, on the steps ahead, on getting back on track. But Silvia felt terrible. It had been her slip-up with the rope tattoo that had caused the whole detour. She'd almost sunk what would be the most glorious event in the struggle of the Camp and the Aryan nation it served.

It had been a fluke, just getting on the team in the first place. She learned, after Burke recruited her, that he'd already had a sniper lined up for Day One of the plan, an ex-military guy from Hawaii who had written to Burke in prison. When he'd backed out, Silvia was called in by her team leader at the Camp to talk in confidence about a mission to further the cause of the brotherhood. Silvia had been teaching sharp-shooting and hunting skills at the Camp to new recruits for only three months. Her leader wanted to know if she could hit a moving target at more than eight hundred yards. Whether she'd be willing to kill for their cause. Silvia knew there were better shooters than her, even in the intake she had been instructing at the time. But Burke was looking for someone who could live up to their word. Who could keep a secret. Who could follow orders. Someone who would show eagerness. Her team leader suggested to Silvia that some of her more visible white power tattoos might have to go if she was going to be a part of the plan. She'd made a booking and had her first laser treatment for the removal of the lightning bolt tattoo from her shoulder that afternoon.

She'd had eight tattoos removed in total. She figured the rope tattoo was far enough up her forearm, and obscure enough, that she could keep it.

"Idiot," she whispered aloud. The sound of her

voice stirred Reiter from a sickly slumber on the food truck floor. The prisoner lay out of view of the serving window with his arms twisted behind his back, secured with cable ties, and his knees and ankles duct-taped together. The duct tape across his mouth was folded in the middle where he had been sucking it between his lips, probably trying to dampen the glue. The fentanyl in his system would make him drool like crazy, Silvia had heard. She wrinkled her nose at the smell of him, but counseled herself that the alternative was worse. She and Willis had been in charge of toileting the captive from the moment he was picked up at Pronghorn, through the journey to the safehouse, from the safehouse to Vegas. Now that they were at their destination, there was no need to bother anymore. Reiter was never going to leave the truck. He would die here, inside the tin walls, in a spectacular fireball created by the gas tanks that lined the cabin around him.

Silvia leaned on the counter again and looked at the ice rink. The first morning skaters were arriving, some of them wearing what looked like brand-new skates probably freshly opened that morning from under Christmas trees. People were assembling around the ice, smiling, rosy-cheeked. Soon the stage would fill with pretty carollers from the Saint Agnes Catholic Girls' School. Those little girls would just be opening their mouths to sing the first chorus of something merry and beautiful, Silvia dreamed, when Burke burst out of the truck and mowed them down. While his primary target was the girls, the painfully adorable angels in their fluffy costumes strung with silver bells, he was going to rake the panicked crowd with as many bullets as he could before heading back toward the truck. The smoke from the explosion would mask him slipping into the car that Clara and Willis would pull up nearby when the shooting began. The police would find Reiter's charred remains in the driver's seat of the truck and, if all went to plan, the rest of the world was going to wake to find their Christmas morning cartoons interrupted with a special news bulletin containing photographs of twelve murdered white babies and a Black man's mugshot right next to them.

And then, Silvia thought, *the war. The beautiful war.*

Burke the commander of the new world. Silvia in his inner circle.

Burke opened the back doors of the truck and slipped in. Silvia backed away from the counter, straightened her spine, awaiting commands.

"It's time to get him dressed," Burke said.

Silvia nodded. She pulled the serving window of the truck closed and went to a backpack sitting behind the driver's seat. She pulled a black ski mask and a pair of black tinted tactical goggles out. As Burke pulled on his own black ski mask, rolling it into a beanie on top of his head, Silvia pulled her mask onto a struggling, groaning Anthony Reiter.

"Urgh," she groaned. "His head's sweaty."

"I saw some of the little girls arriving," Burke said as he worked. "White satin dresses. I thought they might wear red, like in last year's calendar."

"It's going to be so beautiful," Silvia said. "All of it."

"As long as there are no more fuck-ups." Burke shot her a warning glance.

"There won't be."

They crouched together in the small gap between the gas bottles and the stainless-steel cupboards that lined the food truck's interior, surveying Reiter's get-up, his black T-shirt, jeans, boots. An exact match to what Burke was wearing.

Silvia counted silently to three, then said it.

"Burke," Silvia said. "When history looks back on this moment, when it's finally revealed after the war that it was you and me here, preparing like this, I . . ."

The words came in a flurry, then abruptly ran out. Burke was watching her, his eyes hard and his lips taut.

"I just hope they understand how honored I feel," she said.

Burke rose to his feet, flipped the serving window of the truck open again. "Just focus," he said. "Don't get distracted by grand dreams."

"Of course. I won't. I won't."

"You know what you're doing?"

"Yes. Yes."

"Let me hear it."

"When you start shooting, I let him loose," Silvia said. "I get him into the driver's seat, and then I get clear. I wait until you come back toward the truck and give me the signal, then I set off the bomb so you can escape."

"Good," Burke said. "Just memorize that. Go over it again and again. We can't have any more problems."

She nodded.

"I'm going to go take another lap." He pulled up the hood of his sweatshirt and slipped out the doors, slamming them behind him.

Silvia held her head.

"Idiot," she scolded herself.

The bump came as Silvia was securing the serving window open again. Burke was walking around the opposite side of the rink, near the hotel. She was watching him, and a jolt shuddered through the truck that was so hard it almost knocked her off her feet. She stumbled over Reiter, went to the back door of the truck and tried to open it. It was stuck. In bewilderment, she tried again, and the door smacked open against the front bumper of another food truck.

Silvia squeezed out and jumped down from the truck, slamming the door behind her and marching to the driver's-side door of the truck that had rammed her tailgate. The driver was a huge Black man in a blazing yellow T-shirt that matched the truck. On his chest, a little smiley-face button gave his name as Rick.

"What the *actual fuck*, dude?" Silvia mashed her palm on the window.

"Sorry, honey!" The driver wound down the window. "We've all got to move up. They're trying to make room for a churro truck down the back there."

"You hit my truck!"

"Yeah, sorry! Sorry!" He held his hands up, palms out. "It's not bad. Looks like I dented your numberplate. Let me just get set up here and I'll pull it off and pop the dent out."

"I don't want you to do that."

"It's no big deal. It'll pop right out, baby."

"I said I don't want you to do that!" Silvia snarled. Rick the driver reeled in his seat. "Open your big flappy fucking ears!"

"Open my *what*?"

"You heard me, *boy*," Silvia said. "Open your ears. I'm not moving my truck. I booked this spot three months ago. And if you touch my numberplate I'll call the fucking cops on your ass."

Silvia left Rick with his mouth hanging open and headed back to her truck. She opened the back door as hard as she could, smashing the edge into his bumper, and then slammed it shut behind her.

CHAPTER 43

Kradle grabbed Gary Mullins by the front of his nightshirt and dragged him out of bed, kicking him to the ground. The shockwave rippling up through his foot, ankle, knee, hip, from the kick to the man's side made his heart warm. He stood on Mullins's neck, pinning his face to the rug, and pressed the barrel of the pistol to the back of his ear.

"Where's the woman?"

"Ma-Marie, Marie, Marie's," Mullins babbled. "Marie's in Denver w-with her sister."

"Get up," Kradle said again. He didn't give the man a chance to comply. He yanked him up, threw him into the side of the door, bounced him into the hall. While every breath was hot and heavy and filled with the sweet, dark pleasure of revenge, something else was growing in Kradle as he shoved the man through his dimly lit house toward the porch doors. It was disquiet. A kind of empty rattling, the sense of something amiss, a screw loosened or a fixture pulled from its housing. Because, while his fantasy was playing out exactly as it had ten thousand times in his mind since his family died, something about what was happening felt hollow. His punches weren't landing hard enough. Mullins's cries of terror and pain weren't loud enough. Mullins wasn't fighting back. Kradle pushed him out onto the porch. The older man's shoes slipped on the stairs as Kradle forced him out into the yard.

"You know who I am?" Kradle snarled.

"I know. I know. You're John Kradle."

"You murdered my family." His voice sounded thin to him, an impossible instrument for communicating the agony inside. "My son Mason was fifteen years old."

"Listen to me." Mullins tried to turn around. Kradle slammed the butt of the pistol into his face, knocking him down. He followed as the man crawled toward the edge of the yard. Kradle picked him up and pushed him out the small wooden gate in the back fence.

Before them, the hard, unforgiving desert gaped. A featureless slab of cracked clay and sand, bowing and rising toward razor-sharp ridges being lit by morning glow. *This is the place,* Kradle thought. He couldn't replicate the coldness and loneliness and hardness of the bathroom tiles on which his son had breathed his last breath, but he could try. Mullins shuffled along weakly until Kradle told him to stop.

"You're going to die here," Kradle said. "You're going to die in terror and pain, just the way my family did."

"Listen," Mullins said again, his hands up, showing the lines of his palms etched with blood from a split lip. "Listen. What I did was the greatest act of evil a man can do. I know you've suffered. Your son suffered."

"Don't talk about my son!" Kradle barked.

"I was . . ." Mullins shook his head. There were tears running down his cheeks. "I want to try to explain this to you. Please. Please. I want to explain. I was over the edge, okay? I'd been in combat, and I—I was living in a place of darkness. My own son had revealed something to me, and I was confused and traumatized. I was in the valley of darkness, and I hadn't felt God's love—"

"*God's love?*" Kradle said.

"I hadn't heard his word. I'm in a good place now," Mullins wheezed. He rubbed his side, where Kradle had kicked him. "I can, I can look back and see, through the wisdom I have gained, what made me do those things. Those sinful things. I'm—I'm asking for your mercy."

"Where was mercy for my son?" Kradle bellowed. "For my wife? For her sister? Where was—" He couldn't talk. The words felt strangled. "Oh, god. God. This isn't the way it was supposed to be. You weren't supposed to beg me. How dare you fucking *beg me!*"

"I-I-I." Mullins gripped the ground, struggled to explain, his eyes restless, focused on everything but Kradle's eyes. "I needed someone to blame. And it became your wife. After the show, after what happened to me, I needed to direct that anger to someone. My son had just revealed to me that he wasn't . . . He wasn't the person I knew. He was someone else. It was as if he—"

Kradle felt his whole body brace for it. For Mullins to say it was like his son *had died.* Mullins saw the white-hot rage in Kradle's eyes and stammered over it.

"What Christine said to me that day—it hurt. It hurt me. I was a sick man, and I lashed out in a sick way. But almost immediately after I left your house, as I was walking away, I heard the voice of God."

Kradle forced himself to breathe.

"God's word said—"

"What did he say, Mullins?" Kradle asked. "He say anything about coming forward? He say anything about leaving me to *rot* on death row?"

"Listen," Mullins said. "Please listen."

Kradle could hardly focus. The gun was shaking in his hand. He could do nothing but listen, let the useless words wash over him, because what he had wanted was dissolving right before his eyes. He'd wanted to fight his son's killer. He'd wanted to conquer and punish him, to see a flash of the evil that had driven him that fateful day and meet it, quench it, with his own. But all he had before him was an old man simpering and crying and bleeding in the desert, a man who could do no more than die at his hands like a miserable hound.

Kradle had come to the house on Cloudrock Court to be a force of hatred and violence, and now all he felt was disappointment and disgust. He lowered the gun from Mullins's chest, let it hang, impossibly heavy, by his side.

"I can't kill you," Kradle said. "I can't do it. Not like this."

He sucked in a long breath and tried to tell himself that he would find some satisfaction in seeing Mullins behind bars, living in the stale, maddening purgatory he had experienced himself over the past five years.

"If you—"

"No, shut up," Kradle said. "Get on your feet. We're leaving. I'm taking you in."

"You have nothing," Mullins said carefully. "Okay? Think about it. You have nothing left. I took that from you, and I'm so, so sorry. But I have a wife. I have a son. I have people from my parish and my community who love me and need me. So I can't do what you want me to do. I can't go to jail."

"Wha—" Kradle shook his head. "What makes you think—"

"Please say you forgive me. Forgive me now before they take you away."

Kradle felt his mouth twist with confusion.

He took a step back and, as he did, felt two things. He felt his eyes widen as they fell on the shoes on Mullins's feet, as the realization materialized that he'd been wearing them in bed when Kradle woke him and yanked him free of his sheets. Kradle also felt the barrel of a gun against the back of his neck.

"Drop it," a deep voice said.

Kradle felt the man behind him gather a hand around his own. Kradle released the pistol and let the man take it away.

"On your knees."

Kradle did as he was told. He sank to the desert sand. The man side-stepped so that Kradle could see him. He didn't recognize the lone figure nudging glasses back onto his nose, pointing his own gun at him as he pocketed the one he'd pushed against the back of Kradle's neck. Kradle dropped his eyes to the man's wrist and noticed a tattoo that read 4KEEPZ.

"Where's everyone else?" Mullins was shivering from head to toe now, his bloodstream being flooded with chemicals as his terror morphed into relief. "You said there'd be a whole team."

"Yeah. I lied," Keeps said. He shrugged. "It's kind of my thing."

He shot Mullins in the forehead.

CHAPTER 44

Kerry Monahan was lying on her side when Celine entered the hospital room. She was bigger than Celine remembered. Fragments of the hellish moments running with the girl through the forest outside the Rancho Salvaje Wildlife Park lingered in Celine's mind, and from them she had a sense that the girl was small and narrow, like a frightened bird. But one broad shoulder slid from under the sheet as Kerry pushed herself into a sitting position, and her long legs stretched toward the end of the bed, rattling the chain around her ankle that connected to the bed frame. Celine sat down in the only chair in the room.

"Don't even bother," Kerry said before Celine could open her mouth, holding up her good hand. "I know exactly what you're going to say."

"You do, huh?" Celine asked.

"Yeah." Kerry smoothed back her hair, which was still clotted with dirt at the end of her ponytail. "There's been about three versions of you in here already through the night. Good cops trying to tell me they understand me, they feel sorry for me, they want to help me. Problem is, none of you can. It's too late now."

"First of all, I'm not a cop," Celine said. "And second of all, it's not too late. Whatever Burke's plan is, there's still time for you to tell us what it is and save lives, Kerry."

"I've killed," Kerry said. The teenager picked at a bandage around her finger. "That guy from the wildlife park? The one who picked up the bag from the locker? That was me. I killed that guy. I wasn't keeping lookout. I painted the straps of the bag with the stuff that they gave me. The poison, whatever it was. All the good cops who have come in here, the lawyers, they've all tried to tell me they can go easy and charge me with just being a lookout, someone Burke put in position to make sure the target went down. But I'm admitting it. I did it." The girl tapped her chest with one finger. "I want to be a part of the story when it's told."

"Tell me what the story is," Celine said. "Tell me how it ends."

"Forget it." Kerry smiled. "You'll know in less than an hour."

Celine shook her head, overwhelmed with sadness suddenly. The girl in the bed just stared at her impassively, unable to fathom the depth of what Celine was feeling.

"Don't take it personally," the girl said. "You tried to protect me in the forest. I remember it was you. And I'm grateful. I'm not doing this because of you. I'm doing this because I'm trying to make the world a better place."

"The Camp," Celine said. "It was their sniper who shot at you. Do you understand that? They knew Trinity and I were going to chase you down, and they wanted to make sure you were taken out so you couldn't reveal—"

The girl held up a hand, closed her eyes.

"These people aren't your friends. They have no loyalty to you."

"We're all loyal to the cause," Kerry said. "That's what matters."

Celine's phone buzzed in her pocket. She picked it up and stared at the screen. Then she covered her mouth with a trembling hand.

"What?"

"Oh, god," Celine said.

"What? What is it?"

Celine stood, her eyes locked to her phone.

"He did it," she said. Her words came in fitful starts, rushing out of her with horror. "He . . . He did it. Oh, Jesus, no."

"Let me see." Kerry reached for the phone with her good hand.

"Two massive explosions," Celine read. "One inside, one outside the Saint Joan of Arc Church. Emergency response teams estimating several dozen killed."

Kerry's face was a mask of confusion. She reached again for the phone.

"That . . . That wasn't the plan," she murmured. Celine let the phone go. "The plan was the kids at the rink."

Kerry looked at the phone, the lit screen, the small green bar showing the alarm Celine had set to go off only seconds earlier, now counting off a snooze timer. Kerry's mouth turned downward and her small, mean eyes flicked toward Celine.

"What rink?" Celine asked.

* * *

Kradle dropped onto the sand, crawled to Mullins, and grabbed his head, his body working of its own accord while his mind tried to catch up to what had just happened. The first gold beams of morning light made the blood on the sand look purple. Keeps was watching him, his finger still on the trigger, his head cocked slightly and his eyes searching the scene before him as if he was trying to preserve every detail of this moment for future reflection, the gallery viewer assessing a painting: Kradle Over Fallen Man.

"Take a few more seconds," Keeps said. "Then we gotta go."

"Who . . . ," Kradle managed. His hands were soaked in the blood of the murdered man. "Who . . ."

"I'm Walter Keeper. Friend of Celine's. Well, I was." Keeps shrugged. "I'm the kind of guy whose identity changes quickly. Like a chameleon, I guess. Right now I'm prepping to become Mister Millionaire."

Kradle was hardly hearing the words. Fury was unfolding inside him, the ache of knowing that his last chance of proving his innocence was leaking away before his eyes, while the chance to have his vengeance was already gone.

"Second ago I was a killer," Keeps continued, almost to himself. "It's not the first time. Usually I don't mind it, but I wanted to avoid it this time if I could. But I couldn't have this guy going on about the phone call I made to him, pretending to be the police, telling him to get into the bed, that you were coming, that we needed to set a trap for you. Too complicated. And the police don't like to be impersonated, in my experience."

Kradle's hands were balling into fists.

"Look, man, I did you a favor," Keeps said. "I know what the guy did to your family, and that's fucked up. We both know you weren't going to kill him. Now you can go back to Pronghorn and know everything got tied up neatly, even if you didn't do it."

Kradle rose to his feet. He turned in the sand. Keeps raised the gun and pointed it at his chest.

"Don't be stupid," Keeps said. "Don't be stupid! Don't be stupid!"

Kradle kept coming. Keeps shot him in the upper chest. He kept coming.

"No, no, no, no!" Keeps wailed.

Kradle seized him by the throat with one hand and knocked the gun out of his fist with the other. He smashed his body down into the sand, making his head bounce, squeezing hard, the smaller man gripping desperately at Kradle's hands and neck. His nails tore and bit into Kradle's skin, but no pain registered. There was only a deep, heavy silence pressing down on him, making it impossible to break the force of his hands, his arms, his weight coming down on Keeps. The smaller man kicked and flailed, got traction in the sand, somehow, twisted around, elbowed Kradle in the face and scrabbled away. Kradle walked while the other man crawled, gasping for air, toward the house. He didn't get far. Kradle slammed his boot down on the man's back, flattening him against the dirt, then kneeled by his head as Keeps coughed and gasped for air.

"This was the wrong fight to get involved in," Kradle said.

"Yeah. Yeah. I see that now," Keeps rasped. He spat blood on the sand. "Please, please, man. Please just—"

Kradle punched him in the back of the head. Keeps went limp against the dirt, his unconscious breath shallow and rattling.

Keeps was a dead weight as Kradle lifted him and slung him over his shoulder. He walked back through the gate into Mullins's yard, up the porch stairs to the sliding door. He pushed it open and went inside, moving without direction, knowing only that he had to do something with the man he carried, the only man who could testify to his not having murdered Gary Mullins out in there in the desert. Because while losing his opportunity to punish Mullins for his family's deaths, either with murder or with jail time, was cruel enough, Kradle knew serving time for the act would only be worse. He couldn't bear it. Not the sight of Pronghorn on the horizon, nor the feel of its walls enveloping him again, the sound of its clanging gate and buzzing alarms. He fancied he could smell now, in his despair, the other men on the row. His brothers awaiting death. Kradle had no plan. He simply walked across the living room toward the hall with Keeps hanging over his shoulder.

"Reach for the sky, inmate," a voice said.

Kradle turned toward the kitchen, the big windows and the curtains patterned with cheerful lemons.

Warden Grace Slanter was standing there with a bolt-action rifle in her hands, the long black nose of the weapon steady as a rock and pointed right at Kradle's head. The warden was wearing dusty jeans and a flannel shirt, boots caked in desert sand.

"John Kradle," the warden said. "You look awful."

"People keep telling me that," he said. "How'd you know I was here?"

"I got a text," Slanter said.

"Okay," Kradle said. He didn't understand. But it didn't seem to matter. None of it mattered. His shirt was slowly darkening with blood, and his shoulder hurt. He rubbed the hole just under his collarbone and knew there was bad pain, but not death, on the horizon.

"I saw what happened." Grace Slanter took her aim off Kradle for a second, flicked the gun toward the windows. "All of it. Saw you decide not to kill that man out there. Saw that guy you're carrying do it instead."

Kradle gripped the back of Keeps's legs, hefting him higher on his good shoulder.

"If you could maybe memorize that," Kradle said, "say it again when you're asked, I'd be very grateful."

"No problem."

"Anything I can do in return?" Kradle asked.

"Yeah," Grace said. With one hand holding the rifle on Kradle, she took a pair of handcuffs from the back of her belt and tossed them at Kradle's feet. "Put those on him and carry him out to the truck. When we get there, I'll give you your very own set."

CHAPTER 45

Burke stood before the stage, watching the little girls being led on stage and arranged on the platforms. There were twelve of them, mostly blondes, each wearing a satin baby-doll-style dress trimmed in white faux fur. Frilly socks and halos made from wire and white feathers. Around him, people were gathering slowly, some of them clearly the parents of the girls, waving and blowing kisses and giving thumbs-ups. Willis had studied the Christmas morning carolling event that had played out on this exact spot a year earlier, taking segments from the local news and what footage he could acquire online to give a timeline that was as precise as possible. It was 8:42 A.M. With all the jostling and arranging and cajoling necessary to get the girls in position on the stage, the announcer had come out to introduce them and get the first song underway by about 9:03 A.M. Burke wanted the ice rink and the standing area for the audience to be at maximum capacity before he started firing.

He walked back to the truck and, before getting in, glanced down the street to where Willis and Clara would be waiting with the getaway car. He could just see a slice of the front left headlight of the white van, the faithful old vehicle that had seen them from Pronghorn to Vegas, and which would take the whole team safely out of the vicinity of the massacre once it was time to flee. He wondered if the vehicle would end up in a museum someday, along with the rifle, debris from the snow cone truck.

A little girl in the front row of the carolling ensemble was looking at Burke. He raised a hand and waved, and she giggled and hid her face.

"I'm sorry," he mouthed. Because he was sorry for what he was about to do, genuinely miserable, aching in his very bones about it. That it had come to this was not personally his fault—it was a product of hundreds of years of weakness, of the white man laying down his weapons when he should have taken up arms, of listening and bending when he should have remained steadfast, of denying plain realities that were present for all to see. That these little girls should have to be sacrificed so that the world could evolve into a new order was a tragedy, but some futures had to be born out of blood. Innocent blood. The most innocent of all innocent, and purest of all pure. It wasn't going to be easy. But it had to be done.

Burke walked back to the food truck and opened the rear doors, slipped inside, and found Silvia waiting there. He picked up the rifle bag and unzipped it, glancing again at his watch.

"Almost time," he said.

Celine gripped the handle above the window and the edge of the center console of Trinity's car, jamming her feet against the sides of the footwell as Trinity smashed the vehicle over a speed bump at the exit to the parking lot of the Mesa View hospital.

"What if it's not the Planet Hollywood ice rink?" Celine groaned as the car skidded sideways, zooming blindly through an intersection packed with cars. "What if it's a rollerskating rink? What if it's some other—"

"It needs to be this one," Trinity said. "We need to be right about this."

"Because she said kids," Celine said.

"Yes," Trinity said. "If we're wrong—"

"We're not wrong," Celine insisted.

The two women sat rigid in their seats as they turned onto the highway. Trinity slammed on the brakes as a wall of traffic rose before them.

Burke flicked the safety selector on the rifle to fire, put a hand on the handle of the rear door of the food truck and looked back one last time at Silvia, who was standing with her fingernails clawing the edge of the serving counter, her jaw flexed tight.

On the wind, he heard the announcer introducing the choir of little girls. He waited until he could hear the first bars of a carol, smiled as he recognized the tune. "White Christmas." Perfect.

"Here we go." Burke smiled.

Silvia could only give a hard nod.

Burke pushed the handle and shoved against the door.

It didn't open.

He heard a vehicle pull alongside the truck on the opposite side to the serving counter, and the sickening sound of metal grinding metal as another food truck scraped against the counter side, wedging itself tightly against the vehicle so that both serving windows were aligned. Burke stepped back and saw that the kitchen area of a bright yellow truck was now perfectly matched and mirrored with their own, a Black man in a bright yellow shirt standing there with his arms folded. Through the windscreen, Burke saw the truck ahead of them backing up. They were sandwiched between four food trucks, boxed in on all sides.

"Bitch!" The man in the yellow shirt leaned on his counter and pointed at Silvia, standing behind hers. "Me and a few of my friends got together. We thought we'd come over here and encourage you to apologize for what you said to me and—"

Burke stepped up beside Silvia, raised the rifle, and sprayed gunfire through the serving window. The man in the yellow shirt ducked faster than Burke's eyes could follow. He put a foot on the shelf under the serving counter, grabbed the edge of the window, and hauled himself up. Outside the truck, he could already hear screams, shouts of confusion at the sound of gunfire. He could only hope the little girls weren't shuffled off the stage before he could get a few of them.

He tucked his rifle under his arm, pulled down his mask, and raised the goggles over his eyes. He was ready. Game on.

Burke pushed up through the gap between the trucks and placed the rifle on the roof of the truck. He climbed onto the roof of the yellow truck, stepped to its edge, and looked out over the scene before him.

It was just as he'd imagined it. Men and women running for their lives, the flow of people bottlenecking at the natural barriers made by the line of tightly parked trucks and washing up against the wooden partitions that marked out the edge of the Planet Hollywood hotel—human waves of panic. People were trying to find shelter in and around the stage. The inner cordon made by the ice rink was causing terrified families to cower at the edges, no idea where the shooting was coming from, a couple still skittering and stumbling out on the white plain, ripe to be picked off. While some little girls were being dragged off the platform on the stage, a good handful were still standing there, frozen in confusion, their feathered halos bobbing on wires above their heads.

Burke lifted his rifle and aimed at the stage.

His finger had not yet come off the trigger guard and onto the trigger itself when he heard a voice cutting through the screaming, and looked down to see a woman with a bandaged neck dropping to one knee on the grass before the ice rink.

Trinity fired. Burke felt the bullet smash into his thigh. The bullet that blasted through his cheekbone and into his skull was like a punch, a whump that knocked his head back, made the truck beneath his feet feel as if it were a boat rocking on a turbulent sea.

He fell off the truck and landed on the road. The truck that had boxed in his truck from behind had fled when the firing started, leaving the back door free. Burke saw Silvia's shoes as she dropped onto the ground, turned, and tried to sprint away. A second pair of shoes appeared, blocking her.

"Not so fast, bitch!"

Burke looked up in time to see Celine Osbourne punch Silvia in the face so hard she hit the ground and bounced onto her side. But that couldn't have been right. His jailer from Pronghorn could not be here now, cutting off the escape of his comrade. All that must have been fantasy.

So too, he assumed, the distant vision of the white van doing a three-point turn in the street, almost mowing down a mother running with one of the little angel-girls in her arms, as it roared away into the morning. Burke knew his teammates would not abandon them. It must have been the lies of his slowly failing mind, the last desperate pictures of a brain with a bullet lodged in it.

Burke gripped at the asphalt, felt darkness closing out the sounds of people running, crying, screaming.

They were nice sounds to die to.

CHAPTER 46

From the prison van that had driven John Kradle to Pronghorn Correctional Facility for the very first time, he had been able to see exactly zero percent of its exterior. Chained to a ringbolt on a steel bench, he had stared at the floor for the entire trip, resisting the attempts at conversation made by the correctional officer lumped with the responsibility of riding in the back with him.

From where he sat now, in Grace Slanter's truck, Kradle watched as the small hill fell away and the road to the facility opened before them. It was the same road traveled by the bus full of family members of guards only days earlier. He shuffled a little in his seat, his palms flat against the backrest, the chain between his cuffs stretched taut. Grace Slanter had wrapped his shoulder tightly with tea towels she found in the Mullins house before they left for Pronghorn, but the wound felt warm and Kradle knew that the adrenaline that was keeping the pain away was almost used up.

He watched the prison slowly growing, the minimum, medium, and maximum security sections at first appearing as one gray mass against the huge walls, then dividing like cells. In the back of the truck, Keeps still lolled, unconscious, bleeding from the nose onto a seat that was covered in desert dust. Slanter, who had done little in the way of talking on their journey back to the prison, pulled the truck over and stopped it a few miles out from the facility.

"I'm going to make a phone call," she said, and took out her cell phone. As the device came out of her pocket, Kradle watched a thin stream of sand trail onto the bench seat between them. Grace noticed him looking and shrugged.

"I've been out in the wilds for a day or two," she said.

"Okay." Kradle nodded. He watched the prison in the distance, the little cars and vans and helicopters assembled beyond the parking lot, and listened to Grace make a call to the press, telling them she was bringing a prisoner in and to get their cameras ready for her arrival. When she hung up the phone, Kradle met her eyes, and the old warden gave an embarrassed kind of smile.

"I really need this," she said.

"I bet," Kradle answered.

"I'm going to pull up the truck outside the gates and walk you in," she said. "Try to look . . . you know. Defeated."

"Shouldn't be hard," Kradle said.

The warden smiled. Kradle smiled back. She started the engine and pulled back onto the road.

The gold-rimmed glasses with the chain were just exactly Axe's prescription. Lucky thing, he thought. He put them on so he could read a little plaque set into a sandstone block at the edge of the marina. Marina del Rey, it told him, was the largest man-made small-craft harbor in North America. Axe didn't think that was a very impressive claim, but as he straightened and scanned the harbor he guessed there were probably a thousand or so boats in view of where he was standing, which wasn't bad. He picked up his bag, pushing down a Velcro flap that was hanging loose and slapping in the sea breeze, and walked down the harbor, reading boat names as he went. *The Adventurer. Explorer. Distant Sunsets. Flying Free.* The people on the boats didn't much look like they'd ever not been free, Axe thought. He passed a forty-footer that was crowded on the back deck with people in white shorts and long socks drinking orange juice from wine glasses and picking at platters of sliced ham. On another boat, a pair of kids were hanging upside down from a rail, trailing their fingertips in the water, as a bronze-tanned woman in a long yellow dress rushed down from the upper cabin to scold them, reel them in. Axe was heading nowhere in particular, thinking he might stop at the end of one of the piers and look through the bag, when he passed a guy hauling one of those waterproof trunks with the flip-latches on the sides down a short gangway toward the deck of a big white yacht. Axe watched him reach the bottom of the gangway and curse himself, try to shift the heavy trunk up onto his knee so that he could unclip a small chain at waist height that secured the deck. The guy flipped a lank fringe out of his eyes, glanced around, and saw Axe standing there.

"Hey, fella!" the guy said, and threw Axe the smile of a dumbass who should have thought ahead before he started on the path to loading the boat. "Lend us a hand?"

"Sure," Axe said.

Axe made sure his German passport was zippered up in his little undershirt bag, thinking to himself that if it fell into the water it would be a real disaster. He waited for the guy holding the trunk to back up, then went down the gangplank and unlatched the chain. There was nowhere for Axe to go but onto the boat itself to let the guy through. He stood there, holding his bag and feeling mildly pleased with his usefulness, as the guy heaved the trunk onto a table and gave a huge sigh of relief.

"Thanks, buddy," the guy said. "You're a real champ. Stupid me. I put the chain across again, not thinking."

"You headin' out today?" Axe asked.

"Yeah." The guy brushed sea salt that had rubbed off the trunk from his polo shirt. He proudly put a hand on top of the trunk. "Koh Samui, baby. Should take me a couple of weeks. This is the last box of supplies right here. Now I'm all set to go."

Axe smiled and set his bag down on the deck.

CHAPTER 47

Celine Osbourne heard the shunting sound of the toaster lever being kicked down as she rounded the corner of the row. The woodsmoke traveling down from cell eleven was thinner this time. John Kradle was putting the finishing touches on the "t" in "*feet*" when she arrived at his cell. She rested her forearms on the crossbar, her hands hanging near his face as he bent over the slab of wood on his little desk.

She watched him blow gently on the seared letter, then sit back to appreciate his work.

"*Please wipe your feet,*" she read.

"There's room for a punctuation mark," Kradle noted, pointing with the makeshift soldering iron at the end of the piece of wood. "A period, maybe."

"Seems a bit final, doesn't it?" Celine asked.

"What?" Kradle said. "Like you might want to add more?"

"Please wipe your feet before entering."

"Who's going to wipe their feet *after* entering?" Kradle asked.

"Urgh." Celine massaged her brow. "Why do I do this? Why do I talk to you?"

She knew the answer. In the six weeks since John Kradle had returned from the outside world, Celine had done a lot of talking to him. Part of it was wanting to reassure him on his journey to being released.

It had taken a week for police to take Walter Keeper's statement over in county jail, where he admitted to killing Gary Mullins before being apprehended by Kradle. Another day for them to come to Pronghorn and confirm Grace Slanter's story, that she had witnessed Walter Keeper murder the man in the desert while Kradle stood helplessly by. It had taken two weeks for Celine to get an appointment to enter into the official record all that she knew about the Kradle family murders, about Gary Mullins and what she had learned from the unnamed man in the motel room. While Kradle's lawyer worked tirelessly, another week had passed before Dr. Martin Stinway was quizzed by police about his forensic evidence on the Kradle case and Shelley Frapport had given her statement in full about her late husband and his actions around the time of the murders.

While the case had been assembled, and a time arranged to present the findings to an appellate judge, Kradle and Celine had existed as they had before the breakout: him behind the bars and her walking the halls, now and then stopping to reprimand him about his towel hanging on the rail or him drinking backward from his coffee mug. But there was no heat, no hatred, in the banter. Celine took a chair from the breakroom and positioned it in front of the bars, and every night, long into the night, the two talked, Kradle

sitting on his bunk with his back against the wall and
Celine resting her boots up on the bars. Death row was
half as full as it had been, and while three cells on ei
ther side of Kradle's still stood empty, their whispering
and laughing drew complaints from inmates furthe
down the hall who were trying to get some sleep. Par
ticularly vocal about their noise was Anthony Reiter
who took some time to recover from his treatment a
the hands of Burke and his crew. The killer had needed
to recover physically from the ordeal, but emotionally
as well, from the disappointment that his victimhood
at the hands of Burke's crew had not afforded him
some kind of pardon from the killing of his girlfriend
in the backyard of their home.

Some of what caused Celine and Kradle amusemen
long into those evening talks was Celine's updates on
the public life of US Marshal Trinity Parker. Foot
age of her stooping to one knee, raising her gun, and
shooting Burke David Schmitz before he could open
fire on another crowd of innocent civilians had swep
the world, as had the news that Parker was less than
twenty-four hours into her recovery from being sho
in the neck by one of Burke's snipers at the time. Ce
line noted that nowhere in Trinity's many interviews
with journalists did she mention that the wound to her
neck had been caused by shrapnel, not a bullet.

Celine watched Kradle working now, drawing out
the last moments he would remain as she had always
known him, as she had always been comfortable with
him. A man behind bars.

Then she closed her eyes, drew a deep breath, and
slipped her key into the lock.

Kradle looked up from the sign he had made. Ce
line smiled and nodded.

"It's through?" he asked.

"Yeah," she said. "Just got the call a minute ago. They've stamped the vacation of your charge. You're free to go."

Kradle put the sign down, lay the soldering iron beside it. He stood and picked up the box of items he had packed and set on the end of the bed. As he walked through the doorway, something changed in his face, and he turned back and grabbed a stack of envelopes sitting, bound with an elastic band, on the shelf.

"I'll be needing these," he said, showing Celine the label marked MARRIAGE.

"Those women are sickos," Celine said, smacking the envelopes out of his hand. "And they won't want you, now that they know you're innocent."

The envelopes landed on the floor of the cell. Kradle left them there, and she took his arm and led him, uncuffed, up the hall.

She dropped him at the administration building to sign his papers. With the front of the building crowded with press, cameras clicking and people yelling, she was certain he hardly heard her goodbyes, and she barely caught his. There wasn't time for hugging, and he wouldn't have liked it, with all the people watching, she supposed. But just before she turned to leave, he took her hand and gave it a squeeze, and something about the hard fingers she had felt in the car on the way to Vegas told her everything she needed to know. She watched him walk into the fray and march straight over to where the black dog sat uncertainly in the huddle of humans. Kradle's lawyer held the leash, grinning, as the ex-con crouched and ruffled the fur of the dog's head and neck, saying nothing to the journalists that barked all around him.

It was a long, quiet walk back to the row, her swipe card bleeping through gate after gate, until Celine Osbourne was again where she belonged. The smell of smoke still lingered in the air, but the first man she had ever released from death row was long gone, and Celine knew she would probably never see him again.

Past Kradle's empty cell, she saw a hand poking out from one cell, wrist resting idly on the crossbar. Celine wondered if there were more men here who had been deemed guilty by judges and juries, whom she had made it her life's work to keep from the world, who deserved instead to be out there, walking free.

She decided then that she had a new mission.

She was going to find out.

ACKNOWLEDGMENTS

The publication of this novel will mark my millionth word in print. I have no idea which one it was. I hope it was something meaningful and not ordinary (or profane!). Something like "tenacity" or "determination" would have been good, or indeed, "hope."

My career has been buoyed by a ridiculous amount of hope. I hoped, with every waking moment, to be published. That hope was obsessive, exhausting, soul destroying. It flew in the face of so much discouragement in my life, in the media, from other authors, and from my inner critic. When that hope was finally realized, rather than dissipating, it grew. I hoped from one book to another, from one publication territory to another, and my hope ignited hope in other people. I could never have hoped to have a million words in print when I first decided I wanted to be an author. But here I am, deciding what to hope for next.

I have dedicated this book to all the aspiring authors. It's not an easy road. Waiting. Trying. Daydreaming. Being rejected. Having your hopes destroyed and trying to rebuild them. It's lonely, frustrating, and tedious. But whatever you do, my advice is never to let it become hopeless. Only you have control over that.

When it came to research for this book, I am forever indebted to Michael Duffy and Governor Faith Slatcher, who organized a tour for me of Lithgow Correctional Centre, a maximum security institution in New South Wales. Thank you to all of the staff who answered my questions there, and to the inmates, who, for the most part, behaved themselves. I also consulted extensively with Detective B. Adam Richardson of the Writer's Detective Bureau, who was so generous with his time and knowledge.

I am represented in Australia by Gaby Naher, in the US by Lisa Gallagher. My publishers are Bev Cousins, Justin Ractliffe, Linda Quinton, Kristin Sevick, Thomas Wörtche, and a whole host of others across the globe. My main editor is the wonderful Kathryn Knight. I will never be able to repay the kindness, patience, and encouragement these people have provided me.

Never will I reach a point in my successes at which I forget that my ability to write was shaped and developed by my academic studies at the University of the Sunshine Coast and the University of Queensland.

Thank you, Tim, for loving, supporting, and caring for me. Thank you, Violet, for being the most beautiful thing in my world. Thank you, Noggy, for the cuddles.

Read on for a preview of

FIRE WITH FIRE

CANDICE FOX

Available soon from Tor Publishing Group

A Forge Hardcover

FOUR DAYS AGO

Something in the water grabbed her calf. Her brain screamed the word.

Shark.

Mina's body collapsed inward from her elongated freestyle. She twisted and kicked out, the cliffs above and the dusty, gold-lit horizon off Abalone Bay smashing together in her wide-eyed panic swirl. A yelp escaped her throat, making way for sea-foam to be sucked back in. It was a man who'd grabbed her. Not the dreaded white pointer, haunter of her early-morning, high-kneed dash into the dark waves. She was coughing as she tore his hands off her, kicked him in the stomach, the alarms in her brain still sounding even as some other corner of her mind slumped with relief.

"Oh my god! Oh my god!" she gasped. "What the—"

His tattooed, bloodless arm reached for her, and he blew out seawater with the word, "Help!"

He went under again. Mina kicked into high gear: out of survival mode and into rescue mode. She reached blindly into the depths, grabbed a handful of long hair. A wave lifted them both, sea gods thrusting them together, and she caught him under the armpits, clambered around behind him.

"I can't," he shuddered. "I can't keep going."

"I've got you," she said.

She didn't. He was impossibly heavy, not kicking, his head lolling against her shoulder. Now that he'd reached her, he'd given up. She went under, struggled upward, twisted back and forth looking for assistance. When she'd entered the waves only an hour earlier, the horizon smeared red above slate-gray sea, there had been people everywhere. Fishermen standing like black-coated cormorants on the rocks around Portuguese Point. Joggers pounding the distant trails and a small gathering of regulars at the edge of the tidal pool in the cove. Now it seemed as if an uninhabited coast spread before her, the steep hillsides beyond the beach apocalyptically motionless. Mina had no choice. She hugged the man around his chest, turned, and kicked.

She hauled and kicked, hauled and kicked, floating frequently, his naked backside against the hips of her wet suit. She kept telling him that she had him, though time and again when she straightened and kicked down, hoping to feel sand beneath her feet, there was only ice-cold emptiness. East Beach, her destination, grew no closer. Her terror ratcheted higher and higher as she noticed the wounds on the drowning man. A chunk torn from his chest. Bruises and gashes on his arms. Mina waved and waved. No help came. She scanned the swell, every tip a flicking, ink-black fin.

When her feet hit sand, she cried out in triumph.

The man seemed to tap into some reserve of strength as they hit the rumbling breakers, planting his feet, stumbling, hanging a hairy arm around her shoulders. She helped him hobble a few steps before two surfers materialized just in time to stop him from collapsing on top of her.

On the sand, his ribcage expanded and contracted as he fought for breath, making the sprawling blue tattoos rise and fall. She knelt by him, shaking with exertion, her eyes wandering over skulls, eagles, guitars. The surfers were oblivious to the inked landscape, one brushing strands of lank brown hair from the man's battered face and beard, the other heaping a pile of towels and gear at Mina's side. She held a towel against the chest wound while the first surfer spread another towel over the man's naked waist.

"Hey, buddy? Buddy? You all right? Stay with us, bro!"

"Was it a shark?" The second surfer touched Mina's arm. He was older than the other surfer, his bare shoulders peppered caramel.

"No . . . Uh, no," she said. "I don't know. I don't think so."

"So what the hell happened?"

"I don't know."

"Where are his clothes?"

"I don't know! I don't know!"

The drowning man grabbed Mina's forearm, the same death grip he'd used in the sea.

"Phone," he said.

"An ambulance is coming, bro. Just hang on," the younger surfer said. Mina followed his gaze to a pair of joggers who were watching from the trail, one with a phone clamped to her ear, her eyes wide as she recited details, pointing as though the operator could see. Nearby, a flock of seagulls stood watching, wings folded, disapproving.

Mina looked back at the bearded man. His eyes were bloodshot and fixed on her.

"Phone. Now. Please."

Her bag was in her car. But the older surfer produced a phone, put it in Mina's hand and shrugged. Mina realized a ring of observers had formed around them. A flash of anger. Where had all these people been while she was out there in the waves, struggling? The raw exhaustion dragging at her limbs made her feel as if she'd been fighting the current for hours. But maybe not.

Mina handed the phone to the bearded man. With difficulty, he rolled onto his side, one badly trembling hand gripping the phone as the other struggled to dial.

Mina, the surfers, the gawkers, the gulls, they all watched as the man from the sea lay in the sand and defied unconsciousness, waiting for the call to connect. The morning was so still, so quiet, that Mina heard the woman's voice on the other end of the line.

"Hello?"

"Hellfire, hellfire, hellfire," the bearded man said. Once the words were out, he let his head fall back. He was taken so fast, Mina couldn't tell if he was asleep or dead. She pulled the phone from his limp fingers and held it to her ear.

"Hoss?" the voice on the phone said. "Jesus, Charlie! A-a-are you sure?"

TWO DAYS AGO

The sewing needle penetrated the thick, starchy fabric of Lamb's coal-black uniform shirt too fast, spearing the soft flesh of her index finger. She yelped, sucked the digit, looked around the locker room to see if anyone had heard. She was alone. It was her nerves that had driven everyone away, she guessed. Nerves were contagious, and this was a job in which trembly hands, a sickly pallor, and a jolting step weren't useful.

She hunched in her underwear on the worn wooden bench between the stacks of lockers, replaying the past few humiliating moments in her mind. Arriving at the Van Nuys police station and presenting herself at the spit-screened front counter, as she'd been told to do, rather than swiping through the staff doors at the back. Being shown to the locker room to change, her nostrils flaring like a spooked horse at the unfamiliar sights and smells of the ground-floor bullpen. Tripping and stumbling on an electrical cord taped to the carpet, right in front of two plainclothes detectives.

She had noticed the button on her breast pocket hanging loose from a curling black thread as she changed out of her civilian clothes. *Christ. Why now?* All weekend she'd darted back and forth to her bedroom closet, staring at the uniform, reverently touching its spotless sleeves, without noticing the loose button. The sewing kit had been at the bottom of a backpack bulging and sagging with precautionary items. Hydralyte tablets, aspirin, Band-Aids, tampons, snacks, a spare set of civvies, three types of hair ties, in case the one she'd used wasn't regulation. *Why the fuck didn't the handbook say anything about hair ties?* Lamb finished sewing the button back into place with numb fingers and pulled on the shirt, smoothed it out firmly.

She caught a glimpse of herself in the mirror inside her locker before she closed it. There was still no color in her face. She went to the paper towel dispenser, ripped off a handful, reached into her shirt, and dried her pits for the tenth time that day. Then she walked to the door and put a hand on the knob.

She closed her eyes and whispered to herself.

"You deserve to be here."

Lynette Lamb, P1 officer in the Los Angeles Police Department, drew a deep breath and let it out slow. Then she pushed the door open and walked into her very first day on the job.

In the hall outside the locker room, she was the new kid in the schoolyard; frozen, vulnerable. When she reached the bullpen, the officer who'd led her to the locker room was standing at the coffee station, one hand on the counter, the other pinching the bridge of her nose. The *fuck my life* pose. The colleague she was listening to touched her elbow in a consolatory manner and walked away.

Lamb straightened and jutted her chin. She understood. This woman, whoever she was, had probably just been told that Lamb was her baby to sit for the day. Lamb appreciated the disappointment. Rookies were annoying. But Lamb was a fast learner, had excellent retention and an eye for detail. Her grades from the academy proved that. It was black and white, on paper: *she deserved to be here*. Lamb forced a smile and went to the officer, standing at attention.

"Ready when you are"—Lamb looked at the older officer's ID badge—"Officer Milstone."

Milstone wouldn't meet Lamb's eyes.

"Come with me, Lamb," she said instead, and walked away.

Lamb followed eagerly, nodding and smiling at officers who were watching from their cubicles, some on the phone, some peering around their computer screens. Milstone and Lamb took a corridor to a stairwell and climbed in silence to the upper floor. Offices, a row of interrogation rooms, a waiting area. Milstone stopped outside a frosted-glass door with a nameplate that read *Lieutenant Gordon Harrow*.

Of course, Lamb thought. *Meet the boss first.* She gave silent thanks to the universe that the terror in her heart was slowly transforming into excitement. Her cheeks felt hot. She'd studied up on Gordon Harrow in the weeks since she'd been informed of her assignment to Van Nuys. She knew his history, major cases, marital status, love of surfing and golf. Lamb was eager to hear a speech about the valley, how the team operated. *Around here, we work hard and we play hard.*

Lamb was ready to do both.

Milstone rapped once on the door.

"Yeah," a voice said.

Milstone held open the door. Lamb waited for her to go in first. She didn't. When Lamb didn't move, Milstone swept the air, annoyed. *Get in there!* Lamb scooted inside. Behind the battered metal desk stacked with papers sat a tired-looking version of the Gordon Harrow that Lamb had been staring at on her computer screen for a fortnight. He seemed strangely incomplete without the peaked police-issue cap he wore to press conferences. He ran a hand over the brushy cut that crowned his small head and offered Lamb a surprisingly limp handshake.

"Sir, good morning," Lamb started. "It's really nice to meet—"

"Sit down."

She sat.

He consulted the computer screen to his left, appeared to be reading. Lamb felt the wave of excitement that hit her at the door cresting, pausing, plunging.

Harrow turned away from the computer and folded his hands.

"Lynette," Harrow began.

That's when she knew.

Lynette. Not *Officer Lamb.*

This was bad.

"I have to ask you some important questions," Harrow said. "And, look, I want you to understand: how you answer these questions isn't going to affect the outcome for you here today. That's already all sewn up. It's out of my hands. I'm just the messenger."

"Okay," she said.

Lamb waited for a punch line. There wasn't one.

Beyond the frosted glass of the door, people were walking by, talking, laughing, answering phones. She listened, hoped to hear the telltale whispers and snickers of her future cop buddies that would reveal this to be some harmless initiation prank on the new rookie. None came. The world out there was carrying on without her. The wave was crashing down. Down and down and down, impossibly heavy, impossibly fast.

Harrow's gray eyes were fixed on hers. "A week ago, on the evening of the eleventh of October, you went out in the city. You were celebrating your graduation from the academy. You were in the company of some of your friends. Fellow cadets. Is that correct?"

Lamb tried to nod, but her neck and head were locked in place.

"Yes," she said.

"You went to a few bars in the West Hollywood area?"

"Uh. Y-yes. Yes."

"And in the early hours of the morning, around 2:00 a.m. on the twelfth of October, you split off from the group," Harrow said. "You booked an Uber. You traveled home with a man who told you his name was Brad. You and Brad went to your apartment in Koreatown. Correct?"

Lamb couldn't speak. Her tongue was dry, adhered to the roof of her mouth. *It's just a prank,* she told herself. *A hilarious prank!* Cops were about to come bursting in and slap her on the shoulder, ruffle her hair. There'd be a welcome party in the break room. Cake. Harrow waited for her to emit some kind of response, letting the silence drag on and on. When he decided she was incapable, he gave the sigh of a farmer tasked with shooting a sheep that's wedged in the combine harvester.

"Let me just put this all out there." Harrow made a sweeping gesture over the surface of the desk. "The guy you took home that night was a very, very bad man. It's not clear to us whether he targeted you specifically or if he was just trying to get any one of the girls in your group to take him home. But he knew for a fact that you and your friends were all recently graduated probationary officers."

"What—" Lamb's words hitched in her throat. "What is this all about?"

"That guy, Brad Alan Binchley? He's a patched member of an outlaw motorcycle gang called the Death Machines," Harrow said. "You heard of them?"

"N-no," Lamb stammered. "Y-yes. Uh, I've maybe seen a news article—"

"Yeah, well, they're bad." Harrow cracked his knuckles. "And they're clever. Brad flirted with you and you took him home, and while you were asleep, I assume, at approximately four o'clock in the morning, he accessed a computer located at your residence."

"He *what*?" Lamb yelped.

Her mind raced. She remembered Brad's body. His cigarette breath. His laugh. She'd been strangely thrilled to find her apartment empty the next morning, the flipped-up toilet seat the only evidence that he'd ever been there. *Naughty, naughty, Lynette!* She'd smiled to herself. This wasn't her. Nights out in the city, meaningless hookups, her dream job, payment plan paperwork for a brand-new car on the coffee table. This was the new Lamb. The grown-up Lamb.

Harrow continued, shattering Lamb's memories

and bringing her tumbling back to the present. "Brad Binchley used your secure LAPD log-in to access your staff email account."

"That's not possible," Lamb said. "It's just not possible. My password isn't written down anywhere. It's not—"

"There are ways to get around that." Harrow flicked his hand. "Keystroke trackers, whatever. Binchley's a hacker. They're modernizing, the gangs. Bringing in people like him. They have to."

Lamb swallowed.

"Binchley sent an email to a detective named Christopher Keon over at the Civic Center," Harrow said. "Keon opened it. It was internal mail, so he trusted it. The email contained a virus. Brad Binchley and his gang were able to access top-secret police documents through that virus."

"I don't know about any of this." Lamb held her face in both hands, and peered through her fingers at Harrow. "I don't know about *any of this*!"

Harrow plowed on. "Among other compromising details, the gang learned about an undercover officer police had planted in their gang approximately five years ago."

Lamb doubled over, pressed her face into her knees. The wave was crushing her, rolling her, smashing her into the sand.

"They took that officer out to sea on a boat and tortured him," Harrow said.

At this, Lamb reached forward, grabbed the wastepaper basket sitting on the floor at the corner of the desk, and retched into it. Nothing came up, but the retching wouldn't stop. Dimly, she was aware of Harrow lifting a phone on his desk and asking someone to bring her a glass of water. When the retching finally eased, Lamb realized the crotch and armpits of her uniform were drenched in sweat.

Officer Milstone was there with the water and then gone again, wordlessly, leaving the glass on the edge of Harrow's desk. Lamb didn't trust herself to pick it up. She just stared at it, trying to breathe.

"Is he dead?" she managed eventually.

"No. Oh, no, he's not. Sorry. I should have said that." Harrow gave a short, awful laugh that he reconsidered and choked off. "He escaped, swam for shore. Prevailing currents and his efforts ended up bringing him in to a beach near Palos Verdes. He'll be okay."

Lamb nodded, holding her stomach with one hand and gripping the edge of the desk with the other. Harrow sat back in his chair with the groan of a man relieved at having performed his coup de grace and wanting to begin the process of forgetting it.

"I'm going to have to ask you to go back downstairs now," he told Lamb, "and take off that uniform."

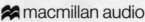